HOMESONG

Misha Crews

Published by CWC Publishing
Because good books are essential for a happy life.

ISBN: 978-0-9857167-3-8
Cover design by Katerina Vamvasaki

Dear Reader,

I'm so happy to finally be able to bring you this re-release of *Homesong*, my very first novel.

For writers, the first novel is a sacred thing. When we start off our careers with the words "I want to be a writer," we have no idea what we're getting into. All we have is the world we've created inside our imaginations and a hazy, dreamy-eyed vision of the day when we'll type *The End* on the final page of our manuscripts.

That's how it was with me when I first began writing *Homesong* so many years ago. It started as a straightforward idea about a shipboard romance, but over the course of time it evolved into a kind of multi-generational/small town gothic/childhood sweetheart/shipboard romance tale. I guess you could say that it's kind of a mess that way! But I hope you find it an enjoyable mess.

Writing may be a solitary pursuit, but nobody really writes alone. With that in mind, many thanks to Marita Golden, Helen Collins, Karen Cantwell and Laura Lucas, as well as my editor Misti Wolanski and the proofreaders at Red Adept.

But the biggest thanks of all goes to the readers who were so enthusiastic about this book when it was originally published. Your encouragement helped keep me writing, and I'm not kidding about that!

For anyone who's reading *Homesong* for the first time, I truly hope that you enjoy it. And either way, I would love to hear from you any time. You can contact me through my website: www.MishaCrews.com. Don't be shy!

Happy Reading!

Misha

P.S. If you like the town of Angel River, then you'll be happy to know that I'm brewing up a whole new batch of stories that take place there. More on that soon!

To my four favorite people:

*My mother, Mary, who always knew I could do this. Thanks
for the incentive, encouragement and unwavering love.*

*My father, Clarence, who gave me a love of reading that
I will always carry with me. Thanks for always being
there, and for making me laugh, even when life wasn't
so funny. I love you and miss you every single day.*

*My sister, Rebecca, one of the most beautiful people I've ever
known, inside and out. When I grow up, I want to be just like you!*

*My husband, Charlie, who read every draft and told me
how good it was, even when it wasn't. There's not enough
space in this book to say how much I love you.*

PROLOGUE

EVERYTHING ABOUT THE LITTLE HOUSE said *dead and gone*.

It stood, empty and alone, at the intersection of two old dirt roads. Scraggly bushes had grown up over the peeling walls, poking their way inside through broken windowpanes. The skeletal remains of an old vegetable garden jutted long bony fingers out of the brown scrap of yard by the front door, and the house's shingled sides had been spray-painted with graffiti. But that too had turned brown, as if even the vandals had moved on to greener pastures.

Reed sat silently in his car, biting his thumb as he looked out at the place where he had grown up. Cicadas, stirred by the heavy heat of the early August morning, whirred their drowsing song in the tall grass by the side of the road. The sun hadn't even crested the far hills yet, and already the inside of his ancient yellow VW felt like an oven. Sweat gathered along his hairline to drip down his neck, sticking his shirt to the small of his back.

It was strange to think that he hadn't laid eyes on the place in almost a year. He had been born in that house, as had generations of Fitzgeralds before him. His grandmother had raised him there: he had crawled along the bare, uneven floorboards, taken his first wobbly steps in the patchy front yard.

The old place had never been beautiful. It wasn't some

picturesque cottage nestled in the heart of rural Virginia. It was a squat, ugly dwelling that had seen too many deaths and not enough births, but which knew the pain of both.

The original foundation had been laid by a long-ago Fitzgerald ancestor in the hardscrabble years following the Civil War — a tough little house built by a tough little man, who had gone on to found the very town that sprawled not two miles from here. Later, the Fitzgerald family had built themselves a home more suited to their own sense of importance: an elegant country house high on the hill. The gracious building had ridden the crest of the hill as pretty as a boat on the water. From the front of its wide wraparound porch, you could look right past this tiny hovel to the town that lay beyond.

The big house had burned down when Reed's grandmother was a child, but money and a kind of careless confidence had resurrected it in the late1960s, just a few years before Reed had been born. A new family had come in from out of town, snapped up the land, and rebuilt the house from the original blueprints. *Outsiders*, his grandmother always said, her voice thick with anger.

Kate's family, Reed reminded himself, trying not to notice the way his heart snaked in his chest at the thought of her. He tugged the handle and pushed the car door with his shoulder, ignoring the painful squeal of rusty hinges as it swung open. He unfolded himself from the front seat, peeling carefully away from the old plastic covers, then stretched his long and lanky frame before leaning back against the car, crossing his ankles with a nonchalance that he didn't really feel.

If he turned his head and looked upward, he would have been able to see that big house — empty now, but still all white and shining with majestic beauty. Instead, he shoved his hands into his pockets and looked down, contemplating the dirt at his feet. He was on his way out of town. Everything he owned was packed into two cardboard boxes on the cracked back seat of his car. One box held his clothes, which were secondhand but clean and carefully folded. The other held a dozen books and what Grand had once scornfully called the family legacy — an old photo album covered in crumbling black leather, and lined with stained and threadbare purple silk.

And that was it. That was all that was left of his family. Generations of men and women who had lived and loved, killed and healed, taught and raised children. And with all of that history, there was nothing left but a broken, faded photo album at the bottom of an old cardboard box. By this time next week, even the shack in front of him would be gone.

And so would he.

College. Reed felt a nervous grin tugging at the corners of his mouth. Two years ago, if anyone had asked him whether he would go to college, he would have scowled and spit a "*Hell* no" out the side of his mouth. Despite all of Kate's enthusiastic dreaming, despite her faith in him, the thought of him pursuing a higher education had seemed so remote that he'd never seriously considered it. He certainly never would have believed that he would end up heading off to university, with a scholarship letter in his pocket and a dorm room already waiting for him.

But anger and desperation could make some potent magic. He had finally gotten his act together, and now he was on his way out of this small town, heading to New York, the biggest big city of them all. The idea made his gut clench with excitement and fear, but he clamped down tightly on both and tried to focus on his purpose.

He had stopped here on his way out of town, knowing that

he had to have a last look, not knowing when or if he would ever return. He had intended to walk through the little house one last time, to say a final goodbye and thank you to his grandmother. But now he felt strangely unwilling to take the first step up the overgrown walkway. As if moving forward would somehow be going back. As if the front door would open and his grandmother would be standing there, instead of lying in the family graveyard half a mile down the road. As if the house would swallow him whole, and he'd be trapped there forever.

He turned to look at the empty fields around him. In his grandmother's youth, all of this land had belonged to his family. The little valley had once been green and alive with corn and tobacco crops. Even after his great-grandfather Gussy had gambled it all away, others had worked the land, given it a purpose and a life. But now that too was gone. The fields had gone to seed, the green grass to dust. In a few days, the house would be bulldozed, the land raked and mowed over, and a condominium community would be built there.

The thought of it made Reed ache in a place that he could not have named. But in a secret place it also made him glad, because now there was nothing to hold him here. It was as if the cancer that killed Grand had also poisoned the very soil around them. When she died, she took with her all the ties he might have had to these few acres of earth that had once been called Fitzgerald land.

Reed squared his shoulders. Time to get this over with.

He crossed the yard in four easy strides. He could remember when it had taken five times that many steps for him to get up the front walk. But his legs had been shorter then. Shorter legs and a lighter heart — that was how he thought of his childhood.

On the tiny front porch, he turned and looked out over the

land again. He imagined his grandmother standing here, on this same exact spot, year after year, watching the world go by. She had been born in 1900, not exactly a time of great opportunity for women. But she had been whip-smart and from a wealthy family — for her, the possibilities could have been endless.

"But life has a way of fucking you over," she once told him, with a gleam in her eye. "The trick is to try to *out*-fuck it."

She had moved into the little house when she was twelve, along with her mother and their last remaining servant. After the big house had burned down, taking her father's life with it. After they had discovered they were bankrupt, and the government seized their land for back taxes. After everything had gone to hell.

For her, there had been no great future, no college, no world travel. There was just this little scrap of land, with its broken-down shack of a house, and the wrenching scrape of poverty.

With effort, Reed swung his eyes upward, finally bringing his gaze to the house that stood on the hill. It was so beautiful that it hurt his eyes just to look at it. When Kate lived there, it had been like his second home. He had run down its wide hallways, scuffed up its glowing hardwood floors with his young feet. He had played under the high ceilings and sat before roaring fires in its carved fireplaces. But Grand had hated the place, and small wonder. To her it had been an abomination, like the resurrected corpse of a dead child. It stood as a reminder to everything that she had lost, everything that had been taken away from her. The two houses faced each other across a great divide — not just the physical divide of hill and valley, but a divide of fortune, a divide of fate.

Which would be worse, looking out the front door and seeing the burnt-out shell of your former home, or seeing that home resurrected, given new beauty and vitality, and knowing others were living there?

Well, there really wasn't any contest, now was there?

The front door was unlocked — it wasn't like there was anything inside worth stealing — and when Reed pushed, it swung open with a horror-movie squeal. He gave himself a minute to allow his eyes to adjust to the murky interior. Then he crossed the threshold.

Weak sunlight slanted through the broken windows, revealing the place to him in patches of dusty light. He stepped forward into the living room, gazing at the space that he had once known so well. The graffiti artists hadn't limited themselves to the outside of the place, they had made use of the interior walls as well, no doubt seeing them as canvases on which they could paint their angry art.

Well, Grand had always been a supporter of the independent arts — not to mention an avid cusser — so he didn't suppose she would have minded.

His footsteps echoed as he walked through the empty rooms. Cobwebs hung like memories in the air. In the kitchen, he touched the faded yellow wallpaper, trying to summon up images of his grandmother from every corner of his mind. Her tiny frame and lined face…gnarled fingers with short-clipped nails…her harsh, uncompromising discipline, and her quick, unexpected kindnesses….

For God's sake, Reed thought with a sudden grin, had he ever given her a moment's peace? There hadn't been a rule that he hadn't broken, not a class he hadn't cut. He smoked; he shoplifted; he vandalized. He was a terror, and he knew it. More than that, he *liked* it. Everyone who knew him knew that he would come to a bad end one day. Everyone. Especially

Reed himself.

But Grand had never given up on him, had she? No, and he had felt the back of her hand more than once as proof of her dedication. But he had never minded that, because he knew that every crime carried a punishment. And eventually, in a weird way, the punishments themselves had become a kind of validation. They made him feel like he was worth protecting.

Besides, he had outgrown his grandmother by the time he was eleven. And by the time he was thirteen, when she backhanded him, it had made him want to laugh at the way she had to reach *up* to get to his face.

But he had never actually laughed at her, of course. Even he wouldn't have been so bold.

He gazed around the kitchen, bereft of its furniture and fixtures. Even the cabinets had been pulled down off the walls and hauled away. But all he had to do was blink, and he could see Grand flipping pancakes over the stove for Sunday breakfast. He could hear the folktales she used to tell him, stories that had been around since before even she had been born. And he could see the two of them seated at the kitchen table on a weeknight, playing cards while she lectured him on politics and he tried hard to catch her cheating.

Reed frowned, remembering that Kate had often joined them, both for pancakes and for cards. And the stories, which were always her favorite. Where his memories of Grand were already faded and dim, his memories of Kate were alive and fully colored.

Anger rose up inside him, making his fist clench and his throat close up. *Kate.* He couldn't get away from her. He wanted to spit out her name, then spit out her memory so he would carry it no longer.

He turned on his heel and stalked out of the kitchen, away from the memory. But there were ghosts of her in every room. In his old bedroom, smaller now than he could ever have believed possible, he saw seven-year-old Kate, dressed in overalls and helping to paint the walls, her hair cut into a wild, curling pageboy. He blinked and saw fourteen-year-old Kate climbing recklessly through his bedroom window, lying on top of his old patchwork quilt, sharing plans for the future and torturing him with her nearness.

And sixteen-year-old Kate, pale and trembling after they had found Harry Block's mangled body in the old barn. Reed had held her tightly and whispered into her ears, and she had clung to him like he was the only thing keeping her from being swept away down the wild, raging river of fate.

His grandmother had always warned him against Kate's family, saying that the Doyles felt they were too good for this town. Reed had never believed it. He had told himself that Grand was just bitter, angry at the way her life had turned out. He knew down to the marrow of his bones that Kate was *good*, that she loved him and would never hurt him. Her parents had always treated him like family.

But Grand had been right. She had been right all along. The Doyles had packed up and left town in the middle of the night. They had left behind no forwarding address, no goodbye, no nothing. Just a thousand unanswered questions, and a raw and aching hole where his heart used to be. They had shaken the dust of this crummy little town off their feet and not looked back.

But then again, wasn't that just what he planned to do?

Damn straight it was.

So what was stopping him? The car was packed and gassed, ready and waiting for him. It was a long drive to New York, and he was burning daylight, as Kate's father used to say.

He had come to the house to say goodbye to his grandmother; it was his only stop on the way out of town. The family burial plot was just half a mile down the road, but he had no desire to visit dead ancestors, people who had once owned half the land in town and lost it. He didn't know what would become of the little cemetery once the house was bulldozed and the land razed. Didn't know, and didn't care.

And he didn't want to say goodbye to his grandmother where she was dead and buried. He wanted to say goodbye to her where she was still alive. And that was here, in this house. Besides, nothing would have gotten her spitting mad like the thought of her grandson spending money on flowers, then standing beside her gravesite, weeping delicately into a handkerchief.

No, Grand would be the first one to tell him to save his money for gas, to save his tears for later. She would tell him to get the hell out of Angel River, and never look back.

And Kate, what would she tell him? What lofty advice would she give him, were she here to give it? Reed thought about that briefly, then realized that Kate had nothing to say. She was more dead to him than his grandmother was. He would never see her again.

Down the road, in another state, his life awaited him. And he was ready for it. He summoned his courage, murmured a final thanks to his grandmother, and headed for his car.

He didn't bother to close the door behind him.

CHAPTER ONE

THUNDER RUMBLED IN THE COLD darkness outside of Julia's big warm kitchen, followed by a fresh spatter of rain sheeting the picture window over the sink. It had been coming down all day — an icy, sweet winter rain that had turned really nasty just in time for the evening rush hour. Kate sat on a stool at the oversized kitchen island, watching with forced nonchalance as her sister turned an innocent head of lettuce into a nearly-unrecognizable mound of shredded green. Julia's arms were stretched awkwardly to accommodate the swell of her pregnant belly, but she could still wield a kitchen knife like a champ. She chopped vegetables with a fury.

No, Kate thought, watching the lightning rise and fall of the knife. Not *with* a fury. *In* a fury. Jules was not happy with Kate. And she had been not-happy since Kate had called from her car and told Julia what was going on.

She hadn't *planned* to tell Jules anything. Not about Mark or the *Sweet William* or any of it. Originally she was just going to leave the firm early and surprise her sister by walking in the door and calling, "Hey, Mom! What's for dinner?" Then they would have a good laugh and a nice visit, and that would be the end of it.

But leaving the office early hadn't worked out, which was her own fault. After she and Mark had left things on such bad terms, Kate had pulled out the Argosy contracts — the ones he had asked about — and thrown herself into re-reading them. No way was she taking them home with her tonight. She'd wanted to finish them right then and be done with it.

So by the time she'd finished up at work, detoured by her apartment for a change of clothes, and was actually on her way out to Julia's house, it had been much later than she had originally intended. When she crossed Memorial Bridge and passed the Pentagon, the traffic had ground to a halt, completely deadlocked, and she'd realized it was too late for a surprise visit. She had to call and let Julia know she was on her way. And once they were on the phone, all Jules had to do was ask, "So how are you?" and the whole story had come tumbling out.

Julia had heard her out in silence, and when Kate had finished talking there had been nothing on the other end of the line except breathing. Kate had waited for Jules to speak, but the silence had lengthened, until she had to bite down on her lip to avoid rushing into excuses and justifications. She knew Julia expected her to say more, but she'd sat stubbornly, groping her way through the rush hour traffic, refusing to be the one to break the silence.

Finally she'd been rewarded with a gentle "Hmmph" from her sister.

"I knew you'd say that," Kate hadn't bothered to hide the triumph in her voice. It was like the staring contests they'd had when they were kids. You blinked first, she thought. I win. Kate knew she was being petty, but she didn't care. "So, what? Does this mean you don't want me to come over for dinner?"

"Of course I do," Jules had said impatiently. "Don't be ridiculous. The kids will love to see you. Sam's working late tonight, so it will just be the four of us. How long do you think it will take you to get here?"

"Probably an hour — maybe an hour and a half."

"Fine. That will give us time to talk about this whole mess before dinner." Then Julia had hung up. No "Goodbye," or "I love you," or "Drive carefully." Just a *click*, and then silence.

Kate had slowly taken off her headset. *Talk about this whole mess.* She was in big trouble, and she knew it. Julia was probably calling Mom right now, and Kate would never hear the end of it. Her family was crazy about Mark, and they plainly thought *Kate* was crazy for not leaping into his arms at the first mention of marriage.

The traffic had continued, bumper to bumper, all the way down the highway. Cold rain sprinkled down on the windshield; the brake lights lining the road were like twinkle lights on a Christmas tree. By the time Kate pulled into Julia's driveway, she'd been worn-out and chilled to the marrow of her bones. It had been a relief to see Julia's house, nestled cozily at the outer corner of a carefully-architectured cul-de-sac. The long front porch had been gently illuminated, throwing streaks of light onto the winter grass in the front yard. Environmentally-friendly solar footlights outlined the driveway and the curved front walk. It had looked cozy and welcoming and very much like a home. Suddenly the chill of Kate's argument with Mark and the cold, wet hours she'd spent on the highway had evaporated, and she'd been flooded with warm comfort.

Julia and her husband had moved into the bastion of suburbia about five years earlier, just after their second child was born. Kate smiled, thinking of Julia's husband. Sam Boccaccio, the dream man. Leave it to Jules to find the perfect guy. He was tall, dark, handsome, brilliant, and also happened to be a real sweetheart. He was a lawyer, of course — everyone in their family either became a lawyer or married one. A few years before, he had become the youngest partner in his firm. He now made what was referred to as "very good money." Kate herself made "good" money, but it was a far cry from "very good."

Now Jules was pregnant again, and Kate could tell that in her parent's eyes, the sibling scoreboard was getting ridiculously lopsided. Three kids, a loving husband, and a big house in the suburbs versus no kids, no husband, and a condo in the city. Julia five: Kate zero.

She got out of the car and stood up. After the long hours on the road, it felt great to stretch. She held her face up to the rain for a moment, ignoring the cold and not caring if she got wet, then grabbed her purse from the back and trotted up the path to the porch. The crocuses in the flowerbed were starting to poke their heads up. Kate and her mother had helped Julia plant the bulbs in October — crocuses, daffodils, hyacinths.

"All Doyle women love spring flowers," Mom liked to say, with her gentle enigmatic smile. There seemed to be a deeper meaning behind the comment, but Mom always refused to explain.

Kate wiped her feet carefully on the mat and used her key to unlock the front door. She called out a greeting as she crossed the wide foyer with its homey, honey-colored hardwood floor and graceful staircase. It looked like Julia had done some redecorating since the last time she was there. The air smelled of fresh paint, and the walls were now a pale butter color. A soft rug with a pattern of deep reds and blues lay on the floor at a rakish angle.

There were some good black-and-white pictures in black frames hanging on the walls. Kate stepped closer, recognizing the photographs that Jules had taken on her second honeymoon to Tuscany last year. Julia had always had a good eye and a way with a camera. Kate had a couple of her sister's photos in her office at work.

Kate had just dropped her purse on the floor and draped her coat over the banister when a herd of children stampeded down the hall, shouting and waving their arms.

They all leapt for her at once, and as she caught her niece in her arms and her nephew grabbed her around the waist, she laughed and gasped for breath. "What, there's only two of you?" she asked. "With all that noise, I thought there must be at least twenty!" She clutched them to her, deeply inhaling the scent of baby shampoo and the good clean smell of childhood. She planted one kiss on Rose's cheek and one on the top of Oliver's head. "Come on. Where's your mom?"

Rose slid to the floor, and each of the kids grabbed a hand and pulled her down the hallway to the kitchen. She tripped along after them, marveling at how big they had gotten. Oliver was eight now, and his head reached almost to her armpit. Tall for his age. And Rose was five — still a tiny little thing, but she had grown, too. They were both wearing karate outfits, and they talked a mile a minute. They had just gotten home from a class, and by the time Kate reached the kitchen, she knew the names of every child in their class and which instructors were nice and how many different kicks they could do.

They jumped around like banshees, asking Kate to tell them one of her stories, asking their mother when dinner would be ready, arguing about which one of them could jump the highest, until finally Julia gave them a snack and shooed them away. Then they stampeded over to the family room and turned on the TV. The sudden relative silence, broken only by the occasional annoying cartoon squeal from the television, was deafening.

Kate turned to her sister, waiting to see how things were going to go. Julia stood at the sink in the oversized kitchen island, rinsing vegetables for a salad. Her face was unreadable. On the stove, a large pot spouted steam and the rich, tangy scent of Julia's spaghetti sauce filled the air. Kate's mouth watered.

"Wow, spaghetti night," she said. "I picked the right day to have a personal crisis and run for your help, didn't I?" She settled on a stool. "Do you need a hand?"

"No thanks. I've got it." Julia didn't sound upset, but her posture told a different story — stiff shouldered, held high and straight, chin jutting out just a little. Ah, the Doyle chin. It was a dead giveaway to any inner turmoil. Rose had it too, whenever she felt stubborn. Oliver, on the other hand, had his father's easygoing personality, and never seemed out of sorts about anything.

Julia stacked up a bunch of dark green lettuce leaves and proceeded to hack them to pieces. Another giveaway. Each chop of the knife sounded like a gavel pounding out a death sentence. Julia was not happy.

Without a word, Kate got up and collected a vegetable grater and a bunch of carrots. When she sat back down, Julia gave her a look and said, "I told you I've got it."

"Idle hands are the Devil's playthings," Kate said lightly. It was one of Julia's least favorite sayings. *That is completely fallacious, and possibly blasphemous,* she would usually say with a smile, *since hands folded in prayer are, by definition, idle.* Dad always said that Julia argued like a lawyer, even though she hadn't chosen to follow him into that noblest of professions.

But this time she refused to take the bait. "Fine," was all she said.

Kate grated the carrots slowly. She wished they could fast-forward through the conversation that she knew was coming. She hated these talks, these heart-to-hearts where she was expected to lay bare her soul and then weep with relief when she was "unburdened." She didn't mind listening to other people's inner secrets, but she hated talking about her own. It was exhausting.

She decided to go on the offensive. "So, you want to talk about this, or not?"

Julia shrugged, and Kate could tell that she was torn between her naturally sympathetic, caring nature, and some idea that she had to mother Kate, which at the moment meant employing "tough love." Kate found this attitude just a tad annoying. Who was the older sister, anyway? And yet she couldn't help but appreciate the concern that came with it.

"I don't know. Do you think it's a story that's suitable for kids to hear?" Jules asked in response to Kate's question. A tentative smile played about her lips, showing that she was willing to thaw.

Kate smiled back, seizing the olive branch with both hands. She looked over at Oliver and Rose, sitting thirty feet away in front of the television. She pointed with a carrot. "Who, them?" she asked. "They're so deep into *SpongeBob* that they wouldn't notice if I rode a starfish through the room and up the stairs!"

"Those kids hear everything," Julia said ominously, shaking her head in warning.

A voice came from the living room. "Mom's right, Aunt Kate."

Kate turned her head, surprised. She knew that Oliver had spoken, but his eyes were still glued to the screen. Then he spoke again, without moving. "We can hear everything you say," he explained. "But we don't listen unless you're saying something interesting."

"Well, thanks a lot, nephew," she said. "So I guess we're safe as long as we continue to be boring, is that it?"

His eyes slid away from the TV long enough to meet hers. He smiled, dimples showing. "Pretty much," he said. Then he was back in the cartoon.

Kate grinned, feeling the dimples in her cheeks that mirrored his. She knew that she shouldn't have a favorite between her nephew and her niece, that she should love them both equally, but Oliver was something special. She could still remember the way she had felt the first time she held him in her arms, minutes after he'd been born. That heartbreaking feeling the first time he'd opened his eyes and looked at her — really *looked*, and Kate had sucked in her breath and thought, He *saw* me. And later, as he grew, the way he would light up when she walked into the room, and the way he would run to greet her on wobbly legs, all smiles and outstretched arms.

He was growing up good, too. Smart, thoughtful, and he had a sense of humor — he always got the joke. He hadn't even held a grudge against his parents for calling him "Oliver." Then again, he had been named after his paternal great-grandfather, a man who had been a circus acrobat in his youth. For an eight-year-old, that was enough to make the name cool.

"See what I mean?" Julia continued to smile.

"Well, I think I can keep my voice down and the profanity to a minimum," Kate replied. "And I'll do my best to be boring."

Julia sighed. "Okay, tell me again, from the beginning."

Kate crossed her legs, trying to affect an air of nonchalance. This wasn't going to be easy. She took a breath. "Well, like I said, this morning I got an email from Dorothea Westlake. Do you remember her?"

Julia squinted, searching her memory. "Vaguely. Friend of

Mom and Dad's, right?"

"Right. She lived here when we first moved up from Angel River in the eighties."

"Oh sure, I remember. We used to go to her house for dinner parties sometimes — it was this huge old Victorian townhouse in Georgetown."

"Sounds about right. Well, I don't know how she got my email address, or why she thought of me, but apparently last year she bought herself a ticket on some fancy cruise ship. She'd been on a waiting list for months; and now, just when her ship's ready to sail, there's some emergency, and she has to fly to L.A."

Julia looked up, concerned. "I hope it's not too serious."

"Oh, it's serious, all right." Kate couldn't help but grin. "Her daughter is remodeling her kitchen, and there's been a problem with the blue marble countertops they ordered."

"Heavens to Betsy," Julia murmured, going back to the salad. "Somebody call the Red Cross."

"I know. It's a blue marble catastrophe. Anyway, for some reason, Mrs. Westlake thought of me, and she said that I could have her tickets if I wanted them — plane ticket, cruise ticket, the whole deal. All I have to do is buy a bikini and step onto an airplane." Kate paused, waiting for a reaction. There was none. "Jules, you should see the pictures of this ship. It's amazing — I've never seen anything like it. After dinner, I'll pull up the email and show you the attachment."

"Sounds too good to pass up."

Kate nodded soberly. "I think this is what they call a once-in-a-lifetime opportunity."

Julia pushed the lettuce aside and reached for a cucumber. "Okay, so that's the good stuff. Now get to the stuff that makes me mad."

Kate took a breath, gathering her strength. This was the tough part, the part that made her seem like a real jerk, even to herself. "This afternoon, just after lunch, Mark dropped by my office. At first he said it was to check on these contracts I've been working on."

"The Argosy thing?" Jules asked.

"Right…." Kate was puzzled. "How did *you* know about that?"

"Dad told me when they were here for dinner last week." Julia was careful not to look up at her sister. "He said this was a big deal for you — maybe you'd get an offer for partnership."

"Well, it's possible, but I'm not getting my hopes up. This is just another account to me." Kate squirmed a little, toying with the stub of carrot she had in her hands. Her career was something else she didn't feel like talking about. "Anyway, Mark came by. We talked business, and then just before he was about to leave, he pulled out this enormous, glossy brochure and put it on my desk."

"It was for a cruise," Julia finished, saving Kate from having to say it herself.

"Right."

"This is the man that you've been dating for five years. The great guy who proposed to you at Christmas, who's given you as much time as you've asked for to consider his proposal, who hasn't pushed you or nagged you in any way. He offered to *take you on a cruise,* and you said no."

"Right."

Julia nodded slowly. "Yep," she said. "That's the part that makes me mad, all right."

Kate didn't know what to say. She had been stunned when Mark plopped that brochure down on her desk. She had leafed through it without seeing really it, groping for the right words, which never came to her. Instead, apparently, only the wrong words had come out of her mouth.

"Well," she finally said, "for what it's worth, Mark wasn't too happy about it, either."

Julia had finished with the cucumber, and she reached over to take the carrots from Kate and finish them herself. Apparently Kate's grating technique wasn't up to Julia's high standards. Kate took a sullen bite out of the stub she held. Suddenly she was very much in need of a glass of wine. Or several.

She got up and took a glass out of the cabinet, then opened the refrigerator and found a bottle of red wine in the door. She took the cork out and sniffed suspiciously. "How long has this been in here?" she asked.

Julia stopped grating long enough to shoot Kate an offended look. "A few days. Why?"

"Well, you're seven months pregnant so you're not drinking, and Sam doesn't like red wine. I wanted to make sure I wasn't about to pour myself a big glass of expensive red vinegar, that's all."

"Mom was over earlier this week," Julia explained.

"Ah." Chilled red wine — another thing Doyle women had in common. Just the thought of it would surely have given Martha Stewart the vapors, but oh well. Kate poured a healthy glass and brought the bottle back to her seat.

"And I clean out my refrigerator every Saturday morning, just so you know," Julia added defensively. "The only expensive red vinegar you'll find in there is the kind I use to make salad dressing."

"Jules, don't be so sensitive. I was just kidding. I know what a great housekeeper you are." Kate settled back onto the stool, took a large drink, and sighed. "I would willingly eat off of any surface in your house, okay?"

"Fine." Somewhat mollified, Julia couldn't help but smile at the image that conjured up. She scraped carrots to the side and moved on to the tomatoes. She rinsed them carefully and then dried them on a paper towel before putting them on the cutting board. She didn't look up as she asked her next question. "Was it really rough with Mark today?"

"It...." Kate wasn't sure what to say. She looked into her glass for answers, found none, and took another drink. As she swallowed, the image of Mark's face floated in front of her, and her eyes welled up with tears. So much for not getting emotional. She drained her glass and poured another one.

"It wasn't good," she said finally. She tried to keep her voice steady. "He was so hurt. I don't think he believed me about Mrs. Westlake, and how can I blame him for that? I mean, here the guy proposes to me, waits with the patience of an angel for my answer, then invites me on a romantic cruise, and I say 'No thanks; I'm already going on a cruise by myself!'"

"Only that's not exactly what you said, is it?"

Kate sighed. "No, it wasn't."

"You two argued?"

"We became very...*lawyerly* with one another."

"That's my Kate," Julia said knowingly. "It's never a fight, right? Never an emotional scene? You don't argue. You just...negotiate."

Wearily, Kate sighed again. "Yes, that's it all right. You've got me all figured out. Congratulations." She topped off her glass again, wondering if it would be rude to just drink right from the bottle. It would save time, anyway.

Abruptly, Julia turned around to face the stove. After a

moment's deliberation, she picked up a large wooden spoon and stirred the thick red spaghetti sauce. Her next words floated casually — too casually — over her shoulder.

"Have you ever told Mark about Reed?"

Kate almost dropped her glass. *"Reed?"* She hadn't heard his name spoken out loud in…ten years? Fifteen? "No. Mark doesn't know about — about Reed. Why would he?"

Julia shrugged, stirring slowly. "Reed, and that whole insane summer before we moved, well, that was a big part of your life. I just thought you might have shared it with Mark."

Kate fingered the bottom of her wine glass. "Mark and I don't talk much about the past." Her voice roughened, and she cleared her throat. "And that's what Reed is. The past."

"Sometimes the past becomes the present," Julia said sagely.

It sounded like a line from a bad sci-fi movie. Kate gave a sickly laugh. "Doesn't the past *always* become the present — unless you're dead?"

Julia threw a look over her shoulder. "Don't try to change the subject. You know very well what I mean."

"Don't you dare say 'The past has a way of catching up with you.' I'm pretty sure Hollywood has that phrase trademarked."

"And don't *you* try to pretend you're not affected by things that have happened to you, Katie. We're all affected by the events of our lives."

The words hit Kate like a ton of bricks, and she felt like something scraped off the bottom of a shoe. Lower than dirt. "Jules…" she said apologetically.

Julia turned around and smiled gently. "It's all right, Katie. *I'm* all right; don't you see that?"

What Kate saw was how the firelight from the family room caught the auburn highlights in Julia's dark hair and sent flickering shadows to emphasize the pregnant swell of her belly. What Kate saw was her baby sister, the young woman she'd once neglected with an appalling result, a young woman who now had babies of her own. What Kate saw was love, and determination, and the power that comes from the two.

Oh God, she thought. I hate sloppy sentimentality.

She drained her third glass of wine and struggled to keep her voice steady. "The guilt just never goes away, you know?"

"Katie, you have *nothing* to feel guilty about. And neither do I, for that matter. What happened, happened. And that's all there is to it."

"I should have been there for you."

"But you *were*. You were there when it counted. As soon as you knew I needed you, you were right there."

"But that man, Harry Block, he's dead, and — "

"And that has nothing to do with us. It was an *accident*. Nothing more and nothing less."

Kate shuddered, remembering blood splattered thickly on jagged metal blades. So much blood. The smell of it had hung heavy in the hot summer air. She had thrown up in the corner of the barn. "The police didn't think so at the time. They even thought that Reed might've killed him."

"They only thought that because Reed was poor," Julia said with contempt. "And the first place the law always looks is to the poor and the defenseless."

Kate smiled weakly. "You sound just like Dad."

"I'll tell him you said that. He'll be thrilled. I think he wonders sometimes if I'm really his daughter." Julia laughed. "He always says there's too much Duncan in me, and not enough Doyle." Duncan was their mother's maiden name.

"Well, there's plenty of Doyle in Oliver, that's for sure,"

Kate said. "That should reassure him. Harry's more like Dad every day."

Julia smiled with pride. "My son," she said with a sigh. "He can't decide whether he wants to be a lawyer like his father and grandfather, an acrobat like his great-grandfather, or the next David Beckham."

"I'm sure he'll be the world's greatest soccer-playing acrobatic lawyer. With a black belt in karate thrown in for good measure. So do you think I should take this trip, or what?"

Kate hadn't meant to spring the question like that. She had planned to play this coolly, with an it's-my-decision-and-I'll-do-what-I-want attitude. That was how she usually did things. The wine must've been making her shaky.

Julia didn't answer right away. She stood looking around the kitchen as if assessing the condition of dinner. The salad had been loaded into an enormous wooden bowl, the sauce smelled ready to eat, and the water boiled for the pasta. "Kids!" she called suddenly. "Dinner's almost ready. Are you two still in your karate gear? Go upstairs and change!"

Her eyes met Kate's and glinted with humor. "Every time I make spaghetti, I end up regretting it. I should put down plastic drop cloths, put the kids in hazmat suits or something. No way I'm going to try to get red sauce stains out of those white uniforms!" She left the kitchen to chase the kids upstairs, and when they were gone, she turned back to Kate.

"We have about twenty minutes before Little Miss decides what she's going to wear for dinner," she said. "Little Miss" was Rose, who, when left to her own devices, tried on at least three outfits before choosing one. "Why don't you show me that email?"

Kate nodded and went to sit at the computer in the family

room. Julia followed her, standing behind her sister so she could look over her shoulder. Kate pulled up the email. The attachment opened, and Julia let out a low whistle.

"My sentiments exactly," Kate breathed.

The picture on the first page looked like a watercolor painted on old parchment. It reminded Kate of something painted by a young lady in a day when all young ladies had learned to paint, to play piano, to speak French, and to give parties. Maybe, Kate thought, the girl had worn a long, flowing dress as she sat by the seashore, her delicate complexion protected by a big straw hat with a blue ribbon around the crown. And her brush, held by imagined fingers in a fancied past, had traced the lines that were so deceptively simple, capturing the graceful spirit of a ship anchored in the harbor.

On Julia's hi-res monitor, the picture took on an almost three-dimensional quality. It seemed to Kate as if she could reach out and touch the roughly-textured paper, stroke the feathery marks made by the strands of the brush, and maybe be transported to that place, where hard-edged reality faded away and a sparkling world of possibilities was unfurled in front of her.

"You didn't tell me the ship was the *Sweet William*," Julia said accusingly.

Kate turned around, surprised. "You've heard of it?"

"Of course," Julia said. "You mean you haven't? It's becoming one of those 'it' spots — you know, where celebrities and society people go to relax. It's for the fabulously wealthy and the wealthily fabulous."

"Oh great, then I should fit right in." Kate shook her head. Then suddenly she realized that her pregnant sister was standing, while her un-pregnant self used the only chair at the computer desk. She jumped up. "Here, why don't you sit?" she offered. "Scroll through that attachment. There are a bunch of pictures of the ship in there."

Julia took the chair without objection, which spoke volumes to Kate about how tired she must've been, then silently went through the pictures, reading the descriptions.

Kate moved to the back door and peered outside into the darkness. The rain had slacked off, but it still drizzled. The backyard was illuminated by a light over the deck, which glinted off the swing set her parents had given to the children last Christmas. One of the swings drifted back and forth in the rain.

"God, I'm tired of winter," she said, almost to herself. "I wish spring would hurry up and get here."

"This is some ship, Katie." Julia's words brought Kate back to the family room. Julia swiveled around and looked at her sister, grinning. "I'm completely jealous, I hope you realize that."

"So come with me," Kate suggested impulsively. She reached out and stroked her sister's hair the way she used to when they were kids, twisting the soft strands around her index finger. "I'll buy you a bikini to show off your belly, and we'll drive all the guys on the beach crazy."

"Don't tempt me," Julia said. Her hand dropped automatically to caress her stomach. "You know, you could ask Mark to go with you."

Kate resisted the sudden urge to pull her sister's hair, *hard*. Instead she turned and plopped into one of the easy chairs by the rustic stone hearth, where the fire was burning with lively mirth. "I guess I could do that."

"But you won't," Julia said just as flatly.

"You have a remarkable ability to state the obvious, sister dear," Kate said. "Look, I know that Mark's a great guy, that he would make a good husband, and that I'm — "

"Not getting any younger," Julia interjected, in the kind of audaciously insulting tone that only a sister can get away with.

Kate held up a finger in warning. "Oh no, don't you start that biological clock stuff with me. I'm only a couple years older than you are."

"Three years, actually." Julia smiled with calm smugness. "And I'm married and I'm pregnant with my third child. My biological clock can tick all it wants to."

"Well, rub it in, why don't you," Kate said resentfully. "I'm not taking Mark on this trip!"

"But you are going," Julia stated.

"*Yes*." Kate spat out the word defiantly, then blinked in surprise. She didn't fully realize that she'd made up her mind until that instant.

"Good," Julia said. "I think you should."

"What?" Kate was thoroughly confused. "Even without Mark?"

Julia paused before answering. She stared meditatively into the fire. When she spoke, her voice was low and tender. "One of my earliest memories is of you, did you know that? You must have been, oh, seven or so, because I think I was about four. It was summer, and it was a Saturday. Dad had gone to the hardware store in town, and he'd taken you with him. I was *so* jealous, because I was just sure that you guys were going to stop at the drugstore for ice cream. So Mom told me we could bake some cookies, and they'd be just for the two of us — just for her and me. We made the first batch, and they were great, of course — you know Mom and her famous 'secret recipe.'"

Kate nodded and smiled, remembering. The girls had been teenagers before they'd discovered that Mom's secret was the recipe on the back of the Tollhouse bag. "Passed down from her grandmother," Kate said.

"Exactly — passed down from her grandmother, who probably pulled the same stunt on *her* daughter! Anyway, we had just loaded the second batch into the oven when you and Dad came home. I was sitting at the kitchen table, and I remember that he was giving you a piggy-back ride, and you were laughing like crazy. Your hair was short then — remember how you used to wear it, cut short in that cute little pageboy? — and it was all wild and windblown. You were completely thrilled because Dad had let you drive his car coming down the Old Back Road. He'd sat you on his lap and let you steer while he worked the pedals. You kept saying how exciting it was — how the road was all bumpy because Daddy was driving so fast…."

"They didn't pave the Old Back Road until 1980 or so," Kate murmured. "It was bumpy even when you crawled down it."

"But that's not how you saw it," Julia said. "To you, Dad's old car was flying down the road, and you were driving it. I'll never forget how your face was all lit up and your eyes were glowing. You looked…golden."

She looked at Kate. Tears glistened at the corners of her eyes. "Do you see what I'm saying?"

Kate shook her head.

"Katie, you were *always* golden. When we were growing up, you were like a force of nature, or something. You would try anything, and you usually succeeded at whatever you tried."

"Your use of the past tense is noted," Kate said, trying to diffuse the intensity of the moment. But the joke fell flat, even to her own ears. Julia ignored her and went on.

"It was after we moved — after that summer — that things changed. You lost something of your old self and became…"

"The poor pathetic creature you see before you today," Kate concluded. She was only half kidding.

Again, Julia ignored her. "That's why I think you should go on this trip. You'll laugh at me for saying this, but I don't care: I think God is trying to tell you something."

A short, unattractive bark of laughter escaped Kate's lips. *"God?"* She looked up and, when she saw Julia's face, quickly put her hand to her mouth, trying to smother the amused smile that she couldn't completely suppress.

Julia sat up a little straighter, her face a stony mask of stubbornness. "Well, it's either God or Fate. But there has to be a reason you were offered this particular trip at this particular moment, right when you needed it most. Don't you think?"

Unease prickled its way down Kate's spine, and she frowned. She hadn't looked at it that way before. She didn't really like the idea of either a bossy deity or some inhuman force of nature tossing a vacation at her like someone tossing table scraps to a dog. Not even if it was a really, really good vacation.

Julia nodded, seeing she'd made her point. "Either way you look at it, when a chance like this comes your way, you take it. Whether it's faith or fate or both or neither. You know?"

"I guess…." Kate said uncertainly.

"Besides," Julia grinned, "if you go on this cruise, you know what that means, don't you?"

Kate was afraid to ask. "What?"

"It means I get to take you shopping!"

Kate sighed. "Oh joy," she said. "My favorite thing."

"That's right, my dear. We're going to toss aside the yoga pants and the business suits and we're going buy some pretty sundresses and tank tops…." Julia's eyes were gleaming, visions of Macy's bags dancing through her head. She gave Kate's skin an appraising look and sighed. "No time for you to get a real tan, unfortunately," she said. Then she brightened. "I know — we'll go to a spa and get you a spray-on tan!"

"You're kidding, right?" Kate was incredulous and more than a little scared. "Spray-on tan?"

"It's the latest thing," Julia assured her. "It's very modern. They put you in this booth, cover your eyes and your hair, start spraying, and *voila!* Healthy glow. All the celebs are doing it."

Suddenly she stopped and looked at Kate, her eyes very clear and keen. "You're going to have a great time, you know that?"

"I hope so," Kate said. She kept her voice low-key, but in her heart a little flower of hope had begun to bud. She looked beyond Julia to the pictures of the *Sweet William* that were still open on the computer screen. It was such a beauty, that ship. During the day there would be the sun and the blue ocean, and at night she would sleep nestled in the heart of that ship of dreams. Or would it turn out to be a ship of fools? And was she the biggest fool of all?

But Jules was right. When a chance like this comes your way, you're supposed to take it. Whether it's fate or faith or both or neither.

CHAPTER TWO

THE CARPET WAS THICK AND deep, the color of a mushroom. It was set in a subtle diamond pattern; half of the large squares were slightly darker and run through with thin gold thread. The effect was almost like a marble floor, ancient and glinting in some Italian palazzo.

Reed walked back and forth across the carpet, his feet bare, balling his toes and watching them sink into the deep pile. The carpet was hand woven — he could see that from small flaws showing here and there. It must have taken a long time to make a carpet like this. And patience, attention to detail, a love for the process of making something that would last.

Those were things he respected, things he understood. Patience and attention to detail were two qualities he had learned to appreciate over the years.

His senior assistant's voice recalled Reed to his telephone conversation, reminded him of where he was and what he was doing. "So how do you like your suite?" Jerry asked. He sounded even more pleased with himself than usual.

Apparently, Jerry wanted a pat on the head. Well, there was no doubt he deserved it. But Reed still took his time in answering. He looked around at the wide sparkling windows that spread over two sides of the living room, opening a panoramic view out into the harbor. When the ship was at sea, the view would be magnificent. Even now it wasn't too shabby—he could just see past the docks and warehouses to the city beyond. He watched a plane take off from Queen Beatrix Airport as he leaned against one of the brocaded armchairs. He bent over slightly to examine the fabric pattern on the chair. Roses. And there was a big crystal bowl of roses on the table in the dining area as well. Nice. He had always liked roses.

"Well?" Jerry demanded.

Reed smiled faintly before putting the phone back to his ear and answering the question. "It's fine," he said briefly.

"Fine?" Jerry's voice took on an offended tone. "It's the best they have! I heard that the King of Jordan stayed there last month. And Madonna stayed there for two weeks last winter!"

"Madonna?" Reed paused and considered. "Well, I guess if it's good enough for her…."

Jerry huffed into the phone, and Reed's smile broadened into a dry grin. Jerry was the only one of his staff that he could tease like that. All of his other employees were too afraid of him to be able to take a joke. And that was fine with him.

He found a short hallway that led to the master bedroom. He peeked inside. Dark oak furniture, and lots of it. Blue French provincial curtains on the long window matched the bedspread. More roses in a bowl on the dresser. He noticed another door farther along the hallway and headed for it.

"How many bedrooms?" he asked.

Jerry rattled off room specs from memory. "Three altogether — master bed and bath, secondary bed and bath, and servant's quarters with its own three-quarter bath behind the kitchen. Living room, dining nook. Plus the private veranda and twenty-four hour room service and butlery service."

Twenty-four hour butlery service? Reed decided not to

touch that one. He pushed open the door to the second bedroom and looked inside. Two double beds done up in navy blue, with coordinating carpet and silk drapes. "Think I've got enough space here?" he asked wryly as he closed the door. "I mean, I do have this huge entourage that I travel with…."

It's a good thing there's carpeting on the floor, he thought as he re-entered the living room, or the echoes would be deafening.

"Hey, you wanted the best, you got it," Jerry said. "Now go look in the kitchen."

Reed did as he was told. The floor in the kitchen was made of some kind of rough marble, and the cool tile felt good on his feet. The kitchen was small — miniature, in fact — but it looked like it had everything kitchens were supposed to have. Sink, two-burner stove, storage cabinets — more oak. He found the refrigerator and opened it. Fully stocked: pâte, cold sliced chicken, assorted cheeses, fruits and vegetables of every color and even — A&W Root Beer!" he said, surprised.

Jerry sounded even smugger now. "You always said it's your one weakness. I made sure they knew to have it on hand for you."

"Jerry, you magnificent bastard," Reed said admiringly. "Maybe I'll make my own lunch and eat it on the veranda."

His assistant paused, then replied hesitantly, "Sir, when you told me you wanted to take this cruise, you said, 'I want a real vacation, Jerry. No billionaire recluse stuff.' Remember?"

Reed closed his eyes. That particular choice of words had probably not been a good idea. He tried to make his voice light and caustic. "Sure. Is that why you booked me into the King of Jordan's suite?"

"I think maybe you should avoid having private veranda meals over the next couple weeks. Go to the restaurant. Eat with the other people on the ship. Have fun."

"Fun, huh?"

"Sure," Jerry said daringly, perhaps emboldened by being left in charge of the office, as well as by the vulnerability he heard in his boss's voice. "You know what fun is. You've seen other people have it."

Over the phone, Reed could hear the sounds of office bustle in the background. Voices, phones, printers, and faxes. He even thought he could hear the New York city traffic in the distance. He felt a weight settle over him as he thought of the next two weeks, and he sighed. "Maybe this is a mistake," he said.

"It's not," Jerry assured him. "I've known you — what — ten years? And never in all that time have you taken a vacation. Or if you have, you've always managed to make it a working vacation — squeeze some sort of deal out of it. Eighty-hour workweeks, hundred-hour workweeks — for a decade? You're a young man, but that's the kind of thing that's going to catch up with you. You don't want to be dead of a heart attack at forty and never have had a chance to enjoy all that money you made, do you?"

"Well, I enjoyed *making* the money…"

"It's not the same thing, and you know it."

Reed did know it. But the simple fact of the matter was that making money was all he was good at these days. It was all he *was*.

And maybe it was time for that to change.

"I don't think I'm paying you enough, Jer," Reed said lightly. It was the closest thing to a heartfelt *thanks* that he could manage.

There was another pause. "Don't I know it," Jerry said, just as lightly.

CHAPTER THREE

KATE HAD FALLEN IN LOVE with the *Sweet William* from the moment she'd laid eyes on it. It was one thing to see it in pictures; it was another thing entirely to see it in three dimensions, to hear the sound of its ropes creaking against the mooring, to smell the ocean air as she walked up the gangway. Sturdy in its navy body and irreverent in the white stripe that ran along its glowing decks, the *William* seemed impatient to be at sea. As if it had only anchored out of consideration for its passengers, those meager human beings who were so dependent on the earth and would never truly know what it meant to ride the curling sapphire waves of the ocean, free of the land and all its encumbrances.

So, it was a ship of dreams, after all.

How could she ever have doubted it?

And now she stood alone on the rear deck, watching the island of Aruba disappear into the distance. Less than an hour earlier, the deck had been crowded with her fellow passengers, waving and calling to the people down on shore. Champagne had circulated, and the captain had led them in a toast to a safe journey. And then gradually the crowd had dispersed, wandered off in dribs and drabs, and Kate had been left on her own. Which was just how she wanted it.

She leaned as far over the railing as she dared and watched the engines churning the ocean into a foamy white wake. Overhead, seagulls dipped and called in the azure sky. They seemed to be escorting the ship out into the open ocean, wishing them *bon voyage* and a safe return.

She felt a crazy impulse to wave at them and call out her thanks, assure them that she would come back safe and sound. But she just knew that the second she did something like that, someone would come around the corner of the deck, see her talking to the animals, and she would thereafter be known as "that crazy lady who talked to the birds." So she contented herself with lifting her face to the wind and closing her eyes to the sun. She sighed blissfully. Wasn't this the very moment she had been waiting for since she had first read Mrs. Westlake's email? Yes, absolutely. And hadn't it been worth all the trouble it had taken to get here?

Again, yes. Absolutely.

But her brow darkened as she thought of that word, *trouble*. She and Mark hadn't spoken since that day two weeks ago, although she had left him several messages and sent him half a dozen emails. And her parents had been baffled, which she knew they would be. Her mother told Kate over and over again that she owed Mark better than that. Kate could only agree with her and stubbornly repeat that she was going, whether they liked it or not.

Getting time off from work had been harder than she had anticipated, but there again she had shown her stubborn streak. She'd worked overtime finishing as much as she could on her pending accounts, then distributed what was left among her colleagues. And lucky for her, the Argosy deal had gone through, smooth as silk, which had earned her a little cooperation. Whether a partnership would follow remained to be seen.

But all that was very far away. She had two weeks to herself. She planned to catch up on her reading, get herself a real tan — she'd managed to talk Julia out of the spray-on kind — and gain ten pounds eating all the desserts she wanted.

As if on cue, a bell clanged, splitting the air with its strident peal. Kate looked at her watch — she'd been out here over an hour. The dining rooms wouldn't stay open all day, and that bell was the signal that lunch was winding down. Of course, she could order room service and eat on the little private balcony off her stateroom, but she wanted to mix with her fellow passengers, to meet some people and maybe make some new friends.

When the bell rang again, she bid a reluctant farewell to her place at the railing, promised to be back soon, and followed signs along the starboard deck that pointed her inside.

Kate pushed through a set of double doors and blinked as she passed from the brightness of the midmorning sun into the cool shadows of the dining room. She paused as the doors swung closed behind her, giving her eyes a minute to adjust to the change. The room came into focus as her vision cleared, and she saw that she wasn't the only one on board who had waited until the last minute to eat. The place was full of people waiting for tables.

She stood on tiptoe and peered around the crowd, wanting to get a glimpse of the dining room itself. It looked opulent but comfortable, in keeping with the rest of the ship. Long windows flanked two sides of the room, giving the dazzling view of blue-on-blue ocean and sky. In contrast to all that brightness outside, the interior was dark and cool, done in earthy tones of green, brown, and ivory. Padded chairs crowded around tables of varying sizes and shapes.

Kate edged toward the hostess table, hoping to get her name

put on a list. Maybe since she was just one person they would seat her at a group table. She liked the idea of sitting with a group of strangers, chatting in comfortable anonymity. It was the sort of thing she would never have done back home.

Out of the dimness, two children came barreling across the room. Kate jumped backward to avoid being trampled and bumped into the man standing behind her. He grabbed her arm to steady her, and she watched with amusement as the kids flew by, followed by a woman yelling in French for them to come back. Those poor kids are in for it when she catches them, Kate thought with a grin.

She turned to thank the man who had caught her. As she tilted her head back and smiled up at him, her first impression was of strength and self-possession — a kind of *sureness*. She had stumbled; he had caught her. He was tall, with wide shoulders and slim hips. Probably a good dancer, she thought irrelevantly. Handsome, too. His blue eyes were set off by the expensive navy polo shirt he wore. The dark blond hair, cut stylishly ragged, accentuated his cheekbones, which looked like they could have belonged to a marble angel in a Renaissance cathedral. His mouth was full and shapely.

Suddenly she stopped. The smile froze on her lips, words of thanks stuck in her throat. Recognition struck like a lightning bolt and shocked through her, electricity ricocheting down her arms and out her fingertips. That face — she knew that face.

It was Reed.

But no, that was impossible. She had superimposed Reed's features over the face of a handsome stranger. This was a mirage, wasn't it? Something that her subconscious had dreamed up for her: a little psychic *bon voyage* present from her overworked brain to her undernourished heart. A silver shimmer of water on a harsh and barren desert.

And then the mirage smiled and spoke. "No, you're not dreaming." His voice was deep and as cool as the ocean. "Hello, Kate. What a wonderful surprise — seeing you here, of all places."

She blinked, and the world refocused. "*Reed*," she breathed his name, then laughed shakily. "I can't believe this. It's really you?"

His eyes blazed a trail over her face as he looked down at her. She had the sensation of being soaked up, drunken in, and then released to pool liquidly in front of him. His mouth twisted briefly into an ironic smile. "Yes," he said, "it's me."

It *was* him. Kate felt happiness breaking over her like a wave, so fresh and surprising that it took her a second to realize what it was. Happiness — joy. Reed. It was *him*.

She moved to hug him, wanting to feel the good solidness of him in her arms, wanting, if only for a second, to be wrapped in his familiar strength. But he was still holding her arm, and suddenly it seemed as if he were holding her slightly away from him, not wanting her to get too close.

As much to oblige him as to try to regain a sense of reality, she took a step back, aware that she missed the warmth of his hand when he released her.

"It's good to see you." She thought about it, then her smile cracked into a wide grin. "Well, that's the understatement of the year."

Reed caught his breath. She hadn't changed. The crooked smile, curving rosy lips into dimples in the creamy-pale skin of her cheeks; the hazel eyes gleaming gold under silky brows. When they were growing up, he had longed to write a poem about her eyes, had ached because he lacked the words to do it.

Now he had the words, but he lacked the passion. And that was a different kind of ache. A man wasn't meant to be an iceberg.

His lips tightened as he worked to maintain his composure. "It's been a long time," he said.

Her grin faltered when she saw the aloofness in his face. "Okay, you win," she rallied. "*That's* the understatement of the year. I mean, my goodness, it's been — what, almost twenty years…?"

She trailed off as a group of people entered the dining room, laughing and talking loudly. Reed took her elbow and steered her aside, saving her from the effort of trying to complete that sentence. She didn't actually know what to say to him. She had imagined this scene a thousand times over the years, being reunited with him in some exotic location. She had pictured herself saying something clever, making his lips turn upward and his eyes glow with warmth. But now her mind was a blank; in the face of reality, all the witty lines she had scripted for herself had vanished from memory.

"Do you…want to get a table, have some lunch?" she asked. It was the best she could think of under the circumstances.

His eyes flickered over her face — lightly this time. She couldn't tell what lay behind them. "I've already eaten," he replied, "but I'll join you for a cup of coffee."

And before she knew it, they were ushered past the crowd waiting for seats. A small table was set up for them next to a wide window. She watched as it was covered with a soft linen cloth and a miniature crystal vase of flowers was placed on top. Her chair was held out for her, and a waiter in a white coat hovered nearby, poised to take their order.

Kate picked up her menu, liking the feel of the heavyweight paper, the dark green cover delicately etched in gold. Inside, the bill of fare was black calligraphy on ivory linen paper. She scanned it quickly, reviewing her options, but then her eyes wandered upward to Reed, and she studied him frankly over the top of the folder.

His words and gestures told the story of a man accustomed to being in charge. When he saw that Kate needed time to make her choice, he turned to the waiter and requested coffee for both of them, waved away his own menu, and told the server that Kate would be ready to order in a few minutes. Then he looked around the room, surveying his fellow diners in almost regal fashion. She thought of a little boy playing emperor and felt a smile tugging at the corners of her mouth. Who *was* this guy, anyway?

When she had looked at him earlier, she had seen him only as a handsome stranger. Now she tried to see the boy she had known inside the foreign person seated across from her. God, he was still so beautiful. His nose was long and elegant, his mouth full and shapely — he looked like something sculpted from clay by the loving hands of a female deity. Proof, Kate thought, that God is a woman. But for all that beauty, something about his lack of expression made her uneasy. It was as if she were looking at a house with the shades pulled down: someone might be able to see out, but she couldn't see in.

At that thought, two images flashed into her mind: Reed as a boy, sturdily built and brown from the sun. And Reed as a young man, his face alight with love and his eyes on fire with passion. A lump rose in her throat, and she blinked rapidly.

"Are you all right?" Reed asked.

"Something in my eye." Kate folded her menu and set it aside. "I don't know if I've mentioned it yet, but it's really great to see you."

"Thanks." He seemed embarrassed by her frankness. "I'm glad to see you, too."

"I've thought about you a lot over the years."

"Likewise." And that, Reed thought, that right there *was* the Understatement of the Year.

Kate smiled. A little of the Reed she used to know seemed to be peeking through. "So," she said, "these cruises aren't cheap. I take it you're doing pretty well for yourself?"

"I suppose you could say that," he said, returning her smile. "What about you?"

She bit her lip, then told him what she did.

His eyebrows went up. "A lawyer — just like you always planned. Congratulations."

Kate stirred uncomfortably. "Thanks. But it's not exactly like I had planned. I mean, I just handle the real estate end of the firm's business."

He kept his eyes on her. "Not quite Atticus Finch yet?"

"No," Kate said quietly. "Not quite yet."

She kept her face composed, but his question stung. Kate had been seven and Reed nine when they had seen *To Kill a Mockingbird* on Sunday afternoon television. Sprawled on the rug in her family room, they had stared raptly at the screen, fairly twitching with impatience during the commercials. Kate had fallen in love with the story, and that very day she had declared to Reed that she would be a defense attorney. Just like Atticus Finch. Just like her father. It was all she could talk about that summer, and all she had wanted to do since then. But she had never been inside a courtroom, except to watch her father as he tried a case.

As if he were following her thoughts, Reed asked, "And how's your father been?"

"He's doing well, thanks. He's still practicing."

"I always imagined that they'd have to carry him out before he'd retire."

"That's just what he says." Kate smiled.

Reed shifted the vase a fraction of an inch to the right, as if it had been a degree off-center and the lack of symmetry was too much to bear. "And your mother and Julia?"

"Also doing well. Julia's married — to an attorney, of course."

The shades behind his eyes rippled, and for a moment the old Reed was visible. "Your little sister is married?" He seemed genuinely astonished. "You mean she's not still eleven?"

Kate laughed. "Sometimes it seems like she is. She still steals my clothes — well, when she's not pregnant."

"Kids, too?"

"Kids two." Kate held up two fingers. "And the third one's due next month."

The waiter returned with their coffee, arranging cream and sugar between them, placing tall glasses of ice water crowned with lemon wedges on the table. Kate picked up her menu and scanned it again. Not wanting to appear to be too much of a glutton in front of her old boyfriend, she temporarily set aside her goal of gaining ten pounds. She ordered a grilled tuna salad and a glass of iced tea, then waited until the server had departed before leaning forward to speak. She spoke softly. "Reed, I was so sorry to hear about your grandmother."

A spasm of pain crossed his face for a moment, and then it was gone as if it had never been there. "Thank you."

"We didn't hear about it until months later, or we would have come back for the funeral." He didn't answer. "I know it must be small comfort for you to hear this two decades after the fact. Did you — did you get my letter? The flowers my parents sent?"

"I got them." His tone was even, but the blinds were drawn behind his eyes again — drawn down and fastened tightly. He was angry. Well, Kate supposed he had a right to be.

She fiddled with her napkin. This was agonizing, but now that she had broached the subject, she had to press forward. She tried to keep her voice gentle. "I always wondered why you didn't call me or write back to me once you knew where I lived."

"I didn't read your letter. I tore it up."

His voice was so matter-of-fact that she couldn't believe her ears. "What?"

"I tore it up." He looked directly at her. "And then I burned the pieces."

Oh, God. Kate thought about the letter, remembering how she had labored over it, written and re-written it, trying to get it right. She had poured herself into that letter, kissed it before she dropped it in the mailbox, thinking that it would make everything all right again. "Why — why would you do that?"

He picked up a fork and drew lines on the tablecloth. "Do you really have to ask?" he asked idly.

She reddened slightly. Now they were getting down to it. "There were things in that letter that you should have read," she persisted, her voice low. She had to make him understand. "Things that would have explained — "

"Explained what?" he interrupted, his eyes challenging her. "Why you left? But I already knew that."

"Did you now?"

"Oh, yes." He smiled without humor.

Kate could feel the back of her neck getting warm, a sure sign that either she was getting really angry or she was about to burst into tears. It worried her that she couldn't tell which. "And just what is it that you think you know?"

"The truth, apparently. Something I didn't get from you."

"And you believed what other people said about me? About my family? That doesn't sound like you."

"How do you know what sounds like me? We haven't seen each other in twenty years. We're strangers now."

"I just can't believe…" She heard her voice falter, and she bit her lip to combat the angry tears she suddenly felt pushing at the back of her eyes. "I can't believe that you would take someone else's word for what happened, and then refuse to hear my side of the story."

"So explain it to me, Kate." His voice was suddenly quiet, almost seductive. "I'm here. I'm listening."

Her anger blew like an icy wind across the table. "You're not here," she said. "And you're sure as hell not listening. Just — just forget it." She pushed back her chair and stood up.

Reed looked up at her, his face inscrutable. "What about your lunch?"

"You eat it. I've lost my appetite."

Reed watched her stalk out of the dining room, dodging gracefully between tables and waiters. He could have handled that better. But when she had bumped into him, when she had turned around and he had seen that beautiful, sweet face of hers alive and real in front of him, it was as if the twenty years in-between had never happened. As if they were still standing outside his grandmother's place in Angel River, and she was looking up at him and telling him how much she loved him, like the last time he had seen her. And then he was wandering through her empty house, dazed and enraged by his own echoing footfalls telling him that she was gone, that she wasn't coming back. The potent combination of love and anger had overwhelmed him, and he had reacted the way he always did now — retreat and fire from a safe distance. No open warfare for him. Why fight fair when you can fight safe?

She reached the far side of the dining room and disappeared through the frosted glass doors just as the waiter returned with her salad and iced tea. Reed considered going after her, but he quickly negated the idea. She was angry, and she had a right to be. He would give her a chance to cool down, then catch up with her later and try to make things right. It was a small ship, and she couldn't avoid him forever. Emotion broiled thickly somewhere inside him, but he tamped it down with long-practiced skill.

Besides, he had lied to her earlier — he hadn't eaten yet. It had been a stupid lie, small and mean and senseless. But it hadn't been the first lie he had told today, and it probably wouldn't be the last. He thought about the chicken salad and root beer in his stateroom refrigerator, then examined the salad she had ordered. The greens were fresh and glistening with champagne vinaigrette, the tuna medallions looked plump and juicy inside their crust of blackened sesame seeds.

What the hell, he thought. Why let it go to waste?

The waiter watched with a practiced veneer as the gentleman at table twenty-one picked up the lady's fork, pulled her salad towards him, and began to eat it. The lady herself was nowhere to be seen.

"Will there be anything else, sir?" the waiter asked, his voice neutral.

Reed swallowed and took a sip of tea before answering. "No," he said. "No, thank you."

CHAPTER FOUR

KATE GOT LOST TWICE ON the way back to her room, making two wrong turns and having to backtrack. That did not improve her mood. She was fuming.

The *nerve* of him, she thought. His behavior defied every rule of common courtesy. Well, maybe not *every* rule. But he didn't have to be such a condescending jerk. "I tore up your letter and burned the pieces"? What the *hell* was that about?

At last she reached her room, opened the door, and closed it hard behind her. Anger still hummed inside her. She needed action, something to take her mind off the whirlpool of emotions bubbling just beneath her fury. She decided to dig out her bathing suit and head up to the pool.

She looked around for her suitcases. When she'd left the room, they were standing at the foot of the bed. Now they were gone. Kate crossed the floor and yanked open the closet doors. Sure enough, her clothes were there. She opened the built-in drawers and found her undergarments, neatly folded. It was then that she spotted a card on her nightstand. It was a pre-printed note from the housekeeping staff, assuring her that her possessions had been unpacked with the utmost care, and that her suitcases had been stored for her convenience.

She replaced the note and plopped down on the bed, feeling slightly deflated. No unpacking for her to do. This kind of efficiency made her antsy. Why would anyone take the time to fold her underwear, anyway?

She lay back and stared up at the ceiling, clasping her hands behind her head. Reed seemed to be doing pretty well for himself, she mused. He probably had someone to fold his undies for him all the time.

We're strangers now, he had said. And he was right.

The grief that she had successfully fought off earlier finally claimed her. Tears welled in her eyes. Ever since she could remember, Reed had been her rock. Even after they parted, the memory of him had been a stabilizing influence in her life. The idea of the two of them being strangers — and awkward, angry strangers at that — was such an alien concept that it hurt to think about it.

She swiped at the tears that had burned their way down her cheeks. This was no way to behave. "You're going to get up and go out," she told herself sternly. "You're going to find something to do."

Instead she closed her eyes, feeling the day catch up with her, feeling exhaustion and jet lag creep over her, numbing her limbs and making them heavy. She was still hungry. She would rest her eyes briefly, then she would go for a swim and maybe order room service before taking a long, hot bath. She would just lie here for a minute....

But a minute later, she was asleep.

She was crying. She was six years old and crying. Her favorite ring, the one Daddy had given her, was gone. She had taken it off in art class, put it on the newspaper that Ms. Twain had spread on the tables to keep them from getting dirty, and then she had walked off and forgotten it. Now it was the end of the day, and the newspaper was gone, and the ring was gone, and her heart felt like it might as well have been gone, too.

All this she had explained to Reed between great gulping sobs. She didn't have to tell him how much that ring meant to her. He remembered when her father had given it to her, the day she had started first grade. She had been so proud of it, showing it to everyone. It was a little silver band with a red stone called a garnet. Reed thought it was the prettiest thing he had ever seen, and he couldn't bear the thought of it ending up in the garbage dump.

"Did you go back to the art room and ask Ms. Twain? Maybe she found it and doesn't know who it belongs to, so she just put it in her desk or something." He doubted that that was the case — Katie had shown that ring to everyone in school at least a dozen times.

"I went to ask, but the fourth graders were having their class. I — I didn't want to go in. I didn't want them to see me *cry.*" Her face crumpled again.

"I'll go with you. If the big kids are still there, I'll go in for you. Okay?"

Kate nodded.

They hurried through the wide halls. Their school was not a big one, but it could have been an entire college campus to their young legs. The art room was at the other end of the building from their classrooms. Kate stood outside on tiptoe to look through the half-glass door as Reed talked to Ms. Twain.

The teacher scurried around the room, giving pointers to the fourth graders as they worked with modeling clay, looking harried as Reed trailed on her heels and asked repeatedly if she had seen the ring. Finally she stopped and asked Reed a question, and he in turn looked questioningly at Kate. Interpreting his look, Kate pointed to the table where she had been sitting. Instantly Reed was there, running his hands over the clean sheets of newsprint that now covered the work area, just in case the ring hid underneath. Then he crawled under the table and scoured the floor, until the girls who were sitting there complained and Ms. Twain had to haul him out by his sneakers. After that, he crawled back and forth between that table and the trash can, examining every inch of floor for a glint of silver, a flash of red. There was nothing.

Kate's lip was trembling as Reed came dejectedly out of the room. Summoning his courage, he told her, "Twain says the janitor emptied the wastebaskets after your class left. We'll just have to go to the Dumpster, find the bag, and look through it."

Kate shook her head. "We won't find it — it's too tiny. Let's just go home."

Reed looked at the misery on her face, the defeated slump of her shoulders. He thought about that pretty little ring spending forever in the dump, with no little girl to wear it.

"Of course we'll find it," he told her. "Don't be silly. We'll look through every bag and piece of paper in the Dumpster if we have to. That ring's out there, Katie, and we'll find it." He grabbed her hand. "Let's go."

The air inside the Dumpster was thicker than gravy. Reed hadn't realized that air could actually be thick. Air was just air, usually. After the first few minutes inside the Dumpster, Reed was sure that the smell would get into his skin and never leave. The kids would call him Garbage Boy, and nobody would play with him or sit next to him at lunch.

"I will, Reed," Kate chirped. The sound came muffled through the metal wall. "I'll always be your friend, no matter what you smell like. And I'll *wallop* anyone who calls you Garbage Boy." A rock skittered across the pavement, fired by a violent kick from her little foot.

Reed hadn't realized he was talking out loud.

It had taken him just over an hour to go through two large bags of garbage with painstaking care. Inside that stinking cavern, however, the hour seemed to have been a lifetime. From time to time he glanced up and was surprised that the sun was still shining. He could imagine that it would have risen and set many times, but that his eyes had undergone a metamorphosis so that now he could see equally well in both light and dark.

"What's a metamorphosis, Reed?"

"It means a change."

Was he still talking out loud, or was she reading his thoughts?

He opened a third bag. It was full of newspaper, so he figured that was a good sign. He had already ruled out several bags that seemed to contain only food and cigarette butts.

He breathed in some more gravy and carefully pulled out a bundle of newspaper. As delicately as possible, he began to pull it apart, mindful of any loose objects that might fall out.

A flash of silver! His heart skipped. Was that it?

No, it was a pencil eraser with the metal part of the pencil still attached.

A glint of red? No, it was just the lid off a tube of red paint.

The sweat poured off his forehead, stinging his eyes. He reached up to wipe them before plunging his hand into the trash bag one more time. His fingers closed around something hard. His heart skipped another beat.

He pulled out his closed fist. He wanted to open his hand, but he was afraid of what he might not find.

"Katie?" His voice was squeaky with heat and weak

with exhaustion.

Her face appeared. "Did you find it?"

He looked up. Her tears were gone, replaced now with confidence. Reed had said they would find it, so they would find it. Nothing to worry about, now.

"Reed, did you find it?"

He looked back at his hand. His fingers unfolded themselves. There, sitting in the center of his palm, glinting merrily, was the ring.

Katie stretched out her hand to help him out. "Oh, Reed. I knew you could do it."

Her eyes opened gradually. Had she been dreaming? Had she slept? Her right hand went automatically to her left ring finger, searching for the garnet ring. Of course, it wasn't there. It was in her jewelry box on her dressing table in her apartment in DC. It was a long way away. Just like her history with Reed.

She sat up and rubbed her hands over her face, surprised to find that her cheeks were wet. Had she been crying in her sleep? Oh, brother. That was bad. She tried to laugh at her own foolishness, but it felt forced and wrong in the wake of the intensity of her dream.

The room was soft with fading purple light. What time was it, anyway? She squinted at the bedside clock. After six. Good grief, she'd been asleep all day. Swell way to start her vacation. Through the open patio curtains a slice of blue sky was visible, just deepening into twilight. Kate thought about how the air would feel up on deck, what the sunset would look like over the water. She imagined a pre-dinner cocktail hour, with her fellow guests laughing and talking, music playing in the background.

She could almost taste the icy smoothness of a well-made martini, the crunchy salt of cocktail peanuts.

Suddenly she felt starved for the company of strangers. She needed to get away from memories and dreams. It was time for new sights and sounds, new faces. She threw back the covers and reached for her swimsuit.

When she got to the upper deck, however, she was disappointed to find that the pool was empty except for a lone swimmer backstroking smoothly through the water. No pre-dinner cocktails, no music, no laughter.

But there was peace here. The gentle lapping sound of the woman's strokes was soothing, blending with the sound of the ocean and the faint cries of gulls. In the west, the sun was just beginning to drop into the horizon, streaking the sky with orange. The swimming pool was a long rectangle, lined with thousands of small iridescent tiles that caught the light and reflected it back, creating an irresistible sparkle. Kate slipped off her shorts and shoes and dove in.

The water was cold and invigorating. It felt good to push her muscles, to work them against the weight of the water. But the exertion couldn't drive away the ghosts that had been stirred by her dream. Reed's recovery of her lost ring had been a forgotten memory, just another stitch in the tapestry of their childhood, but now it seemed like a significant event. Was that when she had first fallen in love with him?

She could remember clearly now the moment he had slipped that ring back onto her finger. She remembered how he looked, his face hot and flushed, his upper lip drenched with perspiration. His eyes had blazed down at her, dark lashes casting shadows on his cheeks. She had felt the heat radiating from his body, and despite the tenderness of her years, she had felt the absolute rightness of their closeness. And she had known that it would always be like that, the two of them, close together.

Yes, that was the moment she fell in love. It had been an innocent love, a child's love; a love that did not conceive of sex or marriage, but was merely a sweet and piercing happiness, deep through the heart. Now, almost thirty years later, she still carried that feeling with her. It had become a part of her, so much so that she had almost forgotten about it.

Until today.

Kate climbed slowly out of the pool, her body heavy with the weight of the water that dripped off her. A soft breeze was blowing in from the west, bringing with it the salty smell of the ocean, and raising goose bumps on her arms as it washed over her damp skin. She reached for a thick white towel from a nearby pile.

"Mind tossing me one of those?" said a voice from behind her.

Kate turned around. A woman stood there, beautifully silhouetted against the backdrop of the setting sun, squeezing water out of her dark red hair onto the deck. Kate had been so lost inside her own thoughts that she'd forgotten there was someone else in the pool when she arrived. She picked up a second towel and handed it over.

"Thanks." The woman blotted her face dry and breathed deeply. "Great swim," she said. She looked at Kate and smiled. "Kind of washes off the jetlag, doesn't it?"

"Among other things," Kate said. The woman looked at her curiously, but before she could speak, Kate went on. "You know, I thought there was going to be a cocktail hour at the pool before dinner. Do you know why they canceled it?"

"They didn't," the woman said. "It's downstairs, on the

Sunrise Deck. This is the Penthouse Deck."

"But I thought the Penthouse Deck had a seawater swimming pool."

The woman smiled at her. "What do you think you've been swimming in?"

Kate turned around and looked at the water in the pool, then surreptitiously licked her lips. Salty. She shook her head. "Well, I'm all turned around today," she said softly. "And don't I just feel like an idiot."

"Don't beat yourself up," the woman laughed. "The need for a good cocktail makes idiots of us all." She held out her hand. "I'm Heather Christie, by the way."

"Kate Doyle. Nice to meet you." Kate studied the woman as she shook her hand. She looked vaguely familiar, but Kate had no idea where she might have seen her before. Maybe in a magazine? She looked like a model: flawless face and perfect body, with lightly tanned skin set off by her dark purple bikini. Kate pulled self-consciously at her own modest navy tank suit, suddenly very aware of her law-library pallor.

Spray-on tan, she heard her sister's voice say in her head. *It's the latest thing.*

Oh, well. Too late now.

If Heather noticed Kate's scrutiny, she gave no sign of it. Then again, she looked like someone who was used to being stared at.

And then something clicked. "Heather Christie," Kate said. "You're an actress, aren't you?"

"Well, that's what I tell people." Her smile was self-mocking as she spread her towel over a deck chair. "But I've read some reviews that say otherwise."

"Last year I was home for two weeks with the flu, and I

watched your show every day. I went through serious withdrawal when I had to go back to work."

"That's the idea. Soap operas are designed to be as addictive as nicotine." Heather settled into the chair. "Speaking of which…." She pulled a pack of cigarettes and a lighter out of a designer duffel and offered the pack to Kate, who declined with a smile and a shake of her head.

Kate spread her own towel over a chair nearby and lay back with a sigh of contentment. Heather tapped out a cigarette and lit it, taking a deep drag. For a moment she looked so deeply relaxed and blissful that Kate was tempted to snatch the thing away from her and suck the smoke deep into her own lungs.

Heather smiled when she saw Kate's expression. "I never smoke in public anymore," she said. "But you don't seem like type to tell on me. You don't have a camera hidden in your cleavage or anything, do you?"

"Not today."

"That's a relief." Heather smoked in silence for a moment, head back, eyes closed. Kate, watching Heather's cheeks suck in slightly as she inhaled, then lips part to release the smoke, was struck by how truly and simply beautiful Heather's face was. The near-perfect line from cheekbone to jaw; the dark eyes, lashes, and brows that contrasted so strikingly with her red hair. TV didn't really do her justice. She wondered if Heather were flaunting her beauty, or if that kind of careless splendor just came naturally to some women.

Kate felt a twist of pure female envy, followed by a wish that Julia were here. Jules would have shrugged off Heather's superior looks and instead pumped her for information, wanting to know all about Heather's skin regimen and who did her eyebrows and all the things that Kate had no idea how to ask.

Suddenly Heather turned and propped herself up on one elbow, facing Kate, who looked away quickly. She had been staring again, hadn't she? But Heather didn't seem to notice — or maybe she was just used to being stared at. "I have a weird question to ask you," she said. Her manner was suddenly very earnest.

Kate laughed cautiously. Well, this was intriguing. And maybe a little creepy. "Okay…."

"Was it my face you recognized, or my name?"

Kate almost laughed again, wondering if this was some sort of test that celebrities put to the common folks. But Heather looked so serious that Kate kept her face straight and tried to answer seriously. "Well, your face, I guess. Why?"

Heather's dark eyes watched her closely. "I just thought that Reed might have mentioned me."

Kate's heart skipped a beat.

"Reed *Fitzgerald?*" Her voice shook, betraying her shock. What was going on here? Was Reed traveling with this woman? Were they — had they — she forced herself to finish the thought. Was Heather Christie — tall, beautiful, famous Heather Christie — Reed's girlfriend? Or even his *wife?*

Kate tried to remember if Reed had been wearing a wedding ring when she had seen him at lunch. She remembered his hands, long and elegant, with slender fingers. She couldn't remember seeing a ring there. But that didn't mean a damn thing. People — men, especially — didn't always wear their rings.

Kate looked at her own hands, at her slender, ringless fingers. They were shaking ever so slightly. She clenched them tight against her knees. This was all too much.

Suddenly she realized that Heather was watching her, taking in every thought and emotion that passed over her face. Kate felt a surge of indignation. She didn't want this woman to probe her most innermost thoughts and feelings. She took a deep breath and tried to get a hold on herself. She groped for calm, found skepticism, and decided that was good enough. She arched an eyebrow and repeated Reed's name, just to make sure they were very clear. "Reed. Fitzgerald."

Heather nodded. "I know Reed. I used to date him."

"Oh," Kate said. That didn't explain anything. And was "used to date" better or worse than married? "And was there a reason you didn't mention this earlier, when we introduced ourselves?"

Heather's expression became apologetic. "I know. I should have said something. But to be honest, I wasn't sure exactly what to say. I thought — well, I guess I was hoping Reed had told *you* about *me*. I saw you two in the dining room at lunch," she explained, watching Kate closely from under those thick, dark lashes. "You argue like a married couple."

"And what makes you think we were arguing?" Kate asked stiffly.

"Body language." Heather smiled without humor. "It doesn't matter how low you keep your voice; body language says it all. I'm an actress — it's my job to know things like that."

"I see," Kate said. But she didn't. She really didn't see at all. How was she supposed to take this woman — this beautiful, poised, interesting woman, who supposedly had once dated Reed, the love of Kate's life? Were they supposed to be friends?

And what about about the situation in general? It had been a one-in-a-million shot that she had gotten the ticket to come on this cruise in the first place. Add to that the chance of running into Reed… and then Heather… those odds were stretching out way past reckoning. Kate was beginning to think that she was in the middle of some sort of elaborate cosmic practical joke. And she didn't like being the butt of it.

"So then I take it the two of you aren't a couple?" Heather asked the question innocently.

Kate shook her head slowly, lost inside her own thoughts. "We grew up together. This is the first time we've seen each other in twenty years." She laughed absently. "We just bumped into each other this morning — literally."

"So this really is quite a coincidence, isn't it?"

Coincidence? That barely covered it. *Impossible, bizarre twist of fate* came closer to an accurate description. Kate wondered if they had taken a wrong turn and were sailing through the Bermuda Triangle. "Do you think there are any more of Reed's old girlfriends on board? Maybe it's some sort of convention that nobody told me about."

Heather laughed, her face transforming from solemn to blithe. Kate was struck again by how lovely she was. "You know," Heather said breezily, "I have to admit that I'm glad Reed isn't married. I'd hate to think he might have dumped me, then turned around and gotten married right away!"

"He dumped *you?"* In spite of herself, Kate was intrigued.

Heather sighed. "Yep. And thanks for looking so shocked, by the way. It does wonders for my self-esteem." She shook her head sorrowfully. "He was never really that serious about me. We were just sort of buddies that slept together." The cigarette went to her lips, and she puffed on it with a dreamy smile. "The sex was great, though."

Again came a wrenching twist of envy. Kate had to turn her head to hide her face. She thought of Reed, so proud and handsome and dear to her. And yet so very, very distant. She thought of how callously he had disposed of her letter, tearing up not only paper, but all their years together, burning their childhoods along with her words.

How could he? she asked herself, feeling the gathering threat of tears behind her eyelids, like clouds before a storm. What was wrong with her, what was it that she lacked, that he would treat her that way? According to Heather, she and Reed had been buddies that had great sex together. But Reed and Kate had been confidants, guardians of each other's dreams, and keepers of each other's secrets. And all that had been torn up, burned, and thrown away.

All of that had meant nothing.

Kate stood abruptly, jamming her legs into her shorts, pulling her T-shirt on over her head. Heather looked up, surprised. "Are you okay?" she asked.

"Oh sure," Kate said, trying to keep her voice steady. Of course she wasn't okay. She felt like running home, back to her little condo and her little job in her little city. It may not be the life she wanted, but it was the life she understood. And there was no one there who would sneak up and attack her from behind. Hello, Kate, how are you, nice to see you, and while we're at it here's a knife in your back. "I mean, I appreciate the girlish confidences and all, but maybe that was a little more than I needed to know."

Heather's hand went to her mouth. "Oh God, I'm sorry. Of course you wouldn't want to know about that stuff. I let my big mouth get the better of me. Did I offend you?"

"No. I don't know." Kate shoved her feet into her sandals, not paying attention to what she said. "It's just that I came on this trip to try to get my life figured out, not to re-open old wounds."

Interest flared in Heather's eyes, then she quickly tried to hide it. "Old wounds?" she asked innocently.

Oh, right, Kate thought. Like I'm really going to confide in you. "It's nothing." She sighed. "Forget it."

She turned to go, but Heather reached out and put a hand on Kate's arm, stopping her. "Wait," Heather said, standing up. "Look, I'm sorry. I can be a real jerk sometimes. I should have been up front with you from the beginning."

Good manners forced Kate to say, "It's all right."

"No, it's not," Heather said, echoing Kate's very thoughts. "Now that I really think about it, that was a hell of a thing for me to do. I guess…I guess it's just that where Reed is concerned, I don't always think straight. Or even play straight."

Well thanks for the warning, Kate thought. But in spite of her better judgment, she could feel her anger start to cool. She wasn't sure she had the strength to stay angry right now.

Heather was watching her closely. "My mother always told me I could lose a friend by lying. I guess I should've listened."

Kate felt herself give in. "Well, it's not like you *lied*, you just…."

"Didn't tell the truth," Heather finished. "I know. Why don't you let me make it up to you? Come to dinner with my friends and me tonight."

Yeah, right, Kate thought. But she toned down her response and simply said, "I don't think that'd be a good idea."

"Oh come on," Heather said. Her voice turned chummy and persuasive. "You'll like my friends. There are four of us — we travel together a lot. We're a pretty motley crew, but we can be entertaining."

Kate sighed. "Traveling with a group of friends," she said. "How Hollywood."

"Oh, yes, all us show-business types travel with an entourage. Without them we'd have to spend all our time telling *ourselves* how wonderful we are. Of course, we do that anyway…."

Kate laughed at that. She had to admit she was tempted. It was hard not to like Heather, but warning bells were going off like crazy inside Kate's head.

"I can't promise you'll grow to love us," Heather said honestly, "but I can *definitely* promise that you won't be bored."

Lack of boredom, Kate thought with heavy sarcasm. Well, that totally clinches it.

But she was surprised to find that, for some reason, it did.

It's just one meal, she told herself. A couple hours, and if you hate it, you can spend the rest of the trip on your private balcony.

Kate nodded slowly. "Okay," she said. "Okay. What time?"

CHAPTER FIVE

I T TOOK KATE OVER AN hour to decide what to wear. She hadn't taken this much trouble to dress since her senior prom. Why had Julia insisted that she bring so many dresses? Sure it was good to have variety, but in this case *variety* meant *too many choices*. She shuffled through the closet again, tossing dresses onto the bed as she went. Blue, red, green… sundresses, tea dresses, even a couple scandalous ones with a long slit up the side. But none of them felt like "her." Not that she knew what that meant, anyway.

She held one long green dress up in front of her and looked into the mirror. The color showed her fair complexion to good advantage, picked up the auburn highlights in her hair. Reed had always liked her in green.

Oh God, she thought, sinking down on the bed. Reed. Would he be in the dining room tonight? He'd have to eat sometime. She'd have to see him sometime soon. She thought about seeing him and Heather together. How was she supposed to stand that?

A couple hours ago, this dinner had seemed like a fine notion, but now doubts crowded in on her again, and she asked herself how she could have been so stupid as to accept the invitation.

Heather had said that she wanted Kate to meet her friends.

She had seemed sincere, but Kate knew that that was just a line. Heather wanted to scope her out, to use Kate's childhood relationship with Reed to somehow find out about him. Or something like that.

It was a control thing, or a dominance thing, or a perverse curiosity thing. Heather's precise motives were hazy, but there was one thing that was clear: Kate wanted to go to this dinner with her as badly as Heather wanted her there. Heather knew Reed in a way Kate never had. And Kate needed to get a grip on who he was now, in this day and time. She felt that if she could understand *him* better, somehow it might help her to understand herself.

She blinked back the tears that had gathered at the corner of her eye and resolutely turned back to the pile on the bed, determined to settle on a dress. Kate searched through the pile until she found a navy blue sheath, with wide straps and no slit. It was pretty, but very respectable-looking. Safe. And Kate was tempted, so very tempted, to go with something safe. Wearing this dress, she would feel completely harmless, totally invisible, not at all competitive with her fellow females.

But that green dress kept drawing her eye. Emerald green, deep and glowing. Spaghetti straps and a low-cut neckline. Wearing *this* dress, she felt, would be a statement — not only to others, but to herself. If she could wear this dress and sit at a table with Heather, knowing that people would be looking at both of them and making the inevitable comparisons, she would have proven something to herself about her own self-confidence.

And that decided the issue.

Later, after she had been introduced to Heather's friends, after drinks had been ordered and the conversation flowed freely, Kate sat in the brocaded dining chair and looked around at the opulence of her surroundings and knew she had made the right choice. This was not the place to fade into the background. This was a place to shine, whatever that meant for her.

Kate found that she enjoyed herself with Heather and her friends. Alicia Whitman was cool, but friendly, mostly satisfied with sipping her drink and commenting on the people around them. Sometimes the comments were complimentary, mostly they weren't, but they were always amusing. Joe King and Elliot Wilde, cousins, were eager to relate embarrassing childhood stories about each other. Elliot had broad shoulders, a long, sloping nose, and a wolfish smile. His hair was blond and just beginning to recede at the temples. Joe, on the other hand, was dark-haired and slender with piercing brown eyes, and possessed a wealth of information about everything around him — the food, the ship, the islands.

He swirled the wine in his glass, admiring the deep red color. "This ship is truly unique," he said. He looked over the rim of his glass and smiled. "Do you want to know why?"

"Do we have a choice?" Alicia Whitman sighed. She leaned across the table towards Kate, dark hair falling sleekly over her shoulder. "He'll tell us whether we want to know or not."

Joe ignored her and went on. "Well, for starters, it's the first ship to be launched by the Phoenix Waters Voyage Line. So in that respect, it's the newest ship on the water. But the *William* was actually built in the '50s — it was part of the fleet owned by Achille Lauro, the Greek shipping magnate."

"Why do all shipping magnates seem to be Greek?" asked Alicia. "Aren't there any French shipping magnates? Or Italian?"

"How about American shipping magnates?" Heather offered.

"Exactly." Alicia gave Joe a triumphant look, as if she'd somehow just scored a point over him.

Again, he ignored her. "The other interesting thing about the *William*," he went on pointedly, "is that despite its age, it's been completely refurbished and modernized. It's totally state-of-the-art. It's got a gym, two swimming pools, wireless Internet — "

"Don't all cruise ships have those features nowadays?" Heather interrupted.

"Some do," Joe conceded, "but most of them carry a thousand people or more. This one is designed to only take on a hundred and fifty passengers at a time. It's the most exclusive ship in the world," he finished smugly. "That's what makes it so unique."

"If it's so exclusive," Elliot said disdainfully, "how did *you* get a ticket?"

"I promised the captain I'd keep you away from the wine cellar," Joe retorted.

"That reminds me, Elliot," Alicia said casually, examining her immaculate nails. "You never did thank me for getting you a reservation."

Elliot raised his glass to her. "My dear Alicia, allow me to express to you my deep and abiding gratitude for your generosity in procuring for me a reservation on this superb vessel. And to your rich daddy, for providing you with the connections to provide me with the reservation."

Alicia smiled, revealing dimples and very white, very straight teeth. "Well put."

Joe stretched his arm along the back of Alicia's chair. Kate watched the motion with amusement. Though his gesture appeared nonchalant, the unspoken message was clear: *mine*. Apparently Joe didn't want Elliot to get any romantic notions about Alicia, but to Kate, there didn't seem to be any danger of that. Elliot's gaze roved freely over every woman in the vicinity — herself included. The possibility of him getting overly-attached to any one female in the room seemed remote, to say the least.

"Well, well," Heather said suddenly. "Look what just walked in."

Kate turned in her chair, following the direction of Heather's nod. Her heart skipped a beat. It was Reed. He had just entered the dining room, and he was standing inside the double doors. Outwardly, he was elegantly handsome in his perfectly tailored suit, and his air of calm self-possession was discernible from across the room. But to Kate he looked like a little boy in the school cafeteria who had no one to sit with him at lunchtime.

"What's he doing here?" Elliot asked sharply.

And Alicia shot Heather a look. "You didn't mention Reed was on board."

Heather ignored them both and raised her arm to get Reed's attention. "You don't mind, do you?" she asked Kate, motioning him over.

Joe spoke up before Kate could answer. "Why would Kate mind?" he asked, his eyes alight with curiosity.

"More importantly," added Elliot, "why didn't you ask us if *we* mind?"

Kate watched Reed's eyes focus on Heather. He looked surprised, and Kate didn't blame him. She could practically read his thoughts. He was asking himself how on earth he had ended up on the same ship as both Kate *and* Heather. Well, he could join the club — Kate had been wondering the same thing.

Reed's gaze slid over the table, taking in Heather's friends, all of whom he probably knew, and finally settled on Kate herself.

When he saw her, his face went rigid — stern, even. Kate had no idea what he was thinking. Was he feeling bad about the things he'd said at lunch? No, that didn't sound like him. Was he blaming her for the things *she'd* said? That was more of a possibility, but it still didn't feel quite right. Was he wondering why the hell Kate was sitting at a table with Heather? Yes, that was probably it.

Kate weighed her own emotions as Reed crossed the room towards them. She was excited, she realized. Her heart beat faster, and she felt her cheeks flush. When they had bumped into each other earlier, she'd had no time to prepare, no time to enjoy the anticipation of meeting him again. But now she could. She was seeing him again, live and in person. It wasn't a dream or some foolish romantic fantasy. They were going to sit at the same table. They were going to talk. This was it.

"Well, hello, stranger." Heather stood up to greet Reed as he arrived at the table. Kate's heart was churning as she watched Heather gave him a peck on the cheek, and then wipe the lipstick mark off his face with a laugh. "Long time no see. Would you like to join us?"

Reed accepted her kiss stiffly, then nodded to the group seated around the table. "Nice to see you all again. I hope I'm not intruding."

"Of course not," Heather said as she sat back down. "The more the merrier."

Reed's gaze settled again on Kate, and their eyes met and locked. Her breath caught in her throat. She hadn't expected this spark of electricity, quickening her pulse and raising goose bumps on her arms. "Have a seat," she said, making an effort to keep her voice steady. "We were just getting ready to order."

A waiter scurried over with a chair. Reed motioned for him to put it next to Kate, and she scooted over to make room. Her heart was in her throat as he sat down next to her. Kate could feel the eyes of the others watching the two of them — Heather with a knowing glint that may or may not have disguised jealousy, the other three with curiosity.

"Well, I take it that you two know each other already, so we're all friends here." Alicia smiled sweetly. "How lovely. Where did you meet?"

Reed was leaning back as the waiter put a place setting in front of him and placed a napkin in his lap, so Kate simply answered, "We grew up together."

"You grew up in Angel River, too?" Elliot said. "Two successful, handsome people from the same little town. What do they put in the water in small-town Virginia, anyway?"

Kate was momentarily confused, simultaneously wondering how Elliot knew the name of her hometown, and somehow thinking that maybe Elliot meant he was also from Angel River.

Joe hastened to explain, "Please excuse my idiot cousin. Putting together coherent sentences can be difficult for him. He was referring to the two of you." He nodded across the table toward Kate and Reed. "Reed's been profiled in a number of magazines, and they mentioned where he was born."

"Oh." Kate suddenly realized that she had no idea what Reed did for a living. Something important, obviously, or else who would write about him?

"From small-town kid to captain of industry," Elliot said acerbically. "That's always been part of the Reed Fitzgerald story." Despite his tone of voice, he looked a little awed.

Reed smiled as he adjusted the placement of his silverware. "Don't believe everything you read in the *Wall Street Journal,*" he said. "I may be from a relatively small town, but my beginnings weren't all that humble."

He shot Kate a look under his lids, taking in the startled

look on her face. "The press likes to exaggerate rags-to-riches nonsense," he added mildly. "Where you're going in life is a lot more important than where you've been."

Kate understood. She knew, better than anyone, how desperately poor he had been while growing up. It made sense to her that he would want to downplay that part of his life.

"Don't be so modest," Elliot said with exaggerated deference. "You're a self-made man, practically a folk hero on Wall Street."

"Elliot, what *are* you talking about?" Kate asked, amused by his overstated obsequiousness.

"Don't you know? My dear, your childhood pal is a now celebrity in financial circles. Everyone who's anyone on Wall Street wants his ear — *Barron's* reports his every move like it was a social column and he was a supermodel debutant."

"Supermodel debutant?" Kate laughed and looked at Reed. "Are you the 'supermodel debutant' of Wall Street?"

Reed laughed uncomfortably. "I wouldn't say that."

"Again, I say don't be so modest. The corporate officers in my firm are thinking of asking you to bless their children after the last financial quarter." Elliot wound up his shtick with an engaging grin. "I bow down to your monetary genius."

Alicia leaned across the table. "Apparently Elliot is hoping you'll give him a job on the strength of his bootlicking ability," she said to Reed.

"Nonsense!" Elliot said loudly. "You know perfectly well that I am *drunk*, not boot-licking. Please, leave me some dignity."

"I think your dignity left when your last drink arrived." Joe looked around for the waiter. "We need to get some food into you." He got the waiter's attention and motioned him over, then looked sternly at the women at the table. "I want you three girls to eat a real meal — not a few pieces of lettuce followed by your third martini each. One supermodel is enough for this table, and Reed has dibs on that title."

The waiter brought their menus and took orders for drink refills. "No more alcohol for him," Heather said firmly, gesturing to Elliot. "Bring him some pre-dinner coffee."

"Yes, ma'am." The waiter slipped discreetly away.

While they looked at their menus, Kate leaned slightly in Reed's direction. "I can't believe that I haven't heard about you — about how well you've been doing," she said in an undertone. There was pride and something like awe in her voice. "I'm so happy for you. Really," she insisted as he shifted uncomfortably. "No matter what else, I am happy for you."

Their eyes met and locked again. The sincerity with which she had spoken communicated itself to him. He nodded, accepting it. "Thank you."

The energy between them was not lost on the others at the table. Glances were exchanged, full of meaning. Alicia was the one who spoke up. "So how long has it been since you two have seen each other?"

With effort, Reed pulled his eyes away from Kate's. "Almost twenty years," he said.

"And you were, what, childhood sweethearts or something bucolic like that? How charming."

Kate's gaze drifted around the table, taking in the frank curiosity in the faces that surrounded her. "Our families knew each other," she explained. "We went to school together, kept each other busy and out from underfoot while the grown-ups were around. Reed was two years older than me, so naturally he was my hero — taught me how to climb trees, how to throw a punch, that sort of thing."

Their eyes met again. They couldn't seem to stop looking at

each other. "When we got older, of course we dated some."

Dated some, Reed thought. That was one way to put it. After they had realized what they had to offer each other — male and female, with all sorts of interesting possibilities arising from their physical differences — they had barely been able to keep their hands off each other.

"I remember the first time I saw you," he said. "You were about six months old. My grandmother had gone to see your parents about something, and she brought me with her. Your mother let me peek into your crib. You were wrapped in a pink blanket, and when you saw me, you started bawling your little head off." He smiled. "It was love at first sight."

The warmth in his eyes touched Kate's heart. There was a catch in her voice when she spoke. "How could you remember something like that? You weren't even three yet."

Someone at the table coughed, and Reed looked up, abruptly reminded that they weren't alone. "Yes," he said quietly. "Well, I guess it's like that old beer commercial: you never forget your first girl."

Laughter rippled around the table as the waiter returned to take their orders for dinner. Reed gave his order, relieved that he and Kate were no longer the center of attention. What had come over him? Sentimental reminiscences weren't exactly his style.

His eyes were drawn back to Kate, and he studied her as she made small talk with Elliot. He hadn't thought it was possible, but she looked more beautiful than she had this morning. Her hair was gleaming and loose against her neck, her lips shiny with gloss. The silky green dress she wore had a long slit in the side, which allowed his gaze to follow the curve of her leg to the middle of her creamy thigh. And here he'd thought that the ocean was going to provide the best scenery on this trip.

She turned her head, suddenly aware of his scrutiny. Her cheeks flushed slightly at the expression on his face, and her eyes took on that knowing look that women got when aware of the effect they were having on a man. He smiled, remembering the first time he had seen that look in her eye, when she had suddenly become aware of her own attractiveness and the power it gave her. The image of her as a young ingénue superimposed itself on the image of her as she was now, and the two pictures blended into one — the past meeting the present and suddenly making sense.

"So where in Virginia is this small town of yours located?" Elliot asked, trying to reclaim Kate's attention, which he had been thoroughly enjoying a moment before she had turned her head to look at Lord-God Fitzgerald.

"Central Virginia," she said.

"I hear it's beautiful there."

"It is. Rolling hills, twisting rivers — the whole country setting. It was a good place to grow up."

"Do you still have family there?"

Kate shook her head. "My father's family moved to Angel River when he was a teenager. My grandfather was a college professor, and he had taken a job at the University of Richmond. I think my grandparents would have stayed in Angel River for the rest of their lives, but my uncle died in Vietnam, and then my father went off to college…. There were just too many sad memories, so the family moved back to DC."

"But then how did you come to be raised there?"

"My mother was also from Angel River. She and my father were high school sweethearts. When they got married, they decided to open up the family house again, and that's where we lived."

"But now you make your home in our nation's capital."

"Correct." Kate took a sip of water and smiled to herself. She was amused at how engrossed Elliot seemed by her prosaic account of her family's history. She wasn't sure if he were trying to make Heather jealous, or one-up Reed in some way, or if he were simply hoping to get her into bed at some point on their trip. Probably all three, she decided.

"I guess that the quiet country life doesn't much compare to the tension of politics and the excitement of life in the big city," Elliot said.

"Small town life has its own tensions," Kate replied musingly. Her eyes found Reed's again and they shared a quiet look.

"Oh do tell!" Elliot said enthusiastically. "What kind of rustic, Carson McCullers-esque sagas unfolded in your little corner of the universe?"

"Carson McCullers is a great writer." Kate smiled and used her best legal-representative-manner to sidestep the question. "Reed's grandmother loved her work — she told us all about McCullers' stories when we were kids. *The Ballad of the Sad Café* was one of my favorites." She looked at Reed. "Remember?"

His face became inscrutable. "I remember," was all he said.

Kate realized she was treading on dangerous ground, bringing up something that would hurt him…or remind him of a past hurt. Her gaze fluttered away from his, then traveled back again. And although she had intended to look away quickly, she found that she couldn't. Their eyes met and locked. Suddenly Kate became aware that it wasn't an old hurt he was thinking about, it was another feeling altogether. She felt a warm flush spreading over her, from the tip of her toes to the roots of her hair.

Alicia leaned forward and stubbed out her cigarette. "Well,

it sounds like you two come from quite a dreamy little burg," she said. "Rolling hills, gurgling streams, and a sweet little granny who tells stories to all the neighborhood children. Charming."

Sweet little granny. Kate felt a laugh sparking wickedly inside her at the description. She recognized the sarcasm in Alicia's voice — recognized it, and appreciated it. After all, sarcasm was Kate's native tongue. Feeling bold, she matched Alicia's tone.

"Oh yes," she said. "It was an idyllic place to grow up. I remember the day that Reed tricked the neighborhood kids into whitewashing the fence for him. And then there was the time we got lost in the cave after the church picnic. Good thing Reed had that long piece of string in his pocket, or we would've been goners for sure. No…wait a sec…." She paused. "That was Tom Sawyer."

Even Alicia laughed at that, and Kate felt confident enough to switch gears. "I have to say, there is a lot of history in that part of the country, though." She looked directly at Heather and smiled. "Did you know that one of Reed's ancestors founded the town?"

Kate could feel Reed shifting uncomfortably next to her, but this time she didn't care. She had always told him that he should be proud of his family. They were pioneers in a lot of ways.

Heather took Kate's look as a challenge — an *I know more about Reed than you do* type of thing. She narrowed her eyes and tilted her head to one side. "I did know, actually," she said. "Reed told me the story himself years ago." She looked around the table. "But my friends here have never heard it, so why don't you tell them?"

Kate's eyes moved again to Reed. He must have read the uncertainty in her face, because he spoke up.

"It's not a very long story," he said. "Because the truth is we don't know everything that happened. But what we do know is that in 1865, right after the end of the Civil War, an ancestor of mine — a man with the improbable name of Gerald Fitzgerald — emigrated from Ireland with his two daughters. The older of the two girls was 'in the family way,' as my grandmother used to say. It's something of a mystery as to why he chose to make such a long and dangerous trip with a daughter in that condition, but whatever his reasons, he found himself traveling through Virginia when she went into labor.

"They were driving a horse cart down an old dirt road when her contractions started. Naturally, they stopped, and Gerald went pushing through the woods to look for water. He came to a creek, which led to a stream, which then led to a small river. That body of water turned out to be a tributary of the James River, although Gerald had no way of knowing that at the time. He brought his daughters to the little clearing that he had found, and the first of a long line of Fitzgeralds was born on U.S. soil. The baby — who was a boy — was named America, after his new home."

"Such a lovely story," Heather said. She had been watching the interaction between Kate and Reed very closely. So far she had refrained from asking too many questions herself because she didn't want to betray her curiosity, relying instead on her friends to gather information — something at which they usually excelled. But tonight they seemed to be slipping, and now her curiosity got the better of her. "So, after all this history that you two share, all the things you have in common, how is it that you haven't seen each other in such a long time?"

Kate mentally bit her lip and again avoided looking at Reed. "When I was sixteen my father got a job in Washington, and we had to move. Reed and I…just lost touch."

"That's so sad. Especially considering how close you were." Heather looked across the table at Alicia. "Don't you think it's a shame?"

Alicia picked up her cue. "I do indeed. It's too bad that you couldn't stay in touch with each other. After all, you knew where Reed was, and he…well, he knew where you were, didn't he?"

Kate was caught off-guard by the sudden change of subject, as well as by the smoothness of the tag-team interrogation. She felt her hackles rise and she opened her mouth to respond, but Reed spoke first.

"Kate's family had to leave very suddenly for personal reasons," he said, calmly meeting Heather's gaze. "Not long afterwards my grandmother passed away, and I went off to college."

His simple statement of fact left little room for further questions. Heather gave in and changed the subject. "We'll be in Bonaire in a couple of days," she said with a smile. "I assume we'll all want to do some sightseeing. We should make plans for all of us to go together."

"We'll be docking in Kralendijk," Joe put in. He, for one, seemed to be glad that they were talking about something else. "It's the capital of the island — supposed to be quite a beautiful place. It was settled by the Dutch in the 1400s —"

"Oh, no," Elliot said. "If you're going to start spouting off again, I'm having another drink."

CHAPTER SIX

FTER DINNER, THEIR WAITER WHEELED over a cart loaded with desserts. The wealth of pastries and confections glistening with glazes, or covered with frothy clouds of whipped cream, was too much to resist.

"How can we refuse?" Kate asked.

"I'm not sure this dress can handle any more food," Heather said, resting her hand on the skin-tight black sheath she wore. "One more bite and the seams may burst."

"Then by all means, have a piece of cheesecake — or two," Elliot encouraged.

After some discussion, they did have dessert, but to Elliot's disappointment, Heather's seams held together. To contrast with the sweets, they sipped biting-hot espresso out of miniature porcelain cups.

When they were done Heather snapped her fingers and said, "All right, kids, it's time to work off those calories. Let's hit the dance floor."

There was a clubroom on the upper deck, which doubled as a nightclub in the evenings. As they climbed the wide staircase and turned a corner, a throbbing Latin rhythm reached their ears. Inside, colored lights pulsated around the room, reflecting off the black floor and the bodies bouncing and gyrating to the rhythm. Heather and Alicia hit the floor immediately, while

Joe and Elliot headed toward the bar in the corner, contenting themselves with cocktails and excellent views of the action. No one spared a backward glance at Kate and Reed, who stood uneasily together on the sidelines.

They shared a self-conscious smile. "Well, this is great." Kate had to shout to be heard. "We couldn't have asked for a more awkward situation."

Reed's lips were moving, but she couldn't tell what he was saying.

"What?" she shouted.

"I said, do you want to dance?" he yelled.

She shrugged.

He put his lips close to her ear so she could hear him. "I'm more used to slow dances. Like when we were kids, remember?"

Oh yes, she remembered.

That was the moment the music was segued smoothly from the pounding salsa beat to a slow, silky remix of Roberta Flack's "Killing Me Softly."

Everything old is new again, Kate thought.

She and Reed exchanged nervous smiles. "Careful what you wish for," Kate said.

This time, he didn't bother to ask. He took her hand and led her out onto the dance floor, sliding his arm around her waist. Close together now, Kate's head rested automatically on Reed's shoulder, and any feeling of awkwardness between them dissolved into the music.

The feel of Reed's arms around her was both wonderfully familiar and tantalizingly new. She remembered being sixteen and held in his arms like this. She remembered the good, warm solidity of his hands on her back, the way it felt to be pressed tightly against him, the scent of his skin. She allowed her hands to slide over his shoulders, and let her fingers twine in his hair. If only everything could be as easy as this. As easy as sinking into him, with the music swirling around them, making it seem as if they were the only two people in the room.

And she was not the only one affected. Reed found himself in a quandary, in danger of losing his grip on the remote façade he had so carefully constructed. His resistance was slipping away like quicksand. She lifted her head from his shoulder and looked up at him searchingly. Their faces were close together, he felt her warm breath on his cheek and saw that she wore some kind of smoky green eye shadow that brought out the gold in her eyes, and her lips shone like they were waiting for him to kiss them until all the gloss was smudged away. He felt faintly dizzy at the thought. Since he'd seen her last, he had spent half his life waiting for this moment, and the other half convincing himself that he didn't want it. Now he didn't know what to think. He wasn't even sure what to feel.

When the song was over they drifted outside, fingers laced together, unaware that several pairs of eyes followed them, all swimming with curiosity.

They walked for a while in silence, without needing or wanting to talk. Each of them wanted to let the other speak first, to set the tone for what was to come next.

It was a beautiful night — perfect, in fact, with a full moon, silver stars sparkling in a blue-black sky. A tropical wind was blowing softly, kissing Kate's cheeks tenderly as it went and gently lifting her hair from her neck.

This is a night made for lovers, Kate thought. Then she pushed the thought away. She was getting ahead of herself. Wasn't she? To cover her confusion, she broke her silence and said the first thing that came to her mind. "We never see this many stars back home."

"Back home? You mean Washington."

"You thought I meant — "

"I thought you meant Angel River." Reed stopped and leaned on the railing, evidently embarrassed by his mistake.

"I guess it is home, isn't it? To tell you the truth, I can't even believe I've started using that word to describe any other place."

"You've lived in DC ever since…?"

"Yes. Ever since we left Virginia." She glanced sideways at him. "Reed, I *am* sorry about — about what happened. About the way I handled things — or the way I didn't handle them, I guess."

"None of that matters now, Kate," he said slowly. "It's all ancient history."

But she could see that he didn't believe that. "It does matter." Kate closed her eyes and summoned her courage. "Look, Reed, until now I wasn't sure I should tell you this, but —"

"No," he said quickly. He smiled apologetically when he saw the look on her face. "No," he said again, more gently this time. "You're under no obligation to tell me anything, Kate. And let's be honest — *I'm* the one who owes *you* an apology. For the way I behaved this afternoon. I had no right to speak to you that way. The only excuse I can offer is that my business accomplishments have made me rather stuck-up — arrogant, even. But then, I've never been very good with people, as you'll probably remember."

"It was the other way around," Kate said, automatically coming to his defense. "What I remember is that most of the people around you weren't good with *you*. You never really got a break as a kid. Growing up that way doesn't exactly foster sympathy for one's fellow men — or one's fellow *people*, I guess

I should say."

Reed waved a hand dismissively. "I appreciate the sentiment — and your politically correct phraseology — but there are plenty of people who had it a lot worse than I did. I have no right to complain. I may not have had a lot, but I did have food to eat and a place to live. And people in my life who loved me."

"Like your grandmother," Kate supplied.

"And you," he added. He turned to face her, leaning one elbow on the railing. "I hope you don't ever underestimate what you meant to me, Katie. What it meant to have you in my life."

Oh God, he was breaking her heart. If he knew, if he only knew half of the things she could tell him, he wouldn't be so appreciative of her presence in his life. He might even hate her. And he was a man who *knew* how to hate, that much she remembered. Abruptly, her eyes filled with tears. She tried to turn away, but it was too late — he had seen them. He reached out and gently took her chin, turned her face to his. "I was given a lousy break as a kid, and I resented it for a long time. But what I've come to realize is that along with that lousy break, I was given a great gift — a wonderful friend." He shook her chin gently, playfully. "I'm talking about *you,* in case you don't know it."

"You had me," Kate murmured gently, very much aware of the warmth of his hand on her skin.

"Yes," Reed said.

"Until you didn't." She backed up slowly, putting space between them. No matter what the consequences to herself, she owed it to him to explain things. "You had me until you didn't. And I need to explain — I need to tell you *why* — "

"I don't want to discuss it!" he said angrily. He ran a hand through his hair. "I don't want to *relive* it. It was the worst time in my life. I see no reason to go back, just on the off chance I might learn something new."

"But there are things that you should know — "

"Why?" he demanded. "Why do I have to know them? Are any of those things going to make me feel better?"

"Make you feel better?" Kate's temper flared. "I'm trying to tell you the truth here, *friend*, and all you want to know is are you going to feel better?"

"Oh, *the truth*. You were always so obsessed with truth. Whose truth, Katie? Yours? Mine? Somebody else's? I have spent years — *years*, do you hear me? — building a world for myself where things make sense. A world where if I'm hungry, I eat. If I'm cold, I can turn the heat up. A world where *I am in charge*. That's all the truth I need. And who are you to try to take that away from me?"

A stab of guilt had her backing up again, shaking her head. She turned away, looking out over the ocean. The infinite, infinite ocean. It made her think of *Romeo and Juliet*.

My bounty is as boundless as the sea,
My love as deep; the more I give to thee,
The more I have, for both are infinite....

They'd read the play in high school, like most teenagers. And for the two of them, young and smitten with each other, the words had unfurled worlds before them, weaving magical pictures of love and eternity. But the world they'd tried to create between them had been as fragile as the paperback copies of the play they'd read — easily torn, growing yellow and brittle with the passage of time.

And Reed had built himself a new world, a place where he could feel safe.

Who are you to try to take that away from me? he'd asked.

She wanted to ask, Who are *you*, Reed? And what is this place you've made, where truth is a threat?

She thought of all the things she had to tell him, all the things that she thought he should know. Some of them would bring him relief, but some of them would hurt. They would hurt to say, and they would hurt to hear — just how much, she didn't know.

Reed was watching her closely, her face turned in profile. He still knew how to read her, knew when the drop of her eyelid signaled her acquiescence. "Let's just...remember the good times," he said gently, coaxingly. "There were plenty of those, weren't there?"

Kate turned back to him, saw the glow in his eyes and felt warmth rush to her cheeks. "There were a few."

"Then let that be enough."

She gazed up at him earnestly, remembering the sweet, serious little boy that she'd loved so much. She had watched him grow into a tough but attractive young man, and it was hard to reconcile that person with the adult who stood before her today — cold, imperious, but somehow still needful and loveable at the same time.

He reached out and took her hand. "What are you thinking about?"

"I was just remembering you as a little boy. It's weird to try to match up those two pictures. Like looking through a kaleidoscope."

"I had the same experience earlier this evening."

"Did you really?"

"Yes. Before dinner I was looking at you, remembering how I used to think it was impossible for you to be more beautiful than you were when you were sixteen. Somehow, you've surpassed even my wildest imaginings."

In spite of herself she flushed at the compliment, then grinned playfully. "So you've been imagining?"

He squeezed her fingers. "Of course."

The heat radiating off him was enough to make her sweat, despite the breeze blowing in from the water. Her hand, held gently in his, was tingling with the touch that she had been missing for so long. He pulled her to him, slowly, deliberately, wrapped his arms around her, and lowered his mouth to hers.

Their lips met while their eyes were still open. Gently at first, brushing with shivering tenderness that turned Kate's insides warm and liquid. She closed her eyes as he deepened the kiss, and the taste of his tongue brought a wave of sensation that turned into a flood of memories. The smell of cut grass, the feel of the air at twilight, the sound of a brook gurgling smoothly over rounded stones. All these met and melded as she pressed herself tightly to him and ran her hands through the thick softness of his hair. She remembered his taste and his smell, remembered the labored feel of his breathing and the joyful rigidity of his body.

She had expected to feel passion when she kissed him. What she had not expected was this overwhelming rush of awareness of all that they were and had been and could be to each other. It turned her over and over, irresistible and devastating, crushing and restorative, until she was not sure if she was standing firmly on deck or tumbling through the clouds.

Maybe, she thought, it was both.

Her lips were still warm and glowing from the touch of his mouth when she sank into a bubble bath later that night. The two of them had plans to meet for breakfast the next morning.

"I have a date with Reed," Kate said out loud to the walls, smiling and not caring if she sounded like an idiot.

After that amazing kiss they'd shared on deck, Kate half-thought that he might expect her to follow him to his bed that very night. And she half-thought that she might have done it, if he had asked. But he had seemed content to walk her to the door of her stateroom, kiss her softly on the mouth, and wish her good night. And that, she thought now, was probably for the best.

Kate sighed as the warm water engulfed her. Now *this* was living. She couldn't remember the last time she'd taken the time for a bath, let alone indulged herself with bubbles. She leaned her head against the bath pillow and let herself relax, floating in the blurry warmth of the water.

She inhaled deeply the scent of the bubbles that floated just under her chin. They smelled softly of coconut milk. Everything on this ship is tropical, she thought, sighing with contentment. She was about as far from the rainy DC winter as she could get. And that felt great.

Her mind drifted back to Reed, and the startling breadth of road that they had crossed together tonight. His sudden flare of anger had surprised her, although she realized now that it shouldn't have. She should have seen it coming — all that talk about how "The past was the past" was such crap. He just didn't want to have to deal with the pain of talking about it, and she could understand that.

Reed was used to being left behind by people who were supposed to love him. His father, dying before Reed was even born, dropping dead on the sidewalk of a brain aneurism. Happened all the time, people said. And his mother leaving town after he was born, never to be seen again. Very sad, people said. And then herself, leaving in the middle of the night. What had people said about that?

Reed was still hurting. That much was obvious.

But then, Kate thought, so am I.

Leaving him, leaving Angel River, had been the hardest thing she'd ever done. Of course, she hadn't had much of a choice in the matter. Her family had left, and she had gone with them. There had been reasons for their leaving, and they were good reasons, even if Reed didn't want to hear them.

After their abrupt departure from her hometown, Kate's family had settled in DC, near her grandparents, and her father had joined a flourishing law firm. Those were difficult days for the four of them — herself, Mom, Dad, and Julia. All of them dealing with different issues, making do as best they could, trying to be supportive of one another without intruding on each other's privacy. It was awkward, and they made mistakes, but eventually they had muddled through.

Kate, for her part, had missed Reed so much it made her ache. There was always something missing: something so basic, it startled her at times. Like the feeling of flipping a light switch when the bulb has burnt out or trying to take a breath underwater and finding no air. And then there was the guilt, the burden of carrying other people's secrets inside her, weighing down her heart.

After a while, not knowing what to do, not knowing how to handle it, she had rebelled. Her final year of high school had been hellacious for everyone. There had been cut classes, Fs on her report card, a little partying — it was all a blur. She could laugh about it now, but at the time, no one had found it funny. She remembered the desperation, the frustration, knowing she was breaking the hearts of the people who loved her most while being unable to stop, unable to control herself or her actions.

She'd been failing senior year — she, *Kate*, who always got perfect grades, who'd never before spent so much as a day in the principal's office. There had been a round of tutors, a round of therapists, a lot of yelling and a lot of tears. And finally, in desperation, her parents had pulled her out of school and had sent her to Europe.

Again, these days she laughed about it — how many troubled teens got a trip to Europe? But for her parents, it had been a last resort.

"Go," her father had said tiredly, his eyes troubled but full of love. "Find your smile. Find what will make you happy — what will make you *you* again. Because I miss you, Katie. We all do."

And so she had gone. Paris had been beautiful, Rome was majestic, but it had been in England that she had finally been able to recover her equilibrium. Like a balm for her soul, the rolling hills of the English countryside had eased her pain. And she had met a boy there. He wasn't *Reed* — no one ever could be — but he was a nice boy, whose smile had quieted the storm in her heart. She had expected to feel guilty afterwards, but when she returned home, she had felt at peace. Still grieving, yes, but at peace. She attended summer school and earned enough credits to graduate. She had gone back to being the faithful, reliable daughter she had always been.

But her life afterwards had been like a movie, like watching someone else go through motions that had already been pre-scripted, pre-planned, and directed by an off-screen presence. She had gone to college, and then to law school, and then had joined her father at his firm. It should have been a dream come true for her. But the truth was, life had been a dreary stretch of sameness. Each day a carbon copy of the day before, until eventually the days had all blended together to make years. Too many years.

And Reed, what was his story? What had happened to him after their world had fallen apart? Somehow he had pulled himself up from the wretched beginning of his life and had made himself into something special. Successful and wealthy, he now had the admiration of people like Elliot and Joe; men born with a silver spoon in their mouths looked up to him, sought his advice, wanted to be like *him*. That must have been satisfying, even rewarding in its own way. But what else was there in his life?

He didn't want to hear the many truths she had to tell him. Well, that was fine for now. She would let him keep his safe, well-built world intact for the time being. And if she were honest with herself, she would admit feeling relieved that she didn't have to be the one to break down the walls of his illusions — at least, not yet. In some ways it surprised her that he was still so angry, and so very adamant that what she could tell him was of no value to him. Wasn't he even *curious?* Didn't he want to *know?*

Apparently not. Apparently, he was satisfied to go on thinking that the world as he knew it was the world as it was.

Well, okay. There would be no life-changing revelations for him, no big emotional scene where she broke down and told him that everything he'd believed about her over the past two decades was a lie. That kind of scenario was the stuff of silly romantic novels, anyway — it had no place in the harsh dry world of reality.

Instead, they would get to know each other as the people they had become. They would get to know each other as adults.

She smiled and sank a little lower into the bubbles as she remembered the feel of his lips on hers. Getting to know each other as adults would definitely have its benefits, she thought.

This was the twenty-first century. She knew that she should be cautious, that she shouldn't rush into a liaison with a man who was virtually a stranger to her. Physically, she would be careful. Emotionally…well, if there were regrets, she would deal with them later.

"I'm going to enjoy myself," Kate said out loud. "For the first time in my life, I feel completely free, and I am going to enjoy it."

It was only later, when she was in bed and beginning to drift off to sleep, that she realized she hadn't thought of Mark even once that evening. Since Reed had first appeared in the dining room that afternoon, her thoughts had been of no one but him.

CHAPTER SEVEN

September 1966

LANA CARLYLE WALKED HOME ALONE from school. Her pace was deliberate and measured. She listened carefully to the sounds of her hard-soled shoes on the pavement, felt her leg muscles stretch with precision at each step. Her carriage was erect and graceful, shoulders square, books carried close to her fifteen-year-old bosom.

Across the street and a little ways behind her, three girls from her homeroom walked home together. Occasional bursts of girlish laughter reached Lana's ears, and at each one, she felt her shoulders become a little straighter, her steps a little more precise. Lana knew that the girls were not laughing at her, but if they happened to glance in her direction, she did not want them thinking that she was jealous of their camaraderie.

This ritual had repeated every day since school had started three weeks ago, and it would be repeated every day for all the months to come. Soon the girls across the street would reach the house of Kathy Duncan, the unacknowledged leader of her little circle of friends. They would go through the gate of the bright white picket fence, up the brick walkway, across the wide front porch, and into the house.

Lana would continue up the street, until it narrowed and

the houses grew smaller and closer together. Here the sidewalk would grow cracked, the street would become pitted, and the air would grow dank and cold. The sunlight never shone as brightly at this end of the street, which was a shame. Its warmth and comfort would have been better appreciated by the occupants of these shabby little dwellings than by their richer counterparts at the "good" end of the street.

When Lana reached her own particular shabby dwelling, she would put her books away and remove her school clothes. She would carefully rinse out her blouse, wash the underarms of it with soap, and hang it over the shower curtain rod to dry. Then she would put on her pink waitress' uniform, and walk back to town with the same uplifted chin and precise, measured steps with which she had left it.

After her shift at the coffee shop, she would make the trek back to her house, rinse out her uniform, and change into dungarees, a casual top, and the gum-soled moccasins that she wore when waiting tables. She would set out whatever leftovers she had managed to bring home for her mother's dinner, gather her schoolbooks and walk back up the street to Kathy Duncan's house.

Then it would be her turn to walk through the gate of the picket fence, up the brick walkway, and across the porch. When she reached the green-painted front door, she would lift the heavy brass knocker and rap three times. The door would be opened by a maid, who would smile at Lana as if she were any other visitor to this important house on the important end of the street. "Hello, Miss Lana," the maid would say.

Lana would give an answering smile and a nod and make her way back to the kitchen, where Kathy Duncan herself sat at the table, milk and cookies at the ready, in dungarees and moccasins like Lana's. And there the girls would sit and study together for an hour and a half, nibbling cookies, sipping milk, chatting together as they had done for as long as either of them could remember.

At some point during the evening, Mrs. Duncan would poke her head in and say hello. Then she would return to the family room, sit down across from Mr. Duncan, pick up her late-evening cocktail, and with a self-satisfied smile, she would say, "It does my heart good to see those girls together."

Mr. Duncan would mumble an incoherent agreement as he turned the page of his newspaper.

Lana and Kathy had been born on the same day in April 1951. They had lain side-by-side in the nursery wing of the county hospital. Their mothers had passed in the hallway, nodded to one another, and gone on, not knowing that their daughters were destined to be friends.

Six months after the births, Lydia Duncan had recovered her figure and wanted a new wardrobe to celebrate that fact. She telephoned the local seamstress, one Mrs. Elizabeth Carlyle. On the day of their first appointment, the two women had recognized each other, inquired after one another's daughters, and agreed that it was a remarkable coincidence that not only had their children been born on the same day in the same hospital, but they themselves had lived on the same street for years and never met.

What neither woman would have dreamed of mentioning was that the reason they had never met was because they lived in different realms of society, the boundaries of which were clearly drawn by the number of digits in one's bank account.

It became customary for Lana to join her mother on her frequent visits to the Duncan household. As the girls grew into toddlers, Mrs. Duncan begged Mrs. Carlyle to let Lana come to them every day because Kathy always enjoyed Lana's company so much.

Mrs. Carlyle knew what kind of opportunity this would be for her daughter — association with the Duncans would bring Lana the type of social stature that just being the daughter of a seamstress could never bring her. And so, with lips pressed tightly together, Mrs. Carlyle accepted the offer. Each day, she would dress her daughter in the best clothes she could provide, admonish her to mind her manners, and walk her up the street to the Duncan house.

But before they walked through the gate, Mrs. Carlyle would always kneel down, take Lana's hands, and say imploringly, "Remember your place, my love, but never feel that you owe them anything."

As Lana grew up, she came to understand those words and to take them to heart. The girls were friends, but it was a friendship that rarely spread outside the borders of Kathy's house. Despite repeated attempts by Kathy to get Lana to sit with her at lunch, to walk home with her from school, Lana always politely refused, saying that she wanted Kathy to have time to spend with her "other friends."

"They could be your friends too, dopey," Kathy had once said with exasperation.

"They might be nice to me because of you," Lana replied calmly, "but they would never really be my friends."

And so Lana walked home alone from school. When she heard Kathy and the other girls going through the Duncan's gate, she turned her head and met Kathy's eye. The two exchanged a little smile and a wave, and Lana walked on.

In the distance, high on a hill, the ruins of the old Fitzgerald place hovered over the town. Lana knew the story of the place as well as anyone. It had burned down over forty years ago, killing everyone except for Mrs. Fitzgerald, her young daughter Pleasance, and a single maidservant. The three of them had moved into a little shack on the corner of the property. Mrs. Fitzgerald, who had the reputation even to this day as a sweet and good woman, had died five years later, and her maidservant had died soon after. This left Pleasance, then only seventeen — not much older than Lana was now — to fend for herself. The girl, who had always been sullen and unfriendly, turned strange. Sometimes she would go years between visits to town. And then, some fifteen years after her mother had died, Pleasance had a baby.

The birth was a strange thing, unexplained. Some said she was a witch, and the child was the spawn of the devil. Some claimed that Pleasance had stolen the baby from a nearby town. Lana's mother always said it was more likely that Pleasance had been seduced by some traveling salesman; and that yes, the baby may have been born out of wedlock, but that wasn't as uncommon as some people liked to think. Nor so sinful.

Not, Elizabeth would add hurriedly, that they should try to befriend her or even speak to her when she came to town. The woman was unpredictable; she had a temper and a mouth like a sailor when she was riled.

Living with those ruins in the distance was like living with a smoking volcano on the edge of town, something violent and oppressive always on the horizon.

By the time Lana reached her house, crossed the small front yard with its short grass and bald spots, and opened the front door, her feet were killing her. She took off her shoes and dropped into a chair, massaging her toes.

"Your pride is killing your feet," Kathy often told her. And she was right. Lana knew that she didn't have to go all the way home to change clothes after school. She could easily have taken her uniform to school with her and changed in the coffee shop restroom.

But if she did that, she would have had to pack her school clothes into a knapsack while she worked, and that would have wrinkled them horribly. It would have taken an hour to iron her skirt each night.

But it was more than that, and she knew it. She didn't want to go straight to work from school. She wanted to walk home with her head held high, to let everyone see that she didn't care if she was alone. It was pride, yes, and she was glad that she had it. There was little enough in this world that she had to be proud of, but her pride came from her independence, from her refusing to be cowed by being poor, from her knowing that she was just as good as every one of Kathy's other friends.

Lana shook her head, amused by her need to reinforce her own importance. It wasn't just a matter of being as good as everyone else. She was different from them, and she knew it. But she didn't try to hide from this difference; she embraced it. And for that, she was proud.

Her stomach growled, abruptly reminding her of the time. Right now, Lana thought, Kathy and her friends were probably lying on the floor of Kathy's room, eating a snack and listening to records. Or maybe they were watching American Bandstand on the color television in the family room.

For a moment, Lana hated them. Really hated them for their complete ignorance of what life was actually about. They would never know what it meant to have to work for their living, to have to count pennies and decide between buying a new pair of shoes and paying the electric bill.

The bitterness that rose within her brought the taste of gall to her mouth, reminding her again how hungry she was. She looked at the clock on the wall. Oh, Lord, she was running late. She would have to skip rinsing her blouse out and would have to hurry to work instead of walking in her usual dignified fashion.

She took the time to spread peanut butter on a slice of bread and pour milk into a thermos before leaving the house. She locked the door carefully, as she always did. Heaven knew they had little enough to steal, but that was no reason to invite thievery.

Lana ate the sandwich as she double-timed it to work, taking small sips from the thermos to wash it down. As she passed Kathy's gate, she felt a wave of shame wash over her as she remembered her earlier violent emotions. It wasn't Kathy's fault that she was born rich, just like it wasn't Lana's fault that she was born poor.

It just is what it is, she thought, calling up one of her mother's favorite sayings.

Kathy was her best friend. No amount of money would change that. The girls had spent hours sitting under the apple tree in Kathy's backyard, planning their futures. College, they agreed, was the best course for both of them.

"We're going to be educated women," Kathy said resolutely. "We're going to be independent and intelligent. We're not going to have to depend on our husbands for anything."

"But we will get married," Lana said, knowing the way her friend's mind worked.

"Of course! We'll have college and then marriage and then babies."

"And who are you going to marry? Hardluck Hank?"

Lana teased, naming a boy that Kathy had dated briefly and in secret the year before. Folks in town pitied him, but called him "Hardluck" behind his back because he never seemed to succeed at anything he'd tried. Her parents would have had a fit if they had known their precious daughter had run around with "trash" like that. Lana had a feeling that one day the kid would drop out, disappear, and no one would ever think of him again. It was a depressing notion.

Kathy wrinkled her nose at the very idea. "Oh, gross! No way." Her eyes became dreamy. "They'll have to be boys from out of town. Mysterious, you know? Maybe even rich…"

Lana didn't bother to remind Kathy that compared to some people, Kathy's family was already rich. Lana could feel herself caught up in Kathy's enthusiasm and didn't want to bring down the mood. "Maybe we can marry brothers," she suggested teasingly.

Kathy pounded the ground with excitement. "I love that idea! Yes, let's marry brothers — twins, maybe — rich ones! And we can get married on the same day, and honeymoon in Paris, and live next door to each other. Oh, Lana, wouldn't that be grand? Then we could really be sisters!"

It was Kathy's determination that they should go to college, which had started them studying together every night. But it was Lana's determination that kept them going. College, she knew, was her only way out of town — the only thing that she could really count on to make sure she didn't spend her life waiting on tables.

But in the meantime, she had to get to work. She redoubled her pace and made it to the coffee shop only three minutes late.

"I'm sorry I'm late, Mr. Brent," she called to the man standing at the stove. George Brent, owner and proprietor of the Angel River Café — Lana always thought it was a very fancy name for a little coffee shop — was a big, beefy man who clearly enjoyed eating greasy food as much as he enjoyed cooking it.

"Never trust a skinny chef," he liked to tell her. "They obviously don't like their own food enough to eat it!"

She had known him all her life. Two years ago, when money got very tight for her and her mother, he had offered her a job sweeping and mopping and helping with the dishes. He had nearly begged her to take it — claimed he needed someone he could trust to do those vital chores. And he assured her that her talents were well worth the generous wage she received. Last year he had promoted her to waitress, where she had the benefit of tips.

George had been in love with her mother since before Lana was born. It was something they never talked about — not Lana and George, not Lana and her mother, and, as far as she knew, not George and her mother. The only thing Mrs. Carlyle had ever said to her about it was that his feelings for her went way back. "From even before I met your father, dear."

George had asked Lana's mother a dozen times to marry him, and a dozen times he had been refused. And so he had done the only thing he could for the woman he loved — he had given her daughter a job, where he could make sure that she had a few extra dollars every week and that she took home a good portion of hot food with her when she left every night.

"What's with this 'Mr. Brent' all of a sudden, Lana?" he asked her, jovial as ever. "You looking for a raise or something?"

She laughed for the first time in hours. "If I was, I don't think I'd be coming in here at three minutes after five!"

"Oh, three minutes after five!" He rolled his eyes dramatically. "You know it won't get heavy in here for another half-hour or so. Why don't you join RJ at the counter and have yourself a piece of pie?"

"That's all right. I ate before I got here."

He eyed her knowingly. "Uh-huh. And I'm sure it was a huge meal, too." He changed the subject abruptly. "How's your mother doing these days?"

"She's…she's all right, I guess. She's working, which always makes her feel better. She hates being idle. Especially when there are bills to pay." George was the only person Lana could confide in about money. She would have died before ever asking to borrow any, but she knew that if things ever got really bad, she could come to him, and he would help her. She just prayed that they never got that bad.

"Everything under control in that department?" He didn't look at her when he asked her this. He was very intent on cleaning the grill, pushing the spatula up and back, up and back.

"It's okay, George," she said reassuringly.

"You know you can tell me if it's not."

"I know that."

Suddenly he was cheerful again. "So how come you're not out on the floor? The place may be nearly empty, but there are a few customers out there, Lana, and I'm sure they could do with a refill on their coffee!"

As she turned and headed to the other side of the counter, he called to her. "Pour yourself a cup while you're at it. And put some cream in that coffee — you are way too skinny to be a waitress here!"

Lana smiled to herself as she tied her apron around her waist. He said some version of the same thing every day. She took him up on his suggestion and poured herself some coffee with cream. As she looked around the shop and sipped her coffee, she saw that George was right, the place was practically empty.

Her eyes wandered idly over the vacant booths, to the three people who were seated at the counter. Two were men she didn't recognize — passers-through, she thought, on their way from Richmond to Lynchburg. When her gaze reached the third man, she was not surprised to see that he was looking back at her, and probably had been for some time.

She smiled at him, and he smiled in return. His wide brown eyes were both kind and bashful as he looked at her. Pleasance's son, Lana thought suddenly. The spawn of Satan. Her smile turned into a grin.

"Hello, RJ," she said. "Can I warm up your coffee for you?"

"Yes, Lana. Thank you." He watched in silence as she refilled his coffee cup.

"How are things at the garage today?" she asked, knowing he wasn't likely to speak first.

"Oh, fine," he said quietly. "Transmission rebuild, timing adjustment, a couple of tune-ups, an oil change. Just the usual — you know."

Lana grinned. "No, I don't know. I have absolutely no idea what you just said."

He gave her a shy smile.

"But I gather business is good?" she asked.

"Business is good," he agreed.

"Glad to hear it." Lana bestowed a final smile on him before moving down the counter to check on the other customers.

She refilled their coffee, brought them each a second piece of pie, and fended off a routine advance with a smile and a shake of her head. She was used to that sort of thing — it came with being young and pretty and serving food to strange men. And, like many fifteen-year-old girls, she looked older than she was.

She could have easily passed for eighteen. Most of the customers knew who she was and were kind and respectful to her. But the occasional stranger who dropped in for a meal usually felt obligated to make a pass.

Then, of course, there were customers like RJ Fitzgerald, whose eyes followed her like a puppy wherever she went. RJ was twenty-four and the best mechanic in town. He had developed a crush on her about six months earlier, right before her fifteenth birthday, when suddenly she had stopped looking like a child and started looking like a young woman. Of course, he was way too old for her, and he knew it. But that didn't stop him from looking.

And really, Lana thought as she refilled his coffee a second time, there were no other customers like RJ. He was there every day just before five, when her shift started. He always left her a tip that was generous, but not extravagant. He always inquired after her mother and asked how their car was running. A couple of times he had performed repairs for a fraction of their cost, insisting that they didn't owe him for his time. He was polite and respectful — when he looked at her it wasn't with a leer, but more with a kind of wonderment.

And today, she noticed for the first time that his hands were remarkably clean for a mechanic. There was only the barest trace of engine grease under his nails, and the skin of his hands shone pink, as if he had scrubbed them for a long time with a brush under hot water.

"How do you keep your nails so clean?" she asked suddenly. "I thought all mechanics had grease under their fingernails. You should be giving hygiene lessons to the other boys at that shop!"

He turned bright red and immediately stuffed his hands into the pockets of his jacket. He stuttered and mumbled, trying to find an answer to her question. "Don't see any reason for you to have to look at dirty hands every day when you bring me coffee, is all," he managed to get out.

And she understood that this was for her, that he probably scrubbed his nails every day before he came in, so that he would be clean and presentable while she poured him coffee and served him pie. And she had never noticed until today.

"Oh, RJ," she said softly. "You are going to make some girl very lucky one of these days."

His face lit up, and right away Lana regretted what she had just said. It sounded like she hoped to be the lucky girl. And the last thing she wanted to do with her life was marry RJ Fitzgerald and settle down in this town. Especially, she thought with sudden and unnecessary cruelty, especially with that crazy bitch mother of his. Pleasance Fitzgerald. What woman would ever be able to stand having her as a mother-in-law? The very idea brought a shudder to Lana's spine. Imagine being tied to that your entire life. It was too gruesome to contemplate, and all of RJ's sweetness couldn't make up for it.

She was relieved to hear the front bell ring, and to see a regular customer come in for supper. She excused herself, got her order pad, and crossed to the booth where the customer was sitting down.

A few more customers came in, and things started to pick up. She didn't speak to RJ again before he left, although his eyes followed her like they always did. She avoided his gaze as best she could. She was afraid that if she caught his eye, she would see hope lingering there, flickering like a candle on a cold, dark night.

But soon he was out of her thoughts, as the coffee shop rapidly filled up. Rosie, George's full-time waitress, came back from her afternoon break at six, and by then there were more than enough customers to go around.

Around nine, Lana had just finished making the rounds of all her tables, refilling water, offering coffee, making sure everyone was happy. She took the opportunity to go behind the counter and lean against the wall, taking the weight off her feet for a moment.

The song on the jukebox ended, and the record was retracted with an audible click. In the few seconds between the record that just ended and the one that had not yet started, the place was filled with a sudden quiet, one of those inexplicable lulls in conversation that occurred every now and then in a restaurant. It was as if every person in there had suddenly paused to take a breath, then wondered why everyone else was so quiet and waited to see if something important was going on. Lana knew that in a few seconds the conversations would start up again, and the happy hubbub of the dinner crowd would continue.

But it was in that moment, in that brief space of time, that the door clanked open and Kathy Duncan entered the restaurant. Lana stared. What was Kathy doing out so late? And why was she here, of all places?

Several of the patrons recognized her and leaned over to whisper to their dinner partners. Lana could imagine what they were saying, could hear the words in her head as clearly as if they had shouted. *There's that Duncan girl. Always heard she was wild. What's she doing out so late on a school night — and without her mother?*

Oh, Lord, Lana thought. When Mrs. Duncan heard about this, there'd be hell to pay. Didn't that girl have any sense?

Then the door clanged open a second time, and the very recognizable figure of Mrs. Duncan glided in. Lana went almost limp with relief, but then stiffened again with worry. Why were Kathy and her mother here? Had something happened to…

Mother.

The word was a stiletto through Lana's heart as she imagined all the things that the Duncans could be here to tell her. Soon after Lana was born, Elizabeth had contracted tuberculosis. It had gotten very bad very quickly, as it did with some people, and though she had lived through it, she had occasional recurrences, which was not uncommon. Fear for her mother was an ever-present emotion for Lana. Was Mother in the hospital again? Had she been in an accident — maybe had a coughing fit while she was driving and run off the road? Or was it…the Worst? It couldn't be.

Not now, Lana thought viciously, not tonight!

She shook herself out of her frozen stupor and stalked across the dining room, meeting Kathy halfway. She gripped Kathy's arms furiously, barely even noticing the way Mrs. Duncan breezed past the girls to a friend she had seen seated in the corner.

"What is it?" she demanded. "What are you doing here?"

The light in Kathy's eyes faded quickly, and her pretty mouth turned itself from a smile into a grimace of pain. "Ouch! Lana, cut it out! Let me go — what's wrong with you?"

Lana loosened her grip, but she couldn't let go. "Why are you here? Is it — it isn't — ?" she couldn't get the words out.

Comprehension dawned in Kathy's eyes, followed by compassion. "It's nothing, Lana," she said. Her voice was quiet but unsympathetic. Lana would never stand for pity. "I mean, it's not nothing — actually, it's *something* — but something *good*. Something so good that I couldn't wait to tell you!"

Lana released Kathy's arm and shoved her hands into her pockets. She was embarrassed by her flash of temper and furious with Kathy for nearly giving her a heart attack. What was it that couldn't wait until tomorrow, for God's sake?

"Well?" she asked impatiently. "Come on, spit it out."

Kathy stood there, grinning rapturously. "Somebody bought the old Fitzgerald place!"

That was the big news? "So?" Lana said. She didn't mean to be rude, but what was the big deal? "I thought that land was seized for back taxes."

"It was. They bought it from the government!"

"Who's they?" Lana asked. Nearby, a customer raised his coffee cup, trying to get her attention. Lana smiled automatically and nodded at him that she would be right over.

"This family," Kathy said impatiently. "The O'Tooles, or O'Doules — something like that. No, wait…." She frowned, her brow creasing prettily with concentration. "Doyle, that's the name. Doyle."

Doyle. Suddenly the name seemed to be rippling around the room like open water in windstorm. Lana, at the center of the whirlpool, heard the voices of the people around her. Doyle, they said. Family who bought the old Fitzgerald place. Fix it up, they said. Like new.

Mrs. Duncan must have also been talking about it, too, Lana realized. That was why everyone seemed to know at once. Mrs. Duncan loved a gossip as much as her daughter.

"That's what's so exciting." Kathy was saying. "It's an out-of-town family! And they have sons — two of them — in high school!" Kathy's eyes shone like the moon at the thought of her fantasy coming true.

Lana laughed, forgiving her friend for the earlier fright. Kathy was so sweet, so innocent in so many ways. "Are the boys twins?" she asked indulgently.

"No," Kathy said. Her disappointment was obvious, but then it was whisked away by an even greater excitement. "But the family's rich! I mean, they'd have to be, buying that old place, restoring it like they are. Daddy says they're going to use the original blueprints that old what's-his-name Fitzgerald had drawn up almost a hundred years ago."

Lana thought of RJ. What would it be like for him, she wondered, to watch that great house be reconstructed in front of his eyes? How would his mother react? Probably not well, Lana thought with a shudder. Whoever that family was, they were in for a rough time, with Pleasance Fitzgerald as their neighbor.

"Miss!" The coffee cup was in the air again, and behind it were the angry eyes of a customer ignored. Lana saw her tip slipping away like quicksand. And she needed her tips.

"Why don't you go sit at the counter," she said to Kathy. "I'll take care of this guy. And by then," she looked at the clock on the wall, "it'll about quitting time for me. Ask George to give you a piece of pie or something while you wait."

"On the house?" Kathy asked hopefully.

Lana was already walking away, but she turned around to laugh. "I think you can afford it."

Lana refilled coffee cups all around, smiling just enough to ensure her customers were generous with their gratuities. She probably could've made more if she'd swung her hips and wore her uniform open to the fourth button like Rosie. But even the idea of using her body like that made her spine stiffen and her shoulders square with dignified repulsion.

But she couldn't hold it against Rosie, Lana thought, watching the older waitress laugh and nudge a customer suggestively. Lana smiled at the hungry look in the man's eye, the way his hand went back into his wallet for an extra bill as

Rosie leaned over the table to refill his water glass. Rosie dimpled prettily and threw a flirtatious glance over her shoulder as she sashayed away.

That attitude suits her, Lana thought. She carries it off with class. But on me, it would just feel…cheap.

She hung up her apron and found Kathy finishing up a piece of blueberry pie. George was behind the counter, loading dirty dishes onto a cart. Kathy chewed and swallowed her last bite, then jumped up from her stool.

"Ready to go?" she asked.

Lana looked at the counter for a quarter. There wasn't one. "Did you pay already?"

George spoke up. "Now Lana, you know I don't let girls that pretty pay for pie in my shop. Especially if they're friends of yours."

Kathy smiled her thanks at him, a sweet and winning grin that was somehow made more charming by the bluish-berry cast on her teeth.

Shades of Rosie's waggling hips, Lana thought irritably, watching the way George responded to Kathy's smile. What was wrong with him? Didn't he know he was being manipulated? Maybe he didn't care.

"George, is it all right if I go now?"

"Suits me," he said agreeably. "It's about closing time, anyway. Here, take this." He produced a large paper bag from behind the counter. It was full and bulging, folded over at the top and tied around with string. Lana thought she could smell the aroma of meatloaf and gravy wafting out of the thick brown paper. Her stomach growled, but her face grew rigid.

"That's not necessary," she said stiffly.

"For your mother," he insisted. His big round face was red

and shiny from the heat of the kitchen and the day's exertions. It was the kindest face she'd ever known.

Lana hesitated, wanting to be won over but not wanting him to think she needed his charity.

"For your mother," he said again, more softly this time.

"Oh for goodness' sake, Lana!" Kathy said. She reached out and took the bag from George, then shoved it into Lana's arms. "Just take the thing so we can go. Mother's in the car. She'll drop you off at home."

"I don't mind walking," Lana said automatically, although her feet hurt and her back ached dully.

"Good grief," Kathy muttered. She grabbed her friend's elbow and pulled her toward the front door.

Lana tried to pull away, appalled at being treated this way in public. Didn't Kathy realize what she was doing? Word would get around. Next thing they knew, people would be referring to Lana as Kathy's maid. Or worse.

"Goodbye Mr. Brent," Kathy called, waving with her free hand. "Thanks for the pie, it was delicious. We're going to be meeting our future husbands soon, so you may have to start interviewing for Lana's replacement!"

"Bye, girls. See you tomorrow, Lana," George called merrily, as if it were completely natural for Lana to be humiliated in his restaurant. She would have a few choice words to say to him tomorrow, that was for sure, she thought. "Good luck with your engagement," he laughed, adding insult to injury.

But by the time they had made it out the front door, Lana was laughing too. Kathy was one determined little rat, she thought affectionately.

"You're a real creep, you know that?" she said when Kathy finally released her. She was smiling.

Kathy smiled back. "Takes one to know one," she said.

"Wow, what a mature response. And this from the girl who's practically planning her wedding."

They climbed into the back seat of Mrs. Duncan's Plymouth, Kathy getting in first and sliding all the way over to make room for Lana, who followed slowly, then was careful to close the door properly — not so hard that it slammed, not so soft that it swung open.

"Thank you for giving me a ride home, Mrs. Duncan," Lana said politely. "I like your new car."

"Thank you, Lana dear," Mrs. Duncan answered graciously. "That bag isn't going to leak, is it?"

Lana held it gingerly, feeling the bottom for wet spots. "I don't think so," she said.

Mrs. Duncan executed a wide U-turn in the middle of the road, resulting in a certain amount of honking and squealing tires from other drivers. Lana's heart seized, and she held her breath, waiting to see if they would make it. They did. As they drove away, some colorful language followed them down the road. "I don't know what those men are so upset about," Mrs. Duncan murmured under her breath. "No one was hurt."

Kathy nudged Lana and rolled her eyes. Lana smiled in spite of herself. She leaned over and whispered, so Mrs. Duncan couldn't hear their conversation. "So, do you really think this family that's moving in from out of town —"

"The Doyles," Kathy interrupted.

"Right. Do you really think that having this Doyle family move in from out of town is going to change anything?"

"Change anything?" Kathy exclaimed, loud enough for her mother to hear. "Change anything?" She shook her head, pitying Lana for her lack of imagination. "No, Lana, it's not going to change *anything*. It's going to change *everything*."

Outside the car windows, houses and trees slipped silently by in the cold autumn night. Lana held her bag of leftovers primly on her knees. She felt the familiar emptiness of her stomach, the aching in her back and feet, and the creeping weariness that assaulted her very bones. The idea came to her that she was too young for this kind of life. Too young for the responsibility, too young for the worries, the aches, the pains. Too young to be so old.

Change everything? Lana thought, blinking at the tears that welled suddenly in her eyes. God, I hope so.

CHAPTER EIGHT

R EED'S EYES OPENED AUTOMATICALLY AT five AM, and once they were open, he found that he could not close them again. As always, he knew precisely where he was and what he was there for. He traveled so often on business that he never suffered any disorientation when waking up in a strange bed.

He threw back the covers and crossed the expansive floor of his bedroom to the dressing alcove. He was used to some physical activity first thing in the morning. Usually he spent forty-five minutes on the treadmill, watching the early news as he ran, but today he decided to go for a swim. After all, he was on vacation. He left his silk pajama pants in a shimmering puddle on the floor and slipped on his swimsuit, a pair of shorts, and a sweatshirt. He picked up the phone as he put on his shoes.

"Room service," he said to the voice-activated dialing system.

A well-modulated female voice picked up on the other end. "Yes, Mr. Fitzgerald?"

"Ms. Doyle and I will be ready for breakfast in the dining room at nine AM. I'll have coffee in my room at six-fifteen."

"Very good, sir. We have the order you placed last night."

"Thank you."

Reed slowly hung up the phone. It was almost the same conversation he had every morning. In hotels around the world, as in his own apartment in New York, there was always someone on the other end of the line who knew what he wanted for breakfast. The only variable was the accent.

Today, he was confirming breakfast for two, not one. Kate didn't know it yet, but he had arranged a special meal for them. He smiled, imagining her surprise. Then he grabbed his room key and headed out the door.

The upper deck was deserted, and the sky was turning light in the east as Reed stripped off his outer layer of clothes and dove into the pool. The water was icy, and he paced himself for the first two laps, allowing his muscles time to warm up. He knew his body well, and he was aware of the moment when it was safe for him to push himself harder, when he wouldn't risk cramps or muscle pulls. As soon as he felt himself make that transition, he opened up and drove himself as hard as he could.

He swam lap after lap, counting them automatically each time he reached the end and pushed off again. When he had done the equivalent of five miles, he rolled over into an easy backstroke, cooling down as his heart rate dropped back to normal.

As he stared up at the sky, feeling the water wash cleanly over his muscles, an image came unbidden to his mind: being ten years old, floating on his back in the Doyle family's backyard swimming pool. Kate, eight years old, had her hands under the water and was supporting him as he floated.

"Let your arms float out beside you," she had droned. "Feel the water lifting you up." Gradually she had removed her hands from under his back, and he had learned to float on his own. From there she had taught him the backstroke.

Reed had been afraid of the water when he was a child, but Kate had been trying to get him to go swimming with her ever since she could talk. Finally she had persuaded him to try by telling him it was like being in outer space. "You're weightless in the water," she had said enticingly. "Just like an astronaut."

Well, that had done the trick. His curiosity had overcome his fear, and he had ventured in. At first Kate had been content to let him splash around and play Marco Polo, but eventually she had demanded more.

And she had gotten it.

The thought stayed with him as he toweled off and re-dressed. Kate had always demanded more of him, had always known he was capable of more than he was doing. She had always had more faith in him than he had in himself.

Until she left you, whispered the Devil's advocate in his mind. Where was her faith then?

But he told the voice to hush. Kate's influence had stayed with him, even after she and her family had left town. The image of her teaching him to swim, helping him with schoolwork — even though she was younger than he was — always insisting that he could do it, had never stopped motivating him to do better. Not even when he had tried to forget her.

When Reed got back to his room, he found it exactly as he had expected: his bed was made, his pajamas had been picked up off the floor and folded neatly away in a drawer. A silver coffee service had been set up in the dining alcove, and there were fresh flowers in a crystal vase. He surveyed the room with pleasure. He liked the quiet opulence of his life, the way order was silently conferred on his surroundings at the mere mention of his wishes.

His mood was high as he headed for the shower, stripping off his clothes as he went. The physical exertion of the swim had left his body feeling taut and alive, and the water streaming down on him was invigorating. His morning shower had become his favorite part of the day. Growing up as the poorest kid in a poor town, hot water had been scarce — most mornings he had sponge-bathed from a heated pan of well water. When he had gone off to college and lived in a rooming house, he had always gotten up early so that he had first crack at the shower. The irony was that now that he was finally in a position to afford as much hot water as he wanted, he was rarely able to spend more than a few minutes a day enjoying it. So that morning he indulged himself, staying in the shower until he had washed everything twice. Afterwards, he toweled off vigorously and donned his favorite blue silk robe.

He poured himself a cup of coffee and took it into the living room. He pulled the silken cord, which moved back the tapestry curtains covering the picture window. As they parted, he drew in a sharp breath. He had been unprepared for what waited for him on the other side of those drapes. Sunrise over the ocean — the exquisite beauty of it hit him almost physically. The water, normally the clear color of blue topaz, had been transformed into a fiery gold firmament. It was oranges flickering into pinks, bordered by writhing, silvery pools where waves cast shadows, and all of it set with glittering diamonds.

Reed stood at the window and sipped his coffee, contemplating the shimmering splendor laid out before him. The sky was a luminous ocean of colored light, awash with undulating waves of radiance. The fiery sun hung weightless over the horizon. It was so unutterably lovely that he was tempted to ring Kate's room, to wake her up and tell her to look out the window. But he didn't do that. He couldn't. It would be a silly, sentimental gesture, something suited to a man half his age, and he wasn't about to try —

He stopped, remembering that last night he had a similar thought about sentimental reminiscences, that they were not his style.

He set his coffee cup and saucer on the low table next to the divan. Apparently, the image he had of himself did not include sentimentality of any kind. But why not? What was wrong with being a little sentimental now and then? With being a little bit overly-romantic, even mushy, now and then? Because it conflicted with his notion of himself as a bad-ass moneymaking machine?

His eyes sought out the telephone and lingered there. Should he start working on his sentimentality — on his warm, gooey, romantic center — by calling Kate? No, he decided. Last night as he had walked her to her room, she had mentioned how much she looked forward to sleeping in. And since he was in the mood to admit things to himself, he went ahead and acknowledged that as much as he was enjoying the thought of seeing her, of getting to know her all over again, things were still a little bit uncomfortable between them.

Besides, if everything went as planned, they would be spending plenty of mornings together and would have plenty of chances to watch the sun rise from his bedroom…or hers, depending on the situation….

With that thought warming his bones, he decided to pull out his laptop and set it up on the dining room table. Old habits died hard, and he had already done more inner-universe examination and improvement this morning than he had in years. He figured he deserved to indulge himself in a few of his more obsessive work habits.

After reviewing the daily news he checked his business email, went over his company's daily reports, and tapped out brief messages to each of his three assistants. He was pleased to see that they hadn't run his company into the ground during the day and a half that he'd been gone, and he thought it was only fair to let them know that he was satisfied with their performances. He smiled as he pictured Jerry's reaction to his dry praise.

With his morning business tasks completed, Reed opened his personal email. And his good mood slipped a notch when he saw the name on the one message waiting for him: Geoffrey Roberts.

Roberts was a private investigator that Reed had used from time to time over the years. Middle-aged, nondescript, with a laser-sharp intellect and an eye for detail, Roberts was a valuable associate, a relentless finder of facts, who attacked his job with relish. But since last night, Reed wasn't sure that he wanted to read any more of Mr. Roberts' communiqués. The phrase "invasion of privacy" circled lazily through his mind, with all its possible ramifications — both legal and ethical.

Reed highlighted the message, but hesitated before opening it. His finger moved over the delete key and hovered there. The impulse to press the button and eliminate the message without reading it was strong, almost overwhelming.

But what if it was important? Almost reluctantly, he shifted his finger to the key marked "Enter," and pressed it. The message flashed onto the screen:

"Mark Levin took Mrs. Doyle to a jewelry shop today. Subsequent questioning of the jeweler revealed that they were looking at engagement rings. Reply if you want photos. No more to report at this time."

Well, there were no big surprises there. Reed had known for weeks that Kate's boyfriend had popped the question. Roberts had been in the restaurant the day that Kate had told her mother about the proposal. That was how Reed also knew that Kate hadn't said yes. Not yet.

He saved the message to the folder marked "Doyle." It was all there: all his correspondence with Roberts, all the information, neatly organized with sub-headings and going back almost three years. His stomach churned with sudden self-disgust as he turned off the computer. The decision to have Roberts find Kate had at one time seemed so simple, so sensible. But after last night…

The kisses they had shared were still hot in his memory, as was the feel of her pressed tightly against him. She was so strong, and yet she had yielded so fully in his arms. He hated to think what she would have said if she had known the truth about him, about what he had been up to. She had been so eager to unburden herself, to be completely honest. She had reminded him of what she had been like as a child: "We should tell the truth, Reed! The truth is always the best choice!"

And for a moment, for one brief, shining moment, he had been sorely tempted to tell her everything. But he hadn't. And now, in the cold light of morning, he knew that silence had been the right decision.

They had loved each other once. He believed that love might be able to be resurrected, that it at least deserved the chance. And there was no reason that she shouldn't know the whole truth. In time. He knew that she would understand what he had done. She had always understood him.

With his resolve stiffened, he got up and moved to the closet. It was time to get dressed and head to the dining room. He was whistling. In a little while, he'd be with Kate.

CHAPTER NINE

THE DINING ROOM WAS SOFTLY lit from within and boldly illuminated from without. Tropical morning sun fell in golden splotches on the floral carpet and filled the room with a warm glow, while discreet light fixtures cast soft illumination on the linen-draped tables and comfortable cushioned chairs.

It was strange. Less than twenty-four hours ago, while standing in this very spot, Reed had seen Kate for the first time in almost twenty years. Had the room looked this elegant yesterday? Had he taken the time to cast an appreciative eye on the carefully chosen décor? He couldn't remember. All he remembered was Kate, her very real presence standing before him in place of his phantom memories.

"Good morning, Mr. Fitzgerald." The hostess interrupted Reed's reverie as she appeared at his elbow, wearing a flirtatious smile and a short blue dress.

Reed recalled himself to the present with an effort. "Has Miss Doyle arrived yet?" he asked.

"Not yet, sir. Would you like to wait for her at your table?"

"That would be fine." He followed her across the room and was rewarded by another engaging smile as he sat down.

"Everything's prepared for you, sir," she said. "Whenever you're ready…"

"Thank you. Wait until Miss Doyle gets here, then give us about fifteen minutes."

"Certainly."

Reed permitted himself a covert but appreciative look at the hostess's figure as she walked away.

Kate's voice came from over his shoulder. "Pretty girl. Should I leave you two alone?"

Reed jumped slightly, and then turned in his chair to give Kate an abashed grin. But the expression froze on his face when he saw her. The sunlight slanting through the wide windows caught the gold highlights in her auburn hair, forming a shimmering halo around her head.

He exhaled slowly, barely realizing that he had been holding his breath. He stood up to hold out her chair for her, and renewed his smile as he sat back down. "You caught me looking," he said.

She unfolded her napkin and placed it in her lap. "No harm in looking," she said easily. "But you might consider putting your eyes back in their sockets. It's sort of unseemly to have them attached to her rear end like that."

He laughed out loud, almost startled by how relaxed he sounded. "It does seem like it would make it difficult for her to sit down," he agreed.

"Or at least rather uncomfortable." Kate smiled, obviously pleased with herself for making him laugh.

Reed recalled his earlier thought that it was a bit uncomfortable, being with her again. But it wasn't uncomfortable. It was the most natural thing in the world.

He decided to go with that feeling. "Did you enjoy sleeping in?" he asked.

Kate gave a sigh that was just sort of blissful. "It was heavenly, up to a point. It's been so long since I slept late that when I finally dragged myself out of bed, I had an attack of Irish guilt. So I did something I may end up regretting: I went online to the ship's activity roster, and signed up for a yoga class later this morning."

"Why would you regret that?"

"Because after I signed up, I read the bio of the ship's yoga instructor. She sounds like quite a character." Kate grimaced. "I just hope that 'character' isn't Torquemada."

Another laugh escaped Reed's lips, this one just as unexpected as the first, and just as welcome. "Well, the nice thing about yoga is that it's healthy *and* a luxury. Not many things in life fall into both categories."

Her eyes were thoughtful as they rested on his face. "Good point."

She seemed on the verge of saying something more when a magnificent black mustache appeared at the table, bringing a halt to the conversation. The mustache was attached to a red-coated waiter carrying coffee and orange juice, with menus under his arm.

Kate and Reed accepted their coffee and juice with the proper deference, but Reed waved the menus away. "The hostess already has our order," he said.

"Very good, sir." The mustache twitched with approval, and the waiter departed.

"You ordered breakfast for me?" A bemused expression came over Kate's face, as if she didn't know whether to be appreciative or irritated. "How did you know what I'd want?"

"I guessed." He smiled when he saw she was still hesitating. "It's a surprise, okay? You don't have to eat it if you don't want to. Relax."

"Okay, okay." She paused for a moment, then a smile broke

over her face. "You're in a good mood this morning."

"Am I?" He sipped his coffee and tried not to look smug.

She arched a brow. "Aren't you?"

"Are you going to interrogate me over breakfast, counselor?"

"Give me ten minutes, and I'll get a court reporter in here," she returned. "We'll make it official."

"Then I'll go ahead and confess — I am in a good mood this morning."

"Well in that case, I think I'll actually stay and eat my breakfast — depending upon what it is you ordered for me, of course," she said.

"Of course," he agreed easily.

She eyed him curiously. Something on his face must have told her to query further. "And may I ask what it is that put you in such a jolly temper?"

Reed shrugged. "What's not to be happy about? Beautiful ocean, beautiful ship, beautiful lady…"

He saw her flush slightly at the compliment. "What's wrong?" he teased. "Doesn't *he* tell you you're beautiful?" That was the wrong thing to say. Reed knew it as soon as the words were out of his mouth. Suddenly Kate looked defensive.

"He who?" she asked uncomfortably.

"He…whoever." Reed tried to keep his voice light.

"What makes you think there's a 'whoever'?"

He chose his words with care. "Like I said, beautiful lady…."

Kate watched him guardedly. Was she trying to figure out if he knew about the boyfriend — or *how* he knew? Reed suddenly wished very badly that he didn't know so much about her. It was painful to watch her sit there, struggling with what to say, not knowing how much she should confide. He felt distinctly like a worm.

He leaned forward, resting his arms on the table and looking at her seriously. "I'm sorry if I was presumptuous, Kate. It just slipped out. It's none of my business who you're seeing. Or who you're not seeing, for that matter."

She relaxed a bit, giving him a tentative smile. "I shouldn't be so touchy," she said. "It's a vacation, right?"

"That's right." He returned her smile. Looking across the room toward the kitchen, he was relieved to see the waiter with the impressive mustache coming through the swinging doors into the dining room. Reed drew himself up, his good spirits returning as he anticipated Kate's reaction to his surprise.

"And now, madam, your breakfast is served," he said, smiling.

It was pure delight for him to watch the surprise on her face as the plate was set down in front of her. He didn't even bother to check the food, he just kept his eyes on her face as she surveyed the breakfast he had ordered: two slices of wheat toast with a fried egg underneath each. The golden-yellow yolks peeked through a hole cut in the middle of the bread.

Kate looked up at him with amazement. "One-Eyed Jacks?"

"Just like Grandma Fitzgerald used to make." He smiled. "I wasn't even sure you'd remember them."

"Not remember? From the time I was six years old, we had these every Saturday after our riding lessons!" She shook her head at the memory, eyes glowing.

At her words, resentment darted through him, causing his grin to falter slightly. He tried to recover, but it was too late. She must have seen the look on his face because she placed a hand over his, as if she knew what he was thinking. His horseback riding lessons had come through the good graces of the Doyle family, as had so many of the good things in his life. The only contribution his grandmother could afford was to prepare the breakfast that became a tradition for him and Kate.

"Sometimes," Kate said carefully, "the greatest memories are the humble ones. You know, I hardly remember riding at all. What I remember is your grandmother's kitchen — so clean and bright and always smelling like something delicious."

Reed nodded, suddenly unable to speak. Her words painted his memories vividly. Images of a thousand happy meals eaten around the tiny kitchen table crowded his vision, bringing the smells and sounds of childhood abruptly into the present.

Kate squeezed his hand. "This is really a great surprise," she said gently. "Thank you."

Her voice and the pressure of her hand blew the memories away like a cool breeze blowing away fog. His vision cleared, and all he could see was Kate.

He cleared his throat and gave her the most honest smile he could muster. "So what are we waiting for?" he asked. "Let's eat."

CHAPTER TEN

KATE HAD ANOTHER PURPOSE FOR scheduling that yoga class, one which she'd decided to keep to herself: she wanted some time on her own. Reed's presence was still overwhelming to her, and she thought it might be a good idea to have a reason to excuse herself after breakfast, to give them both a little breathing room. But as they dug into their meal, it seemed like maybe she'd been worried for nothing. Their conversation flowed as if they'd never been apart.

"I have no idea how to be on vacation," Reed confessed, sprinkling pepper on his eggs. "What are we supposed to do all day, anyway?"

"Oh, lie by the pool, I guess. Read, drink Mai Tais…." Kate trailed off when she saw his face. "None of this strikes your fancy?"

He gave a kind of shrugging grimace that made her want to laugh. She had seen that gesture many times during their years together. "I guess I could get used to it… but by the time I do, this trip will be over and I'll have to go back to work again, so what's the point?"

"Well, we'll be in Bonaire tomorrow, I think — there's horseback riding, sightseeing, snorkeling, scuba diving, shopping — "

"Sure, that takes care of tomorrow," he teased, "but what

about today?"

She sighed and shook her head. "Some people are so hard to please!" she said. "What do you usually do with your leisure time?"

"What's 'leisure time'?" he asked blandly.

She eyed him. "Okay, so you work during your leisure time?"

"Pretty much."

"And what do you do for fun? Wait, don't tell me — "

"I make money."

"Oh, that's fun, huh?"

"Making it is more fun than not having it," he said. Then, as if realizing how weighty that sounded, he rushed to keep the conversation going. "And so what counts as fun for you? Reading legal briefs?"

Kate shrugged. "I do work a lot, I guess. But in between working…I don't know…the usual stuff. Play with my nephew and niece. Read. Watch TV, go to the movies."

"Alone?"

This was her chance, Kate realized. This was her chance to mention Mark. She had avoided bringing him up yesterday and again just a few moments ago. And now….

"When you go to the movies, you're never alone," she hedged.

He looked at her, but it wasn't a serious probing look, it was just a friendly gaze. "Hmm," was all he said.

"Other than that — well, we were talking about horseback riding this morning. I still do it, sometimes, in Rock Creek Park. It's so beautiful there. Have you been to DC much in the last few years?"

"No," he answered. "But it's good to know you still ride. We'll be in Bonaire tomorrow, and there's supposed to be a wonderful horseback tour of the island. Are you interested?"

She was, and she said so. Another date, she thought, feeling color rise in her cheeks.

Suddenly she was very, very glad she'd scheduled some time on her own.

After breakfast, Kate stopped in her room long enough to pick up her yoga pants and the biggest, sloppiest t-shirt that Julia had allowed her to pack. Then she headed down to the middle deck, passing a weight room, a computer lab, and what looked like a beauty salon. All the comforts of home, she thought.

Finally, she came to a halt outside a set of double oak doors. They were each inset with an oval frosted glass panel, etched with the word Studio.

Hesitantly, Kate pushed open the door and peered inside. She didn't know why she was so edgy. She and Jules used to go to yoga together all the time. But then Sam and Julia had moved farther from the city, and as the kids got older, everyone's schedules got busier and busier. Kate's hours had filled up with work, and sisterly-bonding time had gotten scarce.

The studio was medium-sized, maybe fifteen by twenty feet, with the standard wide-planked wood floor and mirror-lined wall. The opposite wall, however, was anything but standard — it was a full wall of windows, giving an expansive view of the ocean, rippling and glittering under the sun.

There was a lone woman at the barre, who looked up as Kate entered. The woman was in her middle age, with a dancer's physique — petite, but long-legged. Cords stood on her graceful neck. She had her hair pulled into a wispy ponytail, and one leg up on the barre. This was obviously Lily Krantz, the yoga teacher whose brochure had so unnerved Kate earlier that morning.

"Can I help you?" the woman asked. She had a thick accent that Kate could not place. Her first thought was Russian, but that was probably some typical American association with Russia and ballet. Tchaikovsky would be pleased about that.

"I'm here for the yoga class," Kate answered.

"You are a dancer?"

"No," Kate laughed.

Lily tilted her head and surveyed Kate with a critical eye. "You look like you could be."

"I was really into ballet when I was a child, but I haven't danced in years."

Again the woman smiled as she gracefully lowered her leg. "Once ballet gets into you, you cannot get it out again, no matter how many years go by."

Oh yeah, this lady was a character. With dialogue that hokey, she could be on the silver screen. Still, she seemed sincere. "I guess," Kate said noncommittally.

Lily nodded to Kate's bag. "There is a changing room in the back."

Kate looked around. "Shouldn't we wait for the other students?"

"No one else signed up," Lily sighed. "I guess they are enjoying their beds too much." She shrugged. "And who can blame them? People who work hard deserve to rest when they get the chance."

She stood looking at Kate expectantly. When Kate didn't hop-to, the woman gestured toward the wall, where cubby holes held tidy, rolled-up yoga mats. "Go ahead. Change your clothes and grab a mat. Your joints will thank you."

And they did. Eventually. When forty-five minutes had passed – feeling more like four hours, of course – Kate lay on the mat, breathing deeply. She felt simultaneously refreshed and exhausted. How lovely. "That was great," she said to Lily.

"I have been teaching people to exercise their bodies for a long time. I started as a dancer in Belgium, then I became an instructor. I retired when I was offered a job on this cruise line; it was too good a chance to pass up."

Kate propped a hand behind her head. "Why did you stop dancing and start teaching?"

"My knee and ankle were shattered when I fell off a horse." Lily conveyed the information with no more emotion than if she'd been describing the discarding of an old leotard. "Why did *you* stop dancing?"

Kate wasn't surprised at the question. Since the true answer was too long and personal to spill out, she kept it simple. "I grew up," she said. "Ballet was a dream of childhood." Like so many other things, she didn't add. "Adulthood is the time for reality, not dreams."

"Adulthood is the best time for dreams — it's the time when we need them most."

Kate smiled. That was a good line. She'd have to remember it.

The door swung open again, and Lily and Kate both turned to see who was coming in. Kate's heart sank when she saw that it was Heather. Heather, who looked as cool and lovely as ever, wearing dark blue yoga pants with a light blue tank top. A thickly-knit cable sweater was tossed casually across her shoulders. Although she was rubbing her eyes and yawning as if she had just gotten out of bed, she looked like she'd just walked out of the beauty salon. Her hair was perfect, rippling down her back like it had just come out of hot rollers. And her skin was smooth and unblemished, even without makeup.

Kate caught sight of herself in the wall of mirrors. She was sweaty and her hair was springing loose from its stubby ponytail to form a sort of frizz around her head. Heather looked cool and remote, like a swan. And I look like an angry duck, Kate thought unhappily, with feathers sticking out every which way.

"Hello, ladies," Heather greeted them with a smile. If she had any clue as to her superior looks, she gave no sign of it. "I decided I had to make up for all that food I ate last night," she said to Kate, "and give myself a good workout before breakfast."

Lily glanced at the clock above the door. "I'm afraid you will have missed breakfast," she said deferentially, "but we will give you your workout before you eat your lunch. How will that be?"

Heather gave Lily her famous smile and said, "Sounds heavenly."

"You may not think so by the time we are done," Lily warned. "Come, toss your sweater over here and pull back your hair."

Kate murmured a quick goodbye and headed back toward the dressing room. She didn't particularly feel the need to be shown up by Heather, whose downward-facing dog was undoubtedly perfect. But Heather stopped her. "Aren't you staying?" she asked. "I didn't mean to chase you away."

"Oh no, it's fine," Kate hastened to say. "I was done anyway."

"Done?" Lily asked. "Surely you have more in you than that! It's been barely an hour!"

That had Kate laughing. "That's more exercise than I've had all year!"

Lily waved her hand dismissively. "One more sun salutation and you will feel like a new woman," she said.

"Please stay," Heather said. "We'll give each other moral support."

Kate returned to the mat reluctantly, as Heather started stretching. Kate tried not to watch as the woman who had been

Reed's lover stretched and contorted in front of her. Not only was Heather's downward-dog flawless, but she performed a variety of other positions that Kate had only glimpsed on the seldom-viewed workout videos gathering dust on her living room shelf. Kate could tell that Lily was impressed, which sparked another ridiculous flame of jealousy in Kate's heart.

Heather must have decided to take a break when she saw that Kate had finished. She pulled three bottles of water from the nearby cooler, handing one to Kate and one to Lily. Kate took hers gratefully.

Up to that point, they'd had the studio to themselves. Now a young woman appeared, escorting two young children, a girl and a boy. Kate recognized them as the two imps who had run across the dining room yesterday the morning before. Was it only yesterday?

Lily got up to talk to them. "My 11:30 ballet class," she explained to Kate and Heather. "You must excuse me. A pleasure to meet you both. Come back soon." She gave Kate a pointed look and turned her attention to the children.

"Those little costumes bring back memories." Heather said, breezily oblivious to Kate's discomfort. "Did you take ballet when you were a child?"

Kate nodded. "Almost since I could walk," she said. Then she smiled, remembering. "I think it was really the costumes that I loved. I didn't understand why I wasn't allowed to wear toe shoes on my first day of class!"

Heather smiled too. She could imagine it — a young Kate, cute but defiant, demanding shoes with the pretty lace-up ribbons, never knowing how wearing those shoes would hurt in the years to come.

"And what about you?" Kate asked politely. "Did you do

ballet when you were younger?"

"There was a YWCA not far from where I lived. I used to take the bus there almost every day after school. I took ballet, swimming — anything that they had to offer."

"Where did you grow up?"

"Baltimore."

"Ah." Kate knew Baltimore a little.

"There wasn't a lot one could do after school that didn't involve some kind of illegal activity, which I guess is why I gravitated to the Y-Dub. I had no intention of spending my life behind bars." Heather smiled ironically and took a sip of water.

"Really? I had you figured as a Rowland Park sort of girl," Kate confessed. She could picture Heather there, where the porches were wide and the lawns green and thick. "You look so…polished."

"Ah." Heather nodded slowly. "The polish was something I acquired on my own, after leaving the old homestead. In my early days, I was pretty rough and tumble."

Kate wasn't sure what to say, so she just bobbed her head in acknowledgement. She was thinking that Reed and Heather had both come from difficult beginnings and had managed to re-invent themselves. They had something in common then, aside from the great sex that Heather had so graciously mentioned yesterday.

"When did you first know you wanted to be an actress?" Kate asked.

"Probably when I read an article that said how much Jeanie Francis was making for *Days of Our Lives*," Heather laughed. "But I don't know, really. It was just something I liked and was good at. And I guess it was a way out for me, too. Being poor was no fun." She gave a small smile, which Kate returned.

"Well, seems like you're doing okay these days," Kate said.

"Not too bad, at that," Heather said. "I've got my first movie role coming up."

"Really?" Kate was intrigued. "Congratulations, that's wonderful."

Heather looked modest. "It's not a big blockbuster or anything. It's a small movie, and my part is tiny. But the director is Maurice Greenstreet. I've wanted to work with him since I was first starting out, so it was pretty cool for me, I have to admit."

Kate stood up. She was starting to like Heather too much, and she wasn't sure how she felt about that. "Well, that's really great, Heather. I'll be first in line when it's time to buy tickets."

Heather glanced at the clock. "Are you leaving?"

"I think I'll change and go up to the pool for a while. Maybe I'll actually get a tan on this trip and surprise my sister."

"Won't you — won't you join me for lunch?"

Kate demurred. "Thanks, but I ate breakfast not too long ago. I think I'll just go lie in the sun for a while."

"Well, maybe we can all get together for dinner again tonight."

"Maybe," Kate hedged. She wasn't sure she wanted to get any chummier with Heather than they already had, and Heather's insistence on the two of them being friends was starting to feel a bit creepy. "Let's just wait and see."

"Fine." Heather seemed a little miffed. Maybe she wasn't used to having her friendship rejected. Not that there was anything she could do about it in this case. "Enjoy the rest of your day."

"Thanks, you too," Kate said. She went into the dressing room to change, remembering to lock the door.

CHAPTER ELEVEN

THE *WILLIAM* ARRIVED IN BONAIRE at dawn on the following day. Passengers flocked on deck to watch the docking as white-coated stewards circulated through the throng, bearing mimosas on silver trays.

Reed's spirits were high as he made his way through the crowd. He and Kate were scheduled to go on a horseback tour of the island later that morning.

The two of them had met up at the pool late the previous afternoon. Kate had looked more relaxed than he'd seen her since they'd arrived. He guessed that the yoga had done her good.

She'd mentioned briefly that she'd seen Heather, but hadn't said any more about it. Reed wasn't sure how Kate and Heather felt about each other. How did women in their position usually feel? He had no idea — he had long since stopped trying to understand inter-feminine dynamics.

He had been surprised and more than a little irritated to find Heather and her entourage on the ship. It made things even more complicated than they already were. But in the end, he decided, it didn't change much for him. Heather was a beautiful woman, she was talented and appealing in many ways, and he had enjoyed their time together. But he had known shortly after first meeting her that they wouldn't have a future together. For him, he figured, it was Kate or no one.

He spotted Kate at the railing. She gave him a bleary-eyed but cheerful smile as he made his way to her.

"Morning," he said. "You look a little tired."

"This is a bit early for me to be up," she admitted. "I usually stay in bed as long as humanly possible." She rubbed her eyes and looked at him again. "You, on the other hand, look perfectly rested and refreshed. Can I infer from this evidence that dawn is not far from your normal rising time?"

Reed snagged a mimosa from a passing steward. "I confess. I'm usually up by four-thirty."

"Disgusting." They shared a smile.

"Here we go!" someone shouted, and everyone pressed forward to get a good look. The ship slid easily between larger commercial ocean liners, nestling snugly against the pier. Ropes thicker than Kate's arm were tossed to the dock and wrapped around squat metal bollards to keep it from drifting away.

"At least now we know that the ship won't run away when we go ashore," Kate said.

"That's a relief." Reed leaned farther over and watched as the tying off was completed. "Is that it?"

"I guess so. I think most of the exciting stuff happens in the pilot room."

"You're probably right." Reed sipped his drink and grimaced. "I hope they're not drinking these."

"Strong?"

"Very. Would you like one?"

Kate shook her head. "I need coffee."

He took her hand. "Coffee it is."

At eight o'clock, they disembarked and joined a dozen other

passengers who were in their horseback-riding group. The dock was alive with people — passengers from other vessels preparing for outings, laborers loading cartons onto trucks, people laughing and calling to each other.

As Kate's feet touched ground for the first time in two days, she felt her equilibrium fighting to right itself. The earth seemed to move under her feet.

"Steady," Reed said, slipping a hand under her elbow.

"Thanks," Kate said. "Guess I've still got my sea legs."

"You're an old salt already." He kept his hand on her arm. "You'll be fine in a minute."

They boarded an open transport, which headed south out of Kralendijk, past Flamingo International Airport to Bonaire Horseback Tours. Kate leaned far over the side, holding tightly to the railing, enjoying the feel of the wind ruffling her hair. The air was wonderfully warm and damp, and fragrant with the sea. The sun was still low on the horizon, casting oblique shadows off the shops and restaurants as they drove through the quiet streets.

Bonaire Horseback Tours was a series of long, low buildings constructed of silvery-gray wood. As the transport lumbered up the unpaved drive, a young couple, blond and smiling, emerged from one of the buildings and stood waiting under a large tree.

"Morning, folks," the young woman said as they got off the bus. "My name is Stacy Haines, and this is my husband. Everybody just calls him Hay. We own this place, and we're going to be showing you all around the island today."

Kate liked her at once. The woman looked to be about Julia's age — young, but with an air of easy confidence. She spoke as if she had been handling tour groups all her life.

"We've got horses to suit everybody, so whether you're an experienced rider or a tenderfoot, we'll make sure you're comfortable and that you have a good time."

Three native boys began leading horses out of the nearby stable, helping the tourists saddle up. Kate noticed that Hay circulated quietly, matching horses and riders with unerring judgment, while Stacy made a point of speaking to every member of the party, exchanging pleasantries while she checked the length of the stirrups and adjusted the bits. Riders and horses alike seemed to find this soothing.

Kate was matched up with a beautiful mare named Chestnut. One of the boys guided her left foot into the stirrup, and then steadied her as she swung her right leg up and over.

"Just like riding a bike," she murmured, eliciting a wide grin from her young assistant before he moved on.

Kate patted Chestnut on the neck and spoke a few soothing words in her ears. The horse seemed very friendly, and Kate looked forward to sharing the day with her.

"You look pretty comfortable in the saddle," Stacy said. "I guess you've ridden before."

"It's been a while," Kate replied.

"It'll come back to you." Stacy double-checked the stirrup length.

"Have you lived on the island all your life?" Kate asked.

"No. Hay and I are from Charleston."

"I thought I recognized a little Carolina drawl in your voice."

Stacy grinned. "You a Southern gal, too?"

"I'm originally from Virginia. I live in DC now."

"Well then we do have a lot in common. My mother's a Washingtonian. She moved to Charleston when she married my daddy. After he passed, she decided to take herself back on home."

"When did you and Hay move down here?"

"About two years ago. We had a windfall and decided to just make the move. We'd come here on our honeymoon and fell in love with the place."

"Sounds like a dream."

"Yep. It's the American dream: inherit some money and move to a foreign country." Stacy grinned as she stroked Chestnut's velvety muzzle. "Well, you're all set here. I'd better move along." She moved on to help one of the other guests.

Kate heard hoofbeats and looked up to the sight of Reed astride a midnight-black stallion. The horse's nostrils flared as Reed pulled up alongside Kate.

Kate couldn't help but laugh. "Stacy said they had horses to suit everyone. I guess she wasn't exaggerating."

"This magnificent creature's name is Necromancer." Reed patted his horse on the neck. "You know, my grandmother used to say that the horse fits the man." The horse huffed through his nostrils to show his approval.

"I'd say he agrees with you."

Stacy's clear voice rang over the crowd. "I understand this is your first day in Bonaire, so I'll go ahead and bore you with a little history lesson. The island of Bonaire is a Dutch province, and has been since 1635. Before that it was mainly the property of Spain, although Dutch settlers had established themselves here for more than 100 years. The first known inhabitants of the island were the Caquetio tribe of Arawak Indians, who reached Bonaire in their dugout canoes between 1375 and 1325 B.C. Many of their cave drawings can still be seen on the eastern shore of the island.

"Today we're going to be visiting the salt pans. These have been used for salt production off and on for centuries, and they are still in use today. The salt company has carefully tailored its operations to avoid disturbing the breeding grounds of the greater flamingo."

Stacy and Hay led the way down a broad, well-traveled path. Stacy chatted about the scenery, relating more historic tidbits of information. The air was warm and wet, and as the morning moved on towards noon, Kate was glad that she'd chosen to wear a hat and a scarf around her neck. The sun beat down on them with relentless cheer. Soon sweat gathered at the back of Kate's neck and at her temples. She swiped at her forehead with the back of her hand.

"Hot?" Reed asked. He held out a handkerchief, and she took it, smiling her thanks.

As she handed it back, she noticed that Reed had managed to remain seemingly untouched by the heat of the day or the moisture in the air. As a child, he had been in a constant state of dishevelment. Something about him had always been dirty or damp, or both. His hair had rarely lain neatly on his head, but always seemed to point in every possible direction. Now it was impeccable despite the heat and the exertion of riding. And his clothing, although informal and well broken-in, seemed to convey a new sense of decorum. The differences were both intriguing and a bit unsettling.

He noticed her studious gaze and turned a questioning eye her way. Refusing to be made self-conscious by her curiosity, she smiled reassuringly.

"What?" he grinned.

Now *he* was the one who looked self-conscious.

"I was just noticing that you look very cool and well-pressed, despite the heat."

"Quite a change from when we were kids, huh?"

"You said it; I didn't."

He smiled. "I guess I left behind all my messy habits when I went to college."

"I see. You had to become a well turned-out young man to fit in with all those yuppie kids?"

"Something like that."

He seemed about to say something more when the path broke through the trees and they came to the crest of a low hill. "Oh, Reed," Kate breathed. "Look at that."

Giant, sparkling white symmetrical hills were lined up before them. Beneath were the salt pans — as pink as the flamingos that dotted their surface. Beyond that, the ocean extended out to the horizon, smooth and blue as a sheet of satin.

"It's almost surreal," Kate said. "Have you ever seen anything so beautiful?"

"Only once or twice." She didn't see him looking at her, watching the changing landscape of her face as raptly as she watched the panorama that was laid out in front of them. No scenery on the island was more beautiful to him than her features.

"Okay, gang. Let's take a break," Stacy called over her shoulder. "I think this is a good place for lunch."

The three boys who had helped the group mount their horses now set to work unpacking lunch. Blankets were spread over the sand, and baskets appeared full of sandwiches, fruit, and bottles of water. Brightly colored umbrellas provided shade as the tour group sat to eat their lunch.

Kate unwrapped a sandwich. "What was it you were going to say?"

Reed laughed quietly. "I'm not really sure." He paused, then spoke quickly, before he had a chance to chicken out. "When I got to college, I learned a few quick, hard lessons about the way the world works. I thought I had it tough in Angel River being

147

the poorest kid in town — that I'd never be able to rise above that label because everyone in town knew all about my family and me. But when I got out of there and got to college, I had to fight like hell just to be considered mediocre."

"You were on scholarship?"

"Of course. It's not like my grandmother had a stash of money hidden under the floorboards. Believe me, I looked. After she died, I found out that she hadn't paid taxes on that place for years. I was seventeen, and being her sole heir, I inherited all her possessions — such as they were — and her debts. I also still had a few months of school left to go, and I had to go to summer school to earn enough credits to help me graduate. I don't know if you remember, but I was always behind in school."

Kate nodded slowly. His grandmother's many illnesses and infirmities had made it necessary for him to drop out every now and then to take care of her or to earn a little extra money.

Reed continued. "Judge Stein — you remember him?"

"Vaguely. He used to come to my house for dinner."

"Well, he would come to my house too, but for different reasons. Any little accusation of petty theft, vandalism, whatever, would bring him around. I used to tell my grandmother that he was sweet on her, and that was why he was always using any little excuse to come to our house. She never believed it, but I think the idea tickled her, even though she would swat me over the head for making up stories. You know, she never asked me if I was guilty of anything that I was accused of. She would just throw back her head — she was a diminutive person, but full of personality."

"I remember. She was the only person I ever knew who could stare you down by looking up at you."

Reed chuckled. "That was her, all right. She would stare down that judge and take him head on. If she couldn't intimidate him out of accusing me, she would remind him about my mother."

Kate could picture it. She remembered well the old woman's husky voice with its Virginia drawl, and she could imagine the woman speaking up in defense of her beloved grandson. "I'm not saying my boy is guilty of anything, Judge, but if he is guilty of something, it's of losing his father before he was born; or of having his mother run out on him when he was just a babe in arms; or of being raised by a no-account, cussing old woman like myself. If he lifted a pack of gum from the gas station, it was only because I can't afford to buy it for him properly. And if he did throw that rock through the drugstore window, it was only because the pharmacist refused to give me my medication on credit, when she knows damn well that I don't get my government check until the beginning of the month. So if you are so certain that it was my boy who did those things, then slap him in irons and take him away, but take me right along with him, because anything he done, he done for me."

Kate had heard the stories related in church or at the table during Sunday dinner.

Reed went on. "I always thought Judge Stein hated me. I was sure he'd use my grandmother's debts to make sure that I never left Angel River, that I stayed there my whole life working to pay them off. But I was surprised to find out I was wrong. He helped me to arrange the sale of my grandmother's place to cover her debts, and he made sure I had a little left over to put in the bank for when I left for college. He even let me stay at his place for six months until I was done with high school and ready to go to NYU. Of course, I worked for my room and board. Even if he had offered me charity, I wouldn't have taken it."

Reed smiled. "He also got me reading about Ben Franklin.

The judge used to quote Franklin all the time, especially that line, 'Having been poor is no shame, but being ashamed of it, is.'"

"Maybe the judge realized that you'd had a bit of a rough start in life. Maybe he could see that your bad reputation wasn't deserved."

"You mean because of my mother."

"Well...."

He said quietly, "The funny thing is I was truly surprised when my mother didn't come back for Grand's funeral. I mean, she had friends in town before she left. Surely one of them might have known how to contact her...I can't believe she didn't know."

Kate shifted uneasily. The naked pain in his face brought a stab of guilt to her heart, and for a moment, all she wanted to do was ease his suffering. But how could she be sure that what she might tell him would make him feel better? Would it do him any good to find out that everything he believed in was a lie? So she kept silent.

Reed continued. "Once I'd gotten out of Angel River and made a name for myself, made myself into a man, I felt I'd finally reached a point where I could say that she was a fool for having left and that maybe I was better off without her."

"Do you ever wonder what happened to her?"

"For years I did. Then one day I decided to stop wondering and find out. I don't know what I was expecting."

"What did you find?"

"I hired a private detective. He found her living in Richmond. She had remarried to a man with three adult children. They were all in college at the time." He paused. "I have two stepsisters and a stepbrother."

"Did you talk to her? Did you see her?"

Reed shook his head. "She has a new life. She's moved on. There's no reason for me to step into their lives and shake things up. Besides, she left me. I doubt she ever thinks of me."

Kate covered his hand with hers. "I'm sure she does. She must. She probably feels guilty about leaving you."

He shrugged, tough once more. "It was the best thing she could have done for me. My grandmother was the best parent I could have had."

"She was one of the most remarkable people I've ever met," Kate said quietly.

Reed talked more about his mother. Slowly, in a stilted way that reminded her of Reed at fourteen, he told her that he had not just left his mother alone. He had used his connections with banks to help get loans to put her stepchildren through school, and a business loan for her new husband to start an auto repair shop. Reed had worked quietly, behind the scenes, to give his mother the life she needed. Kate marveled at the caring and selflessness that he hid behind his mask of coldness. The boy she had loved was still there after all.

Reed took her hand again, leaning over to kiss her. Kate wondered if she would ever get used to the sensation of his mouth on hers — the newness of it and the familiarity, the naturalness of it and the surreal quality. She didn't know if she would get used to it, but she would like to spend a lifetime finding out. Strange how she once again felt like she had lost her land legs, even though she was sitting down.

CHAPTER TWELVE

IT WAS DUSK WHEN THEY finally returned to Bonaire
Horseback Tours. The day had been long, hot, and sticky,
but the scenery was beautiful, and the tour had been
very entertaining.

When Kate dismounted and waved a final goodbye to Stacy,
she was amazed by how tired and sore she was. She had forgotten
how strenuous horseback riding could be. And she wasn't alone
in her exhaustion. The entire group was silent with fatigue as the
transport lumbered back to the ship.

Hot breezes blew through the gathering dark, spiced with
the smell of tropical dishes and ringing with the distant sound of
music. It made Kate long to wander the city and find the sources
of those enticing sounds and smells. But by the time they got
back to the ship, all she wanted was a hot shower, a bite to eat,
and a long night's sleep.

Then Reed gazed down at her with those soulful, luminous
eyes. Holding her hand, he murmured a suggestion, and Kate
found herself nodding in agreement. She trailed after him to
his stateroom, and ten minutes later, she was soaking in his
whirlpool bathtub, up to her chin in fragrant, frothy water. She
had closed her eyes in modesty as he showered in the frosted
glass stall adjacent to the tub, and had promptly drifted into
a doze.

The sound of the shower turning off roused her, and she rubbed her face with wet hands as she struggled to stay awake. "I have to warn you," she called. "I'm falling asleep out here."

"Don't worry," he called back. "The bath balm will help with that."

"What's in it, anyway?"

He opened the door and stepped out, a long towel wrapped around his waist. Although she knew he couldn't see through the frothing water, she folded her arms discreetly over her breasts as he stood looking down at her.

The motion wasn't lost on him. He knelt beside her and stroked her cheek, intensely aware of how close together they were. The steam from the shower enveloped them, combining with the scent of the bath to form a heady fog that seemed to draw them together.

"Lemon and peppermint for energy," he answered softly. "Epsom salts and baking soda for tired muscles."

She felt herself blush as if he had propositioned her.

He let his finger slide along her jawbone and down her neck, pausing as he traced her collarbone. A few inches more and his hand would disappear under the frothy water, slide under her sheltering arms and cup her breast.

He could imagine how soft her flesh would be there — warm from the water, her nipple pressed against his palm. His mouth went dry at the thought, and he couldn't quite get his breath.

He could see the pulse beating hard in the hollow of her neck, and he knew she wanted his hand to drift under the water, wanted his fingers to wander where they would. A smile ghosted around his lips. When his eyes met hers, they were bright with longing.

Reed stood up. Kate swallowed hard and struggled to pull

herself together. His touch on her damp skin had been achingly gentle, sending hot chills rushing over her. She'd had to fight to keep herself from dragging him into the tub, towel and all.

"A lemon-peppermint bath balm," she said shakily. "I never would have pegged you for an herbalist."

He picked up a comb from the sink and pulled it through his hair, feigning composure. "It's all part of the body obsession," he said dryly. "I am a moneymaking machine, after all. I'm interested in anything that will make my body perform better."

It was on the tip of Kate's tongue to tell him that his moneymaking machine looked like it was performing damn well. Having seen him in bathing trunks at the pool, she had known that he had a great physique. But the towel draped around his waist had an erotic quality that a bathing suit could never match. His torso was well muscled without being bulky; the rough-looking hair on his chest was a perfect V dwindling to a point below his navel, somewhere beneath the cover of the towel.

The thought of that hidden region had her heart skipping a beat. She thought idly of dipping her tongue in his navel, wondering how he would taste there. She let her eyes drift upward again, and when her gaze met his, she saw the reflection of her own desire.

He leaned over her and kissed her forehead, lips lingering against her skin. "I'll let you finish your bath," he said quietly.

As he left the bathroom, Kate closed her eyes and sank a little lower in the water, smiling to herself. For the first time she knew without a doubt that they would be lovers. Maybe tonight, she mused, liking the sudden shiver of anticipatory pleasure that went through her at the thought.

The ingredients in the bath balm were beginning to work.

She could feel the ache in her muscles easing, replaced by a feeling of well-being and an infusion of energy. She climbed out of the tub and reached for a thick towel hanging on the nearby warming rack. Reed had left his robe on the back of the door. She wrapped herself in its silky folds and then borrowed his comb to tidy her hair.

She padded across the thick carpet of the living room, for the first time noticing that his suite was quite large and beautifully appointed. When she had passed through earlier, she had been too tired to take it in. Kitchenette, dining nook, living room, bathroom — all were decorated in the French provincial style, with muted colors that conveyed a sense of quiet opulence and drew attention to the magnificent windows, where the lights of Kralendijk sparkled like stars fallen to earth.

"Some view," Kate breathed, conscious of how inadequate the statement was.

"Thanks." Reed's voice came from behind her, and she turned to see him standing in the doorway of the kitchenette, a steaming mug in each hand.

He stopped short at the sight of her in his robe, the sash wrapped twice around her, wet hair combed back from her face. A strange feeling came over him, some sense of inevitability, of a prophecy that was about to be fulfilled. It made him uncomfortable. He cleared his throat and pressed forward.

"I thought you might like some tea," he said, handing her a cup.

She settled on the couch while he remained standing, leaning with apparent casualness against the mantle. But his relaxed attitude was a pose. He had been longing for this moment, when they were completely alone and almost naked, but now that it was here he struggled between desire and his need to maintain control. What he really wanted to do was rip the robe right off her and —

"I like your choice of music," Kate said. Her head was tilted as she listened to the gentle strains of Vivaldi's eleventh concerto drifting softly from a well-concealed speaker. He had learned his love of classical music from her own mother, who had shared her favorite pieces with him. Ignoring how idiosyncratic — almost laughable — it was for a troubled kid like him to be into classical music, he had been the one who taught Kate to love it, too — to love the passion and the story that each piece told so eloquently without the need for words.

Reed caught her look and smiled, acknowledging the shared memory. "This is still one of my favorite pieces."

"Mine, too." She sipped her tea and looked around. "This suite is unbelievable," she said. "I didn't know that cruise ships had rooms like this."

"I think this ship may be special," he said softly.

"Joe would certainly agree with you."

"And do you like your room?"

"I love it," Kate responded enthusiastically. "It's so beautiful — all done in cream and spring green. The curtains are muslin, and there's this big comfy chair in one corner, perfect for reading. It's like my dream room. Very different from my place in DC."

"Oh really?"

She wrinkled her nose. "My apartment is very…beige. I don't spend much time there, so I just have the basics — sofa, TV, bed. The day before I was scheduled to move in, I went to a department store and just picked out whatever was within my budget that seemed moderately comfortable. My sister's always giving me a hard time because she says my place doesn't have 'personality.' She's right, of course, but that doesn't mean I like hearing it!" Kate shook her head. "Maybe it's me that doesn't have personality."

"Oh, believe me kid, you've got personality!" Reed said. "You're loaded with it."

"Aw, shucks," Kate grinned. "What's your place in New York like?"

He thought about it, staring into his tea. "It's beautiful," he said at last, "but cold." He tried to explain. "Very high ceilings, very big windows. It's got a great view, and a huge fireplace, both of which I love. When I bought the place, I tried to decorate it myself, but that was a disaster. So I hired somebody and let him do pretty much what he wanted."

"Disaster? How bad could it have been?"

He looked directly at her. "Halfway through the process, I realized that I was decorating it for you. All those autumn colors that you look so beautiful in. Russet reds, greens, golds…" He shook his head. "I was trying to re-create your presence in my life, I guess. I'm sure some analyst would have a field day with that. I had them take everything away and start from scratch. Now it's mostly black and white. I live with it, but I don't love it. Anyway, I don't spend much time at home either, so I tell myself that it doesn't matter."

Kate didn't know what to say. She was overwhelmed by the notion that someone could love her that much, or had once loved her that much. She steadied the teacup in her shaking hands and tried to shift to a lighter tone. "I imagine you travel quite a bit?"

"I've been all over the world, but always on business. This is my first vacation in…well, too many years to count." He smiled. "How about you? Have you had the chance to do much traveling?"

She shook her head regretfully. "I went to Europe when I was in school, but that's about it."

"It was a family trip?" Reed asked tightly.

"No." She grinned engagingly. "I'd been going through this very wild stage, and my parents just couldn't deal with me anymore. Some friends of theirs were going to England to visit family, and I was invited to go with them. I jumped at the chance to get away."

"*You* went through a wild stage? I wish I'd been there to see that!"

It was an offhand remark that suddenly took on too much weight. "If you had been there," Kate said seriously, "I might not have gone quite so wild."

When he didn't answer, she went on. "That time in my life — it was the culmination of a year without you. At least, that's how I think of it. Once we left Angel River, I just didn't have any direction anymore. I started skipping school, that sort of thing. Mom and Dad probably thought I was punishing them, but in truth I just couldn't pretend that I was okay without you."

The words stabbed him painfully. *She* wasn't okay without *him*? How did she think he had felt? He swallowed the familiar anger that bubbled up inside him. "And Europe made everything okay again?"

She heard the cynical note in his voice but tried to laugh it off. "Of course not. It's not like my parents bribed me with a trip to Europe!"

Or was it? She felt a niggling doubt. *Had* she allowed her parents to buy her good spirits? But those misgivings were pushed aside by Reed's next words.

"Of course not," he echoed. This time he didn't try to hide the sarcasm. "They would never do anything like that!"

Her temper sparked. It was one thing for her to question her own motives, but quite another for him to do it. She set her tea down on the cocktail table and tried to keep her voice level. "So you think they would?"

He tried to keep himself under control, to keep his voice calm and reasonable. This was a painful subject for him, but he didn't want to fly off the handle. Not when things were going so well. "I think they lured you away, Kate. Admit it. You let them come between us, even though that was something you had promised me you'd never do."

"My parents are not the ones who came between us, Reed!" Kate had to bite her lip to avoid saying too much.

Her denial made him angry. Why wouldn't she just admit it? Why did she have to continually try to deceive him, to cover up for what her parents had done? He paced back and forth, working himself into a fury. When he turned to her, his eyes were savage with hurt. "It's the only explanation. I mean, things were fine, right? Then Harry Block gets killed, and a few days later, you leave — in the middle of the night, no less! And not just any night, either — it was that night. *That night*. How can you have forgotten?"

"Forgotten?" Something in her snapped. She sprang off the couch and stood toe to toe with him. She had never wanted to slap someone so badly in her life. "Don't you dare say that I've forgotten! For God's sake, I — "

A sharp rap on the door cut her off. "Who is it?" Reed thundered.

"Room service," said the faint and obviously terrified voice on the other side of the door.

"For God's sake," he muttered in an unconscious imitation of Kate's last words. "I forgot I ordered dinner."

He moved to walk away, but her words stopped him in his tracks. "What did you order?" she asked. "Hot dogs and root beer?"

The look he cast over his shoulder was inscrutable, but Kate knew she had hit a nerve. She turned and walked across the carpet, watching her toes sink into the thick pile as she listened to Reed gruffly accept the room service cart, refuse to allow the steward to set it up, sign the bill, and close the door.

He wheeled the cart into the living room and began to set up their meal. The sight of him performing this domestic task while he fumed visibly over what to say next made Kate's lips want to twitch. But she bit the inside of her cheek and suppressed the smile.

"It surprises you that I remember what we had for dinner that night, doesn't it?" she asked gently. No matter how angry he made her, she had to remember that he had been deceived into thinking the worst of her, and he was acting accordingly. She took a deep breath. It was time to tell him the truth. "Do you want to know what else I remember?"

She took his silence for acquiescence and continued. "That night, I'd snuck out to see you. We drove out to the lake. It was drizzling and muggy. I remember the smell of the lilacs and of those old plastic seats in your car. We sat in the car and ate hot dogs, drank root beer, and talked. We decided that night that we were ready to make love for the first time, but we had to wait one more day." She smiled briefly — a small, sad smile. "In those days, there were no condom dispensers in the school bathrooms, and we didn't want to take any chances that I might get pregnant. You said you would buy some the next day."

"I can't believe that I hadn't gotten them before that." He shook his head, allowing a moment of levity between them.

"What kind of man was I? I should have been ready at a moment's notice!"

"I liked the fact that you didn't have them. It showed that you weren't expecting anything like that from me." She hurried on before they could dwell on that. "You drove me home, parked down the street, and walked me around the back of the house to watch me climb up to my bedroom window. You kissed me one last time before I climbed the trellis, then gave me a boost and watched to make sure I made it okay. I leaned out to wave at you, and you called softly, 'Goodnight, Kate. I love you! I'm going to marry you some day!'"

Her eyes shone with the tears that suddenly filled her eyes. "I could never forget that night," she said softly. "Not if I lived to be a thousand."

For a brief moment, Reed's eyes showed an answering glimmer. Then they hardened abruptly. "But that's why you had to leave town, right?"

"What do you mean?"

"Your parents told people it was a 'family emergency,' but I knew what that meant. They found out that you had been sneaking out, and they had to take immediate action. No way the boy from the wrong side of the tracks would soil their lily-white daughter!" His laugh was bitter. "I don't know what made me angrier — that they would feel that way about me or that it was such a cliché! Couldn't they have been more original?"

Kate shook her head. "No, Reed, you've got it all wrong. It was my sister!"

"Oh, come on. What does Julia have to do with this?"

"She was pregnant!"

Reed could only stare as the words struggled to penetrate his thoughts. *Julia? Pregnant?* But she had only been a child...

fourteen at most. He groped behind him for a chair and sank onto it, waiting to hear the rest.

Kate took another breath. "After I came home that night, I went downstairs for a glass of water. I heard my parents talking in the study. My mother was crying. I thought they'd discovered that I'd snuck out and they were worried about me. I went in to see them, ready to have it out. I was going to tell them once and for all that you and I were going to see each other all we wanted — nothing could keep us apart!"

He smirked, but there was sadness in his eyes. "As if that declaration would have made any difference!"

"I never got a chance to make it. Before I could say anything, my mother told me that my sister — who is almost two years younger than me, remember — was pregnant."

Even after all these years, Kate could still feel her own shock and grief as she recalled that night. She remembered her parents sitting in the living room, a single lamp casting long shadows across the room. Her sister had sat in the corner of the sofa, curled up with her arms around her legs, her eyes red with tears and shame. "My parents looked like they had aged ten years in a few hours. And Julia — oh God, she was just terrified. Angel River was such a small place — she was sure it would be all over town the next day and that she'd never be able to look anyone in the eye again."

Reed wanted to reach out and take her hand, but he didn't. He couldn't. "I can't even imagine how you must have felt."

"I felt guilty," Kate said flatly. "That's how I felt. I had been going around in my own little world — all the drama with my parents over whether I could see you — all the worrying about whether you and I should 'go all the way.' And here was Jules, already having sex, already in an adult relationship. I didn't even know she was dating!" She shook her head. "It's the kind of thing a big sister never gets over. I had completely shirked my responsibility. By the time I arrived on the scene, she had already made a lot of big decisions — like not getting an abortion. She was adamant about that. She wanted to have the baby and let it be adopted. So we all decided we would have to move."

She saw the look on Reed's face. "I know what you're going to say. I guess it *was* my mother who said it first, but really it was a family decision. I wanted to be with my sister. I knew she would need me, and I knew I hadn't been there for her before!"

"But why did you all have to leave so quickly?"

"My mother said she couldn't bear to stay in town one more day. I think she was really scared that someone might find out, and that Julia might do something drastic if she thought people were going to know what had happened."

Plus it was a great excuse to get you out of town right away, Reed wanted to say. But he held his tongue.

"I wanted to call you," Kate continued. "The first moment I was alone, I picked up the phone. But it was two in the morning by then, and I had no idea what to say. I didn't want to be telling Julia's secrets without her permission. So I hung up again. We were up all night packing, making arrangements to go to Washington. We were going to be gone a year.

"We left before dawn. As we drove out of town, I suddenly realized that there was no way I could go without giving you some word of what was going on. I wrote a quick note — I don't even remember what it said — and I forced my parents to turn the car around so I could drop it off at your house. It was just after five-thirty, I remember, because the sun was beginning to come up. I wanted to leave the note by your front door, but when I bent down to leave it, the door opened and your grandmother was looking down at me."

Reed went cold inside. "Grand?"

Kate nodded. "I told her that we had a family emergency and that we were leaving for a while. At the time, I thought Mom and I would be back in a few weeks to close up the house. I had no idea that we would never be back there again. I handed her the note, and she said she would give it to you."

"She didn't," he said shortly. Something inside him wanted to think Kate was lying, but her words rang too true to be disregarded. He could picture the scene: Kate, exhausted and disheveled from her turbulent night. His grandmother would have been wearing her old bathrobe and slippers. The rising sun would cast long shadows on the fragrant vegetable garden by the front door as Kate asked Grand to deliver the note.

Grand would have agreed, but the moment the door was shut, she would have torn it up. She had always possessed what she considered to be very definite ideas about the Doyles and their ilk, but to Reed, all his grandmother's notions had been confused and fraught with prejudice: Don't consort with those rich folks, but make sure you "marry up." Why don't the rich do more to help the poor, but how dare they try to give us charity? I want you to get out of this town and make yourself successful, but don't you dare desert me!

Reed knew that the contradictions in her lectures were the result of being always at war with herself — her desire for him to do well battling with the disappointments and grief she had suffered, and her need to take it out on someone.

Grand had told him that Kate's parents had a family emergency, and she had hinted that it had something to do with Kate. Later there had been gossip in town that one of the girls had started to "run wild." He had thought it was Kate they were talking about, that wagging tongues had turned their innocent love into something sordid. But all the time it had been…

"Julia."

Kate nodded, knowing that he was beginning to see the whole picture. There was more she could say, but the look in his eyes made her hesitate.

"I'm sorry, Kate," he said tightly. "I've been doing you a grave injustice over the years. I've been thinking that you deserted me, without a word of goodbye. I see now that I was incorrect." He had gone stiff and formal. "I apologize, not only for my unfair thoughts, but also for my grandmother's behavior. In her defense, I can only say that however misguided her actions, she thought she was doing what was right for me."

"I know that."

"In defense of myself, I can say nothing at all."

"I'm not asking you to defend yourself," Kate said quietly.

"That's a good thing." His laugh was humorless as his eyes settled on her face. His grandmother's careful rewording of the truth had fanned the flames of his resentment and anger. He had used that anger to fuel his drive to succeed. It could even be said that with her lies, his grandmother had seen to it that he broke the bonds of poverty — with her last breath, she had thrust him out of the life they had both grown to despise. But to what end?

He had become a man who hired a private detective to find and watch an old friend — and more than that. Suddenly those things didn't seem quite so defensible.

Kate was uncertain what to say. Reed's face was as inscrutable as she had ever seen it, but she knew there were emotions running wild beneath the quiet surface.

She closed the distance between them with a few short steps, taking his hand in hers and holding it to her cheek. Fierce emotion engulfed his face, and he rose to his feet. Almost defiantly, he cupped her face in his hands and bent his head to kiss her.

His lips were hot on hers, his hands demanding as they slid around her waist and pulled her to him. For a long moment, she could feel only his desire mingled with her own. But then she became aware of something else. Behind the raging heat of need, there was something hidden — and — and *cold*.

Instinctively she recoiled, pushing him away and taking a few steps back. "Not like this," she gasped.

"Not like what?"

"Not with that cold anger. Not — not for revenge."

At her words, the blinds came down behind his eyes. "I don't know what you mean."

"Oh, yes, you do. You know exactly what I mean. I wish I did." Kate rubbed her face. The day's exertions pressed in on her. "I have to get out of this room."

But should she change back into her dirty riding clothes? She fingered his robe uncertainly. Reed caught her look.

"Wear it back to your room," he said. His voice was icily formal. "You can return it tomorrow. Or keep it — it's up to you."

"You can afford a dozen more like it, right?"

"Easily." The nonchalance in his voice made her want to laugh. Or cry.

He followed her to the door. "Would you like me to escort you back to your stateroom?"

"No, thanks. I can manage."

"What about your dinner?" A humorless smile ghosted around his lips as he recalled their unfinished lunch of only a few days ago.

She returned his look. "You eat it," she said again. "I've lost my appetite."

She didn't bother to close the door behind her.

CHAPTER THIRTEEN

October 1968

I T WAS A **COLD AUTUMN.**

Lana stood behind the counter of the empty coffee shop, watching the rain through the plate glass window. It fell, straight and true, from a slate-gray sky to the Main Street blacktop, water coursing endlessly along the gutters. The day was dark, and it had been dark since she'd rolled out of bed that morning, sleepless and bone-weary, forcing herself to face another day. There hadn't really even been a dawn, she reflected, just a gradual lessening of the night until the streetlamps cut off and the world was illuminated with a dull gray light.

A banner was strung across the boulevard, its colors made brighter by the muted light. HOMECOMING, it said. One of the ties had broken loose, and the corner flapped in the wind. The whole town was wound up, preparing for the parade that was coming up on Saturday, not to mention the dance and football game that would follow.

Lana couldn't even remember who Angel River High was playing against, and she wasn't going to the dance. But Kathy was breathless with excitement. She'd bought her dress over the summer when she'd gone to visit her mother's family in New York. She was on the decorating committee and the Spirit Squad, and she was, as Lana had said to George, in Kathy-Heaven. In fact, Kathy's only real complaint was that Nate Doyle was off at college and couldn't be her escort. But Nate's younger brother, Malcolm, had easily agreed to go in Nate's place. Mal had graduated high school the year before, and he was taking a semester off, planning to start college in January.

The arrival of the Doyle family two years ago had been an unprecedented event, and not just because it had brought Mal and Nate into their lives. The house on the hill, which from Lana's earliest memory had been nothing but a burnt-out shell, was now a glorious mansion, a Phoenix risen from the ashes, visible for all to see. If Lana walked outside and turned right, she'd see it plain as day, even with the rain and the fog. It presided over the town with aloof dignity, eliciting both jealousy and pride from Angel River's gentle citizens.

It was a beautiful house. And quite a marvel, to hear people tell it. Built to the original specifications, but full of modern conveniences. Central air conditioning, modern insulation, and six bathrooms. *Six,* people would say emphatically, sharing looks of envy combined with censure. Surely six bathrooms was showing off? And yet they said that America Fitzgerald himself wouldn't have been able to tell the difference in the place, so cleverly was it built. It might have sprung full-blown from the year 1895.

Pleasance Fitzgerald had put up plenty of trouble as the building had progressed. Minor vandalism on the site — trucks with flat tires, broken windows, piles of bricks scattered all over the place — had been attributed to her, although no one was able to prove anything. But the worst had come when they had started the arduous process of running phone and electrical wires out of town, past her little dwelling, and up the hill.

There was only one way to get to the house on the hill, and that was to take the Old Back Road, which ran right by Pleasance Fitzgerald's shack.

Walter Doyle, Nate and Malcolm's father, had offered to wire up the shack, bringing electricity to Pleasance for free. He had even offered to pay her electric bill for years to come, figuring that one little cottage couldn't be much of a drain, especially not compared to what he would be paying to power his entire house. But each kindness that was offered to her, each concession to the importance of her family, only seemed to infuriate her more. Until one day she had marched through town, straight up to Judge Roberts' house, pounded on the front door and bullied her way inside.

Lana had seen Pleasance stomping up Main Street, fury emanating from her almost visibly, like anger lines in a cartoon. "Oh Lord," Lana had murmured under her breath, wondering what was about to happen. She had thought briefly of RJ, wondered what it must be like for him to have a mother like that, and thanked God that her own mother was so sweet and mild.

Exactly what had happened inside the Judge's house was only known by rumor. The story was that Pleasance had told the judge flat out that if "that goddamn electric company tries to put up one of those goddamn electricity poles in front of my goddamn house, I will take my wood chopping ax and hack it to hell and back! And then I may go after the goddamn family!"

A threat like that couldn't be ignored, and the judge had been inclined to start commitment proceedings. Everybody knew Pleasance was crazy as a loon anyway. But having an old crazy woman living on the edge of town was one thing — kind of gave the town character. Having an ax-wielding maniac chopping taxpaying citizens to bits was quite another thing altogether. Better to have her safely locked up somewhere.

Things had looked pretty grim for a while. Nobody really wanted to see Pleasance locked up. Her family had founded this town, for God's sake. And she may have been nuts, but she couldn't really have been crazy enough to kill anybody. Could she…?

Oddly enough, it was Nate who set the matter to rest. The Doyle family had taken up residence in the local hotel while the house was being built, and Nate had convinced his father to invite Pleasance to a "business meeting" in the hotel's parlor. Everyone thought it was some sort of joke, especially Pleasance herself, but she had come anyway.

And Nate had done the thing that nobody else could do — he had convinced Pleasance to let them build the house. Exactly how he had worked this miracle, people didn't seem to know. Did he flatter her? Did he threaten her? Did he use his famous charm?

Lana had finally worked up the nerve to ask him about it the past summer. He'd smiled easily at her and said, "It wasn't a big deal really. I just talked to her like a reasonable person. It was a business meeting, so I made her a business offer." The Doyles, Lana learned, had paid not only the back taxes due on the big house and the property that came with it, they had paid the back taxes on the land that Pleasance lived on. The offer they'd made her was that they would have that portion of the land parceled off and deeded to her. She would own it, free and clear. It wasn't charity, Nate insisted; it was an equitable exchange. She got her land; they got theirs. Everyone was happy.

Well, Pleasance was never actually *happy*, Lana thought, but she had grudgingly agreed to the proposition. Nate had worked a miracle.

Lana shifted restlessly. She didn't want to think about Nate right now, or the miracles that he could work. Didn't want to think about hot kisses that left her weak-kneed and light-headed. But her heart beat hard as flashes of memory assaulted her against her will. Scorching summer heat, the smell of creek water, and the sound of insects buzzing in the trees. Nate's mouth on hers, his hands roaming her body. She remembered her joy, the feeling that freedom and love were within her grasp, that she was finally able to leave behind her cold gray reality and escape to some place filled with warmth and light.

She remembered feeling happy. That was the worst part.

With a great effort, Lana recalled herself to the present. She willed herself to make her heart a stone, cold and hard and remote. Dreams of love and happiness had no place in her life right now. Right now was for work, and school, and getting through each day as it came. Later, when she had graduated college and gotten a good job and saved enough money so she wouldn't have to be scared anymore, that was when her time would come for love. But not right now. And not with — never with — a boy that Kathy loved the way Kathy loved Nate.

Lana pushed the thought of him away and picked up a sponge to clean the counter. She had wiped it a few minutes earlier, so she could've saved herself the trouble. But George was paying her to be here, so she might as well make herself useful.

In a little while, she would go back and check on him, likely as not finding him with his feet up, reading or doing a crossword. He'd smile at her, but it wouldn't be the bright, energetic smile of the man he'd been two years ago. The past months had taken their toll on him, like they had on everybody. He used to watch the TV between flipping burgers, but he didn't do that anymore.

"I used to think that television was one of Man's greatest

inventions," he'd said to her in June. "I watched JFK's funeral on TV in 1963, and even though I thought my heart was breaking, I was grateful to be able to share in the mourning, as though I was right there with the family, crying the same tears as them. But then earlier this year I watched Dr. King's funeral, and I wondered if I knew what heartbreak even meant. And now it's Bobby's." His voice broke slightly, and he shook his head. "It's just too much. I think I'll give the TV a rest for a while."

Lana had hardly ever seen him turn it on since that day. But then, at the end of August, they'd watched the report of the Chicago police riots, footage of citizens being beaten into unconsciousness with what appeared to be the senseless savagery of men gone mad. George had given the television away after that. "Just tell me when the war in Vietnam is over," he'd tried to joke. "If it ever is."

The door clanged open and Lana looked up expectantly, thinking for a moment that it might have been RJ Fitzgerald coming in for his afternoon pie and coffee. She didn't see much of him these days. Maybe he was too busy trying to take care of his mother.

Or maybe, she thought, as she saw the smiling green eyes and sandy blond hair of Malcolm Doyle walk through the door, maybe RJ was jealous. Everybody in town thought she and Mal were dating. Kathy had seen to that. Maybe RJ didn't want to see her with Mal. The thought made Lana a little sad, although she wasn't sure why.

She smiled back at Mal as he came through the door and crossed the room toward the counter. He lacked Nate's confident stride, lacked Nate's forceful personality and ebullient presence. But Mal had assets of his own. He was kind, for one thing. And he had a good sense of humor and a dreamy charm, a kind of will-o'-the-wisp sweetness that Lana found very endearing. And comforting. She felt comfortable with Mal. She liked being in a foursome with him and Kathy and Nate, despite how things between her and Nate had gotten…complicated, to say the least. But that was her fault, in a way, and it was her cross to bear. And for some reason, it didn't seem to infringe on her affection for Kathy, or for Mal.

On Mal's heels came Kathy, all decked out in her New York duds — a midi-coat over a super-short miniskirt, thick tights, and boots, plus a long, figure-hugging sweater with a matching belt. Kathy had come back from her summer vacation reincarnated as a fashion plate. Lana smiled as Kathy gave her a wave and headed immediately to the ladies' room to check her makeup. Her mascara, worn heavy in true Mod fashion, had melted, giving her raccoon eyes.

Mal settled on the stool in front of Lana. "Hello, beautiful," he said as he always did. "What's on the menu today?"

"Same as yesterday," she said. "Coffee and pie, pie and coffee. Cheeseburgers, fried chicken — you name it, we got it."

"I think I'll go with the pie and coffee," he said.

"What kind?"

"How about pumpkin, in honor of the season?"

"Coming right up."

Lana dished out the pie and poured his coffee, arranging the cream and sugar on the counter in front of him. Kathy came out of the restroom, her mascara fresh and bobbed hair smooth. She headed immediately to the jukebox in the corner and dropped in a dime. She pushed buttons dramatically, then turned and beamed at Lana.

"Oh no," Lana said.

"What?" Mal asked. He had his back to Kathy and hadn't

seen what she was up to.

"Twiggy just chose a song to play, and I think I know which one." She nodded as the first strains of guitar music floated through the air, followed by Arlo Guthrie announcing the name of the song: *This song is called "Alice's Restaurant," and it's about Alice...*

"For Pete's sake," Lana said as Kathy hopped up on the stool next to Mal. "Why that song?"

"It's good economics," Kathy explained innocently. "This is the longest song on the juke. More bang for the buck."

"More bounce for the ounce," Mal supplied helpfully.

"Exactly." Kathy nodded. "Besides, I like this song."

Lana rolled her eyes. "Do you want something to eat, or did you just come here to torture me?"

"I'll have coffee — black," Kathy said. "Nothing to eat, though."

"Uh-huh." Lana looked at Kathy as she poured coffee into her cup. "Are you on a diet?" she asked accusingly. "You know you're too skinny already."

"Look who's talking!" Kathy said indignantly. "You've been nothing but skin and bone since the day I met you!"

Lana smoothed her uniform self-consciously. People were always telling her she was too thin — George especially. She tried to eat, if only to make him happy, but it was hard sometimes. Between school and her work and her worries, food seemed a small priority.

"Besides," Kathy continued, "I'm not that thin, really. You know Twiggy was only ninety pounds when she was my age!"

"Oh brother," Lana said dramatically. "Did I ask what Twiggy weighs? I'm talking about you."

Kathy slumped over sullenly. "I just want to look nice for

the dance this weekend."

"You'll look beautiful," Lana assured her. "You always do." She placed a piece of pie on the counter in front of her friend. "Blueberry," she said encouragingly. "Your favorite. How about it?"

Kathy smiled her concession and pulled the pie towards her. "I am kind of hungry," she admitted as Lana added cream to her coffee. "The Homecoming committee is a total scream, but it's *crazy*, man!"

Mal and Lana shared a look at Kathy's slang. He mouthed the words "*crazy*, man!" and Lana ducked her head, trying not to laugh out loud. He had been quiet during their little weight discussion, obviously knowing that a smart man never interfered with two women in a quarrel — especially not when body weight was involved.

Now he cleared his throat. "Well, Kathy and I both have news for you," he said to Lana. "Since Her Highness here is too involved in her blueberries to tell you her news, I'll do it. Nate may be able to come home this weekend, to take Kathy to the dance." He sipped his coffee, avoiding Lana's gaze.

"Oh," Lana said. She refilled his cup automatically, keeping her face cheerful, but impassive. She risked a look at Mal, trying to gauge his mood. She had never been sure how much Mal knew about her and Nate. From how careful he was not to look at her, she had a feeling he knew a lot. She felt her mouth stretch into a smile. "Well, that's great. It'll free you up anyway, so you won't have to go to the dance if you don't want to."

Kathy scraped her plate with her fork and drained her coffee cup. "Oh no, it won't," she said, eyes sparkling. The sugar and caffeine had brought vitality blooming onto her face, and now she jumped up and pointed at Lana. "It means he's freed up to go to the dance with *you,* my friend!"

"Me?" Lana almost dropped the coffeepot. "But I'm not going. I don't even have a dress!"

"Don't worry about that, Cinderella. Your fairy godmother has taken care of everything. I have the perfect dress for you. It's long and soft and blue to match your eyes. We'll curl your hair and pierce your ears…. It's going to be a perfect night, and we will be the belles of the ball!" Kathy laughed and clapped her hands like a child, then began to waltz herself around the room, completely out of sync with Arlo Guthrie, who still talked-sang with enthusiasm in the background.

Lana watched for a minute in stunned silence, then shook her head and looked accusingly at Mal. "Was this your idea?" she asked.

He shook his head and held up his hands in a *don't-blame-me* gesture. "It's all Kathy," he assured her. "Part of her master plan."

Right, the master plan. The plan for Kathy and Lana to marry the Doyle brothers and live together in the house on the hill. It was the reason that Kathy was always insisting to people that Mal and Lana were dating — because in her sweet, deluded mind, the four of them made a perfect package, and a fairy tale double wedding and happily-ever-after was the only possible ending to their story.

Never mind the fact that Mal and Lana weren't in love. They liked each other a hell of a lot, but that was a far different thing. They weren't destined to be together, and both of them knew it. Mal always seemed to have his eyes on a distant shore. And although Lana didn't know where he'd end up, she was damn sure it wasn't in Angel River. She could only hope the same for herself.

And never mind the fact that from the moment Lana and

Nate had first laid eyes on each other, there had been electricity in the air. It had built slowly, like heavy clouds before a storm, over the past two years, until at last the storm had broken that past summer, when both Mal and Kathy had been out of town. It hadn't gone as far as it could have — Lana had no intention of ending up pregnant and single at sixteen — but there were plenty of things two people could do together that wouldn't result in pregnancy.

During those idyllic fourteen days, Lana had closed her eyes to the guilt she knew she would feel when summer was over and had given herself up to the bliss of her first love, finding sweetness and surprise in the passion that blossomed between the two of them. Then it had been over. Nate had gone back to college, probably on some level glad to escape, conflicted about his affection for Kathy and his passion for Lana. And Lana had learned to live with the guilt of having fallen in love with her best friend's boyfriend.

It was an affair that would not be continued — *could* not be continued, or Lana knew that she would lose not only her friend, but also her soul. Those two weeks had been an island unto themselves. Something to keep safe and sacred inside her, a talisman to be clutched when the nights grew cold and lonely.

And now, she thought, she'd get to go to Homecoming and watch Nate and Kathy dance together. Nate feeling guilty for wanting her, Kathy beautifully oblivious to the emotional tempest raging around her. Sounds like a fun night, Lana thought with grim humor.

She blinked and found Mal's eyes watching her sympathetically. He knows, she thought. He knows what there is between me and Nate. And there's nothing he can do about it except be my friend.

She met his gaze steadily, chin lifting in unconscious defiance. It's all true, she told him with her eyes. Judge me if you want.

But he didn't want to judge, that much was obvious. He reached out and lightly touched her hand as it rested on the counter. His gesture spoke a world of words. I'll be there, it said. I'll be there at the dance and whenever you need me.

Lana turned abruptly, afraid she would dissolve into tears right there on the spot. She placed the coffee pot carefully on its heating ring, composing herself. When she turned back around, she found Mal holding a folded slip of paper between his two fingers, like a magician doing sleight-of-hand.

"And this," he said casually, "is my news. You got an invitation to a dance; I got another kind of invitation."

Lana's heart froze, and she heard a small sound come out of the back of her throat. His eyes seized hers and held them lightly. Don't fall apart, they said.

She swallowed and reached out a trembling hand. After a moment, she gathered her strength and took the paper from him. She opened it and exhaled shakily. "Selective Service System," she read out loud. There was a catch in her voice. "Status Card."

She wanted to crumple the paper in her hands, to smash it between her palms until it disappeared into nothingness. Lana heard a sound behind her and turned quickly. It was George, standing in the doorway to the kitchen. His face, etched in sorrow, told her that he had been listening, that he knew what that slip of paper in her hand meant.

She looked down at it again. It's such a little thing, she thought. It's just a slip of paper. How can a slip of paper look like death and pain and tears to me?

She took a breath. "Well," she said, "I guess you're going to college a bit earlier than you thought you would."

But his face told her what his answer to that would be before he could even open his mouth. He shook his head slowly, still holding her eyes with his own. "I'm not going to college," he said softly. "I'm going to Vietnam."

Again a sound came from the back of her throat, a pitiable whimper at the dreaded word being spoken out loud. *Vietnam.*

"You don't have to go," she said in a rush. "You can stay here, go to school. Or you can go — you can — there are other options."

He shook his head again, more emphatically. "Those other options aren't for me."

"But for Christ's sake, your father is a college professor! He can get you into school. *You don't have to go.*"

"I'm not going to let my father pull strings for me, Lana," he said. His demeanor was so calm, so light, that they might have been talking about the weather. "I'm not going to let my family's money or status get me out of this. I'm going to do what thousands of other Americans have done. I'm going to cut my hair, get fitted for fatigues, and I'm going to Vietnam."

Arlo Guthrie clicked off on the jukebox as Mal finished that last quiet sentence. Kathy stumbled a bit mid-whirl, then recovered and stared at him. Her eyes were as big as saucers. She crept silently toward the counter.

Lana watched her, eyes full of sorrow. I can't bear it, she thought. She looked at Kathy in her fancy clothes, full of impossible dreams for the future. Lana had always felt that Kathy lived on a separate plane of reality from the rest of the world, and she, Lana, liked it that way. She liked knowing that someone she loved could live with her head in the clouds, untouched by the blood and garbage littering the streets of reality. Now Kathy would have to face something serious — something more important than how to wear her hair to Homecoming. And

Lana would have to be strong for both of them. *I can't bear that,* she thought. *I don't have enough strength.*

As Lana had done a few long minutes earlier, Kathy reached out a shaking hand for that piece of paper, the death sentence in disguise. She held it in both hands and read it front and back. "It's not a card," she said softly. "People always say 'draft card,' don't they? It's not a card at all. It's just a piece of paper."

She put it on the counter and took a step back, looking at it. Lana, George, and Malcolm all waited, silent, to see what she would say. As if Kathy could sum up the situation for all of them. As if Kathy could find a way to make it all okay.

But she couldn't. Lana knew that. When Kathy looked up and met Lana's gaze, her face was full of fear and sorrow. Kathy closed her eyes tightly, like a child making a wish, and when she opened them again, Lana was surprised to see strength surging in them. Strength, and defiance.

Kathy turned to Mal and ran a hand through his shaggy blond hair. Only Lana noticed how that hand trembled slightly. "You'll have to get this cut," she said quietly. "But it'll grow back. When you come home, it'll grow back."

She nodded, as if that decided it. She looked back up at Lana fiercely, daring her to contradict that statement. Then, without a word, she went back to the jukebox and dropped in another dime. She pushed two buttons for her selection, and the air was filled with a dulcet swelling of strings. She turned and looked at Lana, unaware that the two of them were locked in a gaze that had been shared by women since man had first learned how to fight — the gaze of two women who loved a man going off to war.

The swelling music reached its crescendo, and the sweet, painful voice of Sam Cooke filled the room. *It's been a long, long time coming, but I know, a change is gonna come....*

CHAPTER FOURTEEN

K ATE'S ALARM WENT OFF EARLY the next morning. She had to force herself awake to shut it off, then she lay back, staring dully into the early-morning gloom, wondering why she had set the clock in the first place. What would she have to get up early for?

She had spent a restless night tossing and turning, punching her pillow with angry frustration. Her body was exhausted, but her mind would not be still. *Reed*, it said insistently, over and over again. *Reed*.

Eventually she had fallen into a deep, exhausted slumber just before dawn. Now, rubbing her eyes, she struggled to think why on earth she would have set her alarm. Then she remembered: she had planned to go shopping in town with Reed and Heather and the others.

Oh, joy. She could see it now: the six of them traipsing through town, picking out souvenirs for the folks back home, she and Reed ignoring each other and trying not to let anyone notice. But they would notice. Those four noticed everything. Not a weakness was ignored, nor a hint of strife disregarded.

What a jolly day.

Well, forget it. She wasn't going. There were plenty of things to do on board. Swimming, tennis, or just sitting in the sunshine and reading…plenty of things to do.

Then a familiar staccato tapping sound caught Kate's ear, and she reached up and pulled back the flowered curtain that covered the window. Rain fell gently, but steadily against the glass, and the sky beyond was a solid mass of gray clouds.

All right, she thought, maybe sitting in the sun and reading is out. But shopping is definitely out.

She dropped the curtain and tunneled gratefully back under the covers. The next thing she knew, she was awakened by the ringing of the telephone. She groped blindly for the receiver and pulled it under the blankets with her. "Yes?"

"Good morning, sunshine!"

"Elliot?"

"But of course!"

Kate pushed herself up, running a hand through her hair. "Why are you calling me? Is anything wrong?"

"What could be wrong on a lovely day like this?"

"Lovely day? But it's — " Kate pushed the curtains aside and peered out again. The sun was out in full force, almost blinding her with its radiance as it reflected off the water. She winced at the sudden brightness and let the curtain fall back into place. "I guess it stopped raining."

"Observant girl, aren't you? Anyway, hurry up and get dressed. We're waiting breakfast for you, and the girls are mad to go shopping — they intend to turn us men folk into pack mules, I'm sure of it!"

Kate hesitated. "And how many pack mules are there to be?"

She could almost hear Elliot smile at the other end of the line. "Why three, of course! Three women, three willing slaves to carry their packages for them. How else could it possibly work?"

"Is Reed there with you?"

"Naturally."

"He — he was a bit under the weather last night, that's why I was asking."

"Well, he looks fine today." Elliot looked across the dining room to where the other four were sitting. Heather had her chair pulled close up next to Reed, and she was looking deeply interested as he and Joe conversed. "Almost chipper, in fact."

"What time did you plan to leave?"

"*We* are leaving right after breakfast — and by 'we' I mean all six of us, in case you didn't catch that. So throw on some clothes and a comfortable pair of shoes, and get down here. The waiters are starting to give us dirty looks for monopolizing their best table."

Once more, Kate hesitated. Did she really want to put herself into such an uncomfortable situation? Again she imagined what the day would be like: Reed cold and unforgiving; Alicia and Heather overly friendly; Elliot overly flirtatious; and Joe, gifting them all with trivia gems.

"I'm not sure I'm up to a big day in the sun — especially after yesterday. My head is still a bit achy…"

Elliot sighed. "All right, if that's the way you feel. I wouldn't want you to exhaust yourself." His voice dropped to a stage whisper. "To tell you the truth, I think that Heather might like to have Reed to herself for a while, without your radiant presence to distract him."

He paused to let that sink in. "Are you sure you don't want to come with us? It's a beautiful old city."

The man is about as subtle as a sledgehammer, Kate thought. Still…"Maybe I should come," she said slowly. "I'd hate to miss it."

"Wonderful! I'll order breakfast for you, and we'll see you in twenty minutes. Don't be late!"

Kate held onto the receiver after Elliot hung up. Was she making a mistake? What she needed right now was to put some distance between Reed and herself, not spend an entire day with him.

Distance between Reed and herself…distance between Mark and herself…was she never going to face up to the men in her life? This was an awfully small ship; was she going to avoid Reed for the rest of the week? And what about when the week was over? Was she just going to scurry away and let all the unresolved issues between her and Reed stay unresolved?

She was tired of all the vagueness in her life. It seemed that ever since she had left Angel River, she had been running away from something, dodging some question or another. Will you marry me? Will you become a partner in the firm? Enough. She was going on this excursion today. She was going to face up to who and what Reed had become. And before this trip was over, she would find some resolution to their relationship.

❧

The buildings in Kralendijk were dazzling, painted bright hues of yellow and orange. The streets were narrow, the sidewalks crowded with tourists and locals, and the very air was alive with the sounds of people.

There were, Joe told them as they crossed a narrow street, three other ships at port besides the *William*, and there were several resorts on the island. "Right now," he said, "there are almost as many tourists on the island as there are natives."

Elliot turned to Heather. "That explains why every other person we see wants to have their picture taken with you," he complained. "We can't walk five paces without someone stopping you for an autograph. How do you live with it, darling?"

"The real question," Alicia murmured, "is how would she live without it?"

Walking a few paces in front, Heather only smiled and shook her head. "Children," she sighed to Reed. "Traveling with them is like traveling with children."

"And you are the patient mother," Reed said. "It's a role that suits you."

He saw the hurt in her eyes. "Seriously," he said quickly. "No sarcasm intended."

She continued to look doubtful, so he continued. "I know you told me that you never intended to have children. That wasn't what I was referring to."

At last she seemed to relax. "Sorry to be so touchy. Sometimes it's hard to tell when someone's trying to hurt you."

"I would never deliberately hurt you, Heather."

"I know." She quickened her steps, and he kept pace with her, so that they began to put some distance between themselves and the others. Heather glanced over her shoulder and saw Kate watching them. Kate quickly looked away.

What was it exactly between Kate and Reed? Heather decided that she had to find out. She took a breath. "Are you enjoying your trip so far, Reed?"

"So far."

"It must have been quite a shock to see Kate again."

He smiled thinly. "The kind of shock I wouldn't mind having every day."

Heather's heart sank. He sounded truly smitten. "She seems nice."

"She is."

"I thought I noticed a little tension between the two of you this morning? Stop me if I'm being too nosy."

Reed shifted uncomfortably. "It's all right. Kate and I have…a complicated history. Tension is almost inevitable."

"It's been a long time since you two have seen each other."

"A very long time."

"And you've both changed quite a bit, I imagine."

"Change is also inevitable."

"Are you sure —" She broke off.

"What?"

"Are you sure that you still know her? I mean, you said yourself that it's been a long time and that you've both changed. Is it possible that she, well, that she just isn't the same girl you used to know?"

"Like I said…"

"I know. Change is inevitable. And I like Kate. She's smart, and she has a sense of humor. But between you and me, I got the feeling that maybe she was hiding something. I know that sounds kind of melodramatic, but…"

Reed was suddenly alert. "Do you have any idea what?"

"No. And, let's be honest, it could just be feminine cattiness. I'm still rather fond of you, you know."

She smiled sideways at him, but he appeared not to notice. He seemed deep in thought. She continued. "Do *you* have any idea what it could be?"

Mark Levin, he thought bitterly. Kate must be more in love with him than she's let on to anyone. She's really planning on marrying him.

Reed remembered how passionately she had kissed him, how electricity had sparked every time she looked into his eyes. Was that all an act? Or was it, for her, a final fling before settling down? But how could she be so deceptive? And how could he be so taken in?

A dozen paces behind, Kate watched as Reed and Heather conversed earnestly. It was obvious to Kate — as it would have been obvious to any woman — that Heather was still in love with Reed. She would take him back if he would come to her. But how did Reed feel about Heather? For that matter, how did Reed feel about anyone? Sometimes it was impossible to tell. That cold mask of politeness had to serve him well in the boardroom, but surely it made intimate relationships impossible. And maybe, Kate thought, that was exactly the point.

"Oh, look!" Alicia exclaimed. She had stopped and was admiring the display in a store window. "What a beautiful carving! Let's go in!"

Like all the shops on the island, this one catered to the tourist trade. They gladly accepted American cash and credit cards. Kate kept to herself as she wandered the narrow aisles, examining the shelves crowded with merchandise. Some of it was truly exquisite. She carefully selected a few gifts for her family. A carved shell for her mother, some wooden figurines for Oliver. She had already gotten a few things for Julia and her father.

And Mark, should she get something for him? She lingered over a wooden box, polished to a dark gloss and inlaid with shells on the top. He would like this, she thought. What was the proper gift etiquette for the man whose marriage proposal one was about to refuse? She didn't think Emily Post had ever covered that.

Suddenly Reed was at her shoulder. "That's beautiful," he said. "Thinking of getting it for your father?"

"I — yes, I was thinking of buying it." She swallowed.

Reed picked it up, opened it, and admired the red velvet interior. "Nice," he said again. "Your dad will like it."

"Yes," Kate said. "Yes, he would."

She brushed by him, leaving the box on the shelf, suddenly needing to be out in the sunshine. When she reached the sidewalk, she stopped, hating herself. As people moved around her, she wondered why she was making such a big deal of this. Why was she being so deceptive — answering his questions with intent to deceive? She should just tell Reed about Mark. She and Reed had been separated for twenty years. She didn't expect that Reed had been celibate; did she think that he would expect that of her?

She was just going to tell him: Reed, I've been dating a lawyer named Mark Levin, and he's asked me to marry him. That box I was thinking of buying was for him.

Yes, she would do it. She would do it as soon as Reed stepped out of the store.

If only he wasn't so cold, so withdrawn, maybe she would have told him already....

But that was an excuse, and a flimsy one at that. She would do it.

Reed exited the store. She heard the doorbell clang as he did. She turned to face him, the truth on her lips.

He was carrying a shopping bag, holding it out to her.

"From me to your father," he said.

And he left Kate standing on the sidewalk, holding the bag.

She watched Reed walk away, disappear into the crowd. Then she went after him. Her guilt was gone now, replaced by anger.

She caught him by the arm, spun him around and made him face her. "What's going on?" she demanded. "What's the idea of just taking off like that? Are you playing some kind of game?"

"Are you?"

She squinted up at him. "What are you talking about?"

"With that box, Katie. You weren't thinking of giving it to your father."

"How do you know that? Are you suddenly psychic?"

He crossed his arms, looking down at her imperiously. "I may not be psychic, but I have a highly developed crap detector. I can tell when someone's lying to me!"

"I wasn't lying — I really was thinking about buying it!"

"Well, if you were, I just saved you the trouble — and the expense!"

Kate was suddenly conscious of intense heat. It seemed to be coming from everywhere. From the sun beating down, reflected off the street, radiating from passersby — and especially from Reed. Heat came off him in waves.

Disconcerted, she dropped her eyes from his and focused on his feet. They were clad in leather sandals...good shoes... comfortable for walking on a warm day like this. His toenails were neatly trimmed and shaped. Pedicured, probably.

Her eyes wandered upward to his ankles. Strong, prominent anklebones. A good swift kick there would hurt like hell, she thought.

Her belly fluttered with amusement, while her face remained impassive. As her eyes wandered upward, past firm brown calves and well-shaped knees, the flutter remained, increased, and she was vexed to realize it wasn't amusement. It was lust.

She didn't dare let her eyes wander upwards to his thighs.

He was looking at her, too. She felt his gaze and awoke to the fact that she had been looking at his legs for quite a long time. And he knew it.

A blush crept into her cheeks.

"I didn't realize you were a 'leg man,'" he said acerbically, not without a touch of amusement.

For a moment she was tongue-tied. He was looking at her as if he knew what she had felt, and as if he was thinking that she wasn't the first woman to be overwhelmed by his magnetism. The combination of her sudden, overwhelming desire and his arrogant self-confidence were maddening.

"I'm just looking for a vulnerable spot in case I decide to kick you," she responded.

He smiled, satisfied that he had won some victory over her, and prepared to overlook the fact that she had obviously lied to him earlier.

"Well, then," he said, "if you're done surveying the landscape, why don't you let me carry those bags? I'm sure there are plenty more shops to see. Maybe you'll find something to buy for your father, after all."

He held out his hand for her parcels, and after a moment's hesitation, she handed them over. She was trying to decide what to say next when the bell clanged once more, and the rest of their party exited the store.

"Hello, young lovers!" Elliot exclaimed. He looked from Kate to Reed and back again. "And what have you two been talking about?"

"Local history," Kate said quickly. "Joe, what were you saying earlier about that church on the corner?"

"That church?" Joe repeated, brightening. Ignoring the moans that came from Alicia and Elliot, he led the way across the street, happily reciting a litany of dates and names.

Reed stood still on the sidewalk, allowing the others to get ahead of him. He knew that he was in over his head. He had known it from the way Kate had looked up at him, with her clear hazel eyes warm and liquid and wanting.

Of course, women had looked at him like that before. It wasn't the look itself that disturbed him; it was his reaction to it. Because when she had looked up at him, he had experienced an overpowering desire to pull her into his arms and crush his mouth down on hers, right there on the sidewalk and to hell with whoever might see them.

In that moment, her lies to him, the years he had spent away from her, trying to hate her — all of it meant nothing compared to his desire for her. If the others hadn't shown up when they did, he might have escorted Kate right into the nearest hotel and let her have her way with him. From the look in her eyes, he didn't think she would have minded.

At length, he crossed the street, following the others into the church. He kept his distance from Kate, but there was something in the air, something vibrating between them, and she seemed to be as relieved as he was to have other people around to act as a buffer, so they would not have to be alone together.

Reed had hoped that the exercise of sightseeing would help calm him, would relax the tension he felt being so close to Kate. It didn't. By the time they decided to stop for lunch, he was ready to break something.

They found a café with outdoor tables and pushed two together to make room for all of them. Kate found herself between Elliot and Heather — an awkward placement, to say the least. Heather was alternately overly-friendly and completely cool. Elliot seemed to be simultaneously flirting with her and trying to make Heather jealous by intimating that something was going on between Kate and Reed.

Something *was* going on, and that was the problem. Or

to be more accurate, *nothing* was going on. They'd been just honest enough with one another to piss each other off and told just enough lies to make them feel too guilty to talk more. Add the undeniable physical attraction, contrasted against their complicated emotional history, and there you go. They were at an impasse.

Trying to be sociable, trying to pretend that everything was fine and normal, struck Kate as being the height of hypocrisy, and she didn't know why she should continue with this ridiculous situation. But she did continue. She ordered lunch, smiled, and made small talk, all the while fighting the urge to turn the table over and tell them all to go to hell — especially Reed.

So when Elliot turned the conversation back to the town of Angel River, she wasn't really in the mood to fence and play with him.

"But my dear," he said, "weren't you ever bored growing up there? So far away from the city — far away from shopping, museums, all the things that make life worthwhile."

"I guess you can't miss what you don't have," she replied tightly.

"But the complete lack of excitement — "

She suppressed the urge to elbow him in the Adam's apple. "I wouldn't say there was a *complete* lack."

"Let's see…someone trampled Mrs. McGillicuddy's marigolds?" Elliot guessed. "Or, no, wait — some of the local boys got a little rowdy and fastened a brassiere onto the statue in the Town Square?"

"How about someone pushed Harry Block under a moving thrasher and turned a human being into dog food?" Kate blurted out, infuriated at Elliot's derisive tone. As soon as she'd spoken the words, she regretted it — this was not the time or place to discuss that issue, raw as it still might be for Reed.

Now all eyes were on her, fascinated in the way that people could only be by a gruesome tragedy that didn't affect them directly.

"Ooh," Alicia breathed. "Murder in Mayberry? Slaughter in Smallville? Do tell; do tell!"

Reed's face was the only one not filled with curiosity — his had a decidedly more annoyed look on it. It took Kate a moment to realize that the annoyance was not directed at her, but at Elliot, for teasing her into speaking. Then Joe shifted uncomfortably. He at least seemed somewhat aware that this might not be a comfortable topic of discussion for everyone present. "I'm sure that the story is fascinating," he said, "but no one will hold it against you if you spare the gory details."

Kate sighed. Maybe she could alleviate their curiosity without making the whole thing as scandalous as it seemed. "Harry Block was a — a bum, I guess you could say."

"A drifter," Reed suggested. She looked at him gratefully.

"Yes. He apparently grew up in Angel River, but he'd dropped out of high school and just…*drifted* in and out of town since the late '60s. Our parents knew him, I guess," Kate said, looking at Reed for confirmation.

"Probably," was his minimal answer.

"Some time in the mid-'80s he started showing up in town again. He did odd jobs — bagged groceries, swept sidewalks, that sort of thing. When he had enough money, he'd go off on a drunk, and we'd see him passed out down by the river, or in the park sometimes. Personally, I never thought much about him, except that he was creepy. And then one day, Reed and I — we found his body in this old barn on the corner of my family's property."

"*You* found him? The two of you?" Heather asked. She seemed genuinely horrified for them. "Oh, God, how awful for you."

"It was a pretty messy scene," Kate admitted cautiously. Memories from that day floated around the outside of her consciousness, but she closed her mind firmly and refused to let them in. No way was she going to relive *that* nightmare in front of this group. "The thrasher was old, and had been stored in the barn ages ago. I don't think anyone even realized that it still worked, but it had been turned on, and Harry had been — pushed into it."

"Or had fallen in," Reed said. "He could've been intoxicated, turned the thing on accidentally, and then fallen into it. Nobody really knows for sure."

"What, you mean they never found out who did it?" Alicia asked.

"They rounded up the usual suspects," Kate answered, this time being careful *not* to look at Reed. "They investigated, but never made an arrest."

"They thought I might have done it," Reed said. Everyone turned to look at him, especially Kate, who was shocked that he would have spoken of such a thing out loud. It was very unlike him to speak so openly.

"You?" Heather said. "Why?"

"Because I was a local...delinquent, shall we say? I was always in some sort of trouble. Nothing violent, but still.... Plus, Block had an argument with my grandmother the day before. She'd caught him stealing eggs from our henhouse. Seems impossibly country-bumpkin now, but at the time it was a big deal. I came home from school and found them screaming at each other, both using some mighty foul language." For some reason, the memory of it made him smile. "If that guy thought he could intimidate my grandmother, he was sorely mistaken. She wasn't afraid of anybody or anything that I ever knew of." He sighed. "Anyway, I pushed him, and he pushed me back. He was so drunk that he fell over, so I kicked his miserable drunken ass right off our property. Two days later, he was dead."

Kate spoke up quickly. "It wasn't like Reed was the only one suspected. I mean, Harry Block was generally disliked by everyone *I* ever talked to. It's just that Reed's family was…." She trailed off and looked at him helplessly. Was she making this worse or better?

Reed spoke. "My family — and in particular, my grandmother — wasn't looked on very highly in town. She had a reputation for being kind of ornery, even a little scary. There were always rumors about her — the old woman who lived at the edge of town. It was easy to think of her as a witch." He smiled and scratched his chin, eyes misty with memories. "She liked the idea, actually. It made her laugh."

Alicia, seeing that Reed was in a talkative mood, was unable to resist digging for golden nuggets of information. She leaned forward and spoke in a soft voice. "But what about your grandfather? Wasn't he ever upset by people calling his wife a witch?"

Elliot couldn't help jumping in with his two cents. "Maybe he liked the idea, too. Maybe he was the warlock."

Reed shifted in his chair, trying to decide how to phrase what he had to say. Kate watched him sympathetically. "My grandfather — well, actually, nobody knows who he was. My grandmother never told anyone his name, which didn't help her reputation any. She was a single woman, past her prime, living alone. And one day, she was pregnant. It wasn't easily accepted by the people in town."

"But it's very understandable," Kate said. She had been watching Reed and had seen the need in his face. He was in over his head with this self-revelation thing, and he knew it. "What happened, I mean. It's understandable. She was a very dynamic person, attractive in her own way, I guess. My mother once told me that she figured your grandfather was probably a traveling salesman, or something like that. Just a fellow passing through. Anyway," Kate grinned, "he got the job done. Your grandmother had a beautiful baby boy. I've seen pictures of your dad — he was a real looker. And you're no slouch yourself, you know. Your grandmother did pretty darn good at carrying on the family name. Good genes." Kate smiled.

He looked at her gratefully, thanking her with his eyes for taking over the conversation. All his earlier frustration had drained away, leaving him feeling peaceful and even mellow. It felt good talking about things, telling people his stories. Why did he always avoid these conversations? He hadn't known what he was missing.

Alicia shook her head. "What a fascinating story," she said. "All of it, I mean." She looked at Kate. "Maybe your family moved to the city to get away from all that country violence!"

It was a good thing to say. Everyone laughed and relaxed somewhat. There was talk of dessert, of ordering frozen drinks with umbrellas in them. There was even talk of more shopping. But eventually everyone agreed it was time to call it a day.

"Let's get a cab back to the ship," Heather said. "I'd love a bath and a nap before dinner."

Reed spoke up with sudden conviction. "I think Kate and I would like to be on our own for a little while," he said. He looked at her. "Wouldn't we?"

Looking into his eyes, Kate felt her heart pound like the ringing of a gong — once, twice, three times. Slowly, she nodded her head in agreement.

Heather's face fell as she looked at the two of them. There was love there; even a fool could see it. Feeling desperate, she started to object, saying that she wasn't ready to go back yet, that it would be more fun if they all stayed together.

But Elliot, who saw a chance to have Heather to himself for a little while, swept aside her protest in a way he knew would work. "Come on back to the ship, my dear," he said. "You know you've been out in the sun too long as it is. You don't want that beautiful skin to wrinkle, do you?"

He offered to take Kate and Reed's packages back to the ship so they wouldn't have to carry them around. Then he hailed a taxi and ushered his companions in the back. Before Kate and Reed knew it, they were standing on the sidewalk, watching the cab drive away.

And just like that, they were on their own.

The sun rolled slowly in the sky. They walked, fingers laced loosely together, along narrow streets, through patches of hot sunlight and cool shade. It was an afternoon of bright colors, sharp to the eye. Red curtains blowing out of a window, blue sky dazzling over crooked rooftops. And then there were the shadows, which Kate had always thought of as gray, but now she saw that they were green, and lavender, and umber as they spilled onto the fiery sidewalk.

They said little as the day moved onward. They walked until they were tired, then found a place to sit until they felt rested, before getting up and walking some more. They looked and smiled and sometimes touched, but they found no need for words.

The bright afternoon gave way to a dim twilight, and finally to night. They found a restaurant on the beach, and they sat outside at a table under an awning. They watched the moonlight glittering on the water, ate a spicy dish of seafood and rice, and drank bottles of cold beer.

After dinner, they walked on the beach, shoes dangling from their fingers, letting the water froth around their ankles.

Reed took Kate's hand. "I'm sorry," he said simply. "Sorry for last night, and again for this afternoon."

She squeezed his fingers. "I'm sorry, too. Let's never fight again." She grinned in spite of herself. They'd always used that line as children.

He gave her a small smile and continued, refusing to let the seriousness of the moment be undermined. "Nothing bad that has happened before matters to me. Right now, there is only this moment, and I only remember the good things."

Kate met his gaze and nodded, inwardly reprimanding herself for always having to make a joke.

"I remember wanting you," he whispered, lifting a hand to caress her cheek gently. "I remember wanting you desperately, before I even knew what that really meant. And I remember loving you...before I'd forgotten how to love."

"Reed...."

"Don't say it, Katie. Whatever it is, don't say it. There will be plenty of time for words later. Right now, tonight, let's just stop talking."

She didn't remember nodding, but she knew she had. Later, she wouldn't remember the taxi ride back to the ship, or the long walk to Reed's cabin. She wouldn't remember anything except the sound of the door shutting behind them, and the feel of Reed's arms around her.

He hesitated a moment, then dipped his head and pressed his lips to hers…gently, uncertainly, as if he had never kissed her before, had never known the softness of her mouth beneath his. He wanted to embrace her, but he waited, his hands hovering inches from her arms, as he reveled in the taste of her, salty and fresh from the ocean air. She suddenly seemed so small, so fragile, as if all her taut strength had evaporated, and she was trembling under his kiss. At last he could wait no longer and he took her in his arms, deepening his kiss as he embraced her.

She gasped slightly as she felt the sweet intrusion of his tongue in her mouth. For a moment, she thought she could smell lilacs and hear the crickets chirping through the moist summer air. She slid her arms around his neck and let her fingers entwine in his hair as she leaned into him.

His lips left hers and traveled down her neck, hovering in the well of her throat before moving along her collarbone. He pulled the fabric of her shirt aside so he could kiss her shoulder, loving the flavor of her skin, the way it felt against his tongue. Then he found her mouth with his again, drinking in her warmth as he pulled her tightly against him. He wanted her badly, wanted her now, wasn't sure if he could wait any longer. But his need to explore her, to know her entirely, was greater than his need for immediate release. He pulled away, kissing her twice more before he unfastened her hands from behind his neck and put them up in the air so he could pull her shirt over her head and drop it on the floor.

He smoothed his hands down her arms, then over her back. She expected to feel him reaching for the catch on her bra, but instead he gathered her close again, kissing her as he touched her bare skin. She pulled his shirt from the waistband of his shorts, running her hands up and over his strong back. She could feel him tremble at her touch. Once again his mouth left hers and ran down her neck. He bent her gently backwards, kissing the well between her breasts, then her breasts themselves through the flimsy fabric that covered them. She shuddered as he took one of her nipples and pinched it gently between his lips.

"Please." She barely knew what she was asking for—but he did. He reached around and unhooked her bra, pulling the delicate fabric gently away from her body as he found her breast with his mouth again. She sighed as he explored her curves with his lips and tongue.

He straightened up, pulling her with him, kissing her lips tenderly, filling her with brilliant warmth. He reached down and caught her behind her knees, lifting her into his arms. He carried her into the bedroom. The bed had been turned down by the housekeeping staff; he laid her gently on the cool sheets, then took a moment to light two candles on the dresser before turning back to her.

He removed her shoes and socks, then took off his sandals before sitting gingerly on the bed next to her. He took her hand and kissed the palm, then put it flat against his cheek. He ran his fingers idly through her hair. He was uncertain of what he should do next. Admittedly he'd had more than a few lovers in his life. But with Kate, it was different. With her, it was almost like the first time.

Kate lay on the bed, caressing his face with her eyes. Silver moonlight steaming through the windows struck his face, throwing his cheekbones into high relief as he looked down at her. She knew what was going through his mind. A lump rose in her throat. To think that this man — strong, successful, a world-beater in every sense of the word — should be so vulnerable…

Gently she took her hand from where he held it against his cheek and began unbuttoning his shirt. He was very still as she slid the shirt back over his shoulders until it fell to the floor. Her bra was still clinging to her body, her arms threaded loosely through the straps. Slowly she removed it, then she reached up and pulled him down to her.

Their lips met again. Kate felt his weight press down against her, trapping her deliciously between his body and the mattress. She buried her face in his neck, breathing deeply, inhaling the good clean scent of him. His nearness filled her with euphoria — the knowledge that after years of waiting, they were together, and nothing could stop them from joining together, uniting as one.

She squeezed her eyes shut and felt a tear trickle down her cheek. Then his lips were kissing it away. She opened her eyes and saw her feelings reflected in his face.

"Oh, my love," he whispered. "We've waited so long for this." He laughed shakily. "I want it to be so good for you."

"It will be."

"I feel almost like a virgin," he confessed.

In spite of the seriousness of the moment, she couldn't help grinning. "Me, too. Although we're both pretty far from that."

He arched an eyebrow. *"How* far from that are you, exactly?"

She laughed, then her face grew serious again. "I'll tell you tomorrow," she whispered.

His lips descended again. His fingers ran lightly over her belly, sending delicious chills racing through her, and awakening deep sensations that had been slumbering too long. She unbuttoned her shorts and slid them off her hips. He pulled them off her legs, then removed his own and climbed into bed, leaning on one elbow.

His eyes raked her body, scorching her with their intensity. Then his fingers followed the trail his eyes had blazed. His movements were slow, almost casual, but he was no longer hesitant. His touch was that of a man enraptured, as if each experience were new to him. But he was also a man with a purpose, and a man who knew how to accomplish it.

Soon his mouth followed where his eyes and hands had gone before. His exploration of her was complete and unhurried. The gentle curve of her breast, the softness of her inner thighs, even the soles of her feet seemed to hold for him an endless fascination.

Time spun out as he touched and tasted. Soon her breathing became ragged, cutting through the darkened room in short, deep gasps. Her hands tangled briefly in his hair, sought out his heated skin and knotted muscles.

At last, when she could bear no more, when every nerve in her body cried out for release, he rose over her, his broad shoulders momentarily throwing her face into shadow. He entered her slowly, inching into her by exquisite degrees. She whimpered as his body struck hers gently, and she knew he was in her, buried completely within her. She opened her eyes and saw him gazing down at her, eyes half open, watching her face in the flickering candlelight.

He pushed gently against her, and she pushed back. They drew apart a little ways, and then pushed together again. "Reed," she whispered. "At last, my love."

His arms slid beneath her, holding her so tightly that for a moment, she couldn't breathe. She exhaled slowly, giving herself up to it, knowing that if she were to stop living right at that moment, she would at least die happy, with the sensation of him moving deeply inside her. His mouth was on hers, his tongue gliding sweetly over her teeth and lips. Then he was rolling onto his back, and she was on top of him, leaning back, hands clasped in his.

She moved forward until the delicious weight of her breasts pressed against his chest, and he was thrusting up into her. He closed his eyes and wrapped his arms around her. In that moment, he wanted to confess everything, be forgiven for all he had done and said. He wanted to bare his soul and have her know him as no one else ever had.

Then he opened his eyes and saw her looking down at him. And he realized that she did know him. She had always known him. No one else would ever be to him what she had been. And still was.

They kissed softly without breaking the stride of their lovemaking, and Reed felt himself beginning to slip over the edge. Not yet, he thought. Not yet. He didn't want to leave her unfulfilled. But he knew he couldn't hold out much longer.

"Kate?" he whispered hoarsely.

"Yes," she answered. Her voice broke on the word.

She cried out, stiffening abruptly in his arms. A moment later, golden lights exploded in his head, and he spilled into her in one long, hot thrust.

Gradually he became aware that they were still moving together, eking out every last bit of sensation that their bodies would give them. He closed his eyes and smoothed his hand over Kate's hair. Lulled by the gentle rocking of their bodies, he allowed himself to doze.

When he awoke, she was asleep on top of him, her cheek nestled against his chest. Gently he eased her to the side, brushed the hair out of her eyes. She stirred, smiling slightly in her sleep. He stroked her cheek and kissed her lightly on the lips. God, how he loved her. His Katie. When he thought of the way she had looked down at him as he was thrusting up into her...had he ever hoped to see that look in her eyes—in any woman's eyes, for that matter? Open and loving and shining down on him as they moved together.

Open...he thought uneasily of the things he hid from her, of the secrets he kept. What would she say if she knew? How would she look at him then? He was determined that he would never have an answer to that question. She would never know how he had deceived her, and he would spend the rest of his life making it up to her, making it right.

He cradled her gently in his arms and allowed himself to drift off to sleep on that thought. He would make it right.

CHAPTER FIFTEEN

September 1938

I T WAS A CARNIVAL THIS time, and probably the last one of the season. It sprawled insolently across a tired brown field about a hundred miles south of Louisville, Kentucky. The pageant lights that had been strung between tents and along walkways glowed a dull yellow in the inky blue-black of night. Those lights were visible from miles around, and they summoned the somnambulant inhabitants of the local towns like a church bell calling the faithful to worship on Sunday morning.

Hands in his pockets, Billy Lewis strolled cheerfully along the "backside" of the carnival shows — the narrow lane created by sideshow tents on one side and old trucks on the other. Moonlight lit his path, and he stepped nimbly over a deep groove that appeared out of the darkness. The dirt beneath his feet was hard and brown, rutted from the weight of old boots and tires, and he had to watch where he was going, lest he turn a delicate ankle and be unable to perform tomorrow. His leaps and bounds in praise of the Lord were one of the audience's favorite parts of the show, and what kind of man would he be if he disappointed them?

How would it look to all those dear Christian souls, baking and sweating in the heat of their own religious fervor, if he were to be glued to the stage like any other mortal sinner? Would he be able to represent himself as a true Man of God if he, injured and unable to leap, merely stood on that old wooden platform and shouted, like some faithless preacher? No sir, he would not. And so he was careful with his body, with his legs especially.

A dry, late-summer wind swept down from the mountains, rifling through the goldenrod in the fields. It scampered along the lanes and aisles of the carnival, making the flaps on the tents dance briefly, then continued on its way, carrying the smells of deep-fried corn batter and spun sugar out across the fruited plains. Billy paused and removed his hat, closing his eyes as he lifted his face to the breeze.

He smiled as he started moving again, picking his way along the treacherous earth. 1938 had been a good year for Billy. Yessir, Mrs. Lewis' boy William had done all right. God had provided, as Billy assured his congregation each and every night that He would. There was the daily jingle of coins in his pockets, his belly never went empty, and there had been no shortage of attractive females to swoon under his holy verbiage. And swoon they had.

He thought back. Had there been even one night in recent history when the Lord hadn't blessed his bedchamber with a willing woman — or sometimes two, if He were feeling particularly generous? To Billy's recollection, he had enjoyed the company of one lovely lady or another every night this week and most nights in the weeks preceding. He had even remembered the Sabbath, and kept it holy by making his girls cry out the name of the Lord as loudly and ardently as was in his considerable power. Hallelujah, Lord, and Amen. God will provide.

He came to the end of the long lane of cars and stopped beside his own vehicle — his pride and joy, a 1935 Ford pickup truck. It was carefully covered by a custom-made tarp that had cost him a month's "cush." But the money had been worth it, to keep his beloved safe and clean amidst all the chaos of carnival life. Billy pulled the tarp back gently on one side, viewing with satisfaction the new paint job that had also cost him dearly. The body of the truck was painted a soft cream color, genteel and understated, the way a gentleman's automobile ought to be. But on either side of the truck was a painted sign that was a merry cacophony of color — an eye-catcher and a brow-raiser, the way a journeyman preacher's vehicle had to be.

The rainbowed letters spelled out the words *Brother Worship — Salvation Awaits*. Originally he had wanted a longer message, something a bit more juicy, with more pizzazz. But space and money had forced him to be succinct, and now he was just as glad. He liked the briefness of the message. It said what needed to be said, and established him as an entity unto his own self — Brother Worship, traveling preacher, Man of God. Come unto me, children. Salvation Awaits.

He smoothed the tarp lovingly back into place, tucking it in and tying it firmly. Then he leaned against the hood and watched the townsfolk go by. Soon the Ferris wheel would be closing down for the night, its gears slowly grinding to a halt as the last strains of music floated through the air. In front of him, the world opened up to a clearing filled with the remains of the night's crowd — the last few stragglers of the evening. There had been a couple of pretty ones at his show that night — young girls enraptured by his quick tongue and his passionate devotion to the Lord. There was one — blue dress, blond hair — who seemed particularly…*intent* on the ferocity with which he spoke. In fact, he'd had a feeling that she might come and see him after the show for a private spiritual consultation.

In the darkness, Billy smiled.

He had been born in the high hills of South Carolina, in a sorrowful backwoods cabin that housed his momma, a dozen assorted brothers and sisters, and occasionally his pa. Pa would come home long enough between drunks to lay his wife, swat the kids on their behinds, and then stumble off again into the wilderness.

Looking at his father, who had grown old and ugly-mean by the age of thirty, Billy had seen with certainty what his own future held, and he had known that it was not for him. So at barely fifteen, Billy had walked away from that cabin, down from those hills and, with the dirt from his front yard still clinging between his toes, he had sauntered into civilization. Barefoot and broke, he'd had nothing to his credit but a sharp brain, a devilish handsomeness, and something that no young man should be without: ambition.

He learned quickly that the fastest way to make a dime was to give people what they wanted. If they wanted their shoes shined, he shined them. If they wanted someone to sweep out their stairwell, he swept it. If you could figure out what it was that people most desired and give it to them, you were golden. And it was not long before he had hit upon the core thing that people were looking for in these devilish times.

Salvation.

The average man and woman walking the street was a seething mass of guilt and fears. They wanted their sins wiped away, their consciences cleansed, and to know that, no matter how bad things got here on this wicked earth, there was something better waiting beyond.

And so Billy, having identified the want, supplied the need as always. And he was doing all right.

"Greetings, Brother!" The call came from a group of solid citizens sitting around a barrel alight with flame, passing a bottle around among them — what Billy's mother used to call a "sinner's circle," God rest her judgmental heart.

"Friends!" Billy called, raising his arm in greeting. "Hail and well met, fellows. How are you faring on this nippy September eve?"

One of the men held up a bottle. The firelight glinted through the clear glass, showing the welcome amber of whisky sloshing within. "A nip to stave off the nips, Brother?" the man offered, grinning.

Billy returned the grin as he took the proffered bottle. "My mother always said it was rude to refuse the hospitality of a friend," he said. He took a swig and then inhaled deeply, drawing his lips back over his teeth in satisfaction as he passed the bottle on.

"Not afraid of the devil's drink, are you, Brother?" The man who had passed him the bottle watched him with glittering eyes.

"'Good wine is a good familiar creature if it be well used,'" Billy quoted self-importantly. He looked around at the faces lit by flickering light and he smiled. "Shakespeare, friends. A man as touched by the hand of God above as any of us poor players, strutting and fretting our hour upon the stage. Anything that's all right by him is all right by me as well."

He took out his handkerchief and used it to wipe a clean patch on the bumper of an ancient Ford, then he sat down and sighed with contentment. "Ah, friends, it's the end of another day here under God's watchful eye. Have you all acquitted yourselves well in His sight?"

"As well as can be expected, preacher man," croaked the man with the glittering eyes, whose name was Rufus, "given these sinful times that we live in."

"You got that right, Brother Rufus. You got that right," Billy said. He wagged a finger at Rufus as he looked around at the shadowy figures surrounding the fire. "Our brother makes a good point here, friends, and let none of us forget it. We live in sinful times. And no one knows that better than we who travel the land, seeing Man in all his good and evil, sin and holiness."

There were murmurs of agreement from around the fire.

Rufus cleared his throat juicily and spat into the dirt. "I always said, no one knows more about sin than a preacher," he said. His voice was deferential, but his eyes smirked.

Billy's eyes glinted with humor, as in his turn he took another sip from the bottle. "We are men of God, gentlemen, each and every one of us," he said virtuously. "Those of us who have received the calling and taken vows are still *men*, flesh and blood, subject to the same evil desires and sinful inclinations as any other mortal creature walking under the sun and the moon."

"You gotta figure, there ain't nobody here who don't have… *intimate* knowledge of one vice or another," Rufus said agreeably. "I myself have always had a particular weakness for women. Any women. All women. All shapes, all sizes, all ages. I love every bone in their bodies — especially mine." He let go a dry cackle that had the man next to him slapping him on the back.

"Uh, preacher?" one of the men said, looking off into the distance. "I think someone's looking for you."

Billy looked up, across the clearing to where the last few townspeople were heading toward the exit. He saw a blue dress, and blond hair. Ah, the girl from tonight's show. So she had come back after all, and she was looking for him. He knew this because she was looking straight at him, shy and brazen at the same time. His mouth watered slightly. Wonderful combination, that.

When his eyes met hers, she smiled slightly, flushed, and looked down coquettishly. Ever the respectful preacher, he started to stand and take off his hat. But she shook her head slightly, looking over her shoulder as if to see if someone was watching. Catching his eye again, she tapped her wristwatch and held up two fingers. Billy got the idea — she was going home, and she'd sneak out later, meet him back here in two hours. He touched the brim of his hat and inclined his head faintly — *Whatever you say, miss* — and smiled as she turned and walked away, prancing ever so slightly.

Rufus looked on in amazement. "How do you do that?" he asked. "How do you get them to come back here, giving you all kinds of crazy signals — " he waved his hands around, extorting guffaws from his fellow lookers-on. "Telling you that she's coming back later to — to — "

"See me about a personal spiritual matter?" Billy finished blandly, with only the traces of a smile turning up the edges of his mouth.

"Exactly!"

"I am a man of God," Billy explained. "I know when someone's in need."

An hour passed pleasantly. Someone rolled a cigarette, and they passed it around. The talk turned to sports, then to politics, then by and by to their own misfortunes. They finished the bottle they'd been working on, and someone else produced a new one. More cigarettes were rolled. And by and by, the talk turned back to women.

"You gotta have a favorite," Rufus insisted to the world at large. He had been enjoying the sharing of liquor and smokes, and now his grin hung loose, floppy and huge on his lips.

"Don't matter if you've been with two women or twenty. If you've been with more than one, you *got* to have a favorite. It's human nature."

Rufus looked around expectantly. "Okay, fine. I'll start. My best ever was Norma Jean Dickens, Kansas City, 1924." He hands, shaky from the drink, described a lopsided hourglass in the air. He whistled and winked. "Yowsah! Let me tell you, the name 'Dickens' described her all too well."

His friends sniggered. "Betty Roberts, 1932," someone said. Then, "Jennifer Clark, 1929." They went around the circle, until every man there had volunteered a name. Then all eyes turned to Billy.

He shrugged and spread his hands magnanimously. "All women are equal in God's eyes, children," he said. "And so shall they be in mine. I loved each of those ladies equally well… though maybe not for an equal period of time."

Rufus shook his head. "And you're telling us that not one of them stands out in your mind? None of them was, shall we say, memorable? Or even — " Rufus licked his lips with salacious enthusiasm " — *unusual* in some way?"

Billy looked up, startled. At his expression, the men around the fire nudged each other gleefully and nodded. Old Rufus had hit on something there, all right. *Unusual.* They knew this should be a good one.

"Well, now, it's funny you should say that, friend Rufus," Billy said softly. "Indeed it is. I do recall this one time — "

He stopped abruptly, staring into the fire. It had been months since he'd thought about a woman named Pleasance Fitzgerald. He hadn't *let* himself think about her, about that fierce night last summer, although there were times when the memory of it would start to creep in around the edges of his mind, bringing with it a subtle dismay that he could never completely define. "I'm not sure if I should," he said seriously.

"Oh, now, well *of course* you should," Rufus said. "We're all friends here, Brother. And what you say will go no further than this here circle. You've got our word on that." He held up his right hand as proof of his allegiance. Half a dozen other hands went up at the same time, all of them eager to join in the vow.

Billy gave them all a knowing look. "I'm sure you're all clean and virtuous fellows," he said dryly, "and that your word is your bond." He considered them for a moment, and considered the story he had to tell. Maybe it was time to talk about it. He threw his cigarette into the fire in a decisive motion.

His audience huddled closer, preparing for a stimulating tale.

Billy cleared his throat. "It was just last summer. I was traveling with Brother Justice's Revival then, and we were making his usual circuit through the southern part of Virginia. We'd set our sights on a big field outside this little town — a town named for the angels.

"I was driving down a dusty back road, headed towards the field where we were to set up for that night, and there she was. Like an apparition. Standing in a garden outside a little run-down shack, just staring at us as we went by. The air was thick with road dust, and I saw her as if through a mist. She was petite, and young-looking, although I realized later that the appearance of youth was an illusion. She looked as if she had been bent over, pulling weeds, and had just straightened up when she heard the rumbling of our caravan coming down the road. A breeze blew up as I was driving by, flattening her dress against her body.

"I slowed down and raised my hat to her — called out, 'God bless, miss, and I hope to see you at the meeting tonight.' As I drove on, I could feel her staring after me, and my heart was lifted by the thought that here was another soul I could save."

Knowing grins were exchanged by the men sitting around the fire, but Billy ignored them and went on.

"That night, I was up on stage, overcome as usual by my love for the Lord. I looked out over the audience, at those eager faces panting for salvation, and suddenly my eyes were seized by the sight of her sitting there."

"Sweet one, was she?" Rufus said, wanting details.

"She wasn't so much pretty as…arresting." Billy shook his head slowly. "Friends, this woman had an aura about her that I had never seen before, nor do I expect to see again within the bounds of earth and incarnation. She was not beautiful, but once I looked at her, I could not look away."

He paused, remembering. She had smiled at him, but it wasn't the usual smile of adoration and longing that he had seen on the faces of the small town girls. It was a mocking smile, a contemptuous smile, a smile that spoke of secret knowledge.

It was a smile that a snake might give to a mouse, right before she slowly squeezed the life out of him and devoured him whole.

He had known right off that she wasn't impressed by his performance, nor would she be awed by his usual flattery and fancy way of speaking. She had sat through the entire show, ignoring everyone around her, eyes for him only, with that same cold, reptilian smile on her face. And afterwards, when the last amen had been spoken and the townsfolk were on their way home, when the air was thick with summer heat and road dust, he had walked outside and found her waiting for him.

She was tiny, this strange woman — barely came up to his shoulder — and solidly built. Her shoulders were stooped and her hand, when he took it, was coarse and calloused from hard work. Up close, she had been older than he thought, and more haggard-looking, like so many women in these dusty, difficult times.

But her black eyes had burned inside her pale, rough face, bespeaking a hunger that could not fail to stir a response. He didn't stop to question it or to wonder why part of him was attracted by this woman, while another part was repulsed.

"She led, I followed. We walked along the dark roads together — sometimes talking, sometimes not. She had an extraordinary voice — young and old at the same time. It was brittle and cracked with bitterness, but underneath that was the sound of refinement, something of education in the way she clipped her vowels and drew out her consonants. She told me that her family had founded the town down the road when her people had come over from Ireland in 1865, after the War Between the States had ended. I remember she said that her family hadn't fought in the war, but had made up for it by fighting every day of their lives since they'd come to this God-forsaken country.

"We walked all the way back down that long, dusty road. I thought we might be headed toward her little rundown shack, and although I generally prefer a more upscale environment, a true man of God does not shy away from a humble abode. We did not stop there, however. Instead of heading up the short cobbled walkway to the front door, she turned me around and pointed upward. I lifted my eyes and beheld a sorry sight.

"High on the hill in front of me, I could see the black-tinged wreckage of what must have once been a home of extraordinary beauty. 'I used to live in that house,' she told me, her voice heavy. 'I was born there.'

"For once in my life, I found myself at a loss for words. So I took the easy road out and stated the obvious with remarkable aplomb. 'It burned down,' I said.

"She nodded, and there was a powerful anger in the way she moved her head, just as there was in the set of her shoulders and the way she moved her hips as we started walking again. Now friends, I have never been aroused by the more...*violent* human emotions, but I don't mind telling you that her anger — the vehemence of it, the power of it — was as intoxicating to me as the rose is to the honeybee on a soft summer afternoon.

"We climbed the high hill, onward to the decaying wreckage of that mighty giant. And she told me how the big house had burned down in 1912, and how afterwards she and her mother had moved into that little shack at the crossroads. Her father, it seemed, had been something of a ne'er-do-well — a hapless gambler. The man had inherited a fortune at eighteen, and had lost it all by the age of forty. When he died in that fire, he left behind his wife, his child, and a mountain of debt so high not even Admiral Byrd himself could have bested it."

Sympathetic murmurs from those around the fire, all of whom had felt the elephantine burden of financial obligation crushing down upon their backs at one time or another. Billy went on.

"In the moonlight, the wreckage of the house looked like the skeletal remains of a giant trying to climb out of its moldy earthen grave, wanting to feel the soft kiss of the night air on its bony limbs. She showed me where the kitchen had been, where the piano had stood in the parlor, how the staircase had curved so gracefully down to the marble-floored foyer. She told me how as a little girl she had dreamed of descending that staircase on her sixteenth birthday, wearing a dress of taffeta and preparing to meet her first beau in the parlor.

"She told me other things about herself, too — personal

things that I'll never relate to a living soul. And all the time she was speaking, I stood mute — *me,* friends, struck dumb, can you believe it? — wondering at how she confided in me, wondering why it was me who she chose to share the burden of her secrets…."

Billy trailed off, looking far into the distance at nothing. He should never have begun telling this story. It depressed him, made him feel cold and lonely. And, for some reason, it frightened him. The woman herself frightened him, to be honest. It was as if her memory conjured up all the baseless, superstitious terrors of childhood. The thing under the bed. The monster in the closet. The darkness of the human soul.

Rufus, seeing that Billy had wandered off somewhere in his own mind, cleared his throat and spoke up. "You said it yourself, Brother," he interjected slyly. "People *like* a man of God."

But Billy shook his head morosely, unable to muster up his usual sly wit. "It was more than that this time, friends. Let me tell you, I have listened with patience and understanding to untold dozens of women — young women who could not find a man to their liking, older women who had a man and no longer wanted him. I have heard their stories, and I have seen their hearts, and I have eased their tensions and their sorrows, but this was different in a way that I cannot explain."

He looked out at the arc of men sitting around him. His face showed plainly his passion and his bafflement, and the men who watched him were silent, understanding his plight. This woman had gotten to him.

"I listened to her pour out her heart, until finally I could stand it no longer. I took her in my arms, and I *had* her."

He paused, breathing deeply at the recollection. "Yes, friends, I had her, right there on the ruins of her family home

— up against the remains of a brick column that had once supported the room that had been her father's study, as she told me later. With the full moon shining down on us, and the summer-hot air burning our throats."

He shuddered as his body conjured up erotic traces of the memory. He didn't know why he had expected her to be a virgin, or why he was so surprised to find that she wasn't. It had irritated him, to be honest. Everything about her had bespoken the words *solitary, reclusive, alone*. Where and when had this woman — especially, he thought ungraciously, a woman as patently unattractive as this one — found a man to take her virginity?

Well, he thought, she found *me*, didn't she? Not to open up the flower of her womanhood, but to satisfy some other carnal purpose.

A fragment of poetry floated through his mind: *And I thought: well, as well him as another*….

James Joyce, he remembered. And it wasn't a poem, it was a novel. Still, there were the words, *as well him as another…*

That summed it up. Any man would have done under the circumstances. And that was a further irritation. Billy Lewis was not just "any man."

The least she could have done was to show a little gratitude, but she hadn't been able to muster that. Instead, she'd just smiled her hard little smile, lit a cigarette, and talked some more.

"She told me that her mama had been a good woman. But the words were said with a sneer. A *good* woman. A good *Christian* woman. The house had burned down, her husband and her fortune had been lost, and what had that good Christian woman done? Had she looked out for her daughter's welfare, gone out West to join her family in San Francisco? No. She'd moved into some ancient hovel on a corner of the property.

Taken a cow and some chickens and started growing her own food. Continued ministering to the sick and the poor, while all the time her own daughter was sick at heart, and they had become the poorest people in town. Played Lady Bountiful and Florence Nightingale up until the day she died, and all the town had turned out to see her buried. Then they had turned to Pleasance to continue in her mother's footsteps. Well, Pleasance was no Good Christian Woman. Any belief she'd had in God had been lost long ago — burned to cinders along with her home, lost amongst the smoldering wreckage of her life.

"She talked about God with the same venom that some women save for their husbands who've beat them, or their fathers who've sold them into married bondage. She spat out the name of the Lord, shaking her fist at the sky and defying him to strike her down where she sat, if he were real and truly all-powerful.

"Then suddenly she turned to me. Looked me in the eye and gave me a smile that chilled my bones. 'People in town think I'm a witch,' she said. The idea obviously struck her as the height of hilarity. 'They say I come up here at night and perform rituals. Animal sacrifices. Carnal congress with the devil.'

"I thought uneasily about the vanquishment of her maidenhead. Certainly it was not I who had done it. Was it possible it had been some supernatural being who had taken her virginity? I banished the thought from my mind. I didn't believe in that sort of thing…did I?

"She was still watching me, still smiling as if she knew my every thought. 'Well, the devil can't give me a child, preacher,' she said, 'and neither could any of those wastrels who've lain atop me and pumped me full of their useless sap. But you… you're different. Potent.' Her eyes glittered. 'I knew it as soon as I saw you.'

"She began slowly unbuttoning the bodice of her dress. 'Shall we really make some noise this time?' she asked. 'Give them something to chatter about in town?'

"I had the grievous but somehow arousing image of her, going through one man after another, trying to conceive a child to stave off the futile loneliness of her life. This was followed by a fleeting thought about how much noise she and I would have to make for it to carry all the way to town. Then her dress fell open, and my mind turned to mush."

Someone handed Billy a cigarette, and he took it, fingers shaking. He inhaled deeply the smoke of cheap tobacco, grateful for the way it burnt his lungs. It was soothing, that burn. It was real. It brought him partway back to the here and now.

Strengthened by the cigarette between the fingers of one hand and the smooth glass of the whisky bottle that was placed in the other, he drew a deep breath.

"That's my last clear recollection of that night. When I woke up the next morning, I was alone, lying on my back in the tall reeds, with the sun burning my face and the stagnant smell of summer in my nostrils. My mouth was dry as dirt. I sat up slowly, feeling sick. My head hurt. I got to my knees, then eventually made it all the way to my feet. I staggered around some, looking for Pleasance, foolishly thinking that I should kiss her on the cheek or exchange some pleasantry that would make the previous night seem more normal." He shook his head, grimly amused at his own misplaced gallantry.

"I opened my mouth to call to her, thinking maybe she was somewhere close by. But before I could make a sound, I heard a rustling in the overgrown trees behind me, and turned around, expecting to see her. But there was no one there. I stared deeply into the heart of those woods, so dark and cold with overgrowth, in spite of the sun. And my heart grew chill with a nameless foreboding. A bird called out — not a pleasant song, but a sharp cry of warning. And even though I knew it was stupid and cowardly, I turned and ran.

"I ran all the way back to the camp, got in my truck, and drove away as fast as I could. I did not say goodbye to anyone, I did not stop to empty my bladder or lace up my boots." He chuckled unpleasantly and took a drag on his smoke. "It's a good thing I had buttoned my fly the night before, or I would have made the journey with my dingle hanging out."

"With a piece the size of yours," Rufus interjected automatically, "you probably would've tripped and broken your nose." Then he looked up guiltily, waiting to see if Billy would be irritated by his flippant tone of voice.

But Billy just chuckled again, with more humor this time. "Well, I don't like to brag," he said. "But it could be you're right about that, friend. Could be you're right."

"Gifts that God gives," Rufus added.

Billy lifted the bottle in a toast. "Amen to that."

"So you shook a leg and scrammed outta there like the devil was on your tail," Rufus said. "And you never saw that dilly-dame again?"

"No. Never."

"So you don't know if you sired her demon offspring or not?"

Billy laughed, dismissing both the idea and his own discomfort in thinking about it. "If God wanted her to have a child, then I'm sure she had one," he said complacently. "And if He worked through me to give it to her, then that's His will, and I've no right to question it."

"And you never think about her, about that strange, spooky woman — all alone, raising your *devilishly*-handsome son,

221

while you go on night after night leaping around on stage and exhorting the name of God?"

Billy faced Rufus across the fire. The flames flickered, sending shadows dancing in strange patterns over Rufus' weathered-ugly face. The other men around the fire laughed, thinking it was just old Rufus ribbing the good Brother Worship again. But Billy knew different. And he wondered if Rufus knew how close he had cut to the bone with that question.

"And say, Preacher," another man spoke up, saving Billy from having to answer. "How come when you told us that *fassss-kinatin'* story, you left out all the good details? You told us what she was like, but what was she *like?*"

Billy didn't take his eyes off Rufus' face. Rufus grinned again, showing his gums and the teeth that stuck out of them.

Details, preacher, that grin said. Your audience wants details.

His eyes broke from Rufus' gaze, and he looked around at his fellow men. A broad grin forced itself onto his face. "Why boys, I could tell you details that would make your hair stand on end," Billy said. "I could tell you about strange positions and muttered incantations. I could tell you about weird noises from the woods and red eyes glittering in the darkness. I could give you details about how her body smelled and tasted, and the evil things she whispered in my ear — "

His eye was caught by a shadow moving through the moonlight. A blue dress glinted subtly, and blond hair shone with a fresh combing. Ahh, his appointment for this evening — there she was at last. He pulled out his watch and checked it. She'd come right on time. He loved that in a woman.

"I could tell you all sorts of details, boys, but that would be ungentlemanly. Besides, I don't think there's enough whisky even in the great state of Kentucky to prepare you for the things

I might say, and I don't want to ruin your innocence."

He stood up and tossed his bottle across to Rufus, then straightened his trousers, brushing dust from his cuffs. "Moreover, gentleman, I have an appointment, and you know that it's not wise to keep a lady waiting. So I'll have to bid you good night, and thank you for a lovely evening."

"And good night to you, preacher," Rufus croaked. He was smiling again, and it was friendly this time. All the challenge had seeped out of him with the fresh bottle that rested comfortably in his hand. "I hope your *prayer meeting* goes well tonight. I expect we'll hear all about it tomorrow."

Billy winked as he settled his hat on his head, tilting it rakishly over one eye. "Good night, boys," he said, "and God bless."

And with that final benediction, he turned and strolled off into the darkness.

CHAPTER SIXTEEN

EATHER RAPPED ON ALICIA'S DOOR, and then entered without bothering to wait for a response. "It's me," she called.

"I'm just getting out of the shower." The muffled reply came from the next room. "Make yourself a drink and have a seat."

Heather was way ahead of the invitation. She stood at the bar and poured herself a glass of vodka, admiring the way the liquid arced from the bottle to the glass. She dropped in a couple of ice cubes and a wedge of lime. Vodka was blessed stuff. Practically odorless, so people couldn't smell it on you, but it sure packed a punch. And she needed it tonight.

It had been two days since their shopping trip in Bonaire. The ship would be departing for Curacao in the morning. Reed and Kate had been fluttering around the island like a couple of damned lovebirds. They were happy, they were in love, and they didn't seem to care who knew. And tonight, all six of them were all having dinner together.

Yes, Heather thought. I do need this drink.

As she flopped down on the chaise lounge, her drink sloshed in her glass. She brushed off the drops that had landed on the watered silk of the chaise, admiring the texture of the fabric. As usual, Alicia had ended up with one of the best suites in the place. Alicia always had the best of everything, no matter where she went. She wouldn't have even considered anything else.

But Alicia had been born with money, Heather reflected. She had never known anything other than wealth and comfort and elegance. Heather shivered a bit as she remembered the hard, grasping days of her own youth. She had worked like a dog to pull herself out of that life, but in some ways she would never fully escape it.

"Stop moping." Alicia appeared in the doorway, wrapped in a silk kimono and smoking a cigarette. She crossed the room and fixed herself a drink.

"I can't help it," Heather confessed. She had no secrets from Alicia. "It's been hard seeing him again. Harder than I thought it would be."

Alicia pushed Heather's feet aside and settled on the end of the chaise. "If Reed doesn't appreciate you — "

"Then he's not worth crying over," Heather finished. She waved her hand impatiently. "That's what I've been telling myself, but I'm starting to think it's all crap. What good is fame and fortune if you don't have someone to share it with?" She smiled bitterly. "Who said that, anyway?"

"Every lonely person with money and celebrity has said it," Alicia snapped. Her annoyance masked the fact that she was worried about her friend. "Are you really that stuck on this guy?"

"Oh, I don't *know*," Heather moaned. "I know I'm being melodramatic, but I can't seem to shake this awful feeling that Reed is the one for me, and I let him get away."

Alicia put out a feeler. "It can't help to see him falling all over Kate."

"I like Kate," Heather said hesitantly. "But it is hard for me to see them together. Especially considering how happy they've seemed these last couple of days."

"If Kate were out of the picture, do you think you'd have a chance with him?"

Heather grinned. "What are you suggesting? That we bump her off?"

"I'm suggesting that we arrange for you to have some time alone with him. Maybe you can remind him why he fell in love with you in the first place."

"That's part of the problem," Heather said sadly. "I'm not sure that he ever was in love with me."

Again Alicia's temper flared. "Well, do you want to find out, or do you want to sit around crying in your vodka? Come on, girl; pull yourself together! Show the world why *Maxim Magazine* voted you 'Most Do-able Woman on Daytime TV.'"

"A dubious honor at best." Heather rolled her eyes, but she pushed herself up a bit on the chaise, set her glass on the floor, and ran her fingers through her flaming hair. "I guess it is better to know, right?"

"Absolutely."

Heather sighed. "All right. You help me get some time alone with Reed, and I'll do my stuff."

Alicia smiled. She loved intrigue better than anything else in the world. She leaned down and stubbed out her cigarette in Heather's empty glass. "Kick ass," she said.

⌐⊸✺⊶⌐

The six of them met for dinner at eight-thirty. With a little finesse, Alicia arranged for Kate and Reed to be seated at opposite ends of the table. Alicia sat next to Kate and kept her occupied to her throughout the meal. Heather caught a fragment of their conversation from the other end of the table. "I'm so glad we're having this chance to get acquainted…" Alicia was saying. Heather smiled to herself.

She kept a low profile during the meal, engaging Reed in innocuous conversation. She was nervous about what she would say later, and she wanted to ease herself into it. She experienced the same anxiety every time she stepped in front of a camera. She knew that once the time was right, she would be able to perform, but in the meantime, she sipped her drink and picked at her food, mentally running her lines as she chatted.

After dinner, Alicia suggested a stroll on deck. Again she managed to steer Kate away from Reed, taking Kate's arm as they walked and saying, "Can I ask you a legal question?" She proceeded to spin a yarn about a "close friend" who was in trouble. The two of them led the way around deck, with Joe and Elliot following.

Heather maneuvered into position next to Reed, mentally took a deep breath, and opened with a joke. "So, are there any other women on board that you used to date?"

Reed smiled. "Kate asked me that very question the other night," he said. "And the answer is no."

Score another point for Kate, Heather thought. "Well, that's a relief," she said gamely. "I'd hate to think I had even more competition on this boat."

"Competition?"

She let the comment dangle unexplained and changed the subject. "I'm actually really glad that we've been thrown together this way. After we broke up, I got the distinct impression that you were avoiding me."

The statement was a challenge. *It's time to deal with me,* Heather was saying. "I guess I was," he admitted. "I felt awkward about ending our relationship. It wasn't an easy thing for me to do."

"That's a relief," Heather smiled. "I'm sure you had your reasons, but I have to confess I was never really sure what they were."

"It…it was complicated," Reed said, "but you should know
— "

"If you say 'it wasn't you, it was me,' I swear I'll punch you right in the mouth."

He held up his hands in mock surrender. "Okay, okay. But I hope you do realize that I've always cared about you."

She rolled her eyes. "I'm just like your sister, right?"

"Not exactly."

The awkward silence that followed gave her hope. It was a silence that was deafened her with possibilities. There were still sparks between them, after all.

Up ahead, the other four turned a corner. She and Reed were alone. This was the moment.

She stopped walking, forcing Reed to stop also, and turn to face her. "You know," she said, "I haven't had a long term relationship since you and I split up."

"What about Elliot?"

She waved her hand dismissively. "We're friends. Sometimes I think he'd like it to be more, but…."

"You're not interested?"

Heather sighed. "Elliot is a charming, intelligent man — his behavior the other night notwithstanding. But we're very different. He's had money all his life, and I don't think that he could ever understand what it was like to grow up without it."

"Well, that's one thing you and I had in common."

She took his hand and squeezed it. "We still have it in common."

He released her hand gently and put his hands in his pockets.

"I don't think that similar backgrounds is the only thing that can make a successful relationship."

"But it helps." She looked up at him, her jade eyes glowing. "Reed, we were really good together. I can understand if you got scared, but you don't need to be afraid of me. I won't ask for more of you than you're ready to give."

Reed was taken aback. The words were so similar to those that Kate had spoken. Was he really so distant that two beautiful women would feel the need to pledge themselves to an uncertain future just to make him more comfortable? The thought had a chilling effect.

She saw him thinking and misinterpreted his expression. She took his hand again, raised it to her lips, and then leaned toward him, eyes glowing. He took a step backward, and she looked up at him, surprised.

Her surprise turned to embarrassment when she realized what she was seeing in his face: compassion, concern…and a complete lack of romantic interest.

"Wow," she said. "I've really made a fool of myself here, haven't I?"

"Of course not," he said, perhaps too quickly. "Most men would have jumped at the opportunity you just offered me."

"Most men. But not you."

"I am sorry."

"Oh, for God's sake, stop apologizing." She smiled. She was an actress, wasn't she? No reason to play this scene as the crying, pitiful ex-girlfriend.

"I really care about Kate," he tried to explain. "In fact, I think I might be in love with her. I didn't even realize it until you wanted to kiss me."

"Kate's a great lady." It didn't help Heather any to know that she truly meant that. "I guess I'm glad I was able to help you realize your true feelings. Hooray for me." She gave him a final smile, dazzling as ever, then turned and walked away before he could see the tears in her eyes.

"Heather." Elliot stepped out from the shadow cast by the stairs as she turned the last corner and stopped before her cabin door.

She jumped. "Good grief, Elliot, what are you doing? You scared me to death!"

She unlocked the door and walked in. He followed her, leaving the door open behind him, as she turned on lights. "Did it work?"

"What are you talking about?" she asked irritably. "Do you want a drink?"

"I said 'Did it work,' but of course it didn't, or you wouldn't have come back here alone."

"Elliot, for the last time, what the hell are you talking about?"

"Operation Reed."

She paused, a bottle of vodka in her hand. "Are you going to clarify that, or should I guess?"

"Don't play that game with me!" In a flash, he was across the room and had her by the arm. "You and Alicia, with your little plots! Are you really in love with him, or is it that you just don't want anyone else to have him?"

She pulled away, smiling slyly. "Why, were you hoping to have a shot at him yourself?"

He looked stricken. "I don't think there's a word awful enough to describe you."

Her face crumbled. It was too much. She couldn't be an

actress twenty-four hours a day. "I'm sorry," she said humbly. "I don't want you, of all people, to be angry with me."

"Why? Because we're such good friends?"

"We are, aren't we?"

He smiled bitterly. "Well, it's certain that I'm a charming, intelligent man, but you could never have a relationship with me because I don't know what it's like to grow up without money!"

She paled. "You heard that?"

"Of course I did! I doubled back so I could hear what you were talking about."

"Sneaky." She smiled. He could always make her smile.

"You should talk!" He glared, then his eyes softened. "Do you really think that I don't understand you?"

"I don't know." She sighed heavily and sat down. "Suddenly I'm so tired. I don't know anything anymore."

"That's the most encouraging thing I've heard in a long time."

Heather leaned forward and took his hand, pressing it against her cheek. "El, darling, make me a drink."

"I'm not sure I should. If you drink, then I'll drink, and I don't want to go staggering back to my cabin again. I'm getting a reputation as a lush."

"So don't go back to your cabin."

He laughed. "You *are* tired."

"Not really."

"Drunk?"

"Elliot, I'm serious."

He studied at her gravely. "You are not allowed to make fun of me anymore, Miss Christie. From now on, if you extend an invitation like that, you'd better be willing to follow through."

"I am." Her face was earnest. "Stay."

Elliot walked to the bar and began to mix martinis, working

hard to control his expression. "Why?"

"Because I don't know if I really love Reed or if, like you said, I just don't want anyone else to have him. I don't know anything except that you are my friend, and you have been for a very long time. And I want you to stay with me tonight."

He took a final look at her face and saw everything he needed to see. He grinned. "If you insist."

He poured the drinks and carried them back across the room to where she sat. "One more thing, Elliot, darling."

"What is it now?" He sighed in mock exasperation.

She smiled up at him. "Close the door."

Kate wasn't buying it. Alicia had been talking her ear off all night, being poisonously gracious and making a big deal out of how wonderful it was for the two of them to finally have a chance to get to know each other. Did she think that Kate wouldn't notice how attentive Heather was being to Reed?

Then there had been that interminable walk around deck, with Alicia's arm linked through hers like they were old chums. Joe and Elliot trailed along behind like ducklings, which again left Heather and Reed conveniently on their own.

"I know that you and Reed have been busy getting reacquainted, hon," Alicia said with a twinkle, "but I'm sure you won't mind if I say how nice it's been for me to see Heather and Reed together tonight. You know, when they were dating, everyone thought that they made a perfect couple. We were all surprised that they didn't get married. By the way, where did you get that gorgeous dress you wore the first night we met?"

No, Kate wasn't buying it at all. And although she was getting very tired of this game, she wanted to let it play itself out. She had known for some time that it was coming.

And now here they were, just the two of them, in Alicia's room, trying on clothes like longtime girlfriends.

"There," Alicia said. She was standing behind Kate, sliding up the zipper on the dress that Kate was wearing. "I told you it would look better on you than on me."

Kate looked at herself in the mirror. The dress was green velvet, strapless, with a high waist and a full, sweeping skirt. She spun around, admiring the way the fabric moved.

Alicia peered over Kate's shoulder into the mirror. "It brings out the green in your eyes," she said, "just like the one you wore that first night at dinner. And that cut is much better on you than on me. Why don't you take it?"

Kate hesitated. She had to admit, the dress was beautiful, and it did look good on her. But something inside her was strongly resistant to the idea of accepting anything from Alicia — especially something as beautiful and expensive as this dress.

"Oh, I couldn't," Kate said.

"You most certainly could," Alicia replied. "And you most certainly should. It might have been made for you!"

"Oh, I get it," Kate said. "I take the dress, and Heather takes Reed?"

Alicia looked taken aback, but then she laughed. "Am I that transparent?" she asked. "I thought I was a good deal more clever than that!"

"I'm sure you're very clever," Kate said. "But I'm afraid you're also that transparent. Would you help me with this?" She turned slightly so Alicia could undo the zipper.

"I appreciate the offer," Kate said, stepping out of the dress, "but I'm afraid I'll have to decline it."

"You're sure?"

"I'm afraid it wouldn't do as a conciliation prize."

"Is a good man so much harder to find than a good dress?"

Kate smiled. "You tell me."

"I would, but I'm afraid I don't know any good men!"

"What about Joe?"

"Joe?" Alicia looked blank for a moment, then she smiled. "Joe's all right. Joe's lovely, in fact. I'll probably marry Joe one day. But not until I've had some fun in life first!"

Kate stepped behind the fabric-covered screen, unhooked the bustier that she had borrowed from Alicia, and proceeded to put her own undergarments back on. Suddenly Alicia's head popped around the side of the screen. "Dressing so soon?" she asked. "Sure you wouldn't rather slip on that robe and have a drink?"

"I can have a drink just as well with my clothes on."

"True, but what if…what if later you wanted to take them off again? Wouldn't you rather just save some time?" Alicia eyed her up and down, speculatively.

For a moment Kate was shocked. But then she threw her head back and laughed. "Well, well, aren't we modern?" she said. "Again, I appreciate the offer, but I'll decline that one too, thanks all the same."

Alicia shrugged. "It never hurts to ask." She withdrew her head. "Now, how about that drink?"

Kate shook her head as she continued dressing. "I think I'll head back to my room."

"Will Reed be there waiting?"

"Reed will be where Reed will be," Kate said. "He's an adult, and he's capable of making his own decisions."

"Who's being oh-so-very-modern now?" Alicia shook her head. "You're not fooling me, sweetie. Any woman who tries to take him from you won't get away without a fight!"

"You may be right," Kate admitted. She came around the screen and slipped her shoes on. "Yes, you may very well be right. Goodnight, Alicia. Thanks for…an interesting evening."

"You're very welcome. Goodnight."

Alicia held the door for her and closed it after Kate had departed.

"Well, Heather," Alicia said to herself. "Guess you're on your own."

Kate walked slowly back to her room. The evening had left her bemused, thoughtful. She wasn't sure what to think about anything anymore. So, Heather was in love with Reed — at least according to Alicia. While she had always expected as much, Kate was still surprised at how the actual news had affected her.

The question was, how did Reed feel about Heather? Always the gentleman, he had never discussed her with Kate. But as Kate thought about it, there were moments when she could remember his affection showing through. Nothing too obvious — the curve of his lips as he had talked with Heather at dinner, the way he had helped her with her bags when they were shopping, a certain glint in his eye when she made a joke. Could be love. Could be anything.

As she reached the door to her room, Reed was just rounding the opposite corner. He looked tired and preoccupied as he leaned against the wall.

"Hi," she said. Her heart was in her throat.

"Hi." He paused, scratched his head. "I've been looking for you. Where have you been?"

"With Alicia…trying on clothes."

"Trying on clothes?" Reed arched an eyebrow.

"Don't ask."

"I won't. With Alicia, that could mean anything."

"Want to come in?"

"Yeah, if you don't mind. I have something I'd like to talk to you about."

Kate's stomach dropped. She let him take the key from her fingers, which had suddenly gone numb. This was it, then. He would tell her that he was in love with Heather. *Thanks for the push, Katie. I never could have done this without you.*

He unlocked the door and held it open for her. Kate roused herself and entered, murmuring her thanks as she passed him. She made herself busy by circling the room, switching on lamps, creating interconnected pools of light that gradually illuminated the room.

"This is a nice room," Reed said. Strange to think that with all the time they'd been spending together, this was the first time he'd been inside it. "I can see why you like it so much."

"Thanks," Kate said automatically. Then she added, "I guess I shouldn't really say 'thanks,' though, should I? I mean, it's only mine for the week, after all. Do you want a drink, or something?"

"No," he said, sinking into that deep, cushy chair she had told him about.

"Do you mind if I...."

He waved his hand. "Of course not. Go ahead."

She opened the mini-fridge, extracted a full-sized bottle of red wine, and poured a generous amount into a glass. Reed sat silent, watching her without really seeing her. He smiled absently.

"Red wine," he commented. "Isn't that supposed to be served at room temperature?"

"I like it cold, so sue me." She shrugged, dropped into a

chair across from him. She took off her shoes and crossed her legs, flexing her toes.

His eyes cleared, then narrowed. Something in the nervous, automatic way she moved caught his attention. "You all right?" he asked.

"Fine." She sipped her wine. "So what's up?"

His eyes clouded again. He got up, started pacing, reminding her of an earlier conversation they'd had…was it just three nights ago? No, it was another lifetime.

"You know that Heather and I were…together a few years ago."

"You had a relationship. Of course I know."

"I broke it off because I thought things were getting too serious. I was sure she had marriage on her mind." His mouth twisted into a bitter smile. "After all, I'm so irresistible, right? What woman wouldn't try to land me?" He shook his head. "The truth is, as I realize now, that she scared the hell out of me. Suddenly it seemed natural to be thinking of living together, maybe even getting married…."

"Having children," Kate finished, working to control the tremor in her voice.

Reed shook his head. "That was one thing we definitely agreed on — neither of us wanted to have kids."

"No heirs to carry on the Fitzgerald name?" Kate couldn't help but smile. "I remember when you were twelve you told me that you were going to have five sons and name them all Reed Fitzgerald, Jr."

"Oh, right. But that would have been kind of rough on them, wouldn't it?" Reed shook his head ruefully. "When I became a man, I put away childish things. Five years ago, I couldn't have imagined having children. But suddenly the idea of marriage didn't seem so far-fetched."

"So you dumped her," Kate supplied, wondering why she felt obligated to help him with this conversation.

"To put it bluntly, yes."

"And now you regret it."

"I regret that I hurt her. I regret that I lied to her and to myself. How unbelievable is it that I saw her again on board this ship?"

Kate couldn't help but feel a little stung. But she kept her voice mild as she said, "No more unbelievable than you seeing me, I guess."

"Seeing you? Seeing you." Reed stared at her, then waved his hand dismissively. "Kate, seeing you was an act of God, or Fate, or whatever. It was a total inevitability. You and I had to meet again someday. There was just no way around it."

"I had no idea you were so philosophical."

"But that's just it — I wasn't. I am now. Tonight Heather took me for a walk, and she told me that she still has feelings for me — that she might even love me. When she said those words, it was if suddenly it was five years ago, and no time had passed. I looked down at her, I felt all those things that I had felt then. And I knew."

"You realized you loved her."

"No," he said simply. "I realized I loved you."

Kate felt a shock go through her. "What?"

He knelt down before her, took her hands in his, and kissed them. "I love you, Kate." He looked up at her. "I always have. I love the girl you were and the woman you've become. There could never be anyone else for me but you."

She felt her eyes fill with tears. She turned her head and blinked rapidly, but not before he had seen the emotion in her face. He kissed her hands again, waited for her to speak.

"I — I don't know what to say."

"Tell me you love me."

She looked down at him. "I do love you. I have always loved you, I will always love you."

She inclined her head slowly, until her lips rested on his. It was a gentle caress that quickly became a passionate embrace.

He gathered her in his arms, carried her into the bedroom, and closed the door.

CHAPTER SEVENTEEN

August 1969

L ANA STOOD ALONE ON THE street corner. Her suitcase sat next to her on the concrete, its scuffed, shabby sides made somewhat less scruffy by the dim light of early evening. The summer dusk was fading softly around her, sky growing faint and stars beginning to peek out from the veil of night. The streets were deserted, and she was alone. Well, almost alone. Her hand drifted downward to her belly and pressed lightly. There was a slight bump there, nothing more. Three months, the doctor said. Soon she wouldn't be able to hide it.

She was exhausted, but she was used to exhaustion. Her feet hurt, but her feet were always hurting. Her heart ached, but she was accustomed to that pain. What she wasn't used to, what she couldn't handle, was the anxiety, the sense of urgency that was clawing inside her — the knowledge that there was something she had to do that she wasn't doing.

Across the street, glowing faintly with fluorescent light, was the garage where RJ worked. In spite of the late hour, he was still inside, working on a car. She could see him from where she stood. On the side of the building, a set of stairs led to the second floor, where he had his own little apartment. When he finished work, he would scrub his hands, turn out the lights, and go upstairs. Before this spring, Lana had always thought he lived with his mother, in that little shack on the outskirts of town. But she had been wrong — he was independent, he had his own place. The fact that he lived alone was just one of the many things she had discovered about RJ Fitzgerald in the past few months.

She had been standing on that corner for what seemed like hours, mentally exploring her options. She'd opened up the diner on her own that morning, even though customers were scarce these days. She'd made the food herself, carried the trays out to the diners, collected the money, and rang it up. She accepted only cash and pocketed what there was. George would've wanted it that way.

By seven o'clock, the place was empty. No dinner crowd to warm the dining room with laughter and noise, no one to play the jukebox. So she'd cleaned up and closed down, locking the doors for the last time. The new owners were coming tomorrow to look the place over. There should be some sort of ceremony, she'd thought, that goes with putting a place like this to rest. But there was only Lana there to pull the shades and lock the door. And after that, she'd had nowhere to go.

She'd walked up and down Main Street for a while, looking in store windows and trying to ignore her own reflection in the glass panes. Her eyes were dark and heavily circled; her skin was pale. She looked like a walking corpse, and she felt like one. There was no life left in her, except for the one growing in her womb.

Eight months of tragedy, Lana thought. How could anyone live through that and not be changed?

They had buried Mal in January. The whole town turned out for the funeral, black-coated mourners huddling around the grave, their breath fogging up the frigid air. The ground was cold and frozen hard, like the hearts of those who loved Mal had been frozen by his death. *Malcolm Doyle, war hero,* people said tearfully.

Nothing was the same after that. Not for the Doyle family, not for Lana, not for the town. Mal was the first son Angel River had lost to the war, but everyone knew he wouldn't be the last. And now that Mal had died, a cloud of fear hovered over the town. It was as if some invisible barrier had been broken. One boy dead — when would it be two? People went about their daily business in the midst of a silent terror, like a mouth poised on the verge of screaming. Waiting for something to push a piercing wail out of the throat, past the lips, and into the open air. Waiting for the next boy to die.

Kathy and Nate had grown closer to each other after Mal's death, while Lana had grown apart from both of them. Nate came down from college almost every weekend to see Kathy. In September, she would start college, and after college, she and Nate would be married. They weren't officially engaged yet, as far as Lana knew. No announcements had been made. But it was there, an undercurrent of coming nuptials running swiftly under the waters of their romance. The future was already decided.

Whether it was out of guilt or sadness, Nate tended to avoid Lana when he was in town. And because of that, Lana and Kathy saw less of each other than they ever had before. There were no more evening study sessions, no weekends spent lounging under the apple tree in Kathy's yard. They smiled at each other when they passed in the hallways at school, spoke briefly and quietly from time to time, but that was it. Their friendship as they had known it was changed forever.

Lana had let go of that part of her life with a mixture of

regret and relief. After Mal died, it made her sad to be with Kathy, sadder to be with Nate. There were too many unhappy memories associated with their past together, and she couldn't spend her life looking back.

Instead, Lana looked forward to the future with a steely, stubborn optimism. She had been granted a partial scholarship to Agnes Scott College in Georgia. She had been hoping for a full scholarship, but she refused to feel disappointed. The amount the school was offering was still pretty good. She would have to work her way through college, but she'd been working all her life, so that was nothing new to her. She would succeed, one way or another. She would get out of this town, away from Mal's grave and the ever-watchful face of the Doyle house high on the far hill. She would make a life for herself. It was a dream she had guarded fiercely inside her heart, and she wasn't going to turn away from it.

At least, that had been her attitude during the months between January and May. But at the end of May, the world had turned upside-down. The only family she had ever known was gone forever. She pressed a hand to her belly again. And then *this* had happened. Now nothing about the future was certain.

Her mother had died on a sunny day in May. The weather had been gray and rainy for almost two solid weeks before, and the return of the sun had made Lana feel peaceful, almost optimistic. The tulips and azaleas were in full bloom. Lana had always loved spring flowers. School would be over in a few weeks, and she was energized by the thought of moving out of the "school days" phase of her life to the "college days" and onward toward the days of independent adulthood.

The diner was empty that afternoon, quiet before the dinner rush. Except for RJ, of course, who sat in his usual place at the counter with his afternoon coffee and pie. Lana had been feeling more kindly to him of late. She tried not to encourage his ever-present crush on her, but at the same time, she recognized him as being one of the few unchanging elements in her life — along with George and this diner. They were some of the few things that hadn't changed after Mal died. And in a couple short months, she'd be headed south to Georgia, where everything would be different. So she tried to be more friendly to RJ, who always seemed to be a nice guy: harmless, if somewhat pitiable.

She refilled his coffee and gifted him with a smile, then turned and headed in the back to see if George needed anything. She heard the phone ringing and doubled her pace to answer it, but George beat her to it, picking it up and grinning at her, as if he'd beat her in a game of chess instead of merely winning the privilege of being the first one to the phone.

But the grin faded quickly, and his face turned gray. His eyes found hers, and in them she read fear. *Mother*, she thought. Something's happened to Mother. She heard a rushing in her ears and reached out to steady herself against the wall.

George said a few words into the phone and hung it up. But it missed the receiver and clattered to the floor. Lana looked at it lying there, the cord like a shiny black snake.

George spoke softly to her in words she couldn't really understand. He told that Mother was in the hospital. She'd been at work and started coughing blood, and they'd taken her to see the doctor. We have to go *now*, George said. Lana heard him speaking and knew what he was telling her, but it was as if she didn't comprehend the individual words. She simply knew that it was Mother, that it was serious, and that they had to go. *Now.*

RJ was already on his feet, turning out lights and putting out the "closed" sign. He offered to call Rosie and tell her what was going on so she wouldn't arrive for her shift and find the place locked and dark.

"We'll take my car," George said. He'd grabbed his jacket and was pulling it on while at the same time pulling Lana towards the door.

"I'll talk to Rosie, and then I'll follow you to the hospital," RJ said, looking at Lana. George nodded his thanks.

Outside, they squinted against the brightness of the spring day. George's car was parked right outside the café. He unlocked the passenger door and opened it for Lana, then went around to the street side to get in behind the wheel. The afternoon sun beat down on her head, making her feel slightly sick as she stood there, looking at the inside of the car. It looked like a cave to her, or the open mouth of a monster. Her stomach roiled. She didn't want to get in.

You're so stupid, she thought fiercely. What's wrong with you? Mother needs you, you have to go.

George unlocked his door and opened it. He leaned forward and looked at her across the roof. "Lana, sweetheart, get in the car." His voice was kind but impatient. *Move,* his tone said. He looked at her in frustration, saw she wasn't moving, and pushed away from the car.

He's coming back over here to help me in because I'm too stupid to do it myself, Lana thought. Why won't my feet move? Why can't I just get in the car and close the door? Poor George. He always has to take care of me.

She watched as he took a step back and reached out to close his door. Later, Lana would wonder if he ever heard the squeal of brakes, if he saw the truck that hit him, if he knew he was flying ten feet in the air, if he felt the impact of the pavement under him.

She screamed as the truck slammed into the car, into George, sending his body flying down the street along with the car door. The car jumped sideways at the impact, her hair was blown back from her face with the rush of air, and she felt as if the open mouth of the monster was roaring at her, lunging at her, trying to eat her. She reeled backwards, arms out, trying not to fall.

The truck glanced off the side of the car, kept moving at high speed, and slammed into a lamppost on the other side of the street. The driver went through the windshield, landed on the sidewalk outside the bank. All Lana could see was blood and glass.

RJ came stumbling out of the store, his face slack with shock. He stared blankly at the scene in front of him, then shook himself and turned to Lana. Gently, he turned her around to face him, looked her up and down to make sure she wasn't bleeding. Then he was down the street, kneeling next to George. People were starting to gather, but no one was doing anything.

RJ ran off, away down Main Street. He's going, Lana thought desperately. He's running away. I need him; where's he going? But he was back a moment later, driving his pickup truck. There was a conversation with several men on the street. Carefully, as carefully as they could, they loaded George into the back of the pickup. RJ arranged some blankets around him, then came back to Lana.

"We're going to take him to the hospital," RJ said. He spoke slowly and carefully, looking into her face to see if she understood him. "I'm not leaving you here alone. You come along with me."

Lana nodded, absurdly grateful for his presence, and for his presence of mind. She allowed him to put his arm around her and guide her to the truck. But when he opened the passenger door, she shook her head emphatically. "I have to ride in the back with George," she said.

He didn't want to let her. He tried to argue. He told her it was almost an hour's drive to the hospital, that they'd be on the highway, that it wasn't safe. But she was stubborn, and in the end, he gave in. He helped her climb in the back of the pickup, helped her settle next to George. As soon as she saw George's face, white as a sheet under the rusty-red blood that was spattered everywhere, she wished she hadn't been so insistent.

The truck pulled off, RJ trying to drive smoothly, but quickly towards the hospital. Lana eased George's head onto her lap, trying to give him some comfort.

His breath was ragged, but regular. She looked up and down the length of him, trying to ascertain how much damage had been done to his poor, fragile human body. But he was so swaddled in blankets that she couldn't see much. And in the end, she realized that was probably a blessing.

She smoothed the thinning hair back from his forehead. She had known him all her life, and she had never looked at him this closely, this intently, before. She wanted to memorize every line, to burn them into her brain so she never forgot him.

He's always been so kind to me and Mother, Lana thought. He can't be dying. He *can't*. How can someone so good be leaving the earth like this? Broken and covered in blood.

And then she realized that this was how Mal must have died. They said he had been killed in an ambush, but that he had pushed another soldier to safety before being shot himself. He must have lain like this — bloody and torn, life slowly oozing away. Far from home, without anyone around who loved him.

Lana found George's hand inside the folds of blankets, and

slipped hers inside it. His fingers gripped hers weakly, and when she looked back at his face, she found his eyes open, staring at her. She could only stare back, speechless, as the bright blue of his eyes shone starkly from the pale white of his face. They were so alive, those eyes, so bright and intent.

He wants to tell me something, she thought. He wants to say something important.

She held her breath and waited, counting seconds as he stared up at her. But his eyelids fluttered closed again. And suddenly she knew that this was one of *those* moments — the ones she avoided — the moments in life that are too real, too final, too painful for words. George was dying, and she may have just seen his eyes close for the last time. She was feeling his last breaths as she held his hand tightly against his side. He would never speak to her again; she would never hear him laugh. He was going, and she was witnessing his departure. And all she could do was watch him leave.

Tears welled hot in her eyes, spilled over, and rained down on his motionless face. They fell softly — sorrowful kisses from the daughter he'd never had, to the only father she'd ever known.

He never regained consciousness. Lana held his hand the whole way, murmured to him in a soft voice. When they got to the hospital, George was whisked away down a long corridor and disappeared behind two swinging doors. RJ helped her fill out the papers the nurse gave her, then sat and held her hand until the doctors came out and told her that George had died.

Lana wanted to cry, but she had no tears left.

Afterward, they'd gone upstairs to see her mother. Elizabeth Carlyle, once so bright and trim and full of advice, was now frail and shrunken and silent. She was unconscious, sleeping under an oxygen tent.

"She's stable," the doctor said, "and she should last the night, but it's only a matter of days."

Lana looked at him with hollow eyes and nodded, understanding but not accepting. She wanted to stay the night, to sleep in a chair in case her mother woke up and needed her, but the doctor took out one of his instruments and tilted her head back, looked in her eyes, then felt her pulse.

"She needs to go home," the doctor told RJ. "Get some food in her and let her sleep. It's the best medicine. You can both come back tomorrow."

RJ had kept his arm around her the whole time, holding her up. It wasn't until they were back in his truck, driving down the highway, that Lana realized the doctor had probably thought she and RJ were married. Strangely enough, she found she didn't mind the idea. It was comforting to be thought of as belonging to someone, part of a couple, instead of always being on her own. Even if it was make-believe, it was still good.

She reached out and touched RJ's hand, tough and cracked from work, rough but kind. After all that had happened today, Lana felt deeply ashamed that she had always considered this good man to be pathetic, ineffective, someone to pity. She slipped her fingers into his palm. "Thank you," she said. "I don't know what I would've done without you today."

Grief welled up inside her again, making her voice crack. God, could this possibly be happening? She thought she would break in two from the pain of what she was feeling. With effort, she swallowed the pain, pushed it down deep, where it couldn't hurt her. She looked out the window, at the scenery rolling past. It was still light out, the sun hadn't yet begun to set. Nothing seemed real. In a few short hours, her entire universe had blown apart.

"I don't want to go home," she said helplessly, almost to herself. "There's no one there. I don't want to be alone."

"The doctor said you should eat something," RJ said. "Do you want to stop…somewhere?"

Lana had the feeling he had been about to suggest stopping at the diner, but then quickly changed his mind. That was the last place they wanted to be.

"You mean do I want to go to a restaurant?" The effort of thinking was painful. "I don't care." But then she shook her head. "I don't much feel like being around people, though."

RJ thought in silence. Then he cleared his throat. "We could — we could go to the river," he suggested hesitantly.

"The river?" No. There were too many memories there — she and Nate had spent time there just last summer, when life was good and before everything had fallen apart.

RJ became stubborn and slightly embarrassed. "Well, we can't go to my place," he said. "It wouldn't look right."

Lana wanted to laugh at that. With everything that had happened today, what did she care about what looked right? But then she saw RJ's face, and she realized that *he* cared what people thought about her. He cared a lot.

"Fine," she said. "Let's go to the river." It didn't really matter, anyway. Not now.

They stopped by the garage to pick up some food. Lana wasn't hungry, but RJ was adamant about following the doctor's orders. "He said you need something to eat," RJ said stubbornly.

So they stopped. That was the first time Lana realized that RJ had his own living quarters, a little apartment over the garage. When he had referred to "his place," she assumed he meant his mother's little house. But no.

He wanted her to wait in the truck, but she was insistent. She didn't want to be alone, even for a few minutes. She followed him up the stairs, close on his heels all the way. He left the door open after they entered. She smiled to herself. He wasn't taking any chances — he didn't want anyone to think there was any "funny business" going on.

He gathered up some food and blankets, then made her sit on the steps while he went downstairs to "see to the truck." This time he wouldn't take no for an answer. Lana paled slightly at his words, knowing that what he had to do was remove the bloody blankets from the back and wash George's blood away with a hose.

George. Her heart twisted painfully as she thought of him, lying cold and alone in some distant part of the hospital. It wasn't fair, she thought bitterly. Grief and frustration welled up inside her, like a volcano which was about to erupt. She wanted to stomp her feet and wail like a child. It just wasn't *fair*.

When RJ returned from his gruesome task, he found her sitting with her head on her knees, arms wrapped around her legs. She looked up at the sound of his footsteps. Her face was red from weeping. She sniffled and wiped her eyes as he held out his hand to her. Wordlessly, she reached up and took it, allowed herself to be pulled up and escorted to the truck.

He opened the door for her, then closed it after she had climbed in. It took a moment for her to realize that he was still standing there, looking down at her through the glass. She turned and peered up at him, into his face — a face so full of love and misery that she wanted to turn away again. But she didn't.

RJ *loved* her, she realized suddenly. It wasn't a crush or a kind of mindless lust that drove him to the diner day after day.

It was love — for her. She reached up and touched her fingertips to the cool glass of the car window, her eyes on his. She wanted him to love her today, she *needed* it today. Because after Mother died, all the love in her life would be gone. *Mal, Kathy, Nate, George...Mother.* She could count on the fingers of one hand all the people who had loved her during her life, and all those people were gone. Except for RJ, the one she never would have counted to begin with.

She smiled at him, a sad smile, and he smiled in return.

The streets of Angel River were deserted on that late spring afternoon. It was like a ghost town, Lana thought. She knew that by now everyone in town must have heard about George's accident, and that he had died at the hospital. Bad news travels faster than whitewater raging down a wild river. Lana hoped that people were crying for George, that they were shedding tears for the life that had been lost so senselessly, for the friend who had been taken without warning.

They crossed the Main Street bridge and turned right onto River Road. What most people in town usually referred to as "the river" was actually a small clearing near a picturesque curve in the tiny tributary known as Angel River. Families picnicked there on Saturday afternoons; teenagers used it as a Lover's Lane on Saturday nights. That was where Lana thought they were headed. But to her surprise, RJ passed the lane that would take them there, and headed farther down the road, into the woods.

"Where are we going?" she asked.

"I want to show you something."

He drove almost to the end of the small road. The river twisted and turned to her right, disappearing and then reappearing through the woods. Eventually RJ turned right, drove through a clearing that looked like it hadn't seen human traffic in a hundred years. On the other side of the clearing, the woods opened up, and the river appeared before her, like magic. RJ stopped the truck in the grass beyond the woods and got out.

He opened her door and smiled at her. "Come on," he said.

She got out slowly, thinking of stories she'd heard about stupid girls who went into the woods with men and never came out again. "What about the food?" she asked, gesturing back inside.

He shook his head. "We'll be right back."

His smile reassured her. This was RJ, after all. She'd known him all her life, and he loved her. He held out his hand and she took it unquestioningly, allowing herself to be led down a winding path through the woods.

It was almost sunset, and the cool dark of the woods was soothing, reminding her of the time they had read Robert Frost in English class.

"The woods are lovely, dark and deep," RJ said suddenly, surprising her.

"I was just thinking of that poem," she said. "It's one of my favorites."

"Mine too," he confessed. Then, giving her a bashful look, he recited the next lines, "But I have promises to keep. And miles to go before I sleep."

"Miles to go before I sleep," Lana echoed softly. Her eyes welled with tears, and she blinked. She didn't want to break down again.

"You always have miles to go, don't you?" RJ asked. She stole a glance at him, trying to gauge what he was thinking about. But his eyes were fixed straight ahead, and he held her hand loosely, easily. She couldn't read any hidden agenda on his face, but she didn't know how to answer the question.

"No more than most folks, I guess," she said finally.

He shook his head. "No, I think you do — I think you walk farther and try harder and want more than most people," he said. Now he looked at her. "More than most people in this town, at any rate."

"You mean, more than most of the *poor* people in this town," she answered bitterly. She surprised herself with her own fervor. "I want the same as the rich people want, but I have to work harder for it. And even then I may never get it."

"Oh, you'll do all right," he said easily. "You're going to college, then you'll get a good job and marry some nice fella." A wistful tone crept into his voice. "I think you'll have everything you're wanting — you'll have to work hard for it, but in the end it will all be there for you."

She looked at him curiously. "Do you really think so?"

He squeezed her hand and smiled down at her. "Yep."

She shook her head in slow amazement. She had known this man almost all her life, and today she had seen a side of him that she would never have imagined existed.

RJ stopped suddenly and looked around. "I think this is it," he said.

Lana looked, but she didn't see anything — just leaves and trees on all sides of her. It didn't look any different than the woods they had been walking through. "This is what?" she asked.

He pointed, and suddenly she saw what he was talking about. It was a large rock, flat on the top, lying low to the ground. It must have been six feet long. It was unusual-looking, out here in the woods, and certainly impressive in its size, but she didn't know what the big deal was supposed to be.

He spoke again, saving her from asking him. "The first Fitzgerald born in this country was born right there."

"Really?" Lana tried to muster some enthusiasm for the subject.

"The Fitzgeralds founded this town, you know," he said earnestly.

She smiled ironically. "How could I forget? Your mother does a pretty good job of reminding everyone."

He scratched the back of his head, embarrassed, and Lana felt like a jerk for what she'd said. "Yeah," RJ said, "she's pretty, um, *enthusiastic* about our family's history."

Enthusiastic, Lana thought. That was a nice way of putting it.

RJ kept talking. "She's harmless, you know — my mom, I mean. She's just been through a lot in her life, and it's made her kind of unusual."

Lana nodded. "Unusual" was an understatement in her opinion, but she didn't feel like mentioning that.

"Anyway, I thought you might like to see this. Nobody knows about it except for my mom and me. It's kind of a special place. I haven't been here in years, though."

Lana released RJ's hand and walked over to the rock. It was unusual, as he'd said — special, in a way. If the story was true, she thought skeptically. The first Fitzgerald, grandson of the man who'd founded their town of Angel River, was born right here. She squatted down, touching the cool hardness of the rock, breathing in the smell of the woods — dark and leafy and sweet. What would it be like to give birth here, to feel that pain and fear and wonderment in this foreign land, deep in the darkness of the woods?

Lana turned and looked up at RJ. "They came over after the Civil War, didn't they?"

RJ lit up, gratified that she was interested in his story. He nodded emphatically. "It was 1865. My ancestor — his name was Gerald Fitzgerald — came over here with his two daughters. The older one was — well, you know." He blushed.

"Pregnant," Lana supplied.

"Right." RJ blushed deeper, then shuffled his feet and went on quickly. "His daughters were Melinda and Angelica. Melinda was the older one. She was in the family way. Angelica was younger, but people said she was special. She had a power."

"She was visited by angels," Lana said, recalling the detail from stories she'd heard in her childhood.

RJ hunkered down next to her. "So they said. She was the one who delivered Melinda's baby. They ended up settling here. They built the little house where my mother still lives, and they started farming. Just enough to get by, you know? But once word got out about Angelica's gift, people started coming to see her. They'd ask her to bless their children, that sort of thing. Some of the people who came to see her ended up settling here, and eventually there was a town. And they called it Angel River."

"In honor of Angelica's gift."

"That's right."

Lana smiled. It was a sweet story, and she was glad that he'd told her. She looked up to find RJ staring at her.

"What?" she asked self-consciously.

"Your face — " he reached out as if to touch her cheek, but his hand hung in mid-air. "For a second you looked…almost happy."

She stared at him, then impulsively reached out and took his hand, placing his palm flat on her cheek. He looked uncertain, scared almost, at this new and intimate contact between them. Before she knew what she was doing, she leaned over and kissed him.

His lips were soft, and cool with the evening air, but they warmed quickly under her own. He pulled away suddenly, looking worried. "No — " he said.

"Yes," she answered and kissed him again, deeper this time. She could feel the hesitation in him, the worry that he was doing something wrong. She knew he was thinking that he was too old for her, that she'd suffered a terrible loss today, with another one waiting just around the corner. He was thinking that he should stop her, that he should take her home, let her regain her wits. But he was also thinking that it felt so good to kiss her, that he had wanted to kiss her for so long, for so many years. And here they were, alone in this place.

He was so transparent, Lana thought. She could read him so easily. She wanted to laugh with triumph when he finally put his hands on her shoulders, gripping her with barely-concealed desire. Fate might sweep like a hurricane through her life, stealing away all her loved ones and leaving her bruised and gasping in its wake, but here was something she could do, something she could control, something she could conquer.

But Fate had the last laugh. Standing on a darkened street corner three months later, alone except for the unplanned life growing inside her, Lana's lips tightened with bitterness. She had been so close to getting out, so close to escaping to college and moving toward the life she'd always dreamed of, and then *this* had happened.

And she wanted this baby — that was the real irony of it. When she had realized she was pregnant, she had been ecstatically happy. It didn't make sense. While she was counting down every breath she took in this town, at the same time she was thanking God for giving her a baby. She couldn't wait for it to be born, to hold it, to kiss its little feet and hands. Someone to love, she thought, and someone to love me.

So the question became, what did she do? She was alone, she was poor, she was unmarried, and she was pregnant. She had no parents or family to go to. She had her high school diploma, the suitcase at her feet, and a few dollars in her pocket. That was it.

Except for RJ.

RJ, who had been her salvation on the day that George had been killed, who had made love to her with such an enticing combination of reticence and ardor, who had held her chastely and let her cry on the day her mother had finally died.

Lana watched him across the street, hard at work in the garage. He took a lot of pride in his work, and he was good at what he did. She wondered if he would ever consider moving out of Angel River…maybe getting a job someplace else, like maybe Georgia….

She shook her head. She had to stop these wild flights of fancy. What was she planning to do? Marry RJ, have her baby, and still go to college? Girls like her didn't do things like that.

No, if she told RJ about the baby, they would have to get married. And if they got married, she was bound to stay in Angel River. She wouldn't have to stop dreaming, but her dreams would have to get smaller. A house instead of the place over the garage. A few more children, maybe a car of her own. She could keep working. Maybe RJ would own his own garage some day, you could never tell.

Did she love RJ? Lana asked herself the question for the hundredth time. No, was the answer. But she liked him a lot now. She felt safe with him. She knew he would not hurt her or allow her to be hurt, if it was in his power to stop it.

And what were her options? She had money in her pocket

for a bus ticket out of town. If she took that bus, where would she go? What would she do about her baby? She knew there were places she could go, homes for unwed mothers. But she shivered at the image that conjured up — long dark hallways, cold rough sheets, hard-faced nurses with coarse, unkind hands. There would be the discomfort of pregnancy, the pain of childbirth, and then what? Give her baby up for adoption? Give up the chance to hear it laugh, to watch it take its first, toddling steps?

Of course, there were other options for girls in her position. She had heard it whispered about in the bathrooms at school. There were people who could take care of these things — illegally, it was true. But what kind of an option was that? Knitting needles, clothes hangers. Pain, possible infection, sickness, maybe even death. And what about this child that she loved so much?

No. She shook her head stubbornly. She would just as soon cut off her right arm as give up this child — whether it was to strangers to raise or to that other, more sinister, option.

And given all that, there really wasn't a choice, was there?

She looked up and down the empty street. This was her home, after all. She'd been born here, raised here, lived and loved and lost here.

And it was here that she would raise her own child. In Angel River.

Lana leaned down and picked up her suitcase. She squared her shoulders, gripped the handle, and nodded resolutely. She had made her decision.

She took a deep breath and crossed the street.

CHAPTER EIGHTEEN

KATE AWOKE TO A LOW knocking. She decided to ignore it and shifted a little under the soft feather quilt, searching for sleep. But the knock was repeated, and she came more fully awake. The second knock was followed by the sound of the door opening. Then there was a muffled murmur, a brief exchange of syllables spoken too softly for her to understand.

Finally there was the click of the door latch and the gentle movement of the bed as Reed leaned over and nuzzled her ear. "Breakfast is served," he whispered.

Kate smiled and opened her eyes. "But I'm still sleeping," she protested as she rolled over onto her back.

"Well, wake up!" He bent his head to kiss her, but she clapped a hand over her mouth and shook her head in objection.

"Uh-uh," she said, her voice finger-muffled. "I haven't brushed yet!"

"Too bad." He moved her hand and pressed his lips briefly to hers. He gave a mock grimace, and she pushed him away playfully.

"Well, you're minty fresh, anyway," she said. She pushed herself up to sit, keeping the covers up under her armpits for the sake of modesty.

"I used your toothbrush," Reed explained. He pulled the

drapes back, letting the strong mid-morning sun come tumbling into the room. Kate held up her hand to shade her eyes. "Hope you don't mind."

"Oh, I think I'll come to terms with it eventually," she said dryly. A dining cart was in the middle of the room. The sunlight glinted like diamonds off the high-arched lids of the silver serving dishes. Something smelled phenomenal. "Who was at the door?"

"*Whom* do you think?"

"Room service?"

He smiled. "No, it was the two hookers and the midget from last night. They finally decided to leave."

"There's no need for sarcasm," Kate said. Then she grinned and blushed at the same time. "It *was* kind of a wild night, wasn't it?"

"I think it's safe to say that it was," he said.

Their eyes met, and Kate shivered, remembering the intensity of it. Their lovemaking last night had been just that — the deepest expression of their feelings for one another. It was as if every time he moved inside her, he was whispering that he loved her; and every time she rose to meet him, she was doing the same. Later they had turned playful and robust, each trying to outdo the other in inventiveness and enthusiasm.

She smiled again. "Anyone call security?"

"What, with noise complaints?" She nodded. "No," he said regretfully.

Kate batted her eyes. "Well, we'll have to try harder tonight."

"Hell with that," he said, moving toward the bed. "Why wait for tonight?"

She held up her hands. "Oh, no! Not until I have a shower and a cup of coffee!"

"And?"

"And not until I brush my teeth!"

"Thank God!"

She threw a pillow at him.

❧

Breakfast was enormous, and they ate with enthusiasm. Fresh fruit, omelets, pancakes, and sausage, with coffee and fresh-squeezed juice — they had no problem finishing it all. Afterwards, Kate took advantage of the shower while Reed cleaned up and wheeled the cart into the hallway. The thought of him fiddling with the silverware and bundling up napkins had her grinning under the cool stream of water that was raining down on her. Why did the idea of this Wall Street tycoon doing simple domestic chores make her want to laugh?

Kate couldn't remember ever having been this happy. There was a peacefulness riding high in her heart that she had never felt before. He loved her. He *loved* her. And she…God, she loved him too. That delicious feeling that she remembered from her Angel River days had been real, not a lie her heart had told her. It had been real, and she had been right to trust it.

After a while, Reed opened the bathroom door and poked his head in. "Hey, lady," he called. "Don't use up all the water! You're not the only one on this boat who needs to bathe."

She turned off the tap and reached for a towel. "We *are* in the middle of the ocean, you know," she said. "Water, water everywhere!"

"And not a drop to drink. Or shower with. Come on, hurry up. It's my turn!"

❧

Reed had used Kate's laptop to log onto his email, and had

forgotten to log off. Good grief, Kate thought with a smile. First my toothbrush, now my computer. Is there no end to this man's intrusion into my life?

She sincerely hoped not.

Kate had a brief but almost overwhelming urge to snoop through Reed's email. It was so tempting — it was all laid out there in front of her. Maybe there were some old messages to Heather, Kate thought with a smile. Maybe there were other emails to other girlfriends. Hmmm…

She started to close the browser when a name caught her eye. *Her* name. That couldn't be right. Why would Reed have an email file labeled with her last name? She squeezed her eyes shut, then opened them and looked again. *Doyle.* It was.

Kate told herself it must be a coincidence, but a dark gray suspicion was beginning to creep in to her sunny little world. It was with a trembling hand that she moved the cursor over the file with her name on it. She watched it light up, and she clicked. Her heart froze. The long list of messages in the folder made her feel physically ill. She scrolled down… down… they went back months, years. Oh God.

When Reed came out of the shower she was still reading. He was smiling, his hair was mussed, and he had a towel around his waist. She noticed dimly that he looked incredibly sexy. The observation didn't make her feel any better.

"You had me investigated," she said. She heard the helplessness in her own voice, the anger and the sadness.

He stopped short and stared at her. The smile faded from his face.

His lips parted as if to speak, but she cut him off. "You hired somebody to investigate me. Why?"

Reed cautioned himself to stay calm. He had known this

was coming; it was time to face up to the actions he'd taken. Nothing had happened that couldn't be fixed. "Because nothing in my life had been right since you left. Even after I made my money — even after I had made *millions, Kate* — I still wasn't happy. I needed *you.* I've always needed you."

"I think you'd better tell me everything."

Reed swallowed. "It was just after I broke things off with Heather," he said. He held up his hand as she started to speak. "I know how bad that sounds, but believe me, it wasn't like I hadn't been thinking about you. Every woman I met, I compared to you, and I found them lacking. I became obsessed. I was tired of not being able to fall in love. I had to find out if I was really missing *you,* or just some memory of you. So I hired Roberts to find you."

He walked over to the window and looked out over the ocean. "At first it was only to find out where you were — if you were married, what you were doing with yourself. I didn't even know if you were alive...I didn't know anything. So Roberts found you. And for years, I did nothing but get him to keep tabs on you. I told myself that I wanted to make sure you were okay, to find out if I could help you in any way, like I had with my mother. But I think I really wanted to make sure you were still single, and I wanted to know if you were as miserably alone as I was."

That struck a chord with Kate, which she tried to ignore. She didn't want to sympathize with his motives. "Go on," she said.

He turned around. "At the beginning of the year, Roberts found out that the man you had been seeing — that Levin guy — he had proposed to you. And suddenly I was frantic. I was about to lose you forever, or so it seemed to me. So I decided to do something about it. It took me a while to set it up, but finally

I had everything in place. I had bought the *Sweet William* only a few years ago, and she'd been sailing for — "

"Wait, what?" Kate looked around, astonished. She hadn't had any idea how hugely wealthy Reed had become. "The *William* is yours? You *own* it?"

Reed nodded, for the first time appearing somewhat sheepish. "And one or two others. Phoenix Waters is one of my companies."

Kate sat silent. This was too much. "So my ticket from Mrs. Westlake, that was your doing? You set that up?"

"She's a friend of a friend," he said. "I told her it was a surprise for an old sweetheart, and she was very agreeable. She thought it was sweet, actually — "

Reed stopped talking. Kate was shaking her head. "How can you sound so calm? How can you stand there and tell me all of this so matter-of-factly?" Her voice cracked, like her world was cracking, and she turned away.

The phone on the nightstand started to ring. They both ignored it.

"Katie…." He wanted to take her in his arms.

She held out her hand to stop him, and raised her voice to carry over the ringing telephone. "Don't. Don't touch me." She started getting dressed. "Your relationship with Heather ends, so you track me down, and find out all about me. Then, instead of getting in touch with me, you wait. Why? What were you waiting for? And for how long, exactly? Two years? Three?"

She didn't wait for him to respond. She was on a roll now, pumping up her anger. Anger was better than heartache. She raised her voice again — this time just because she wanted to.

"You wait and watch and find out what I'm doing. You find out that I'm seeing someone seriously." She glared over her shoulder at him as she looked for her shoes. "You arrange this 'accidental' reunion. For your own amusement, I can only assume — "

"That's enough!" He pulled on a robe, feeling vulnerable. "Yes, everything you said is true. Except that I didn't arrange this because I wanted some sort of amusing diversion."

The phone stopped ringing abruptly. His voice seemed very loud in the sudden silence. "When I found out that you were getting married, I was frantic. I thought that I had missed my chance to become part of your life again. I thought that if only we could see each other, spend time together, maybe I could…."

"What?"

"Make you love me again."

She seized on the phrase. "Make. God, that speaks volumes about you, Reed. I don't want to be *made* to love anyone. But you think that you have the right to arrange this meeting, and then have the nerve to act angry with me for leaving you?"

The phone sounded again. "I *was* angry!" Reed shouted over the shrilling. "And uncertain, and confused! None of it was an act!"

Kate threw up her hands, started toward the nightstand. "Damn phone!"

"To hell with the phone!" He picked it up and hurled it against the wall. The plastic casing shattered.

Kate jumped, shocked at the savagery of his actions.

He continued to shout. "I'm still angry. You had to leave town because of your sister. I understand that. But let's not forget that for years afterwards *you* knew where *I* was, and you never said anything. You could have called, you could have written — "

"I did call; I did write!" Kate spat. "Your grandmother told me that you never wanted to speak to me again!"

His anger seemed to evaporate into shock. Color drained from his face. He looked stricken. "That's not true. She would never — she *knew* how I felt about you. She knew how miserable I was when you left."

There was a knock at the door. It made them both jump. The knock became an insistent rapping.

A voice came muffled through the door. "Sorry to disturb you, ma'am, but there's an urgent phone call."

Kate stalked across the room and jerked open the door. A steward stood there, cordless phone in hand. He apologized again for interrupting. "It's a satellite call, ma'am. They say it's an emergency."

Emergency? Kate took the phone from his hand and put it to her ear. "Hello?" She paused. "Dad? Is that you?"

Another pause, longer this time. Her face paled.

"Oh my God."

Reed stepped close. "What is it? What's wrong?"

"It's my mother," she whispered. "She's in the hospital. They think she had a heart attack."

Reed took the phone from her. "Mr. Doyle? This is Reed Fitzgerald. I don't know if you remember me...Yes, that's right. From Angel River. Kate and I met accidentally on the ship.... Yes, quite a coincidence. What hospital is your wife in? Georgetown University Hospital? All right, I'm going to give you the number of my personal assistant. Are you ready to take this down?"

He recited a phone number. "After you and I hang up, wait ten minutes and call him. That will give me a chance to call him first. I am going to tell him that he is to get a hold of the best cardiologist in the business, and that he is to help you in any way you need it. You spend the next ten minutes finding out everything you can about your wife's condition. Any information you can give to Jerry will help him when he tracks down the doctor. You understand? All right. Kate and I will leave right away. We should be there in…." He checked his watch. "Eight or nine hours. Kate will call you once we're underway."

He gave the phone back to Kate.

"Dad?" Kate said. "I'll see you real soon. Are Julia and Sam there with you? Then you're not alone? Good. I'll see you in a few hours." She paused. "Tell Mom…" Her voice broke. "Tell her I love her, and that she has to hang in there, okay? Tell her that I love her and I'll see her soon. Okay. I love you, Dad. Bye."

Kate handed the phone back to Reed, then covered her eyes with her hands and stifled a sob.

"Hey, none of that," Reed said. "She's going to be fine. And anyway, you have packing to do. I want to be off this boat in half an hour."

He turned to the steward, who had retreated to a discreet and respectful distance. "Can I call out on this thing?"

"Of course, sir."

"Good."

Reed punched numbers furiously. "Jerry? Jerry, *pick up*; it's me. He's the only person I know who still has an answering machine," he told Kate tightly. "And thank God he does." He spoke into the phone again. "Jerry, I know you're there."

A second later he heard his assistant's voice on the other end of the line. "Hello, Jerry. I have an emergency on my hands." He briefly explained the situation. "I need you to find the best cardio man in the country, and get him to DC as fast as possible. Mr. Doyle is going to be calling you on this line in a minute, so you'll have to make your outgoing calls on your cell phone. I don't want that man to get a busy signal. Find out all you can from Mr. Doyle, then give all the information to whatever genius doctor you track down. You give the matter of Mrs. Doyle's health your full attention, and *carte blanche* on whatever expenditures are necessary to make this thing happen. Understand? Good. I'm on my way. We should be there in eight or so hours." He paused. "What? No, don't waste your time on that. I'm capable of making my own travel arrangements. All right, Jerry, get cracking. And thanks."

He clicked off and looked around again for the steward. "Would you get the captain for me, please?"

"Certainly, sir." The steward disappeared down the corridor, visibly relieved to leave the emotional atmosphere behind him.

"Reed, you're not going to try to get the captain to take us back to Bonaire?"

"Of course not," Reed said. He was already dialing the next number. "I'm going to tell him that in half an hour, a helicopter will be landing on deck."

⁘⤳⋙⊱⟢

Reed helped Kate to pack a few essentials and then sent a steward to do the same for him. "I'll have them send the rest of our things back to DC," he told her.

Less than an hour later, a small helicopter did indeed land on the upper deck of the *Sweet William*. Kate and Reed were ready, and they boarded quickly. Word had spread rapidly through the ship that something unusual was going on, and a crowd had gathered behind the security barricades. They waved and shouted as the aircraft lifted off.

Kate watched the ship get smaller and smaller as they sped to Aruba, the closest island with an airport. She thought briefly about Heather and her friends. There hadn't been time for her to say goodbye.

At the Aruba airport, there was a small plane waiting to fly them to Washington.

"We'll make a short stop for refueling in Miami, and there'll be a car at Reagan Airport to take us to the hospital," Reed explained as they settled in. "We may just set a world record for traveling from Bonaire to DC."

Once they were in the air, the pilot got on the intercom and announced that it was now safe to use the phone located at the back of the plane.

"Call Jerry's cell," Reed suggested, and wrote down the number. "If I know him, he'll be at the hospital by now, with your father."

Kate wasn't sure if she'd be able to get through, but Jerry answered his phone promptly, sounding pleasant and competent. When she told him who she was, he immediately turned the phone over to her father.

"Dad?" Kate said anxiously. "How is she?"

"Still critical," her father replied, "but the doctor that Jerry contacted arrived a few minutes ago, and he's with her right now."

Kate could hear the relief in her father's voice.

"What's the doctor like?" she asked.

"Typical medico: aloof and noncommittal; but there's something about him I trust."

"That's good to hear. How's Julia holding up?"

"She's shaken, but she's a strong person. Both my girls are."

"We get that from our parents," Kate said tremulously.

There was an emotional pause.

"I love you, Dad," Kate said. "She's going to be all right."

"I know. I love you too. See you soon."

"See you soon. Bye."

Kate hung up, then bit her lip to get control of herself. Exhaustion rolled over her like a fog.

As she wearily returned to the front of the cabin, she noticed for the first time the luxury of her surroundings. This was no ordinary little plane. The twenty or so seats were wide and covered with leather. The carpet was thick and eggshell white.

"This is some plane," she said as she slipped back into her seat.

Reed looked around, as if seeing it for the first time. "How's your mom?"

"Still critical, but the doctor Jerry found just got there, so Dad is feeling much better. He sounds better, too. Julia is with him, and they'll hold each other up until we get to them."

"That's a relief."

She looked at him, impulsively reached out and took his hand, pressing it to her cheek.

"Thank you," she said firmly. "I don't know what I would have done if you hadn't been there."

"You would have raised hell until somebody found a way for you to get back to Aruba."

"That's not what I meant, and you know it." She didn't let go of his hand. "I don't know what I would have done if you hadn't been there *for me.*"

He squeezed her fingers. "I'm glad I could be. And…I'm very sorry for the way I acted earlier. I hope you know that I would never, *never* purposely hurt you — emotionally or otherwise."

"Of course I know that. And I'm sorry, too."

"What do you have to apologize for?"

"Being a hypocrite, I guess. I was so angry with you because you had kept something very important from me. But I've been keeping something from you, too."

"You were under no obligation to tell me about what's-his-name," Reed protested. "You don't have anything to apologize for."

Kate smiled faintly. "His name is Mark, and I'm not talking about him." She paused. "Reed, I know why your mother left town and never came back."

"What?"

"I've known for a long time, and I've been torturing myself these past three days trying to decide whether or not I should tell you. I was afraid it would hurt you. But I've realized during the last hour that no matter how painful the truth is, lies always hurt more in the end. I don't want there to be any secrets between us anymore."

"Neither do I," he said quietly. "I think you'd better tell me."

Kate looked into his eyes for a long moment. Then, sending up a quick prayer for strength, she took a deep breath and started talking.

⁂

Two days after the Doyles had left Angel River, Kate tried to call Reed. By that time, the family had settled into a hotel. Julia had seen a doctor, her father was ready to start at his new law firm, and her mother was looking at houses.

She picked up the phone at precisely four o'clock, knowing that was the time Reed usually got home on Wednesdays, since he didn't work that afternoon. She thought he would be there, and she was looking forward to hearing his voice. Even forty-eight hours apart seemed way too long.

But it wasn't Reed's voice Kate heard on the other end of the line; it was his grandmother's.

"Reed's not here," Pleasance had stated coldly.

"Oh." Kate caught her breath, trying not to let disappointment show in her tone. "Do you know when he'll be home? I really need to speak with him."

"He's at Vera Milner's house. They're studying together," was the reply.

Kate suspected it was a lie and ignored the obvious implication that there was more going on than studying. "All right," she said politely. "Would you please tell him I called? I'll call again tomorrow at four."

Pleasance had hung up without saying she would pass on the message. When Kate did call back the next day, there was no answer.

After that, she called every day, sometimes more than once. But she could not get Reed himself on the phone. Either there was no answer, she got a busy signal, or his grandmother was there to say brusquely that Reed wasn't available, or that he didn't want to speak to her.

She tried writing letters. The first three or four went unanswered. After that they started coming back marked "Return to Sender."

This went on for weeks. Kate's parents complained about how much the phone bill would be, but she didn't care. She wanted Reed to know why she left, where she was, and when she was coming back.

One night she got Pleasance on the phone, and she refused to be put off.

"I'm sure he's there," Kate said. "It's eleven o'clock at night! He never stays out that late."

"Plenty of things have changed since you've been around,

girlie," Grand said. "And there were plenty of things going on before you left that you didn't know about. Now stop calling. I've given him your messages. If he wants to talk to you, he'll call. But don't hold your breath." She hung up.

Kate stared at the phone, desperate and suddenly furious. Either she was being lied to or Reed was a coward who refused to tell her himself that he didn't want to speak to her. Well, she wasn't giving up this time until she got an answer directly from him, one way or the other.

She dialed again and listened to the phone ring. Ten rings… twenty…thirty…on it went. Each ring was like a knife in her heart. Pleasance could have unplugged the phone. Well, then, she'd let it ring a hundred times, and if it didn't work, she'd call Mr. Donovan who lived down the road and say it was an emergency, could he please drive over to the Fitzgerald place and see if everything was all right? Or she'd call the police, or the fire department, and say there'd been an accident. Or —

"Are you stupid or just rude? I told you not to call anymore!"

Kate suppressed a triumphant yell. Score one for me, she thought. I got through again.

She knew she had to be tactful, to keep Pleasance on the line. "I'm sorry for being such a pest." *Liar.* "I know that Reed is angry with me, but if I could just speak to him, I know I could explain everything. He loves me. I know he'd forgive me."

But his grandmother refused to be mollified. "If you want him to keep loving you, stay away from him!"

"I don't understand. What do you mean?"

There was a pause. Then: "How much do you think he loves his mother, since she ran off and left him?" A smiling note had crept into Pleasance's voice.

"But this is different! I didn't — "

"Neither did she!"

Kate drew an exasperated breath. To hell with being polite. "If you have something to say to me, then say it. You're not going to scare me off with insinuations."

"All right, I'll tell you plain, like you ask, and no more beating around the bush!

"Reed's mother was a treacherous snake. She tempted my son and when he was dead, she tried to take my grandson away from me. As if I would let her!

"So I told her, 'Sure, honey, you go look for work. But leave the baby here so you won't have to worry about him. Once you're settled, why then you can come back and get him!'

"She was so grateful for my help! She couldn't thank me enough for supporting her through all that had been going on. She left at night, took the bus to the next town to try to find work and a place to stay. She called almost every day. I laid my trap — set it up real nice.

"First time she called, I said the baby was fine. 'He's just got a little fever. Nothing serious.'

"Next time I said, 'Just a little cough. Doctor said there's nothing to worry about.'

"Finally, I told her he had died. It was easy, really. 'I'm so sorry, dear. Yes, we buried him already. We didn't think it would be fit to wait. No, there's no headstone. No place to put flowers, no reason to even come back. In fact, the folks in town aren't too kindly disposed to you right now, what with you leaving so soon after the baby had been born. They've been saying some nasty things about you, I'm afraid. I tried to tell them different, but of course they didn't want to hear it! If you came back now, it wouldn't be to a warm reception. There, there, dear, you're young. You can marry again and have more children….'

"But I'll never have more grandchildren. Reed is the only one. And I will not let you get your clutches into him!"

Kate's ears echoed with the insane tale that had been spun for her. She hadn't realized that hatred like that which lived inside Pleasance was possible. Summoning her strength, she swallowed and said, "But I only want to talk to him, to explain why I left. Afterwards, if he doesn't want to see me — " Her voice broke at the thought. "If he doesn't want to see me again, I'll live with it. But won't you please just let me talk to him?"

"No! I won't give you the chance to beguile him with pretty words!" Grand's voice again turned sly. "What would it do to your family if a rumor started that one of the beautiful and chaste Doyle girls was going to have a baby?"

Kate gasped. "How did you know?"

"Oh come, dear, haven't you figured out by now that nothing goes on in this town without me knowing it? What do you think it would do to Reed if it turned out that the pregnant sister was you — who he thinks he loves so dearly?"

"You'd say that? You'd lie to Reed and hurt him just to keep him from me?"

"A little hurt is better than a big one! He'll get over you, *Kathleen,* and he'll go on to better things. Better women. If you stop calling, stop writing, I'll say nothing. Reed will be angry and hurt for a while, but he'll get over it. But if you try to contact him, I swear I will tell him that your family had to leave town because his precious Katie is a slut!"

"Why are you doing this?" Kate cried tearfully, her dignity gone. "Why do you hate me so much? What have I ever done to you that you should hate me this way?"

"Nothing yet. But like I always say, an ounce of prevention is worth a pound of cure!" Grand slammed down the phone.

Kate sat stunned, tears streaming down her face. She had lost, and she knew it. The woman was clearly crazy. She would spread all sorts of rumors, with no thought of what it would do to Reed or to Kate's family. Just to keep Kate away from her grandson.

When I go back, I will put it right, Kate vowed. When I go back, I will put it right.

"But we never went back. My parents decided that DC was better for us than Virginia, especially Angel River." Kate had avoided Reed's face as she had told the story, but now she forced herself to look.

It was devoid of expression.

"That explains a lot," he said carefully. "It explains an awful lot. It never made sense to me that you…." He trailed off as he looked away from her. "I just knew that you had more class than that, I guess."

Kate watched him, waiting. She could imagine him looking this way at board meetings, with lawyers telling him that the stocks were down, they should cut their losses and get out before they went down with the ship. He uncrossed and then re-crossed his legs, straightening the crease in his trousers, maybe preparing to tell the attorneys that they would ride out the storm, that he had faith in the company and knew it would work out. Had what she'd said about his mother even sunk in? She laid her hand on his arm. "Reed," she said softly. He turned and looked at her. "Did you hear what I just said? Your mother thinks — she thinks you *died*. She didn't desert you when you were a baby. You weren't abandoned. She doesn't know you're alive."

He nodded. "I know. I mean — I realize that now. And that

makes sense, too." He looked at her, but his eyes were far away. "I guess I should be angry at my grandmother?"

It puzzled her that he stated it as a question. "I don't know," she said simply. "*I* was angry with her, for a long time. First I was scared, then I was angry. I think I still am, but on your behalf. I mean — she did rob you of your mother."

Reed waved a hand dismissively. "Oh, I don't know. I think that's putting it a little melodramatically, don't you? She did what she thought was right. She had a hard life, Kate. There were disappointments, hardships…things you and I can't even know about."

Kate shook her head, feeling a surge of anger at his unreasonable calm. "But that was her excuse for everything! She was antisocial — but it's okay because she had a hard life. She never had a kind word for anyone — but it's okay, she had a hard life. Well, lots of people have lives harder than hers. *Heather* had a hard life and look how great she turned out!" Kate hadn't intended to thrust Heather's perfection in Reed's face again, but that didn't make it any less true.

"My grandmother *raised* me, Kate!" he flared, finally giving her the emotion she was looking for. "She fed me, clothed me, put up with all my rebellious teenage bullshit…she took care of me when no one else would!"

"But she told your mother you had died. Your mother never even had a chance to do those things for you!"

"How do you know that's even true?" Reed asked. He dragged a hand through his hair, tugged at the collar of his shirt. Agitation showed in every ragged breath he took, in every trembling motion he made. "My grandmother, she — she always had a weird hatred of your family. She respected your father, I know that, but she hated him, too. And she was afraid of him. Maybe she just wanted to drive you away, maybe it was just a stupid, outrageous lie that she told you."

Kate shook her head gently. "I don't think so," she said. "I think that your grandmother was a lonely, bitter old woman, and she wanted you all to herself. I think that she didn't care if she deprived you of your mother. I think she thought she could raise you better than anyone else could, and that she wanted you all to herself. And maybe that is an excuse, of sorts. If nothing else, I guess it's something we can sympathize with. I don't think you should hate her, Reed, but don't make excuses for the things she did wrong."

Reed turned away and looked back out the window. Far below, the water glittered like quicksilver, with cloud shadows making cool islands on the rippling surface. That was how his heart felt. Cold, and sharp, glittering with icy pinpoints of pain. And remote, like the blue sky above.

"Maybe I'm too much like her, then. Doing the wrong thing for the right reason — or what seems like the right reason. It's difficult sometimes," he said, "so difficult to know what to do, what to feel at any given moment, about any given situation. I love you."

He said it so quietly, so matter-of-factly, that it almost didn't make her heart stop in her chest. Almost.

He turned back to face her. "I have loved you all my life. For the past twenty years, I've been wondering if what I loved was the *idea* of you, instead of the reality. But regardless of that, I've held on to the love I felt. It's been the only constant thing in my life, you know?"

Kate nodded. She understood that, all too well.

He went on. "And now that I've seen you again, I know that what I've felt for you is real. You are every bit as — as magnificent as I remember you. I still love you, Katie, and I'm sorry I lied to you."

"I'm sorry I lied to you, too — or that I didn't tell you everything. I thought I was doing you a favor by keeping it a secret. And then I thought I was doing the right thing by telling you. It's difficult sometimes, like you said, to know what to do, and to do the right thing." She took a deep breath, mustered a tremulous smile. She knew what had to be done, what had to be said. But it was taking more courage than she knew she had. "And I love you, too. But I don't think that you and I — "

"Don't say it."

"I have to. You know it, just like I do. We're not going to work out. Too much time has gone by, too much has happened. We're not going to make it." She fought to hold back tears as she met his eyes. She could see him going cold inside, retreating to whatever safe place he had made for himself. She saw him struggle with it, and it was a struggle for his very own humanity.

Abruptly the cold was replaced by fire, and he reached out and grasped her hands with his. "Please," he said. "Please don't say that, Katie. I'll never find anyone else like you."

"And I'll never find anyone like you, either. But maybe that's not what this is about. Maybe it can't be what this is about. We — both of us — have to find a way to create a future. We've been living in the past too long. And I think — I really do think — that if we hold on to each other, we'll always be living in the past." She started to speak more quickly, forcing the words out so that they tumbled over each other like puppies. "I want a life. I want a family and children of my own. I want to find some fulfillment somewhere — God, anywhere. I need to find some peace."

He reached out a hand and tilted her chin up until their

eyes met. His touch was very gentle. "What do you think you're going to do? Marry that man of yours?"

Kate shook her head. "He's not mine. I never claimed him, really, never wanted him the way I should. I'm going to tell him as soon as possible. It's not fair of me to keep him on the line. He needs to be free, too." She met Reed's gaze with an unwavering stare. "And so, I think, do you."

"Is that what you think you're doing? Setting me free?" He released her chin, dropped his hand back into his lap. "You're condemning me to a life without you."

She shook her head again, more forcefully this time. "I'm not doing anything to you, Reed. I'm just telling you what we both know. You and me — it's not going to work. If we try to force it, we'll only end up hurting each other all over again. And I think we've both had enough of that for one lifetime." She searched his eyes with her own. "Don't you?"

Helplessness welled up in his eyes and was backed up by the pride that she knew so well. "I can't fight you, Katie," he said. "And I won't force myself on you. Like you said, that would only lead to pain for both of us. But won't you think it over? Before you put an end to us, won't you give it a little time? At least until we get to DC and see your family?"

Kate wanted to agree. She wanted to say that she couldn't fight any more either, and that whatever he wanted would be fine with her. God, she was tired. But she shook her head resolutely. "I'm sorry," she said, "but I can't do that. I *won't*. I've had enough indecision to last me a lifetime. I need to follow what is true for me. You and I — we're haunted by too many old ghosts. And I'm tired of what's old and dead and gone. I want what's living. I want a *life*."

Her throat ached with unshed tears. She swallowed over the

pain and gave him a small smile. This decisiveness thing was really fun. She laid her head on his shoulder. "Now let's stop talking about it, okay? I don't think I can bear to talk about it anymore."

He looked at her for a moment, then put his arm around her, and she nestled her head against his chest, where it had always fit so well. Together, they looked out the window, watching the blue sky go by, counting the wispy clouds.

CHAPTER NINETEEN

I<small>T WAS A SHOCK TO</small> the system, coming from the warm, humid air of the tropics to the dry, frigid cold of DC in February. The sky was blue here, too, but in Aruba it had been an embracing blue, vibrant and welcoming. Here it was a pale, distant turquoise, with a lemon-colored sun just starting its drop towards the horizon.

February was an unpredictable month for DC, weather-wise, and as they tipped their wings over the monuments and started their sharp descent over the Potomac River, Kate counted her blessings that there was no snow or freezing rain to delay their arrival. The plane glided to a smooth stop on the tarmac, where a car and driver were waiting to meet them on the runway. The driver was well-prepared — there were thick wool coats and hot coffee waiting for them.

"Sorry it's not a limo," Reed said as he bundled Kate into the backseat.

"I think I'll survive." Kate managed a small smile as she leaned back against the plush headrest and looked at Reed. She had napped some on the flight from Miami, but she still felt drained. She was grateful for Reed's presence — he felt sturdy and comfortable, and he radiated strength from every pore.

But she could feel him stiffening as they crossed Memorial Bridge. GU Hospital wasn't that far away. They would be with her family soon. What would that be like for him? He hadn't seen her family in twenty years, and he had spent that time blaming them for taking her away. She slipped her hand into his, and he gripped it appreciatively.

It was already late afternoon in DC, and traffic was thickening into rush hour. They passed the Kennedy Center and the Watergate. The weak winter sun glinted off the silver ice that lined the shores of the Potomac. It was a very different body of water than the warm, jewel-toned ocean they had left behind in Aruba.

"DC's a beautiful city," Reed commented.

Kate nodded. "I do love it most of the time," she said. She looked at him curiously. "Have you been here much in the past few years?"

He shook his head. "Only once or twice in the last decade, I guess. I think I was avoiding it."

For some reason that made her laugh. "Because of little old me?" she asked, giving her best Southern belle impression.

He looked serious. "I know it seems silly, but DC's not a big city. I didn't want to just run into you on the street, somewhere. I didn't — I wasn't sure how or if I could handle that. I knew I wanted to see you again, I just — "

"You just wanted to engineer the whole thing, so it could be on your terms." Anger rumbled inside her, like thunder in the distance. But she pushed it aside. There was no sense in being angry over that anymore. She looked over at Reed, and at that moment, the sun dropped behind the steep slope of a hill, throwing the planes of his face into deeply-shadowed sharp relief.

She leaned her head back and looked at him, at the beautiful line of his nose, at the long lashes around his ocean-colored eyes, and she felt a surge of love that she quickly stifled. There was no sense in *that* anymore, either. Love and anger — both had become relatively useless emotions when directed toward him. All she could shoot for now was friendship.

It left her with a hollow feeling inside the pit of her stomach.

It was fully dark by the time the car rolled to a stop in front of Georgetown University Hospital. Kate opened the door and stepped from the warmth of the car into the cold night air. She was grateful to have the borrowed coat, and she pulled it more tightly around her.

Reed got out behind her, and the car was about to pull away when she called out "Wait!" and turned around to get the bag she'd brought with her from the *William*.

Reed gave her a look as she slung the bag over her shoulder. "You know, you can leave that in the car if you want. I'll give you a ride home later."

Kate shook her head. "Thanks, but it's okay." She offered no further explanation, unable to admit that she wanted to be able to make a quick getaway later if necessary. She didn't want to be dependent on Reed to take her home, didn't want to risk the possibility that they'd end up spending the night together.

The car drove off, leaving the two of them in front of the hospital. Reed looked at Kate and saw the worry on her face, the fear. He took her hand and gripped it firmly. She squeezed back.

"Come on," he said. "Let's go."

The hospital managed to be dim, bright, quiet, and buzzing with life all at the same time. They checked in at the front desk to get Kate's mother's room number, then Kate and Reed walked the wide hallways, following signs until they finally found the right floor, and on that floor, the right room. The door was closed. Kate took a breath, pushed it open, and walked in. If she hadn't known Reed was behind her, she didn't know if she would have made it.

Although she was dimly aware that the room was full of people, Kate focused only on her mother's face.

Kathy Duncan Doyle sat up in bed, looking tired and pale, but she was still as pretty as ever. Her dark hair was cut into the same bob that she had worn most of her life. The thick hair had lost some of its shine and was now lined with strands of silver, but it was still beautiful. And her eyes were the same as they'd always been — dark and snapping, full of life.

She was propped up against a mountain of pillows, managing to make her limp hospital gown look classy. She looked like she had just finished laughing at something that Kate's father had said. She was looking up at him with an adoring smile, her eyes crinkling at the corners and her lips slightly parted. She looked sixteen, and she looked sixty. She looked like Mom.

When Kate and Reed entered the room, half a dozen heads swiveled their way. Kathy's face lit up, and she held out her arms. "Sweetheart!" she said. As Kate rushed into her arms, there was a flurry of words spilling out over each other.

"Can't believe you came all the way back — "

"Of course I couldn't stay after I heard — "

"Is this Reed?"

Kate turned around, brushing tears away. Reed was shaking hands with her father, who stood by the bed. It gave her heart a turn to see these two men that she loved so much standing side by side. Kate looked around the room. Julia was sitting in a chair by the bed, Sam stood behind her. She hugged them both, and in answer to her query, they told her that the kids were with

Sam's parents. Then she gave her father a hug and a kiss.

There was a handsome, dark-haired man that she didn't know standing against the wall. "Jerry?" Kate asked tentatively. He smiled and nodded, introducing himself.

"I can't thank you enough for everything," she said. "You're amazing."

He waved away the compliment and turned to have a murmured conversation with Reed. And as he did, Kate saw Mark. He had retreated into a corner, away from the family, but he was here. She stumbled slightly at the sight of him.

"Mark," she said tearfully. "I can't believe you're here."

He stepped forward. Everyone else seemed to turn away slightly, to give them some privacy. "The mother of the woman I love is in the hospital," he said in a low voice. "Where else am I supposed to be?"

Her heart sank. She had thought — hoped — that she would have a few days to collect herself before having this conversation with him. She took a deep breath. "Maybe we should step out into the hallway," she said.

He nodded. She turned and touched her mother's blanketed foot. "I'll be right back, Mom," she said. She was careful not to look at Reed as she led the way out of the room.

Despite her apprehension, Kate couldn't help but smile as she and Mark faced each other in the hallway. Some things never changed. Although it was after six in the evening and he had likely been working since early that morning, Mark was as immaculate as ever, giving the impression that he rolled out of bed coiffed and ironed to perfection every morning. His overcoat was folded over his left arm; his suit looked crisp and fresh and was tailored within an inch of its life. The grey wool scarf that hung around his neck set off his green eyes to good advantage.

Kate's smile faltered. Her mother had once predicted that their children would also have green eyes. Heredity was in their favor, she said.

Heredity. Their children. Hers and Mark's. Kate swallowed.

"I wanted to thank you again for coming today," she said, wishing she didn't sound so formal and distant.

"Like I said, where else would I be?"

Kate nodded. She was stuck for what to say. She felt that she should make some sort of speech. She should say something sensitive and intelligent. She should apologize for not being able to make the commitment he wanted her to make. She should find the words to make all this sound understandable, and maybe even *right*. But all she could do was nod.

Finally, Mark gave some ground. "Did you enjoy your trip?"

It was a good question. Gave her another reason for nodding. "It was lovely," she managed to say.

"You look really beautiful. You're glowing," he said. "I think the sea air did you good."

The wistful note in his voice made her heart twist. "Thank you." She winced at her own words and went on in a rush. "Mark, it's not going to work."

He drew in a sharp breath and looked away. A young couple walked by. The man was holding a flower arrangement with a balloon tied to the top. Mark waited until they had passed, then looked at Kate with sharp eyes. His voice was low and intense. Hurt. *"It's* not going to work? What you really mean is that *I* am not going to work. You don't want *me;* you want *him*." He gestured towards her mother's room, where Reed was. "Isn't that right?"

Kate forced herself not to look away. "He and I — we're not together, not in the way you think."

"Oh no? He brings you all the way here from the Caribbean, and you're trying to tell me you're not together?" Mark turned and walked a few paces away, then turned back sharply. "Who is that guy, anyway?"

"Reed Fitzgerald. We were friends when we were kids."

Mark's eyes narrowed. "Oh, I see. Childhood sweethearts, unexpectedly reunited. Shipboard romance? *Please*," he said disgustedly.

"I know it sounds unlikely. That doesn't mean it's not true." Kate decided that it wasn't the time to bring up that her trip had been arranged by Reed.

Mark didn't respond to her statement, just gave her a disbelieving look.

"I know you think that this is about him, but it's not." Kate reminded herself to be patient. Mark was the wronged party here, after all. "This is about me, about my mistake in not telling you months ago that I can't marry you. I can't," she repeated. "It wouldn't be fair. I don't love you enough." She knew how awful that sounded, but she had to be blunt. She had to make him hear her.

"So that's it? It's just over?" His face was taut with anger. "You don't love me enough, goodbye?"

Kate moved her hands in a small, helpless shrug. "I don't know what else to say."

The anger suddenly drained out of his face, replaced by sadness. "And what am I supposed to do? Thank you? Congratulate you on your insight?" He shook his head. "I can't do that. And I won't try to convince you that you're wrong."

The words were so similar to what Reed had said on the plane that Kate felt a chill.

"You're an adult, and you have the right to make your own

decisions. I'm going to go home." In an uncharacteristically sloppy gesture, he tossed his overcoat over one shoulder. "I've had a long day, and I'm exhausted. Please give my best to your family. I'm sure your mother will have a speedy recovery."

The exit was behind Kate. Mark started toward her on his way out, but he paused as he passed her, and he leaned close. For a moment, Kate was afraid he would kiss her or whisper something sweet and terrible in her ear. But all he did was look at her for a long moment.

"Goodbye, Kate," he said. And he was gone.

Kate leaned her shoulder against the wall and sagged a bit. She lifted a trembling hand and rubbed her eyes. She had that floaty feeling again, semi-euphoric, semi-panicked, like she was drifting away, cutting all her ties to the warm and familiar.

A hand dropped on her shoulder, and she looked up. It was Julia. Sam was with her. She and Julia embraced, and Kate felt tears again squeezing from inside her eyelids.

"We're heading home," Julia said. She dropped her hand to her belly. "I'm wiped, and Sam's got to get up early tomorrow for a conference." She looked around. "Did Mark go home?"

Kate could only nod.

"So it's done, then?"

Kate nodded again, and Julia echoed the motion, only with more energy and with a certain satisfaction. "I always liked Mark," she said. Kate stiffened, prepared for a scolding. Julia continued, "And I'm glad to see that he's been set free, to find a woman who can fall in love with him."

She squeezed Kate's shoulder affectionately and added, "Instead of a woman who's already in love with someone else." Julia looked meaningfully into their mother's room.

Kate followed her sister's gaze and saw Reed sitting at

Kathy's bedside, holding her hand.

The look on his face struck Kate forcefully. He gazed at her mother with an expression both tender and yearning. Love hit her again, crashing over her like a wave. Kate felt herself being drawn forward, a step at a time.

"I'll call you later," Julia said from somewhere. Kate turned slightly and nodded, then continued her stumbling pace into the hospital room.

"You look so much like both of them," Kathy was saying, gazing into Reed's face. "Seeing you brings back so many memories." She laughed softly. "So much time has passed. Hurts to think about it, actually."

She looked up and smiled as Kate sat on the corner of the bed. "I was just telling Reed how much he looks like both his parents." She turned back to him. "You've always had your mother's eyes. She had such beautiful eyes. I was always jealous of the color, although I would never tell her that! And those cheekbones." She reached out and gently touched his face. "Those are your father's. I think you must have some Native American in you from somewhere. So beautiful. I never knew your father well. He and I...traveled in different circles, I guess you could say. I wasn't at the wedding."

Kathy looked pensive and re-arranged her sheets with restless hands. "So much happened in that year before you were born. Nate's brother was killed in Vietnam. It was such a tragedy; he was a beautiful human being. One sees these things clearer with the perspective of time, I guess. Your mother and I grew apart. Too many changes, too much hurt. I think we both needed the distance from one another. I wish I had been smarter...."

She shook her head. "But there's no sense wishing, is there? After high school, I went off to college, and Lana — your mother, dear — she stayed in Angel River. I didn't realize at the time that she was pregnant with you. She was always holding so much inside her. Your parents were married in September 1969, while I was away at school. I don't think it was a very big ceremony. And then suddenly your father died. You were born, and your mother ran away." Another head shake. "I never understood that. It wasn't like Lana to shirk her responsibilities. She wasn't weak or cowardly. She was strong…and brave, too. She was the bravest person I ever knew, I think." Kathy's eyes grew distant. "I never told her that, either."

Reed cleared his throat. "My mother didn't abandon me," he said slowly. He looked up at Kate. "I found out that my grandmother told her I had died. That's why she left and didn't come back."

Kathy's eyes filled with tears. "Oh, that explains so much." She squeezed Reed's hand. "Your poor mother. To think that her only child had died. How she must have suffered. She was all alone in the world. Her mother had passed away, and then George was killed. He was the man who ran the diner; he was like a father to her. And Mal dying, and Nate and I getting married…." Kathy's eyes met her husband's, and something unspoken passed between them. "I can't bear to think of it. Your poor mother," she said again.

Reed continued to look at Kate, and as Kathy's words began working their way through to his consciousness, he began to look increasingly taken aback.

He's never thought about this from his mother's perspective, Kate thought. *He never thought about what she must have gone through.*

Kate opened her mouth to speak, but her mother interrupted. "I have to tell you all something," Kathy said abruptly. She looked suddenly frightened, unsure, as if she was wondering if she were making a mistake. But then she nodded. "Yes," she said, "this is the time — maybe the only time. Things happen without warning, and then sometimes, it's too late to say what needs to be said."

She looked at all of them. "I'm sorry. I know I'm not making sense. It's just that I didn't expect to be telling this story today." She looked at her husband. "This is going to be a shock to you too, my darling. You who have known me for so long. You probably think that you know everything about me."

But Nate shook his head. "All human beings are a mystery," he said. "I hope I'm never so arrogant that I think I know everything about anyone. Why don't you just — "

"I killed Harry Block," Kathy blurted. Then, as Kate gasped and Reed sat up straighter in his chair, Kathy clapped her hands over her mouth.

But Nate just raised an eyebrow. " — Say what's on your mind," he finished. Ever the good poker-faced attorney.

Behind her hands, Kathy's face grew very white. "I never thought I'd say those words out loud," she whispered, dropping her hands onto her lap. She studied her fingers intently before speaking again. "It was such a long time ago." She grew red, remembering, then pale again as she looked at her husband. "You know some of this, Nate," she said. "Thank God we talked about this years ago, or I don't know...."

Kate looked at her father. His face was calm, but she sensed a tautness in him, a dread of what he was about to hear. To his credit, he reached over and took his wife's hand, squeezing it gently to give her strength.

Kathy took a breath and started again. "I actually dated Harry when we were teenagers. He was always a hard case, and some girls like the bad boy." She looked indulgently at Kate, who suddenly remembered her mother saying, years ago, *I understand you better than you think.*

"The people in town called him Hardluck. Hardluck Harry. Nothing ever did seem to go right for him. We ran around together for a while, then I got tired of him. Plus, I was saving myself for marriage." Another indulgent look, this one directed at her husband. "And Harry wasn't really interested in being with a girl who was so fond of her virtue. He drifted in and out of town for years afterwards. In the early '80s, he drifted back in and stayed until he died.

"You won't be able to understand this, I'm sure. But when you girls became teenagers, I began to feel...stale. I was restless. Your father was away a lot, remember? He was always coming up here to the city to consult on a case. You and Julia didn't seem to need me as much, and you'd also started into that phase where girls lose their obsessive love of their mothers." Her lips tipped up at the corners. "I do love to be loved, after all. I — well, this is uncomfortable, but I guess there's no way around it — I had an affair with Harry."

She lifted her chin a little. "It's not something I'm proud of, but I can't do anything about that now. These things have to be faced, and the fact is I did have an affair with the man." She looked at Kate sorrowfully. "I'm so sorry, my darling, for you to have to be hearing about this now. After all that you've been through, I know it must be a shock. You always set such store by my marriage to your father, didn't you? Much more so than your sister, I think. But nothing's perfect, darling; remember that. People do get tired; they do get bored. Marriage is always work, regardless of how wonderful the person you're married to may be."

She looked again at her husband, although her words were directed at Kate. "I told your father about Harry years ago, after we moved to Washington. I knew it had to be a fresh start, completely new and unfettered by old lies. So I told him about Harry…but not everything.

"That barn where he died, that was where we used to meet. It was a musty old place, but it seemed to suit the sleaziness of what we were doing." She blushed again.

"That last day, I went to meet him in the afternoon. I wish I could say that I went to break things off, but the truth is, I was still infatuated. I hadn't yet confronted what a wretch the man truly was. Harry was excited because he'd gotten the thrasher working. He had an idea that he would make some money with it come wheat-harvesting time. He kept tinkering with the motor, turning the blades on and off. I sat up on the platform, looking down at him.

"I was worried. That morning I'd found Julia throwing up. I'd tried to get her to tell me what was wrong, but she refused. I had noticed certain things about her…I was afraid she might be pregnant, young though she was. I was distracted, rattling on to Harry about it, all the while knowing that he couldn't care less. Then all of a sudden, my words seemed to penetrate the noise of the thrasher and his thick skull. He looked up at me, very white. And he sneered. 'So young Julia got herself knocked up, did she? I should've known that — '

"He stopped. And suddenly I knew. I *knew*. He had been having an affair with me, and somehow he had managed to seduce Julia at the same time. My daughter. My *fourteen-year-old* daughter. Oh, God, I couldn't stand it. It was so ugly.

"He must have seen something in my expression. He climbed up to the platform, nimble as a monkey, and pushed his face close to mine. 'If you tell anyone, I *will* kill her,' he said. Even in that moment of terror, I thought of how clever he was. Threatening me would not have made a difference. I was disgusted with myself, with my infidelity and willful blindness to the man I'd been having sex with. But threatening my child, that got through to me."

Kathy gave a bitter smile. "Oh yes, it did get through. But not in the way he expected. I pushed him. He fell right into the blades of the thrasher. I watched the whole thing. I wish I could say that it was awful, but in a way, I found the carnage very satisfying. Harry got what he deserved. I only wish he could have suffered more."

"It was an accident," Kate said swiftly. "You didn't intend for him to die. You didn't intend to kill him." She blinked as she looked at her mother. *"Did* you?"

Kathy's pretty hands fluttered in her lap. "Oh, love, after all this time, even *I* don't know what I did and did not intend. I know that in that instant, I hated him for what he had done to your sister. I wanted him to suffer. I wanted to annihilate him." She looked at her husband. "Does that count as criminal intent, dear?" She was only half joking.

But Nate Doyle was all seriousness. "It doesn't matter," he said, "because a jury will never hear your story."

"You mean you're not going to report me?"

"Even if you weren't my wife, I wouldn't report this," Nate said. "As far as the world is concerned, Harry Block's death was an accident. And so it was. He was not a good man, not even a little bit. He seduced a fourteen-year-old girl. He threatened an old woman — Reed's grandmother. He made choices in his life, and those choices lead to his death."

"Justifiable," Kate murmured. She looked at her mother.

"Even if you went to the trouble of confessing, even if they took you to trial, which they probably wouldn't, Dad's right. Harry's own behavior would condemn him as a man who deserved to die." She paused, trying to absorb everything her mother had said. Harry Block had fathered Julia's child? No wonder Jules had never wanted to reveal his name. The very idea made Kate want to retch; how must Julia have felt about it? Then Kate recalled the gentle, happy look on Julia's face when Sam had put his arm around her, and Kate realized that Julia probably never thought about it. She had put the past behind her and was creating a blissful present for herself and her family. Kate wished she could follow that example.

"All these years, I thought my grandmother had done it," Reed said. He looked at Kate. "It's one of the reasons I didn't go after you, didn't try to find you back then. I was afraid she had killed him. I needed to watch her, make sure she didn't give anything away. I think I would have even gone to prison to protect her if I had to." He stopped, thinking. Then he looked at Kate again. "You thought I had done it, didn't you?" It wasn't an accusation.

Kate shook her head slowly. "There were moments when I was afraid you could have, yes. But I never truly believed it. Not in my heart."

"Oh," Kathy said. She had begun to cry. "When I think of all the trouble I've caused for the two of you. I thought I was doing right by not saying anything, but…."

Reed spoke for all of them. "But we can't go back," he said gently. "None of us can go back. And if we did, there's no guarantee that the choices we'd make would still be the right ones."

"What can I do to make it up to you?" Kathy asked Reed.

"Would you tell me about my mother?" Reed asked. "Would you tell me every little thing you can remember about her? I've spent my entire life hating her, and she didn't deserve it." His voice broke. "I want to know who she was, who she *really* was, and you're the only one who can do that for me."

"Not the only one," Kathy said, looking significantly at Nate.

"But will you?" Reed asked.

"Of course, child," Kathy said, grasping his hands as he clutched hers. "Of course."

❧

Kathy talked for a long time. She told them about how she and Lana had been born in the same hospital on the same day, how they had grown up together. The nurse came in and tried to shoo them out, but Reed made a phone call and they weren't bothered again after that. Kate stretched out on the narrow bed next to her mother, with her head on her mother's chest like she had not done since she was a child. Kathy stroked her hair absently with one hand; the other held Reed's as she talked, as she told him of the remarkable woman who was his mother. Kate's father sat quiet in his chair, close enough that Kate could feel the warmth of his body against her back. Kate was dimly aware of being hungry, but that was overpowered by the fatigue she felt creeping through her. Her eyes drifted closed, and eventually, she slept.

❧

When she woke, Reed was gone. Her mother said that he had gone downstairs to make arrangements for a hotel room and to make sure the driver of the car hadn't frozen to death in the limousine parking area. Kate saw her chance, and she took it. She kissed her mother goodbye and promised to return tomorrow for a visit. She slipped downstairs and called a cab from a payphone. Her cell phone battery had died.

She braved the cold and waited outside for the taxi. She didn't want to risk running into Reed. She knew she was taking the coward's way out, knew that she would have to see him again, probably soon, but she needed some time to herself. She needed some time to think.

CHAPTER TWENTY

THE TAXI GLIDED SMOOTHLY THROUGH the cold, wet winter night. Kate leaned her head against the window and watched her breath fog the icy glass. Outside, DC looked like a foreign land. Streets and buildings that should have been familiar looked strange: smaller, less impressive. After everything that Kate had seen and heard and done in the past twenty-four hours, her whole world seemed different.

But it felt good to be home. The taxi came to a halt on the dark street, brakes squeaking ever so slightly. Kate paid the driver and climbed wearily out of the cab. She looked up, waiting to cross the street until the taxi drove away. The lights from her apartment building welcomed her, pulled her across the street, inside the building and into the elevator. On her floor, she paused as the elevator door slid closed behind her. The hallway looked the same as it always had. In that dimly lit, carpeted world, it might be any hour, any day of the year. There was something soothing about that.

The sound of the key sliding into the lock on her apartment door also had the comfortable ring of familiarity. She opened the door to darkness and warm, stuffy air. Dropping her bag on the floor, Kate let the door close behind her and flicked on the light in the foyer. She leaned back and closed her eyes. Her muscles ached with exhaustion; she felt like she'd been run over by a freight train, but she was home. She'd made it.

When she opened her eyes with effort, she saw that the dim foyer bulb cast just enough light for her to make out the beige bulk of her sofa in the living room and the TV lurking in the corner. The place looked plain, almost empty, without so much as a houseplant to add a sense of life. Home, she thought, but what kind of home is it? Did she really live here, or was this just some hotel room that she had stumbled into by mistake?

"Ugh. Enough of that." She shook her head at her own melodrama. She was being maudlin, feeling sorry for herself to disguise the guilt she felt for leaving the hospital so quickly, for running out on Reed again like she had twenty years earlier. She shrugged off her borrowed coat and kicked off her shoes. "Knock off the fussing. Mom's okay; I'm home safe — I've even ended things with Mark, relatively amicably. The world is my oyster. It's time for some good spirits."

But just saying it out loud wasn't enough. She went into the kitchen and poured herself a glass of wine, then made a point of going around the apartment and turning on all the lights. When that didn't work, she turned on the television and flipped the switch on the gas fireplace. Ah. Light. And sound. And dancing shadows on the wall. That was better — at least it was something.

She needed a bath, a nice long, hot soak to drive away the cold in her bones. Then a long sleep in her own bed. Everything would look better in the morning. Everything always did.

But then her stomach rumbled loudly and insistently, changing her mind. She realized it had been almost twelve hours since she'd eaten. Instead of a bath, what she needed was a hot meal: comfort food, and preferably something that was not at all good for her. Then she remembered that she'd seen the lights on at the Szechuan Delight — her favorite Chinese restaurant across the street. Oh, that was perfect. She'd cut down on her takeout meals in the past few months, but the thought of a brown bag with grease stains on the corners of it pushed aside all trivial thoughts of health.

She glanced at the clock and saw she had time for a quick shower and a change of clothes before heading across the street. She'd get moo shi pork, she decided, with egg rolls and extra plum sauce. And when she got back home, she would watch *The Philadelphia Story* while she ate — the combination was a guaranteed mood-elevator.

The smell of her own shampoo was comforting, as was the feel of her favorite sweatpants and her thick cotton socks. She decided to skip wearing a bra and pulled a faded blue T-shirt over her head, followed by a soft sweater. Sneakers and her own winter coat made her feel like herself. As she rode the elevator to the lobby, she caught her reflection in the stainless steel walls. Wow, what a sight she was in her old clothes and no makeup. "Hey, glamorous." She combed her fingers through her damp hair. "Nice to see you. You're starting to look like yourself again — only happier."

She was still smiling as the elevator doors slid open. She crossed the lobby briskly and pushed open the thick glass doors to the street. But she pulled up short when she saw Reed standing on the sidewalk.

Streetlights glowed dully through the misting rain. Their light glinted coldly off his golden hair, but his face was silhouetted in the darkness. His breath fogged out into the damp air.

Kate leaned back against the door, groping for some support. She didn't say anything at first, just stood quietly, trying to gauge his mood. His appearance wasn't completely unexpected. She had known that he would get in touch with her at some point before he left town; she just hadn't thought he would come after her tonight. Was he hoping for reconciliation, or did he just want to tell her off for disappearing from the hospital in such a cowardly way?

In one hand, he held a package. When he saw that she was looking at it, he held it up silently. It was a large brown bag, folded over and stapled at the top, with grease stains on the corners. Even from this distance, the smell of Chinese food was unmistakable. Kate gaped, feeling a superstitious chill go through her as she wondered if he had read her mind.

"Is that from across the street?" she asked.

He nodded.

"How did you know?"

Reed lowered the bag and shuffled his feet. "You told me about that place, remember? That night in Bonaire? I figured that after the long day and everything that's happened, you might like a bite to eat."

"And you want to come up," Kate asked, although she did not phrase it like a question.

Reed took in her posture — legs apart, arms crossed — and prepared for an argument. "We have things to talk about," he said.

She started to shake her head. "We've had this conversation already."

"What conversation? How do you even know what I'm going to say?"

She didn't answer. She just stood, with her chin raised stubbornly. "I need some time to be alone," she said. "I need to think."

"No, you need to stop thinking and start acting," Reed said impatiently. "God, Kate, you can meticulously figure things out, stuck inside your own head, computing tiny details and possible outcomes until the end of eternity. But it won't get you anywhere." He paused and took a breath. "This food's getting cold, by the way."

Kate eyed the bag. "What did you order?" she asked.

He sighed. "Moo shi pork, string beans, fried rice, egg rolls. Happy?"

She lit up. "Moo shi pork? You remembered my favorite food?"

"How could I forget? You made your parents get it for you on every birthday."

Her stomach was still growling. She eyed the bag again. "Did you get me my own container, or do we have to share?"

Reed sighed again. "Your own container, plus extra plum sauce and extra pancakes. *Now* are you happy?"

Kate stared at him, amazed. Maybe it was really true love, after all. How could he remember all that?

Grudgingly, not wanting to seem like she was giving in, she held the door open and stood back to let him go by. In the elevator on the way up, they didn't speak. Kate caught sight of her reflection again and smoothed down her hair self-consciously. Suddenly her old-clothes-and-no-makeup look didn't seem so glamorous and funny. She glanced at Reed. His eyes were tired, and his face showed a day's growth of beard. But the whole disheveled thing looked good on him — it was sexy, appealing. It made her want to rub his shoulders and wrap her arms around him until she soothed his cares away. It was annoying as hell.

Having him in her apartment felt weird. He made the place

seem smaller, less colorful — more beige. Feeling unsettled, Kate took the food into the living room and put the bag on the coffee table, then went to the kitchen for plates and utensils. Although she couldn't see him, she could hear him wandering around, and she just knew that he was moving like he owned the place, looking at the few pictures she had on the mantle, checking out her view to the street below. When she came out of the kitchen with the dishes, she was surprised to find him walking out of her bedroom. She gave him a look, and he held up his hands innocently.

"I was just washing my hands. Hope you don't mind."

"Next time, use the door from the hallway." She made herself sound irritated to cover her discomfort, and set the dishes down on the coffee table with a clank.

Knowing that Reed would sit on the sofa, Kate chose to settle on a cushion in front of the fire. She wanted to be able to keep her distance.

He surveyed the table and, without a word, went into the kitchen for wine and glasses. He poured them both a glass and sat down.

Kate hesitated for a moment before reaching for the food. She was flustered by his presence, more so than she liked to admit. She felt a little like sulking, turning up her nose at the food, ordering him to go away and darken her door no more. But her appetite got the best of her, and soon she had dished herself out a plate and was dousing her food with sauce.

"So do you want to tell me what you're doing here?" she asked finally.

He also fixed himself a plate, manipulating chop sticks with ease. "I told you," he said. "We need to talk. I was surprised to get back to your mother's hospital room and find that you'd left.

You didn't say goodbye."

Kate looked down. "Okay, that was spineless of me, I admit it," she said softly, speaking into her plate. She looked up again. "But I'm not going to apologize for it. I didn't want to have an awkward goodbye scene with you. We said everything we needed to say on the plane."

Reed nodded slowly in acknowledgement. She could tell that he was chewing over what she'd said while he chewed his food. And when he swallowed, she knew he'd decided what he wanted to say. She stiffened, trying to prepare herself for whatever was coming.

"So then, let me sum this up," he said. "You love me, but you don't think we have a future together. And the *reason* you don't think we have a future is that our past history is so full of tragedy and deceit that there's no way on earth we could ever get over it and find happiness. In fact, if we did get married and have children, we would probably pass our myriad of neuroses on to said children, thereby ruining their lives as well as our own."

His tone was insulting, but at the same time, Kate had to bite back the urge to laugh. While it was annoying to hear herself parodied like that, there was something endearing about it too. He could always sum up her thought processes so well.

Reed paused a beat, waiting to see if she would respond. When she didn't, he went on. "And so your solution to this inescapable catastrophe is simply to avoid the whole goddamn mess and break things off now. I'll go my way, and you'll go yours." He looked at her. "Is that about it?"

She swallowed. "You could have been a little less sarcastic about it, but yes, that's about it."

"And would it do me any good to point out the gaping holes in your logic?"

Kate was surprised to realize that she wanted him to do just that. She wanted to be convinced that they belonged together. But she couldn't bring herself to admit it. "Not even a little bit."

"Fine. Then I won't." He pushed the food around on his plate. "And so what are you going to do with yourself, now that you've decided that you don't want *him*, and you don't want *me*. Any idea what you *do* want?"

She did her best to ignore the derisive tone of his question and tried to answer honestly. "I'm going to take a leave of absence from my job and do some traveling. I have a little money saved up. Maybe I'll find a place where I feel like I belong, a place where I can be happy."

"Where do you think you might start your travels?"

She smiled slightly. "I was actually thinking I would start by going back to Angel River. It's been twenty years. I'd like to see the old place again."

"I don't know," he said warningly. "Didn't Thomas Wolfe say that you can't go home again?"

"Mr. Wolfe never met me," Kate retorted, joking. "Although I know where I'd tell him that *he* can go. No, I know it will be strange. I know things will be different. But that's okay. I'd like to see it in the present time. Whatever's different, whatever's still the same, I think it will be okay."

"Did your mother tell you that she's going to get in touch with *my* mother?"

Kate blinked. "No, she didn't say anything about it. When did she decide that?"

"I guess it was while you were still sleeping. Kathy — " He laughed a little. "It still feels strange to call your mother by her first name, but she was insistent about it. Writing the letter was her idea. She's going to write to my mother and tell her that I..."

he trailed off, his expression awkward.

"That you're alive?" Kate supplied. It wasn't surprising that he couldn't finish that sentence on his own.

He nodded slowly. "I don't know how my mother will take it. I *hope* she'll be happy. Kathy said that Lana deserves to know the truth, that no matter how happy she's been with her husband and stepchildren, she would want to know about me. And so I agreed to let her do it."

Kate stared at the thinly-concealed emotion on his face. "And then you're going to go and see your mother?"

"I hope so," he said. "If she wants me."

Abruptly, Kate's eyes filled with tears. "Oh, my old friend, of course she'll want you. Who wouldn't?"

He looked at her with eyes dark and hurt. *You* don't, his expression said.

She dropped her gaze. "I'm very happy for you," Kate said. "Will you let me know how things work out?"

"I don't think so," he said quietly.

She looked up. He was watching her intently. She was afraid to ask the question, but she couldn't help herself. "Why not?"

"Because I want you to come with me."

She shook her head in exasperation and climbed to her feet. Angrily, she gathered up their food and dirty dishes and took them into the kitchen. He followed her.

"For God's sake, would you talk to me?"

"There's nothing left to say!" She banged the tray down on the counter. Food splattered on the wall. The wine glasses fell over. One of them rolled to the floor and broke. They both ignored it.

"Oh no?" he said. "How about 'I love you'? How about 'I need you, and I can't live without you'?"

"Those are just words!"

"No." He shook his head seriously and looked into her eyes. "No, they're not. They're facts. They're truth. I do love you, Kate. And I need you."

He gripped her shoulders. "And you love me, too. You said you did." She opened her mouth to speak, but he cut her off. "Earlier today, you said we're haunted by too many old ghosts. You said we'll just end up hurting each other again. Well, you're right, on both counts."

She blinked up at him. That wasn't what she had been expecting him to say.

He continued, appreciating the fact that he had surprised her. "But I have an answer for that: so what?"

"So *what?*" Now she was indignant.

He grinned. "Yeah. So what? Say you and I decide to make a life together. Settle down, get married. Sooner or later, we'll end up hurting each other. There's no way around that. We'll have a misunderstanding, we'll fight, then we'll make up and move on. It happens all the time. Look at your folks, for God's sake! Look at all they went through, stuff you never even knew about. Would you say that they're unhappy?"

"No," Kate admitted.

"And what about Julia and Sam? Are you going to tell me that they never argue?"

Kate smothered a laugh, remembering some of the knock-down-drag-outs that those two had. "Of course they do."

"Of course they do," he echoed. "And so will we. But, Katie, *so what?*"

"So what." This time it was not a question. A reluctant grin started to form on Kate's face. Nothing was going the way she had expected. She had thought she could argue him into apathy, drive him away, and that then she would be alone with her misery. He never ceased to surprise her.

Seeing the change in her face, Reed slid his arms around her waist, pulled her close. "None of us can ever predict exactly what will happen in the future. All we can do is try to make the best decisions now, based on the information at hand. I know three things: that I love you, that I need you, and that I'll never be completely happy without you. I want you in my life — for all of my life, all the rest of it, no matter how long it is."

He reached a finger into the pocket of his slacks, pulled out a tiny silver ring, set with a single garnet. He looked at it for a moment, and then slipped it onto her finger. It only fit down to the base of her nail. They both laughed shakily. "Will you marry me?" he asked.

"Where did you find this?" she asked in amazement.

"I snagged it from your jewelry box when I went to wash my hands," he confessed.

"But how did you know it was there? How did you know I still had it?"

"I asked your mother about it — she told me where she thought I could find it."

For once, Kate did not mind her mother's interference in her life. She looked at the stone as it glittered against her nail and remembered the first time he had slipped it onto her finger. "I can't believe you remembered."

"Of course I did. I fell in love with you the day I first slipped this on your finger, and I've loved you ever since." He paused, waiting. When she didn't say anything, he prodded gently. "Well?" he asked. "You haven't said yes yet."

"Yes," she said and threw her arms around his neck. "Of course, yes!"

He scooped her up in his arms and carried her over to the couch. He sat down, keeping her in his lap, keeping her close. He took her hand and kissed it.

"We'll go to the jewelry store tomorrow and get it re-sized," he said, touching the tiny gem. "How would you feel about getting a couple of diamonds on here, too?"

"I think I could live with that," she said.

"And we'll add one for every baby we have," he said. He looked at her with loving eyes. "Have to give Oliver and Rose some cousins, after all."

She got a little misty at the notion and blinked her eyes to disguise it. "I think I could live with that, too."

"So where do you want to go for our honeymoon?" he asked. "Back to the *Sweet William?* I think I could probably get us a reservation."

"How about the Angel River Hotel?" Kate laughed. "I hear the accommodations are wonderful."

He bent his head to kiss her. "Sounds perfect," he said. "Sounds absolutely perfect."

They stayed that way for a long time, listening to the rain.

CHAPTER TWENTY-ONE

1865

HIS DAUGHTER'S PAINS HAD BEGUN with the morning light. Little ones at first, stabbing her unexpectedly, making her bend over suddenly, with her hand to her swollen belly. They were on the road already, just the three of them in the cart, the pack mule tied behind. Gerald knew that they should stop and make camp, that he should allow little Angelica to prepare for the delivery to come, but he was driven to go on, to go always just a little further towards the summit of the next rise, though he knew not why.

As the sun had risen in the sky, the horses had pulled them higher, and so had poor Melinda's pain increased. Always a docile child, though slower than most, she bit her lip and tried not to cry out. But before long, her face was white and slick with sweat, and she could no longer contain her cries.

While Gerald drove the cart, Angelica made her sister as comfortable as possible, holding her hand and whispering soothing words while she dabbed Melinda's forehead. And when even Angelica's considerable gifts could no longer soothe her sister's pain, she slipped her soft tiny hand into his big rough one and whispered, "Da."

Gerald nodded, a great weariness growing on him as he

realized that though they would go no farther that day, the day was far from over. Angelica had already warned him it would be a long and difficult birth, that the narrowness of Melinda's hips and the greatness of her swelling told that easily enough. Gerald should have blushed to hear his nine-year-old daughter speak of such things, but he pretended to himself that she was speaking of one of the cows or sheep on the farm from which they had fled. Had she not tended many a birthing beast since she was but five years old?

She had seen more of nature and the intimate messiness that accompanied the creation of life than any man he could name, so why should she fear to speak of it bluntly, and why should he fear to hear it? There was no one here to be embarrassed of, not a soul for miles around in these dark Virginia hills, so let the child speak as she must.

All of this Gerald told himself as he climbed down from the cart and tethered the horses to a nearby tree. He took a moment to stroke each one on the neck and speak a few words to them. They were good horses, strong if not beautiful, and of a middling age. They would live years yet and give a good day's work every day it was asked of them. Gerald congratulated himself on making a good buy of them some weeks before, and then thanked God that he had made at least one right decision on this reckless journey.

"When we get where we're going," he said companionably to the horses, "I'll tell you of Ireland and of the horses we had on the farm where I grew up. You would've liked Ireland, my friends. The rolling green hills, the brooks in the little meadows…"

When we get where we're going, he thought. If only I knew where on God's green earth that was.

He turned at a cry from Melinda, and he gritted his teeth

at the sight of her white, frightened face. Poor child. Simple-minded, but pure of heart, until some rich and handsome devil from a neighboring village had seduced her and left her to bear both the child and the shame on her own.

But she was not really on her own, Gerald reminded himself, for she still and always had her family, small though it might be. Only himself and the two girls remained, their blessed mother having been taken nine years ago at the birth of his little Angelica.

And that selfsame child was blessed with gifts the like of which Gerald had only heard of, but never before seen. She could talk to the birds in the trees and the beasts in the field, and she said they talked back to her. But even more amazing, she had a knack for seeing people that weren't there, people with a glow around them. Angels was what they were, and so from the time she was old enough to tell of these heavenly visitors, they had called her Angelica.

Some people said that it was an ancient gift, that there was witchcraft in his dear wife's family, and that the angels were actually demons in masquerade, but Gerald would have none of that. This…*talent*…of his young child's was a gift straight from God himself, and no one would ever convince him otherwise.

And perhaps it was not so startling after all, her having grown up on a farm and all. The little lambs and calves were her playmates from the time she was walking, so was it not natural to think that she would have a special relationship with them, even until it seemed that she could talk to them and they understood her, and that she could soothe their fears and even seemed to lessen their pain when they were suffering?

If it had not been for Angelica's gift, would he have dared to bring his two daughters across the ocean to America at a moment's notice, Melinda gone with child as she was? No, Gerald didn't think he could have done it. They would perhaps have fled to England, maybe even gone on to the continent. But to take that hazardous journey across the wide and willful ocean, which no man alive could predict, let alone control, with no idea of what they would do when they got here?

But Angelica did have the gift, and he trusted his older daughter to her care as readily as he would have to the local doctor back home — more so, in fact, for the man was a notorious drinker, and what did he know of the pain a woman had to bear? Better a female to attend to her needs when the time came, as had been done for centuries.

And sure'n he felt safer here, with an ocean between him and his sin, than he would have felt in England or anywhere else on that side of the world.

Melinda's blue eyes squeezed shut, foretelling the agonized cry that ripped from her lips a moment afterward.

"How long?" Gerald asked tersely.

"An hour, maybe two," Angelica said, her face calm. Melinda groaned with dread at the thought of two more hours of agony. Angelica held her hand and kissed her temple, whispering words that Gerald could not hear. Melinda nodded and closed her eyes, face calm, but still white. As Gerald watched, two tears slid from behind her lids and washed down her face.

"We have to get her comfortable," Angelica said. "We need somewhere we can settle for the night."

Gerald nodded. The road they were on was an old one, hardly used anymore, but still, he preferred to get his girls and his goods off to a sheltered spot. The trees here were not as dense as they had been farther down. He looked up at the sky, where the sun had crested and was starting its long, slow slide downward. His eyes went back to the road, winding its way up the hill. How desperately he had wanted to get to the top, though he could not have said why.

"Well, dearhearts, the weather's with us, and that's a blessing," he said cheerily. "Sure'n it's a good time of year for traveling. Springtime, when the world is alive with possibilities."

Possibilities. His eyes traveled upward to the summit again.

"Da!" Angelica said sharply. He looked back at her. Her eyes blazed a bright blue, her red hair stood out against her head, making her pale skin look paler, almost transparent. Against each of her white cheeks stood a patch of red.

She was angry at him. The knowledge penetrated his mind slowly. He had never seen Angelica angry with anyone or anything. Always a child of the mildest temperament, her patience seemed endless. Until now.

"Not up there!" she said firmly. She lifted a slender arm and pointed towards the woods behind him. "In there! There's a path. Find us a place to shelter for the night, somewhere with water nearby. By midnight, your grandchild will be born."

His grandchild. Gerald turned around. There was a path, all right. Why had he not seen it before? Wide enough even to take the cart, if he were careful about it. He had been daydreaming, that was why he hadn't seen it.

He shook his head and started forward, suddenly angrier at himself than even Angelica had been. Daydreaming, at a time like this! Daydreaming, when his fifteen-year-old daughter was about to bear her first child, with only a nine-year-old girl and his bungling self to help! But that nine-year-old girl was worth a hundred of him, and he knew it.

And so did Melinda. Gerald knew that she would rather have Angelica attending to her than anyone else in the world, unless maybe it was her own dear mother.

Oh, the pity of it, that Melinda should be so sweet and simple-minded that she didn't even blame the boy who had put her in this condition! Never could she bring herself to speak a word against him, and Gerald suspected that in some corner of her heart, she fostered a dear hope that the whole thing had been a mistake, that the boy was alive and well and would follow them here and beg her to marry him.

But that was not to be, and none knew it better than Gerald. Gerald, and God…and maybe little Angelica. How oddly she had looked at him that night when he had come home. He had carried the rifle as casually as he could, as if he had been out on a bit of a hunt and had come home empty-handed. But something in her eyes told him that she knew what he had done…and that she did not disapprove.

The Devil had been in that boy, no doubt about it, been in his casual grin and charming manner, in his black hair and blue eyes, in his dimples and good white teeth. And he had seized on Melinda, as did every boy who took in her fair face and handsome figure. But that one had gone farther than any other before him. Charmed her, lied to her, seduced her, left her.

When Gerald had found the boy, he was on horseback, headed back to school after the summer holiday. No groom rode with him, nor was he carrying any baggage other than his horse's saddlebags. This young man was brave, to be sure. And foolish.

Gerald had not set out to shoot him, that was certain. But when he insisted — as was his right, as Melinda's father — that the young lad take responsibility for his actions and marry the girl whose virginity he took, the young man had laughed. Laughed, while Melinda wept at home into her pillow. While a scandal that could ruin her forever grew in her belly. The young man had laughed, and Gerald had shot him.

Stupid, impulsive, foolhardy. These words had repeated themselves in his head as Gerald dragged the young man's body into the woods.

Sacrilegious, sinful had then taken their place as he rifled the young man's pockets and the horse's saddlebags. He then slapped the horse on the rump and set it galloping off, knowing that it would return to its home stables and a search would start for the young man himself. Stealing his possessions would make it seem as if he had been set upon by thieves along the roadway.

At least, that was what Gerald had hoped would happen. What people would think when they found he had been shot with a hunting weapon was not so certain. For an instant, Gerald considered burying him, hiding the body. But the thought of even that devilish young man lying forever in an unmarked grave, with no Christian service said at his internment, with his mother forever lost in the mystery of what had happened to her favorite son, quickly put that idea to rest.

A dry branch snapped loudly under Gerald's foot, making him jump and then laugh at himself for being so easily startled. *Somewhere with water nearby* was what Angelica had specified, but Gerald had doubts about finding such a place. The river was far and away to the south of them, they had seen no signs of brooks or streams for miles, and he had that very morning started to worry that their last barrel of water might run dry before they could refill it.

The shadows in the woods had grown very long, and Gerald glanced anxiously at the sky. Sometimes they lost the sun too quickly here in the hills. It had happened once or twice in the past weeks, and this was no time to be taken by surprise. He needed to get the girls settled, to build a fire, and go in search of water and perhaps a rabbit. Angelica had told him that Melinda would need to eat as much as she could take after the child was born.

There was a clearing up ahead backed by a small swell of a hill, and the path — if indeed it was such — seemed to end there. A large flat rock, the very size and shape of a bed, seemed the perfect spot for Melinda to lie on — off the ground, where she could stay dry. Very well, he would bring those that waited out by the road in here and make a camp. Then he would go search for water, and if he could not find it, he would make what they had last somehow. Shelter, rest, and food was what they all needed more than anything.

So much relief did Gerald feel at making those resolutions that he realized just how frightened he was. He straightened his back, and it was with a resolute step that he returned to his girls.

He wouldn't allow them to see any fright in him or nary a weakness. Certain it was that he would bow to Angelica on any issues dealing with the birth of his grandchild, but he would firmly maintain his authority on all other things. He was, after all, the man and the master of this family. He had led them into the wilderness, and with God's help, he would lead them through it and to a better place.

Such self-assured thoughts did not stop him from feeling somewhat more composed at Angelica's approving glance around the clearing once he brought them there. She walked around, took in the roll of the tiny hill, the softness of the pine needles covering the sizable rock, and the thickness of the branches overhead. Then she turned, smiled, and nodded at him.

They set about making camp very quickly. Melinda helped, as was her custom. At first Gerald tried to bid her sit down and rest, but Angelica stopped him, saying that the movement might make the baby come more easily.

And as soon as Melinda heard *that*, she could not be made to sit and rest for all the world. Until at last, all was done that could be done, and there was nothing to do but wait.

Gerald checked the water barrel and found it comfortably full. Angelica said that it would do, provided that she and her father didn't drink much of it themselves. Gerald pointed out that he had a smaller barrel full of ale, and it would be no hardship on him to drink that instead.

He had good luck with hunting, and he brought back two rabbits, which he skinned and spitted over the fire. Angelica had set up Melinda as comfortably as she could, with blankets beneath her and a pack of clothes at her back. She sat and held Melinda's hand, talking her through the pains as they came, closer together and more intensely now.

In between the pains, Angelica murmured to her sister, words so soft and low that Gerald could scare hear them. When the rabbits were cooked through, he pulled them off and ate his share, then put by the rest of the meat until the birthing was over, for Angelica had said she would not eat until Melinda did. As he stored the meat carefully in the cart to keep it away from the prying noses of ground scavengers, a few of Angelica's words floated to him on the wind.

"Never you mind about the wind in the trees," she murmured. "'Tis not ghosts, after all. The trees whisper secrets in our ears, if we care to open them and listen."

"Are any of *Them* about?" Melinda whispered, her eyes filled with both hope and fear.

"Sure'n They're all about this place," Angelica whispered back. "Who do you think lead us to this spot, and guided Da to find this perfect little clearing? This is the place where They mean you to have your child, and They'll help you all They can. Lie back now, and try to rest a little."

Gerald met Angelica's eye and saw that his little daughter was worried. A great fear gripped him, but he stifled it as best he could. Strong, he told himself. You must be strong.

It was a long night, like something out of a fevered dream. Gerald sat at Melinda's back, holding her up as Angelica had instructed. He tried not to think of how he had done the same for the girls' own mother, how he had felt the life slipping out of her as Angelica had made her entry into the world. Instead he tried to remember happy times and imagine what their future would be like, here in this country of endless possibilities.

Melinda's moaning brought him back to reality, and he shifted, trying to give her more support. She quieted some, breathing deeply as Angelica told her to, and Gerald wished he could do more for his girls than just sit like a toad on this rock.

The night wore on. Gerald couldn't see the moon through the thick twining of branches overhead, but he knew when it was up and could sense its slow progression across the cold and distant sky. Here, in the clearing, there were screaming cries and the smell of blood. There was the paleness of their faces, lit with the flickering light of the fire. He could feel Melinda's fear, could almost taste her pain and desperation in the back of his own throat. But through all that, he could also feel her happiness, a blissful awe that her baby was about to be born. Regardless of its illegitimacy — even because of it — this baby would be a Fitzgerald, raised as Melinda herself had been raised. That brought her comfort and a measure of peace, and Gerald reveled in both.

And later, after many tears and much willing suffering, Gerald's grandson made his first appearance into the great, wide world, announcing his arrival with a robust cry that echoed through the night. Melinda, who despite her fragile appearance had been strong and determined through the whole ordeal, held him lovingly and fed him his first meal before giving him over to Angelica to be bathed and swaddled.

They persuaded Melinda to take a little food, and Angelica helped her clean herself as best she could. Afterwards, when mother and child were settled as comfortably as possible, when Angelica had washed and eaten, the baby had his second meal, and they sat and watched him.

"A boy, Da," Melinda said. Her voice was quiet with wonder. "I wouldna believed it." Then she looked up, her pretty brow creased with concern. "I don't know what to name him," she said. "If he'd been a girl, I would've named her after Ma, but now…"

"Da will think of a name," Angelica said drowsily. She had curled up in her cloak, head pillowed on her arm. "Don't you worry, Melinda, Da will take care of it."

Melinda looked at her father and nodded. "You choose a name for him, Da. Will you?"

"Of course I will, if you want me to," Gerald said. He tried to keep his voice steady. "But not right now. Now is for sleeping. I think we could all do with a bit of rest, don't you?"

And Melinda, ever the good girl, closed her eyes promptly and was asleep within moments.

Gerald tried to stay awake, but when he heard his grandson whimpering, he opened his eyes to find his head had dropped to his chest. He got up and made his way over to where Melinda lay, trying to feed the baby.

"I don't know what he's crying for," she said worriedly. "I fed him, and he's not wet."

"He just wants to walk around," Gerald said. "He wants to get a look at his home country. I'll take him to the road and walk him back and forth, shall I? If you need anything, your sister is right here."

Melinda looked over at Angelica, asleep by the fire, but still close enough to be reached if she was wanted. "She's young to be bearing the burden of her gift," Melinda said, sounding suddenly mature. "Do you think she'll be all right?"

"She'll be dandy," Gerald reassured her. "She's got the angels looking out for her, and we whom she loves have them, too. So don't you worry, little girl. Just get some rest. After a few days, we'll be moving on."

"Where will we be moving, Da?"

"You just let me worry about that, all right? Now, give me my grandson." Gerald cradled the baby in his arms. So tiny, this little one. So fragile, and yet there was sturdiness in his face already.

"You're a Fitzgerald all right, lad," he said. As if in agreement, the baby yawned.

Gerald looked down at Melinda. She had fallen instantly back asleep. He made his way to the edge of the clearing, then turned and looked back. His two daughters. He was proud of them both. They were strong, like their mother. They would weather the hard times ahead.

He passed the horses, stopping to stroke them, and to introduce them to the new member of their party. "It's four of us you'll be pulling tomorrow," Gerald said. "But I don't think you'll mind this little bit of extra weight, will you?"

The horses nickered softly in response. He bid them look after his girls, then headed onward.

When he reached the road, the baby stirred. "Feel the call of the open road, do you boy?" Gerald asked. He looked up toward that hill, the one that had so entranced him earlier. "Let's just get us a better vantage point, shall we? Take in the lay of the land, so to speak."

The night was cool and quiet. Gerald's feet made scuffing sounds on the hard-packed dirt as he trekked up the hill. The moon hung low on the horizon, but the stars still glittered in the blue-black sky. "It'll be getting on to dawn now shortly, and then you'll really have a sight to see," he told his grandson. "There's nothing like a sunrise to lift a man's spirits and energize him for the long day ahead."

And what, he wondered, would the days ahead bring? Sure'n they couldn't stay here and live in the woods like savages. His daughters needed a roof over their heads; his grandson needed a good floor to crawl on. And he needed a patch of land to farm, a place where he could work the earth and coax good green things to grow from its soily depths. He needed sheep and pigs and chickens to give the place noise and smells. He needed a home. They all did.

At length, he made it to the top of the hill, huffing and puffing as he did. Exhaustion was creeping its paralyzing way through his bones, but he shook it off. "I must be getting old, lad," he said. "Twenty years ago I could go for three days straight with no sleep — work all day, drink all night, and come home whistling in the morning light. But don't you go telling your ma and auntie about that, my boy. That's to be kept just between us men, you hear me?"

He pulled back the blanket that had slid over the baby's face and admired the way the boy squirmed in his arms. "Impatient to be up and around already, aren't you?" he said. "Well, soon enough, my boy; soon enough."

Gerald lifted his head to get a look at what lay on the other side of the hill, and as his eyes lit upon the landscape that sprawled away in front of him, he gasped. "Jesus and Mary," he said breathlessly. "Would you look at that?"

At the top of the hill, the road made a sharp turn to the left, following the crest of the steep hillside. Below him was the most beautiful valley he had ever laid eyes on. The land was long and wide and flat. Good farming land. Even in the silvery light of night, he could tell that the grass was thick and vibrant. The tall stands of trees which dotted the landscape would provide good wood to build a cabin.

Best of all, from out of the thick woods came a curling, silver ribbon of water. It made a crescent in the middle of the valley, then wandered off. It was a river — small, to be sure — but it was an actual river.

"Why, this is it, boy!" he said excitedly. "This is where we'll settle. First a cabin to give us shelter." He scanned the terrain and saw a little creek bubbling up at the foot of the steep hill. "There," he said with satisfaction. "True it is I'm getting old, but my eyes can still find water good enough. We'll build our cabin there, and someday — someday — we'll build us a grand house, right where we're standing now. Can you imagine it, my boy? How fantastic it'll be. And we'll *farm*. We'll turn all this land into an ocean of crops."

The baby moved again in his arms, and Gerald looked down. "What's that you're trying to tell me, boy? You're trying to tell me that this land may already belong to someone, is that it? Well, land can be bought for gold, my son, and gold can be earned if necessary. No, don't you worry about it. The angels brought us here. They showed us the way, and they won't disappoint us. This land belongs to us."

In the darkness, his eyes glittered, showing the gentle sheen of tears. "It's not been for nothing, boy. We'll work hard, and we'll have what we're needing, never you fear."

He held the boy up in the night, wanting him to get a look at his future, his destiny, his birthright. "The world is yours if you want it, boy, and if you're willing to work for it. You, the first of our family to be born on the soil of this new country, will be a living testament to that."

And as he lowered the baby back into his arms, rocking him gently back to sleep, he knew what name he would choose for his grandson.

"America," he said. "America Fitzgerald."

The End.

AUTHOR BIO

Raised in a family of book lovers, Misha's mother first encouraged her to read by offering to pay her two cents per page of 'Hop on Pop,' by Dr. Seuss. At first Misha was happy just to be raking in the cash, but before long she traded the pennies for the riches of the written word, and since that time she's seldom been seen without a book in her hand, in front of her nose, or at the very least in her purse!

Misha is married and is currently living and working in Northern Virginia. She welcomes messages about writing, reading, workshops, ice cream, antique typewriters, stuff that make you laugh, etc., and can be contacted via her website: http://www.mishacrews.com/